Wolf Laurel

Also by Lee Martin

The Third Moon is Blue
The Six Mile Inn
Starlight, Starbright

WOLF LAUREL

A Novel

Lee Martin

iUniverse, Inc.
New York Bloomington Shanghai

Wolf Laurel

Copyright © 2008 by Lee Martin

All rights reserved. No part of this book may be used or reproduced by any means, graphic, electronic, or mechanical, including photocopying, recording, taping or by any information storage retrieval system without the written permission of the publisher except in the case of brief quotations embodied in critical articles and reviews.

iUniverse books may be ordered through booksellers or by contacting:

iUniverse
1663 Liberty Drive
Bloomington, IN 47403
www.iuniverse.com
1-800-Authors (1-800-288-4677)

Because of the dynamic nature of the Internet, any Web addresses or links contained in this book may have changed since publication and may no longer be valid.

ISBN: 978-0-595-49602-0 (pbk)
ISBN: 978-0-595-61169-0 (ebk)

Printed in the United States of America

This is a work of fiction. All of the characters, names, incidents, organizations, and dialogue in this novel are either the products of the author's imagination or are used fictitiously.

Cover Art "A Quiet Place"

from a painting by
Robert E. Tuckwiller, artist
www.tuckwillergallery.com

To West Virginia …

*… where the moonlit meadows ring with the call of Whippoorwills,
always you will find me in my home among the hills.
And where the sun draws rainbows in the mist of waterfalls and mountain rills,
my heart will be always in the West Virginia hills.*

—E.W. James, Jr.

"And make ready against them all you can of power, including steeds of war, to threaten the enemy of Allah and your enemy who you may not now know. The Gates of Paradise are under the shadows of the swords. A martyr's privileges are guaranteed by Allah and he forgives with the first gush of blood, protected from the test of the grave and assured security in the Day of Judgment. Declare war with your hearts and your bodies against the Great Satan and cause the blood of every man, woman and child to run in its streets."

وأعدوا لهم ما استطعتم من قوة ومن رباط الخيل ترهبون به عدو الله وعدوكم وآخرين من دونهم لا تعلمونهم. إن أبواب الجنة تحت ظلال السيوف. امتيازات الشهيد مضمونة عند الله، وهو يغفر عند تفجر أول نقطة دماء، ويحمي من عذاب القبر ويجعلك تأمن في يوم الدين. أعلنوا الحرب بقلوبكم وأجسادكم ضد الشيطان الأعظم، واسفكوا دماء كل رجل وامرأة وطفل يجري في شوارعه.

"… the predator will become the prey."

Acknowledgements

There are many people in my life from whom I gather my inspiration to write these books and it is their simple goodness, friendship and sense of family that continues to sustain me. They always appreciate the books and that makes me want to work harder to be a better writer. I sometimes even weave their personalities into some of the characters ... only the good characters, of course, considering that thus far all my novels are murder mysteries.

To family: my wife, Sandy, most of all, and to our children and grandchildren. To Wilma, Linda and Dan, Rick and Janet, Karen and Rick, and Mike. And then there's my Uncle Red Martin whose stories of our family and West Virginia are always mesmerizing.

To my Vietnam War buddies, Kyle and Lanny. And to my true blue West Virginia State chums, Joe, Brenda and Chris ... I am happy we have continued to stay in touch. You will always be in my heart.

I've acknowledged other friends in previous novels who assisted me personally and with my research; but specifically this time, I thank my comrade in arms Special Forces Warrant Officer Mario De Carvalho and his beautiful wife, Jane Robelot. Mario, a major network photographer and former action guy (FAG), provided technical information in places and is responsible for the author photo on the book cover. You did the best you could with a difficult subject, Mario.

To all my buddies from GMS, both those who have passed on and those who remain. Greenbrier Forever; her name will never die.

And to the three thousand ...

Foreword

So we are now engaged in a global conflict against an unconventional enemy that may number one or three or twenty, whose battlefield is the street and whose target is the sky scraper, the shopping mall or the marketplace. Anywhere there are large numbers. He strikes and then shields himself within the populace like the coward that he is. But conversely he may be the one who chooses to give up his *own* life willingly and with a smile on his face in exchange for favor and rewards from his God. He may think of himself as the blessed and chosen one, a seeker of Allah's favor; but as he slaughters the innocent indiscriminately, without conscience, he is instead nothing more than a bilious disciple of *Shaitan*, the Evil One.

"A martyr's privileges are guaranteed by Allah; forgiveness with the first gush of blood, he will be shown his seat in paradise, he will be decorated with the jewels of belief, married off to the beautiful ones, protected from the test in the grave, assured security in the day of judgment, crowned with the crown of dignity, a ruby of which is better than this whole world and its contents, wedded to seventy-two of the pure Houris and his intercession on behalf of seventy of his relatives will be accepted."

Osama bin Laden, 1996, Dark Prince of Terrorism
From the Qur'an, Suras 44 and 61

Chapter 1

It doesn't matter. It could be pouring one of those bone-chilling, mind-numbing rains. Or in the dead of winter, the landscape may be painted brown and gray with dirty patches of snow hanging on until that first warm and hopeful spring morning. I don't care. Whatever the weather, the temp or the season, I am good there. It is the place I have always called home. I have lived a great number of places in my life, seen every state and worked and played in most of Europe and Asia. I have been intrigued, fascinated, enticed and enchanted by so many of these places. But I always go home. Not often. But when I do, it's my needed shot in the arm.

Each time I cross the state line into God's country, my heart bristles and swells as I sweep my eyes along great defiant mountains that finally level off to the west into lush, peaceable meadows. In the summer the hills can change color, from hazy blue to violet, from deep green to gold, depending on where the sun is positioned on any given day. The land, rich and munificent in its bounty, is now left relatively undisturbed by those who would defile it in their search for gas, coal, salt and iron. The environmentalists and entreating lobbyists have seen to that. Still, this beautiful state so greatly advanced by those industries that have often spoiled the air and earth, never fails to provide for the comfort and prosperity of its people.

Well, I'm not exactly a poet. Although I can *get* pretty poetic at times, you won't see it coming out very often. But there are still a few things that continue to bring out the Robert Burns in me. One of those is Caroline, the love of my life, who happens to be my daughter; another, an ice cold six pack of Heineken that when sucked down my swallow pipe on a hot day, cools my arteries as well as my jets; and lastly, my Austin Healey 3000, to which I have visitation rights once a month while it sits in my ex-wife's driveway. But the odes and sonnets that sometimes dance in my brain are never more prolific than when I do go home from time to time to the extraordinarily beautiful land called Greenbrier.

✶ ✶ ✶ ✶

I know it sounds all dramatic and clandestine, but I simply can't tell anyone what I do, who I work for or where I'm going from one day to the next. Not even my daughter, my ex-wife or my brother. What I *can* say is that I'm a contractor and these days my services are pretty much in high demand. It's not really one of those jobs where if you asked me what I did, then I would say "if I told you I'd have to kill you." Well … maybe it is; but I wouldn't necessarily go through with it.

It's a hell of a lot more dangerous world we live in now; and seeing as how we're slammed into World War III, a war like no other, you could say I'm a modern day battlefield soldier … a for real Army of One. The difference is I don't wear a uniform, have a sophisticated, high-tech weapons system at my fingertips nor do I take orders from skin-head Colonels. When I was in the Army's Special Forces a hundred years ago, I used to carry a card for fun that listed my job responsibilities like '*villages plundered, despots exterminated, terrorists castrated and virgins deflowered.*' The card that I carry now provides no information about me or my job responsibilities as a government operative. It's actually pretty generic. Across the top it reads *United States Department of State,* over which you will find the department seal, and under which is my name. The only other items on the card are my State Department web site and the main office phone number which patches the caller directly to my cell phone.

Let's just say I fix things ... and people ... both good and bad. But the thing I'm most proud of is that I do my damnedest to facilitate life, liberty and the pursuit of happiness for American citizens. My tasks and methods, however, are a little unorthodox. Call it what you will ... deactivation, extermination or perhaps a fancier word like *extirpation*. But if you're fishing to know exactly what I do, please don't ask and I won't tell. It may end up changing your impression of me.

I'm in kind of a sales and service business for the government. Actually, mostly service. Here's how it works. I get a call from my boss at the Counterterrorism Team (CTT, not to be confused with CTC or Counterterrorist Center), an elite, covert and classified department of the Bureau of Intelligence and Research. He has no name on his door nor supervises a department known or recognized by ninety-five percent of all government law enforcement organizations. He has a code name like Falcon, Condor or some other freaking bird ... that is in times of crisis ... which would make one think he's James Bond or the Man from U.N.C.L.E. This is a sapient guy with steely eyes who walks and talks like Joe Friday and would never ever admit he was breast-fed by his mother ... that is if he ever had one. But I have to admit he is a good guy; and as tight-lipped as this distinguished, silver-haired dude is, whenever he speaks, anyone in CTT had better listen. To everyone else in the State Department, he is the Preceptor of CTT. But to us on his Special Ops field team called Zulu, he is affectionately known as *Birdman*.

Officially, our mission is to collect and analyze intelligence about foreign state-supported terrorist groups and warn appropriate government agencies and branches of impending terrorist operations or threats. As necessary, we will employ 'defensive' measures to prevent terrorist attacks from occurring or at the very minimum weaken the enemy's infrastructure. Selected members of Zulu will be fluent in a half dozen languages, and depending on their ethnicity, may actually infiltrate the terrorist organization.

There are six of our strategically located teams throughout the Continental U.S., mostly situated in or near the larger metropolitan areas. Four additional teams are in Europe, the Middle East, Asia and South America. Each team is comprised of four to seven agents who mostly operate individually, but will come together as a Special Reaction Team (SRT) when a threat is realized. Our goal will first be to capture the subject or subjects, conduct preliminary interrogation, assess the threat, and then transfer the element to the Company's (CIA) Counterterrorist Center in Langley or Guantanamo Bay.

The Preceptor will tell one of us he was contacted by an operative or informant who has secured information about a customer of the 'imported' persuasion with a product that will unwittingly attract our services. But unfortunately for the customer, he will not appreciate these services. It will be up to one of us to approach the customer, give him our sales pitch and insure that any concerns he has are extinguished forever. I must be good, because so far, I have never heard back from any of my customers. Furthermore, neither has anyone else.

My twenty years with the Bureau behind me, I had planned to settle down, rust away and become a slug, operating a bar in the tropics somewhere or growing some tobacco on a little farm in North Carolina. But after my first week in retirement of doing absolutely nothing except eating and drinking everything I could get my hands on, I decided that as this FAG (Former Action Guy) would soon end up either in a funny farm or on a fat farm, I would make some calls. One of the calls I made was to another recent Bureau retiree by the name of Charlie Green who I knew had gone through the same post partum blues and took on an afterlife with the government in a different capacity.

"Sending up the old S.O.S., huh fella?"

"Help me, Charlie," I replied. "I feel like a '58 Edsel, broken down, unloved and upon blocks. I need something to do. And I don't mean handcuffed to a desk, my friend."

He laughed. "So, a case of the D.T.'s, huh? All right, I know a guy, okay? All I can tell you is that people are being recruited for this new kind of organization that operates out of the State Department. It's still on the drawing board and has been for quite some time from what I understand, but they plan to implement it some time this year."

That's when I was put in touch with a man named Brent Sawyer who ultimately got me an interview with Birdman. I guess because I was a true FAG and knew a thimble full of Arabic, not to mention being pretty astute in English, I was in. In three weeks I was undergoing training with the Delta Force at Ft. Bragg in the Close Quarters Battle (CQB) course. The Combat Application Group was doing much of the training which included modules such as terrorist profiling and assessment, Intel ops, sniper M-24 certification, selective targeting and what is called double tap engagement (making sure the target does not get up).

We were to be the first line of defense where it came to counterterrorist warfare. The CTC and other global counterterrorist groups would still do their strategic stuff, but *our* ears would be closer to the ground. And by the time we sought out and destroyed the element, the spooks and FBI would just be getting out of bed. For the most part, we would only share our information with them when the action was over, if in fact it was a matter of national security, and then we were selectively resistant. That meant we wanted no one else in the way, especially large bureaucratic Intel groups who were in competition with one another and who were compelled to run their plans and operations by special congressional panels to determine whether something was indeed of national security interest, a violation of the Geneva Convention or human rights, congruent with U.N. concupiscence or politically correct.

Well anyway, what it comes down to is that I'm sort of a government cop, but I carry no badge. I do have an ID with a barcode on it that can be read by select people at certain federal agencies; however, I will not necessarily be recognized by other law enforcement, especially the local yokels. Basically, I have no rank, title or position. One other thing; it is imperative in my work that I have zero visibility. For this reason I am not always the person I appear to be. Let's just say there would be fewer questions if my vehicle were stopped by a *federal* cop versus a *local* ... especially if they found my deadly accurate cryogenic-treated Remington 700 .308 complete with sniper scope. And then also somewhere on my person are usually my Glock and .380.

My name is not a code (except when I'm on a mission) or a number, like Mr. Bond. But although I sometimes change my name temporarily to protect the innocent (me), I generally go by the name my Scottish-American parents laid on me some fifty-four years ago, Bruce McGowan.

It wasn't but a month after I joined up with CTT that the Birdman dropped my first mission on me. The Intel came down the chute in April just a year ago where two young Islamic idealists, both disciples of the militant sheik Omar Abdel Rahman, the convicted mastermind of the 1993 World Trade Center bombing, had been spotted reconning the Sears Tower in Chicago. Their mugs had appeared just once too often on cameras in the vicinity of the building, looking around suspiciously, scratching notes and crotches, and taking photos. As there was nothing incriminating about their activity, there would not be enough cause for law enforcement to pick them up for questioning. These guys would argue that besides them, a great many people pass by or stop and look at the building day after day, which was true; and if they, the Islamics, were hauled in just because they had been admiring the building, that would be a case of ethnic or religious profiling and a complaint would immediately be filed to the Council on American-Islamic Relations.

Anyway, I staked these guys out for about three weeks, finding also that a Chicago FBI team was on their case. A self-made problem for the Feds was that their black Ford Crown Vic with plain wheels was just a wee bit too conspicuous. The suspects' casing of the Sears Tower then suddenly stopped cold. But knowing where the Arab boys lived, I rented an apartment in the same tenement just two doors away. When all they had to do was look out their window to spot the Crown Vic, they did as I expected them to do ... took the fire escape down the back side of the building. Each time they did, I trekked down my own set of stairs, followed them at distance and recorded their activities.

And then there was that cold, blustery evening in early April when I tailed the suspects' Pontiac Grand Am from a parking garage to the empty lot at Soldier Field. I watched from about fifty feet away through my telephoto lens while they made contact with another Middle Eastern man in a white cargo van. The boys disappeared through the rear doors of the van and then reappeared about three minutes later with a large suitcase. I snapped shots of the license plate on the van as it pulled away, then advanced quickly on the Grand Am. They never saw me coming. Before the driver could throw the car into *drive*, I jumped into the back seat, cracked him on the head with the butt of my Glock and stuck the muzzle into the passenger's ear.

"Touch the suitcase and a .40 caliber round will split your head open like a ripe watermelon," I barked.

The would-be terrorist didn't go for the suitcase, but instead reached down under the seat for a handgun. Since I had thought in advance to attach the silencer, it wasn't a very loud report. Instantaneously, the passenger's head exploded, coating a section of the windshield with a smattering of goopy red and white stuff.

I retrieved the bloodied suitcase from the man's lap and returned to my car. In case it was booby trapped, I did not open it. Popping the cover of my cell phone, I called Ramon, the team leader for Zulu Chicago.

"Ramon, this is Scorpion. Cleanup on Aisle C10 at Soldier Field. I have one DOA and one sleeper. Bring an EOD expert and a disposal unit."

Well, we *did* find that it was an explosive device which was meant for the Sears Tower. As for the would-be terrorists, the dead guy disappeared altogether. The *driver's* brain, scrambled as it was from my whack, somehow still remembered the names of the two cohorts in the van. And a few days later, after further interrogation of all three at Gitmo, they seemed happy to give up details of the plot.

I drove back to my tenement, got out and strolled up to the Crown Vic, still parked in plain sight, and tapped on the window. When the startled driver dropped the window down, I said, "Give it up Bureau Boys and call your office. Your boss has something to tell you." I just love spreading good news.

So, anyway, most of the time, thanks to guys like me, the general public never finds out that a threat like that even exists nor that the purveyors of such plots suddenly and rudely exit from society. We Zulu guys not only keep Americans from developing unnecessary fears about their security, but our way of doing business keeps us from being subject to all those pesky civil rights concerns.

But then something happened a few months ago where for the first time in the year and a half since I had hired on with CTT as an operative, not only did certain members of my family find out more about me, I ended up breaking my policy of secrecy. And I also found myself compelled to collaborate with people and agencies that I usually keep in the dark. But I needed them … and they sure as hell needed me.

✳   ✳   ✳   ✳

I drove slowly over the old bridge on Route 136, glancing down occasionally at the now unused and broken tracks, then pulled my Suburban onto the dirt shoulder at the end of the guardrail. Sitting for a few moments with my wrist propped atop the steering wheel, I allowed the sweet memories of childhood to fill my head. In the past thirty years I had been home, as I still called it, perhaps a dozen times, but the visits had generally been short. Short except for when I came back for the funerals of my mom and dad and the one-time fishing sabbatical I took at my brother's cabin up on the Greenbrier River. I reckon I needed those days in the woods on the water to recuperate that year just after a perp's bullet drilled my lung out. And scantly a month after I was released from the hospital, my divorce was final. Not a good year, to say the least.

I stepped out of the Suburban to greet the sweltering afternoon sun and adjusted my Ray-Ban flight glasses to shield my eyes from its piercing glare. In late August the mountain air is generally tolerable and even down-right cool, especially just after a front has passed through. But that afternoon, the dog-day haze was heavy and consuming after the rain, after the sun began again to heat up the soggy earth, making it hatefully humid if you will, making it difficult for me to suck enough oxygen from the atmosphere into my damaged lung. Summer just didn't want to give up.

It was peacefully, even deafeningly quiet on the bridge which allowed me to barely pick up the noise of whining tires and tractor rigs running through their gearboxes on I-64 near the Lewisburg exit. Obnoxious crows called and answered one another from the white oaks that towered over magnificent mountain laurel, some of which had crept cautiously toward the tracks over the years. It had been twenty years or more since the last coal train passed under the bridge on those tracks on its way from the Raleigh mines, over the Alleghenies, through the Shenandoah, and then on to Norfolk.

I placed one of my Tony Lamas onto the lower abutment and leaned over the railing to spit out a gnat that just had to find a moist cavern to fly into. Fortunately for my sinus cavity, it hadn't flown up my nose. My chest hurt a little that day where six years before, an emergency room doctor had cut a hunk out of me. But otherwise I felt pretty good. I'm still in fairly good shape, considering both knees were blown out by shrapnel from an NVA .122 rocket back in 1970. Oh, and did I mention I had actually been wounded when I was with the Bureau … *twice;* once in a shootout with a bank robber and then by a mob henchman (ergo the sucking chest wound) after my partner and I cornered him in an alley. And then there was that time I rolled a Bureau Crown Vic and banged up my head when I was chasing an escaping wife killer.

By the way, the bad guys I mentioned got the worse end of the deal. But at least I can say I'm proud to be an American economist at heart; no tax-payer money is generally shelled out for trials and incarceration. *My* services are both expedient and cost effective.

At six-two and a hundred seventy-five pounds (with Glock), I can still hold my own in any scuffle, damaged goods and all. Except I choose not to do that anymore. 'Cause if you *are* the bad dude and you run on me, two of my rounds will take out each leg at the back of the knee. Of course, I would warn you first. The law mandates that. But if you continue running after the warning, ten yards is all you get.

Anyway, I'm still a pretty good-looking guy who hasn't let age ravage his body, although Heaven knows I've beaten it up over the years by allowing bullets, booze and babes to have their way with it. The babes and booze, of course, I allowed into my life voluntarily. One thing is, though, I can still run … bad knees, bad lung, bad years and all. Five, six mornings a week you'll see me pounding the pathway on the D.C. Mall, from the Capitol to the Lincoln Memorial, or maybe some trail off the beaten path wherever I happen to be.

Upon hearing the limo approach, I turned my head and watched the car pass by. I kept my eyes on it until it pulled off the road to the right and to the front of my Suburban. For a few moments the driver stayed put, but then the door eventually opened and a man of fifty with hair as black as the coal in them thar hills, wearing a black suit and tie, exited the Lincoln. He approached me slowly, but with purpose. "Special Agent McGowan, I presume."

I took off my glasses and shook my head. "Not anymore."

"You're not going to jump, are you?" he asked, gluing his eyes to mine.

"Any reason I shouldn't?"

"Yeah, you'd probably miss the ground. I know what a bad shot you are. Dad always said you couldn't hit water if you fell out of a friggin' boat."

I smiled wryly. "Contraire, little brother. I could drill a hole in your belly button at two hundred yards. And that's with a .45."

Joe McGowan out-stretched his arms and walked over to embrace me. We patted each other's back and then separated.

"You look good, Brucious. Obviously, even with all the holes in you, you're still running. Either that or you've been shacking up with some split-tail who's giving you a good workout."

"Definitely not the latter. Still making it on my own. I just can't seem to get a woman to accept my being gone ninety percent of the time. I had a goldfish once, and it lived, I think, three days. I found out you have to feed the little bastards."

Joey laughed and turned to the railing to look down. A couple of the N&W tracks were missing, but mostly, the rails remained intact. He followed them with his eyes until the rails grew together at a point a half-mile away. "I miss the old trains, Brucie. Gawd, it had to be forty or more years since they ran the last of the steam engines from the coal camps through here. We'd stand and watch them come under the bridge, black smoke puffing with every chug, and then after the train was gone, the gray fog laid all in the trees. I remember that smell of the burning coal." Joey closed his eyes and drew in a deep, nostalgic breath.

"Yeah, I know," I said. "And do you remember when we used to bring our model planes up here and pretend they were WW II fighter-bombers. We'd hold our P-51 Mustangs in one hand and drop cherry bombs with the other down into coal cars as they passed under. They'd go off and scatter bits of coal like shrapnel."

Joey grinned. "The thing I most remember like it was yesterday was when you thought the train was longer than it was and dropped a bomb on the caboose when it went by. Man, the brakeman jumped out of the back and started cussin' and shaking his fist. We took off like a couple of scalded dogs."

We both had a good laugh with that. I also remembered that the brakeman reported us and somehow it got around that it was *us* on the bridge. That was one of the few times I wish I had been wearing asbestos underwear. Dad sure as hell lit our britches on fire.

I found my smile quickly fading when I thought of how simple and innocent those days were and then how complicated we had all made our world since. Those childhood years were stocked with good times. And although there would be many more good days to come in my teens and twenties, bad days were soon to follow. Days of heartache. Days of pain and disappointment. Some of which would be thrust upon me by fate. Most of which, however, was of my own making.

It was McGowan and Sons Funeral Home for more than seventy years. First there was my grandfather and his three sons. Then when Pops died, Dad took over and kept the name, hoping both his sons would go to mortuary school, become licensed funeral directors, and settle into the family business with him. Little Joe did; I didn't.

Dad thought it family treason to reject the business, and considering the business was our very life growing up, he never understood why I hated being around the dead. It was just a natural thing for him to embalm, bathe, dress and primp corpses in preparation for viewing. When Dad married Mom, she knew that to be his wife, she had to become comfortable with it all. And that she did. She washed and set the women's hair, helped loved ones pick out just the right burying clothes and held the trembling hands of the bereaved at wakes. I ignored the whole sordid atmosphere. I had too much living to do to spend my life with the dead. Anyway, corpses always gave me the heebie-jeebies. The first time I saw Dad push that needle up under somebody's arm to drain the veins, I passed out cold on the floor. Dad just smiled, checked to see if my heart had stopped, then went on flushing.

And then there was that one day I remember with shocking exactitude when I was feeling sorry for myself, being an outcast like I was, I was bound and determined to join the family business. I also guess I was tired of my dad calling me a pansy or a pantywaist. It all started with ol'man Cunningham who up and died of a heart attack after he climbed on top Prissy Purcell, the town whore. Although Dad was normally tight-lipped about picking up people who expired in such compromising situations, I did overhear him telling Mr. Bartholomew, the barber, that he had to strap the old man's erect penis to his leg with duct tape. The damn thing wouldn't go down, he said. Of course you can't tell the town barber, bartenders or butchers anything in confidence. You might as well set up a PA system in the middle of town. Old man Cunningham's wife gave Dad the devil for inadvertently spreading the story around and even threatened a lawsuit. But after a few days it all simmered down.

My point here on the Cunningham corpse is that right after Dad brought him in and dropped him on the embalming table, he received a phone call and left me in the room by myself with the stiff, telling me 'don't let him go anywhere.' Dad smiled and patted my head before going to his office, like he was elated that it was finally going to be *McGowan and Sons* after all. And when little brother Joey would get into *his* teens, the 's' on Sons would be for real.

It was deathly quiet in that room (no pun intended). Just old man Cunningham and me. I could swear the corners of his mouth were turned up. I guess he had every reason to smile when he drew his last breath. What happened next Dad says occurs sometimes by reflex, but *that* didn't make it make it any easier for me and my stomach. One moment ol' Cunningham just laid there with a sheet up to his neck and then the next … well, suddenly he sat straight up and exhaled a burst of air. Then his head plopped back down hard on the metal table with a clunk. I let out a scream that brought Dad back into the room and then I yelled *"He's alive, he's alive!"* Sometime thereafter I recalled I must have sounded like Dr. Frankenstein just after he jolted the monster to life with channeled lightning. Dad laughed like I'd never seen him. Mom whisked me out of there quickly and held me while I muttered and sputtered something unintelligible. At twelve, that was the last time I set foot in a room with the dead. I still don't hang around the dead. I've *made* quite a few of them that way, but don't usually stick around to pay my respects.

Back to the bridge. "So, what's up, Joey? Why the phone call?"

"Well, you haven't been home in more'n two years, Brewster. Thought maybe you'd like to take some time off ... maybe go up to the cabin again."

He had called me the day before and said he had something I needed to see and that I should get there as soon as I could. But he was reluctant to tell me over the phone what it was. I *knew* Joey, he being my brother and all, and it had to be more than a concern that I was working too hard and needed a vacation.

"You'd better have a more compelling reason than *that* to get me back here, Joey Boy. You said on the phone you had something to show me. Something that would interest me because of what I do for a living. With the urgency in your voice, I thought somebody died."

He nodded and shuffled a bit. "Somebody did, Bruce. And I thought you'd like to go to his visitation."

"What are you talking about?"

"Well, I know you've really never told me what you got into after the FBI, but it *does* have something to do with hunting down subversive types, doesn't it?"

"Let's just say I investigate people suspected of planning or conducting activities against the United States. Does that sum it up for you?"

"Okay, then you *may* be interested in this. I've got a dead A-rab on my slab."

"A what?"

"An A-rab."

"And?"

"Well, I think he may be connected to some kind of terrorist organization."

"Because he's Middle Eastern?"

"No … look. I know you had been working in some kind of counter-terrorist organization and were on the USS Cole bombing. And I know you've been involved in bringing a number of the A-rab guys to justice."

"Yeah, but that was when I was still with the Bureau. The A-rab … er, Arab, Joey. What about him?"

"Well hell, Bruce, these kinds of people don't live around here or hardly anywhere else in the state for that matter. Then one ends up prostrate, face down on Washington Street."

"Uh huh. So how did he end up that way?"

"The stupid bastard stepped off a curb and got flattened by a UPS truck."

I had to stifle a smile, listening to the way Joey was prone to put things. "And you think I'd be interested in him *why?*"

"Well, as I said, when did you ever hear of any Middle Easterner visiting or taking up residence in good ol' Greenbrier County?"

"The world's a global community now, Joey. People can live anywhere. But, you think he lived somewhere around here?"

"I don't know. Rufus Morgan, you know, he still runs the Western Auto, says he thought he saw the guy two or three weeks back at Spurlock's Grocery. You know old Griffin Spurlock, right?"

I nodded, even though I really didn't. In fifty odd years of compiling information about people, places and things, stuff has been steadily seeping out of the seven holes in my head. But maybe I did remember the Spurlock girl. Nobody ever looked better in a knit sweater. "Go on."

"Anyway, the EMTs picked him up and took him to the hospital where he was then transferred to the county morgue. He had no ID on him and no one has claimed the body in over six days. A public notice ran in the paper a couple of those days."

"You're still the assistant coroner, aren't you?"

"Yes."

"Did you or anyone do an autopsy?"

"Yep. Harvey Tucker the M.E. did it. No alcohol or drugs in his system and he obviously died at the scene, according to the paramedics.

I shoved my fingertips into my jean pockets and shrugged. "I still don't see anything suspect here. This is why you called me? About a dead, unidentified Middle Eastern man? And by the way, how do you know he's of the Arab persuasion?"

"He just looks like it ... like he's from Iran or Libya. Maybe Iraq, I don't know. He doesn't look like he's from India or Pakistan. We've got a couple of them in the county running motels between here and Ronceverte. They're more chocolate in color and have glossier hair."

"The next time I see an ad in our system for a bigoted government profiler, I'll be sure to give you a call, little brother."

"Very funny. I *can* tell the difference in ethnic origins, you know."

"I still don't have my question answered, Joey. What's so special about this John Mohammed Doe, other than him not blending in with you mountain WASPS here in Greenbrier County?"

"Tell you what. Follow me down to the shop and let's finish our conversation there."

"Why do you have him there and not at the morgue?"

"I dispose of all the unclaimed and indigent in the area. The county pays me. Before I cremate him, I wanted you to have a look."

I shuffled a bit, kicking a loose stone over the bridge to the old tracks below with one of my roach killers. "Look, Joey. I don't know if this is a carcass I'd be interested in. Hell, I thought somebody killed somebody and that's why you called me."

"You're not far off, Bru. I think somebody was planning to kill a hell of a lot of people. And there *is* something about this guy that will interest you."

"What?"

"You'll see when we get to the shop."

"If you have suspicions about the man, why haven't you taken this to the State Police or Feds in Charleston?"

"Hey, you're the only anti-terrorist guru I know and I thought you'd like first crack at him. Anytime I can help my big brother get another feather in his bonnet, especially if this turns out to be something, I want to call you."

"You're being way too mysterious and dramatic about this. Whatever you've found out about this schmuck better be worth my trip out here."

He grinned. "Wouldn't you have come here just to see me, Cora and the girls?"

I squinted my eyes at him and shook my head. "Let's get it on with it, Joey Boy."

I turned to walk toward my vehicle and he followed. The butter-bright sun was oppressive and the piercing heat radiating off the Suburban created a shimmering effect, making the trees in the distance lose their clarity. I suddenly needed a burst of air conditioning. It's really hell to get fragile like this. I do love my comfort.

Before I entered the SUV I said, "So you have reason to believe he's a terrorist, huh?"

"Was. *Was* a terrorist. Now just a stiff. Just follow me to the shop. You can make up your own mind. By the way, is this how a G-Man dresses these days? Jeans. Golf shirt. Cowboy boots."

"Not a G-Man anymore, Joey. I'm just making a living fighting for truth, justice and the American way."

"Right," he replied with a smirk. "I don't see you wearin' any blue underwear on the outside of your pants and that shirt doesn't have a big 'S' on it. But come on, Mr. Kent. I may actually have an exclusive for you."

Chapter 2

▼

I have never forgotten how incredibly beautiful this Eastern West Virginia landscape is. The low hills between the Alleghenies and the Appalachians slope gently into green velvet pastures that on most crisp mornings lay blanketed with a haunting fog. When the ten o'clock sun floods the valley and dissipates the opaque wisp, the colors of summer and fall are then gradually and vividly magnified. Almost Heaven, they call it.

I followed the McGowan family car west along the highway for four miles until it turned left at Saturday Road. Small, white-frame houses with ten to fifteen year old sedans and pickups sitting in gravel driveways popped up on either side of the narrow two-lane. Further along, the terrain widened again into rolling, majestic farm land stocked with fine, brawny Herefords and Guernseys, owned by Greenbrier's more affluent barons. What they call the opulent society.

The covered bridge over Nathan's Creek appeared to be standing as strong as ever. A few of its panels were missing and it needed a coat of paint, and although it creaked a little, it had never given an inch after sixty five years. I did see where it had been reinforced by new timbers and pylons some time back. The bridge was an important piece of the county's history. It had carried both the living and dead to points of destiny since the days of my mortician grandfather.

As the road curved uphill and to the right, Rest Lawn Cemetery, a veritable city of monuments stood silhouetted against the hazy late summer sky. Beyond the grave markers was the old board-and-batten church where I was baptized eons ago by Pastor Billy Tompkins back when God used to smile on me. I guess I've been a major disappointment to the Great One over the years.

Joey finally turned into the mortuary ... the shop ... as he called it. For some reason Dad's weathered face and guttural voice popped into my head as McGowan and Sons Funeral Home came into view. Dad used to crack corny one-liners about the business that made Joey and me nearly gag. When someone would ask how business was, he'd say "dead" with a straight face. "People just die to get in here." And "*rest* assured, we're the last people to let you down." Yet, the man actually committed these quippy atrocities wearing a dead-pan face.

I sat in the Suburban for a while as Joe went to the left of the building to unlock the large double doors out from which a thousand coffins had rolled to the hearse parked under the huge carport. I hated this place, mostly for the reasons mentioned earlier, but also because I took a lot of heat from my friends growing up around the area. Most every other kid's dad was in the farming business, but the only thing my old man planted was bodies. Hell, I couldn't get a date on a bet. No girl wanted a guy to touch her if he had touched dead bodies. Even when I tried to convince them I didn't ... ever, I guess they thought I was lying. One of my buds, Bobby Crawford, even joked that I was into necrophilia. I was nineteen before I learned *that* meant having sexual relations with corpses. I was thirty before I actually did. But it was with my ex-wife, Darlene, and she only pretended to be dead.

Joey motioned for me to come on, but he stayed by the door without going inside. His face appeared urgent. He yelled to me, "You got your piece on you?"

"My piece?" I knew what he meant, but didn't know why he asked. "Why? Aren't people already dead in there or is business slow and you want to kill old Lester?"

"Lester's off today. The door's been rifled. Looks like someone broke in here."

I reached across the glove compartment and took out my Glock. Holding it at my side, I moved in toward Joey. "Stay here."

After assessing the broken lock and the chewed up facing, I swung the left door open and propped my gun atop my left wrist. I scanned the lobby through the sight and swept the Glock around the room. Joey was right on my heels, the disobedient little shit.

"No one's ever broken in here," he said. "What would they want?"

I didn't answer, but continued my canvass of the lobby. It was quiet, as it should be in a funeral home, and no sign of a fleeing burglar. I moved from room to room, Joey with me all the way. "I thought I told you to stay."

"I'm your brother, not your dog."

The place seemed to have been left intact. Joe didn't readily see that anything was missing. But what would someone take from a funeral home? No money was kept around. People didn't buy caskets and funerals with cash. Of course, if it were kids, they probably didn't know that. In Joey's office, two desk drawers were half open and papers strewn about. The safe was still locked and anyway it would only temporarily contain valuables, like dead people's jewelry, mostly costume, until the family claimed it. There was no attempt to pry it open or blow it. I told Joey not to touch anything; he needed to go ahead and call the locals to dust for fingerprints.

"If our stiff had a friend, I believe I know what he'd be looking for," Joey said.

"What?"

"I'll show you later. But first, come take a look at the body."

I had searched every room, including the viewing rooms to see if an intruder was hiding out. We even popped open the caskets in the selection room. Only *the* room remained. *The* dreaded room of my psychological pain and childhood nightmares. The room where I last saw Mr. Cunningham, the old letch.

Joey pulled out one of the refrigerated body drawers, number ten. Fully expecting to see a corpse, I was surprised when he grabbed a bottle of Evian and tossed it to me. "Would you like a snack? Let's see here ... got some cheese, beef stick ... how about a boiled egg?"

"You've got to be kidding. You made a refrigerator out of one of these drawers?"

"Yeah, why not? Embalming makes me hungry. Some people whistle while they work; I get the munchies."

"Sheesh! You're sick, man." I let that picture filter on through for a moment. "So, is your John Doe in one of the drawers?"

"Number Six there."

"Anybody in any of the other condos?"

"Nope, he should be the only one."

"Should be?"

"Unless our intruder decided to take a nap."

I smiled. Joey had a pretty good sense of humor, but he was still not as funny as me. Or maybe as funny as I *used* to be before bullets and ex-wives scarred me for life and made me rather grumpy. "Pull him out," I said, shoving the Glock into my pants at the butt crack. "Whoever broke in here is long gone, now."

Joe opened the fridge drawer. John Mohammed Doe was still there. He hadn't been stolen, but I could see the alarm in Joey's face.

"Obviously, our intruder was interested in our friend here. The sheet I covered him with is now down around his ankles."

"Maybe your perp is into necrophilia."

"No, that's *you*, remember?"

"Damn. You talked to Bobby Crawford."

Joey just looked at me with a confused expression on his face.

The John Doe looked to be about twenty five, had light brown skin and a half dozen black moles on his face. The body was well-developed without an ounce of fat. He did look Middle Eastern and could have been from twenty different countries across the pond. And he looked very dead. Actually, mangled. But you would expect that, being kissed by a big brown truck. The head was swollen and one eye was partially open and puffy. There were comminuted fractures of the humerus and tibias on both sides, and major torso bruising. I took out my Nikon and snapped several shots of his face.

For whatever reason, I started becoming intrigued. Obviously the intruder or intruders could have been kids, breaking in on a dare. It was the same kind of challenge they may pose to one another like in spending a night in a haunted house. And that's what I told Joey.

He shook his head. "I think the intruder was likely another A-rab, looking for something. And that *something*, big brother, is in the safe."

"Okay, I'll bite. What?"

I followed him back into the office and he went directly to the safe. "Eh, eh," I chided. "Fingerprints."

Joey reached into a box on his desk and pulled out a single latex glove. Snapping it on his right hand, he began fiddling with the combination. After some left and right spins, he pulled the lever and the door popped open. He pulled out a box which did contain some unclaimed jewelry, several envelopes, some photos and a pistol. He withdrew the photos and one of the envelopes.

"Here are several police photos taken at the scene. You may want to see these. Most of them are of Mohammed back there. He was killed instantly and dragged about twenty feet before the driver got stopped."

I looked them over. "Okay. Nothing unusual here."

"Inside this envelope is what was found in his pocket. No one's seen this except for the medical examiner. As I said, there was no ID or green card on him. Just what you see here."

Inside of the envelope were a small pocket knife, a twenty and about two dollars in change, a green capsule and a small photo of a young woman in headdress, probably his wife or girlfriend. There was also a sheet of printer paper on which there were some words scribbled in Arabic and a hand-drawn map. I studied the paper for a few moments, then turned to Joey.

"My Arabic is a bit rusty, but one of the words here is *factory*. Whoever sketched this put a lot of detail in it. That line there is a road and has a 6-0 on it. Maybe Route 60. There are two gates indicated, seven, no eight buildings, and two circles which could represent storage tanks which have internationally recognized radioactive symbols by them. Well, I can see why you'd find this interesting. A map of a factory on a Middle Eastern man who by the way was found dead in Podunck, West Virginia, with no ID."

"My thoughts, exactly," Joey replied, looking pretty proud of his detective work.

Then I believe I must have scowled. Joey gave me a funny look when I held up the sheet of paper to his face. "If you recognized the importance of this map and had suspicions about this guy being some kind of terrorist, why didn't you take this immediately to the FBI or State Police?"

"I called *you*, didn't I? And the state cops didn't act much interested in the man. They took one look at him and thought he was a derelict. I knew that you being Bureau and all, you'd be the guy to look into this."

"I'm *not* the FBI anymore, Joey. I'm retired and doing contract work for the government, only."

"Which some day you're going to tell me *what* kind of work. Of course, I have it on good authority that you're some kind of terrorist hunter."

I gave him an irksome glare. "Don't concern yourself about that, little brother. I'm making a living and the government pays me what I'm worth, which isn't much on either account. You actually broke the law, you know. They call it *suppressing evidence*. Getting this information in the right hands on a timely basis could be the difference in whether a very real plot is choked off. Something could have already happened in the time it took for me to get over here."

"Well, apparently it didn't or we would have heard about it."

I dropped the sketch map back in the envelope. "I need to get this to the Bureau as soon as possible. First, I'll call the Charleston office and see if I can meet with one of the agents this afternoon or tomorrow morning."

"So, should I go ahead and cook this guy?"

"No. How much longer can he stay in the fridge before he starts to … you know …?"

"He can go another two days; then, he starts to melt. We don't embalm those destined for the cooker. You should know that, or did you forget your Mortuary 101?"

"Probably. Look, Joey, you need to go ahead and report the break-in to the county or state. I'd say this is up the sheriff department's alley."

He nodded and picked up the receiver at his desk.

I needed to call the boss, so I pulled my cell phone from its holster and hit 2 on speed dial.

"Hello," the familiar voice answered.

"Is this Vulture?"

"Very funny. Where are you?"

"Home."

"In D.C.?"

"No. Home, like as in *boyhood*. West Virginia."

"What are you doing there?"

"So what kind of bird are you today?" I answered his question with one of my own.

"Never mind. Where are you exactly?"

"I'm still wearing my locator chip. You should already have me pin-pointed with that sophisticated satellite toy you've got."

I had almost convinced myself that during the psychoanalysis performed on me by CTT that first day of service when they put me under with sodium pentothal to check out any deviancies in my personality, they injected a chip in my forearm. A chip that is both a listening and a locator device. That's the only explanation I have for Birdman ringing my cell phone immediately after I get too engaged with a vixen over a couple of drinks in a bar or if I wander too far off his radar screen. And then every time I hear his voice on the other end, the lump under my skin becomes irritated.

"You taking a few vacation days?" he asked. "You need to tell me these things, if you are. Give me your location."

"Should I send it in the clear?"

"You're not in a combat zone nor are you on assignment, Bruce." He paused. "Ah, there you are. You went to a military school near there, didn't you?"

I was just kidding about the satellite toy. He really *did* have me located. Damn chip. And then I wondered how he remembered the military school. "You're either psychic or have the memory of an elephant. But I suspect you're reading my file."

"It does make for interesting reading. Okay, enough small talk. What's going on there?"

"I'm looking at a dead Middle Eastern male in my brother's freezer drawer … you remember me mentioning Joey … has a bad habit of draining blood from people and sticking them in the ground …"

"Yes. Go on."

"Well, the Arab schmuck tried to make love to a delivery van going 30 miles an hour. Found on his person was a hand-drawn map of a factory which appears to be on the Kanawha River near Charleston. Looks like he or someone else sketched in great detail the interior of the factory, specifically high-lighting buildings containing radioactive, possibly nuclear or chemical material. Also in his possession was a capsule. It's not for acid reflux or high cholesterol, either. I suspect it's cyanide."

"Hmmm."

"Is that a reply of interest?"

"I assume you'll be nosing around, then."

"I thought I was on vacation."

"Okay, then. Combine a couple of days with this. Yes, do some digging. I suspect a colony of roaches. Where there's one, you know there's a nest somewhere."

"So, do I put out bait or just pull out my can of Raid and start zapping?"

Joey rolled his eyes at all my gobbledy-gook while he was waiting for a deputy to come on *his* line.

"Your mission," began the boss, "should you decide to accept it, would be to take out the colony if one does exist. But I need to know beyond any doubt there is good evidence. Of course, we would disavow any knowledge of your activity." For a stoned-faced, no-nonsense ex-CIA chief, he enigmatically loved to quote those lines.

"Got it, Preceptor. I do need a Bureau contact in the city. They have to know I'm here in case I misbehave and get taken for a Company man. You know all too well the two families don't get along. But I can show them my Junior G-Man barcode card and decoder ring, and I'm sure they'll let me keep my pea-shooter. Will have to avoid the locals, however."

"I'll make the call to Charleston for you."

"Thanks, Chief. Now warble me something soft and melodic." I heard the click and he was gone. "I stayed on the phone and continued a one way conversation for Joey's benefit. "This cell phone will self-destruct in five seconds. Phelps, out."

Joey, who was still waiting on his line for somebody ... anybody ... had a pained expression on his face. "That was the weirdest conversation I ever heard. Do they call you Phelps?"

"They do, Bro," I replied. I remembered that Joey was probably too young or too disinterested to watch *Mission Impossible*. When that show was on, he was only into *Captain Kangaroo* and *Romper Room*.

"I take it you got the green light to stay and check out our Doe, huh? What are you going to do with the map?"

"Let the Bureau see it and then try to find out where the factory is. Maybe the map itself will provide clues as to what 'dead guy' was up to and if there are anymore out there like him."

"You think there are?"

I shrugged. "Maybe. By the way, when you do get hold of the locals, ask if anyone has seen any other Middle Eastern types around the area. That question would much better come from you than me going to them. An undertaker and assistant coroner would have reason to follow up. I can't afford to get into a dialogue with anybody."

"I don't understand why you have to be so mysterious around me as to what you do."

"Don't concern yourself with it, little brother."

He sighed in resignation about the time a deputy came on the line. Joey began filling him in on the break-in and then was told a car would be dispatched in about twenty minutes. After he hung up from the call he returned all the contents to the safe except the map and capsule, which I kept. I would have the powder inside the capsule tested.

"You *are* staying at the house, aren't you? Cora and the girls will expect that."

"I don't think so, Joey. I'll need to be in Charleston early in the morning, so I'll probably go on in and stay there tonight. Maybe tomorrow night I will. But my lodging gets paid for with my government credit card and as I'll be coming and going at a lot of strange hours, I don't want to disturb anyone. I'll likely get a motel between town and the interstate."

"Okay, but it won't be a bother."

I swept my eyes around the 'shop' and realized that I didn't miss the place one iota. Missed the old home place and countryside, though.

"By the way," I said, "are you planning to drag the girls into the business? You'd have to change the name to McGowan and Daughters, you know."

"I haven't decided yet. Molly has some interest, but Casey gets the willies, just like you used to do. She definitely wants no part of it."

"Smart girl."

"Not exactly. She's decided to be a gourmet chef. But what does *she* know; she's only sixteen."

"Well I think that's a good thing. Maybe I'll be visiting *her* more than *you* if I don't one day find a wife who can cook."

"But I remember visiting you and Darlene a couple of times when you were in San Antonio and I thought she did okay on the meal."

"Ha! She thought *Cook*ing and *Ba*king were cities in China."

Joey laughed. "Man, you could never hang on to a good thing. Speaking of good things, how's Caroline?"

"Super. She graduated from Columbia last year with honors and is now in Quantico."

"In the Marines?" he asked, grinning ear to ear. That was Joey ... once a jarhead, always a jarhead. Could it be his only niece was joining the Corps?

"No. Don't get excited. She's in the FBI Academy."

"Then I guess she'll soon be following in her old man's footsteps."

Not finding myself particularly elated about her being there for any reason, I replied,

"I sure as hell hope not."

Chapter 3

▼

Around five I set sail west on I-64 toward Charleston. Almost immediately after climbing a long five mile grade and reaching the apex of the mountain just east of Beckley, the temperature cooled a bit. It had actually turned into a pleasant afternoon; so I continued the two hour jaunt with my driver's side window down. On hot days, I have to admit, I'm a wuss. I run the air conditioning most of the time during the hot months, especially in D.C. where it can get into the mid-nineties with no breeze any given summer's day. The blacked-out windows also do much to keep the Suburban comfortable inside. But I love the mountain air … invigorating to the lungs and smells delightful. Every once in a while there's a whiff of wood smoke or the sweet scent of lilac, tweaking the olfactory sense that much more. The state's stunning beauty is promulgated by showy rhododendrons, towering blue spruces, and majestic waterfalls that splash over huge black boulders along side of twisting roads. I heard say that Bob Denver, you remember Gilligan, having moved to the Bluefield area, once told a reporter 'they oughta put a fence around the whole state and charge admission to get in here.'

After another hour on the WV Turnpike, and reluctantly paying that 'admission' at a toll plaza near Cabin Creek, Charleston loomed ahead. The area was much as I remembered: cracker box houses crammed together from the base of the mountains to the banks of the Kanawha. People had better be able to get along under such close conditions. The few who actually own little more than postage stamp front yards would be considered land barons around there.

Then there's the Kanawha. It begins way up stream at the Gauley, that treacherous tourist attraction with Class Five rapids, mellows out and runs gently through the locks at London and Marmet, snakes past the Capital City and its factories, and finally works its way to the Ohio.

Soon the familiar gold dome of the Capitol building, a somewhat smaller replica of the U.S. Capitol, came into view. It is clearly the most recognizable feature of the city. I jumped off at a Holiday Inn in Charleston, took a quick shower and put the old jeans back on. I did change into a nice pink polo, however, which by the way is not a threat to my masculinity. After sitting down for a light Italian dinner of ravioli, a side of spaghetti, salad and hunk of garlic bread, I sipped on a glass of Merlot on a neat little terrace over-looking the city. After that glass was gone I ordered another, taking a good bit of time to do a little reminiscing.

I had visited Charleston a few times when I was a boy, mostly when my dad went there to pick up the body of some poor bastard from Greenbrier County, who had left home to find both his fortune and a new family, only to be planted back in his hometown bone yard. I had remembered Charleston as being a rather dirty and old looking industrial town. Factories to the east and west along the Kanawha emitted a retching font of chemicals that stunk up the city air with that rotten egg smell, then passed over the river valley, finally settling into the surrounding hills. There was the seedy red light district called Fry's Alley, where scantily-clad whores sat in the windows of seamy bordellos, and Capitol Street, the only real shopping area around, both of which venues kept Charleston on the map. I didn't recognize the newly-rejuvenated Capitol Street with its tree-lined sidewalks, modern curbing and sprightly store fronts. Somewhere along the line, Charleston went from old and feculent to modern chic. Hip coffee houses, quaint epicurean-style restaurants and neato book stores had sprung up here and there, all within the past twenty years. It almost reminded me of a minute Greenwich Village. And although many of the factories and mills still remained, the air ultimately got cleaned up. Like in Pittsburgh. I guess the EPA had a lot to do with that.

The lights of Charleston were now on, which did not exactly give me the impression of a New York night life scene. But what did I expect in a small river city? I went back into the bar and had a cold draft. Sweat from my frosted glass formed and drained into a pool on the mahogany bar. The bar-keep seeing this egregious violation of bar room protocol quickly plopped down a cardboard coaster and placed my glass on it, giving me a stern, silent lecture with his steely blues.

It was just me, a couple of businessmen talking about plastics over their scotch, and a lonely-looking redhead in a tight skirt stirring a fruity drink in a martini glass with a swizzle stick. Ten years ago I might have hit on her with my "I think I can make you very happy" routine. I don't do that anymore. The last time I tried to be bar room suave I opened a dialogue with a very svelte vixen with this line: "Hi. I'm a photographer and I've been looking for a face like yours." Her reply was, "Hi. I'm a plastic surgeon and I've been looking for a face like *yours.*"

My eyes left the redhead and returned to the TV screen behind the bar where Kramer was having an animated dialogue with Seinfeld and Elaine. The sound was down low or even off, which was a good thing. And I was damn glad there was no mediocre lounge singer with a guitar and stool singing overly done renditions of *Margueritaville* and *Brown Eyed Girl.* Please!

I returned to my five diamond room around eight, stripped to my tee shirt and boxers and sat down with a carafe of spring water at the desk. Retrieving Dead Arab Guy's (DAG for short) map from my valise, I unfolded it flat to study the drawing again. Why would a sketch-map be on DAG unless he and others were plotting to blow up the place and kill a lot of people? That factory could be one of five or six such plants that lay along the Kanawha. It had to be somewhere around Charleston as there was a river drawn, represented by wavy lines with a 'K' on it, and a road that tracked along beside it bearing a 6-0 (Route 60). I guessed that tomorrow I could drive by each plant to see if I'd recognize the buildings as they were positioned in the sketch. If DAG did have designs on some kind of terrorist act in the Kanawha Valley, why was he in Greenbrier County? Perhaps he and others thought they'd attract more attention staying in and around Charleston's factories. On the other hand, Middle-Eastern men would certainly be more visible in the state's rural areas, living among the farmers and shopkeepers versus a conglomeration of people. But I stopped thinking about it all for the evening as I had fallen victim to the devil wine that I had consumed earlier. I snapped off the desk lamp and lost consciousness on my pillow in no more than thirty seconds.

The seven-thirty sun poured its dollop rays rudely through the vertical slats on the window blind, painfully opening my eyes. While still working for the Bureau more than a year ago I would bounce out at five-thirty, drain the lizard, and run my five miles. Then I would shower, drown myself in a pot of java, and was at headquarters by seven with a breakfast bar in my hand. It helped having an apartment seven blocks from J. Edgar's place. Now-a-days in semi-retirement, I'm out of bed a little later, run less far, and go into the D.C. office probably three days a week. The breakfast bar is still part of my routine, but my stomach rarely allows me to go beyond a second cup of coffee. But the good thing is, my agenda is no longer structured. I'm no longer attacking each day with a tenacious sense of purpose. Mostly, I just make it up as I go along. Granted, I can be up any time of the day or night, canvassing, following, questioning, probing or exterminating, although the latter thing kind of ruins my day, not to mention the exterminee's day.

After I donned my light blue oxford and khaki slacks, I threw on my Navy blazer, looking rather G.Q. in the motel mirror. This is about as dressed up as I get. I haven't worn a suit since I used to be *known* as one of the 'suits.'

I arrived at the Charleston FBI Headquarters at 9:30. A lovely young thing greeted me with a sweet smile and asked me to wait. I had hoped Birdman had telephonically introduced me yesterday, which would prepare him for our meeting. In a couple of minutes Special Agent Jack Fuentes appeared in the reception area with his hand extended. I took it, finding the grip a little wimpy, not to mention clammy. It has always made me think that a guy like that was either a Nervous Nellie or perhaps had a glandular problem.

"I'm Jack, Mr. McGowan. Please come back to my office." Jack was a nice looking chap of Hispanic descent, I later learned to be Cuban, but he was as stiff and uptight as they come. He motioned for me to sit down in the chair facing his desk and then he quickly retreated behind it to his leather wingback. I always hated the scenario. It made me feel like I was either in the principal's office or interviewing for a job. In *my* office, I had always made it a point to sit in the companion chair adjacent to my guest.

"Well, Mr. McGowan, I did get a call from your boss in New York. He told me you're retired Bureau *and* a West Virginian to boot."

Jack had gotten right to business, so I suspected he was not one who was comfortable with small talk. He neither asked me how my trip was or if I got lucky last night.

"Call me Bruce, Jack. Yes, I finished out my twenty. I was twelve years with the Army before that."

"Special Forces, right?"

"You *did* talk to my boss. But … right."

"Where did you go to college?"

Did I say he was not comfortable with small talk?

"WVU."

"No kidding. Same here. I graduated in '88. How about you?"

"Let's say we weren't in the same class."

He chuckled. I figured it was because he knew I had twenty years on him. Jack was a handsome dude with his black, thick hair and square jaw, but a little paunchy in a couple of places. A picture of his wife and two kids, boy and girl, was on his desk. She looked like a typical former high school cheerleader, blonde, beauty pageant smile with perfect white teeth. Even the kids were blonde, and the little girl, who looked to be seven, was in a miniature cheerleader get-up. Perfect family. I'll bet he even had a white picket fence around his house in South Hills, a Honda Odyssey in the driveway and a Jack Russell that wears an Izod sweater in the winter. His daughter, he said, was into ballet and tap, and his son who was five was an All-American soccer player. There's some sarcasm in there, but maybe I was just jealous of this golden boy and his sublime, ideal life.

"Beautiful family, Jack."

He looked at his photo and beamed proudly. "Thanks. My wife's name is Diane, and my children are Jessica and Jack, Jr."

It just suddenly hit me and I almost giggled out loud. "So you kids are from the heartland and doin' the best that you can."

"I beg your pardon?" Jack said, looking very confused.

I finally laughed. "I'm sorry, Jack. It just made me think about *Jack and Diane*, you know, the song?"

"No," he searched his mind, rolling his eyes around thoughtfully. "Can't say as I know that one."

"You're kidding, right?"

"*Jack and Diane* was a song?"

I just kind of stared at him with my own dumbfounded look, but then nodded. I finally changed the subject because right about then I was feeling very old. "Well, I guess you know why I'm here."

He nodded. "I got the gist of it from your boss."

"He told you about the Arab John Doe and the map."

"He did. Do you have the map with you?"

I pulled it from my inside coat pocket and handed it to him across the desk. Before looking it over, his expression changed like he had just performed a social faux pas. "Hey, Bruce, where's my hospitality? How about a cup of coffee or a pastry?"

Obviously, this guy was not your father's Oldsmobile … er, FBI agent. He looked like some light-loafered accountant or stock broker at Smith Blarney with not one ounce of macho in his entire body. In my day we Special Agents were a cross between Robert Stack and Sean Connery.

"By the way, Jack, what is your degree in?"

"Accounting. Why do you ask?"

"Oh, no reason. Just small talk." *Damn, I'm good*.

Jack looked back down at the map on his desk. He studied it for more than three minutes. I thought he was going to diagram it like a sentence or dissect it like a frog. "Hmm. I would agree that finding this on a deceased Arab gentleman would create a concern or even a suspicion of a potential terrorist threat."

Brilliant, Jack.

I pulled out my digital camera and showed him the photos I took of the corpse.

"This man died when?"

"About six days ago."

"Why is this information just now coming into our hands?"

I definitely didn't want to give Joey up for his evidence suppression indiscretion. "I think it may have been overlooked by the locals or just not been given that much attention when first found. My brother got hold of it and called me. He's a mortician and has the body." I have this unique way of filtering my lies so that a little truth will squeeze out every once in a while.

Jack looked at me over the map as though he didn't quite believe me. And with good cause. But then he replied, "You know, that's just typical of local cops. Many don't have the nose or investigative insight that government cops do. Does your brother still have the body?"

"Yes. The mortuary is in Greenbrier County, McGowan and Sons."

"McGowan. Like you."

"Family business."

"Interesting. Did you pick up anything significant about the body? Tattoos? Birthmarks?"

"No, not really. He has a bunch of facial moles. But he won't have them long. He will soon have a pauper's funeral and be put in the oven. The county M.E. has the stiff's prints and DNA sample for posterity purposes."

"Well, I'm glad *somebody* over there is on the ball. Your boss said you believe there could be a network of these people in Greenbrier County or here in Charleston. Do you have any evidence to support that?"

"No, none. But it only figures that if the dead guy had a map of a factory on him, he's not the Lone Ranger. In my experience, these guys work in packs, three or four together."

"That's right," added Jack. "As you know, we have developed profiles on these types of elements. Their purpose is to assimilate into the American society and then find opportunities to wreak destruction. And even though their determinant is terrorism, paradoxically they're deeply entrenched in their Muslim faith. It is the most troubling of all paradoxes."

"That's all well and good, Amen and Hallelujah, Jack, but you failed to mention that they're ruthless cutthroats, have no value as to human life, kick their women around, and are programmed and committed to annihilating the infidels, namely us. Their mission is to demoralize America and bring down our economy, our government and civilization as we know it."

Jack nodded. "We know they're out there ... trying to blend into the mainstream."

"Yeah. They integrate our society by pretending to be students and business people, all the while plotting to kill Americans in mass. What makes them dangerous and difficult to stop is that the bastards are willing to sacrifice their own lives. And all it takes is one suicidal son-of-a-bitch and one bomb to take out a building, stadium or marketplace. We're long overdue in this country, Jack, to experience the same type of activity we see in Israel or Lebanon."

"I see you're very passionate about this, Bruce."

I did realize I had stood on my soap box a little too long and was actually preaching to the choir. And, hell yes, I'm passionate about this. So, I thought this was a good time to inject a little levity into the conversation. Maybe then Jack would void the corncob he was sitting on.

"Hey, Jack. Listen to this. Two Islamic terrorists are chatting. One of them has his wallet out and is flipping through pictures. He says, 'Yeah, this is my oldest. He's a martyr. And here's my second son. He's a martyr, too.' Then there's a pause. The second terrorist says, wistfully, 'Ah, they blow up so fast, don't they?'"

Jack sat there with a slight frown between his eyes. No guffaw ... not even a smile.

"Well, how about this one," I tried again. "Why don't Muslims celebrate Valentine's Day?"

No response.

"Because camels couldn't care less."

Well, I laughed at my jokes, but there were no yuks from Jack. He just stared at me, eyes transfixed like he was looking into a kaleidoscope at complex patterns. Listening to what was coming out of my head, maybe he was.

"Yes, well that was entertaining, Bruce," he said. I took it that Jack had no sense of humor and was all business. "Were you this frivolous when you were with the Bureau?"

Fair question, I guess. I think early on in my career I was quite a bit like Jack ... professional, matter-of-fact, dignified, anal. But then I answered him. "I suppose I've let my hair down in my old age, Jack. I think somewhere along the line I got tired of being a regimented stuff-shirt for twenty years."

I actually believe Jack took offense to that and felt maybe it was directed toward him. "It *is* expected that at our level we must maintain a certain decorum."

He was beginning to bore me now. This thirty-four year old kid sounded like somebody sixty-four. Obviously his training officer was from the days of J. Edgar and had instilled in the little bastard an unhealthy degree of self-purpose and demeanor. Nonetheless, I was determined to give him the respect of his position. When I occupied a similar office in Hooverland, I may have been put out with some 'frivolous' guy making light of *my* demeanor. But I still couldn't imagine I was as stiff as this kid.

"So, Bruce, what are your plans from here?"

"I'm going back to Greenbrier County and look around for any other Middle Eastern gentlemen who merit watching."

"And if you find any, then what?"

"If I see something that deserves my attention, I will provide it."

"And what does that usually entail?"

What's with the twenty questions?

"Surveillance, information gathering. You know, the usual sneaky-peek stuff."

"What will you do with the information you obtain? You're not a federal cop anymore."

"Jack, I'm still in law enforcement working for the Department of State."

He eyed me with what I thought to be a look of contempt … or something like it.

"I'm pretty sure I know what you do, Bruce."

"Really? I'm glad *you* do, because half the time, I don't."

He kept his third-degree eyes on me. "Let me tell you what I know about the Counterterrorist Center. It has a collaborative alliance with the FBI, but responsible only to provide intelligence information about suspected or known terrorist groups for Bureau use. It does not 'dish out' justice; its purpose is to help the FBI to wield justice."

"Jack, I am *not* CTC. My organization operates independently from other intelligence groups. We are a smaller Special Ops organization with a specific purpose."

"Which is?"

"To take whatever measures are necessary against terrorists and other subversives to assure the protection of the American people. In other words, my friend, the predator becomes the prey."

"You know what I think, Bruce? I think you're some kind of government-directed renegade who will flirt with crossing the boundaries of the law whenever it suits you or your boss. And I further believe you would take somebody out, just on suspicion. You know, 'kill 'em all; let God sort 'em out."

Wow! This guy is insightful. And that impresses me.

"No. That was my motto two jobs ago, Jack. You know, the Special Forces."

"Right." He kept his steely blues on me for a moment, then added, "I'll ask that you keep this office informed about any findings, Bruce."

"Okay, Jack. Right after my boss is apprised of whatever it is I find, you'll be the second to know."

"Can we trust you to not go off on tangents and killing sprees, Bruce?"

"Cross my throat and hope to choke."

He actually half smiled and I thought his face would crack open like a glazed donut.

"And before you leave, I need a copy of the map. We're going to work on this on our end."

"Fine. Now Jack, would you do something for me?"

"Okay. If I can."

"Do you have a secure fax line?"

"Of course."

"I want you to fax the Arabic message on the map to this number. The recipient, Mr. Abu Narziz, one of our operatives, will translate it and send it right back. I'll write a note to Abu so he'll know this is from me. Then, guess what? *You'll* be the first to receive that information."

I knew Birdman would call me right away with the translation, but I wanted to make good ol' Jack feel important in the matter. He would get the impression of willing cooperation on my part. And I *would* give him that, at least partially. I may at some point need his unwitting collaboration, not to mention backup.

"No problem. Anything else?"

"One other thing." I took the green capsule from the envelope. "Can you have your lab check the contents of this? It may be some kind of cold capsule, but as there are no trade letters or markings on it, I suspect it's a cyanide capsule."

"That was found on the dead Arab?"

"Yes it was."

Jack's eyes widened. I don't know that he'd ever seen one. "If it is cyanide, then we'd know for sure that he planned never be taken alive and submit to interrogation. The average law-abiding Joe Citizen would have no use for one of these, would he?"

No, Jack, he wouldn't.

Jack continued. "I may skip away tomorrow to take a look at the body. Will you be accessible?"

"Probably."

"When will you return to Washington?"

"I don't know. Maybe two or three days. It depends on what I find out nosing around. Anyway, I would go to New York to brief the boss. He always wants a face-to-face when it comes to things like this."

Jack pulled a business card from his desk and I reciprocated with one of mine. He looked it over. "It's pretty plain, Bruce. It has the Department of State Seal, your name and a web site. No title indicated, like Assassin or Terminator."

Well, the junior G-Man did have a sense of humor after all.

"Funny, Jack," I replied. "You know … I think we're going to get along just fine. Beneath that tight-ass Jack Webb exterior, I actually think *you're* a bit 'frivolous.' Maybe in twenty years, you could even be me."

"Not likely," he replied. This time the half smile was rather smug. "You've got my number, Bruce. Stay in touch. Oh, and see you tomorrow."

Chapter 4

▼

Hey it's good to be back home again.
Sometimes this old farm seems like a long lost friend.
Hey it's good to be back home again.

—*John Denver*

I caught a burger at the Cedar Top and started back toward Lewisburg. I do a lot of driving across America, but I find that few states broadcast the grandeur beauty of West Virginia. For nostalgic reasons, I decided to stay on Route 60 and go the way of the Gauley and Sewell. These are majestic mountains with hair-pin curves, some so sharp that the brake lights you see in front of you may in fact be your own. Occasionally, one catches a glimpse of the New River snaking through its chasm two thousand feet below and it is both frightening and humbling to think that allowing one wheel to drop off the pavement will send one tumbling through firs and hemlocks to the gorge below … and certain death. After descending eight to ten percent grades and negotiating challenging, seemingly impossible turns, the driver levels off into quaint little towns inhabited by sweet, unpretentious people. Then after the last wood frame house or store front is passed, the wayfarer starts yet another climb to do it all over again. The land, a perfect wilderness of rapturous rhododendrons and garish Virginia bluebell, is so wild and wondrous that once afforded a taste, it remains forever ingrained in the soul.

So why here, I thought? Why West Virginia, a state that should be far removed from terrorist interests? It's not Washington, New York or Los Angeles. But I also realized that one of the goals of terrorists is to demoralize a people by striking where least expected with the element of surprise. So then, why not a place known for its innocence and simplicity? To get to the throat of America, attacking the very heart of its people, the terrorists make their statement … "we can attack you anywhere." An attack plan involving a Charleston factory was *very* plausible. I reminded myself that since the beginning of the Cold War, the area around the capital city had been known as the Chemical Center of the World. Depending on what kind of chemicals the plant manufactured, a bombing on any one of them could release a lot of nasty pollutants into the air. Some of the stuff would be deadly.

The ride back had made me even more determined to get to the bottom of why an unidentified Arab with a detailed hand-drawn map of a West Virginia factory in his possession lay dead in a Greenbrier County mortuary. That is, other than getting mashed by a big brown truck. If there were others out there, I would find them.

I called Joey and told him I was on the way. He said he had to finish up on a teenage girl from Alderson who was killed in a car wreck just south of town. She had just gotten her license and had become the victim of inexperience and speed. She had misjudged a curve at over seventy miles an hour and T-boned the driver's side into a large oak. Joey was doing his best to wire her back together. As feverishly as he was working on her face, her casket would still likely have to be closed. It saddened me to hear that. I remember as a teenager looking down on the dead faces of two of my friends after they had failed to realize that youth was not invincible. There was nothing that pained my father any more than having to work on the body of a child. And I knew that my brother was feeling the same pain, especially considering he had two teenage girls of his own.

"You're coming for dinner tonight, aren't you big brother?"

"I wouldn't miss it, Joey. It's been weeks since I've had a good home cooked meal."

"Good. Go by the house anytime. I'll be there a little later. Dinner is usually at six."

Joey's wife, Cora, was a fine-looking woman at forty-five. About an inch taller than her husband who stood five-nine, she was a little humped over like many tall women are. I guess they think by lowering their stature, their partners will not look so conspicuously short beside them. But she had a pretty face with her high, chiseled cheek bones and full lips. Their two girls, Casey and Molly, sixteen and fourteen, were cute, but tall like their mother. And they were personable and talkative around adults, unlike most teenagers. As they were six and eight years behind Caroline, they had not gotten an opportunity to know her very well. Of course, the fact that Caroline had mostly lived with her mother in Maryland, distance made it even more difficult for the cousins to know one another. One of my biggest regrets.

Cora and I had a nice conversation in the kitchen to catch up while she was chopping up carrots and peppers on the carving board. She was a sweet gal with a marvelous personality and genuine smile. Her eyes were happy eyes, sparkling nearly as brilliantly as the diamonds on her earlobes. She and Joey were perfect for one another. Had been since the day they met more than twenty years ago. Their utopian little marriage had made me quite envious, not jealously so, but in a good way. Sometimes, though, seeing them go on with each other like they did summoned remorse within me for not trying harder in my own marriage.

Joey bounded in the back door after an hour or so, bellowing lively that he was home. I don't know how he did it … working every day with corpses and bereaved families seven days a week, then turning on the laughter and jocularity with his family when the day was over. But I knew Cora and the girls were his end-of-day catharsis. His sanity. And I did admire and respect him for hanging in there with the business.

We all sat down at the dinner table and about the time I picked up my butter knife, Casey put my left hand in hers and Molly picked up my right. "The blessing," Casey said.

As Joey was talking to God, I tried to remember the last time I said 'grace' or was in the presence of someone who did. More than anything, it made me not only realize my heathen status in this world, but that I never said a blessing over a meal with my own daughter. And then instead of listening to Joey pray, I thought about the probable terrorist lying in Joey's drawer and all the other jihad and al-Qaeda types who pray religiously … excuse the play on words … then go out and blow up innocent Americans. This kind of hypocrisy I will never understand, and I have had tons of courses in Psychopathology, Criminology and yes, even Religion.

"… amen."

I didn't hear much of the sermonette, mainly because of my A.D.D, but it did make the vittles taste that much better.

"Joey says you're not going to stay with us, Bruce," began Cora.

I chewed and swallowed the bite of roast beef before answering. "I told Joey I'd stay tonight, but will go to a motel tomorrow."

"Nonsense. We have plenty of room and you know you'd be more comfortable than in some stinky motel room."

"Thanks, Cora, I really would like to, but I need a kind of base to work out of, to come and go without bothering the girls." I winked at them and smiled. "The type of work I expect to do may require that I stay out part of the night or even all night. I'm used to it. Don't think I've had any decent circadian rhythm since before college."

"What kind of work do you do, Uncle Bruce?" asked Molly.

"Well, sweetie, I still work for the government. I locate and investigate people."

Casey was now interested. "What kind of people?"

Joey shot me a glance and formed a half-smile, like "talk your way out of this one, Brucie."

I hate explaining things to children, especially *these* inquiring minds. I definitely wanted what I do to remain in the dark where they were concerned.

Joey bailed me out. "Your Uncle Bruce hates talking about work, girls. And he's been traveling for two or three days and tired. Now let him be. Look at the bags under his eyes."

All three women looked at my suitcases and didn't say anything else.

I nodded my thanks to Joey.

After dinner Joey and I stepped out onto the front porch. He lit a Swisher Sweet which I'm damn glad he finally went to after those nasty Marsh Wheelings. I propped a foot up on the railing and inhaled the cooling air. Joey was still thinking about his young wreck victim he was working on just before dinner.

"She was the same age as Casey, you know. The whole time I was working on her, I thought about the horror of seeing one of my girls lying there. It made me almost demand the keys to Casey's Honda."

"I'm with you, Joey. I think of Caroline every day there in Quantico. A hundred different things could go wrong. She could get hurt or even shot by accident in training. I can't even call her except on certain evenings. Trainees can only receive calls if there's an emergency. Hopefully, she'll call me tomorrow."

"Caroline will be fine, Bruce. She's in great physical conditioning and she's smart. She'll take care of herself and she'll make a good agent."

I nodded, but didn't respond. I was afraid the lump in my throat would give me away. Real men don't bawl like little girls.

Joey changed the subject. "Well, the deputies came out and gave the shop the once over. They did dust for prints, checked the door, looked at the Arab and said if I find out I'm missing anything to call them."

"In hindsight, maybe the State would have been more thorough. Maybe you should have called *them* instead."

"Maybe. But these guys thought it was just kids who broke in."

"What did they say about DAG losing his sheet?"

"Dag who?"

"Sorry. Dead Arab Guy."

"Good acronym. They thought it was still kids. The kids likely took a peek and left out screaming. Some guy was probably showing his girl what Arab equipment looked like."

Joey grinned; then it went away. "So, how will you find out if there are other people of his persuasion in the area?"

"I'll take DAG's picture and float it around the shops downtown, the post office and all motels in the area. Believe me, if there are others and they look like him, they'll be remembered by someone."

"Yeah, but you know that people don't often recognize ethnic differences. They may see a darker-skinned Mexican or I-talian and think he's the kind of guy you're looking for. And there are scores of Indians, you know, from India, around here running Seven-Elevens, Dairy Queens and motels."

I nodded in agreement. "After Pearl Harbor, not only Japanese Americans were rounded up, but Chinese, Koreans and Siamese were as well. Let's face it, Joey; we all tend to profile when a person doesn't look like you and me."

"Well, I don't envy your task. Good luck." He paused for a drag. "By the way, what motel are you going to stay in?"

"I haven't decided. I was thinking about the General Lewis or the Best Western."

"Not the Greenbrier?"

"Yeah, right. I'm lucky my expense account allows me to stay at a Motel 6."

"Why don't you stay at Wolf Laurel?"

"What's that?"

"It's a Bed and Breakfast. I don't think the cost is extravagant, although the accommodations are."

"I can't say that I remember such a place around here."

"Actually it was the old Wolf estate. I don't think it became a B & B until the early '70s when the owner died. He left the house to his son, Mason, who turned it into a country inn of sorts. And do you remember Adrianna Randolph? She now owns the place. She was three or four years in school behind me. Ended up marrying Mason. Then Mason died a couple of years ago of an aorta dissection at forty-eight. Was as healthy as any one I've seen his age and he just dropped over one day. No warning."

"Bummer. Yeah, I remember her. Pretty little girl. Pretty name. I'll never forget when I went off to WVU, she was about ten. I used to kid around with her and do some innocent flirting. I cut her dad's grass for an entire summer when Mr. Randolph got hurt in a saw mill accident. Then one day we were coming out of church, the day before I left for Morgantown, and she said out of the blue, "Skip McGowan, I'm going marry you one day." I thought that was real cute. I winked at her and said, "Okay, I'll wait for you to turn eighteen. Can *you* wait that long?" You know, I haven't seen her since. That must have been more than thirty years I reckon. So what's she look like now?"

"Forget it, Brewster. She weighs over two hundred pounds, got bleach blonde hair and a huge mole or wart on her upper lip."

"Cute little Adrianna?"

"Cute people can grow up and become beasts, Bro."

"Well, whatever. Maybe I'll go by there to see if a room is available. That is, if I can get Birdman to pay for it."

"Birdman? Who's that?"

"You know, the guy I spoke with on the phone."

"Oh." Joey was still puzzled by all the bird references.

Our old house was a handsome looking place with its white frame and bronze cedar-shake roof. It was built in the early Twentieth Century by our granddad when he was a young man fresh back from WW I, the war to end all wars. Joey had done a lot of work on the house, like replacing all the distorted windows, adding R13 insulation throughout and overhauling the decrepit wiring system. There was a fair amount of acreage around the old home place. Some of it was being farmed by Homer Ridgeway just down the road and the rest of it was being mowed continuously by a herd of Joey's Billy goats.

I remember going there on weekends as a child with my parents, listening to Dad and Pops talk funeral business. It wasn't enough that they talked it all day at the shop, but they brought it home with them. Mom and Grandy, as we called her, just sat in the kitchen snapping green beans or husking corn, saying very little to one another, but hanging on every word the men had to say in the parlor. Sometimes there was stuff talked about that pricked their ears, like what they found on the decedents or what the dearly departed were doing when they kicked off. Like old man Cunningham, for example. When it came to men talk, Mom and Grandy were sure to keep the door between the kitchen and parlor open.

I remember a movie that came out way back when called *The Loved One*. It was based on a book by Evelyn Waugh and was a kind of satire about the funeral business. Jonathan Winters played the part of twin brothers. One mortician owned a very respectable business while the other, a kind of black sheep brother, ran a pet mortuary. My dad, who took us to see it, mostly for curiosity reasons, was incensed about the movie. He said the mortuary service was one of dignity and shouldn't be parodied and degraded by cartoonish comedians. Dad was serious about the business. But I guess death *is* pretty serious business. I don't remember much about the movie, but I did like looking at Anjanette Comer. Can't believe I actually conjured up her name. She must have made a hell of an impression on a kid like me slammed almost overnight into puberty.

Well, back to the old house, Joey and I would be camped out in front of the black and white Zenith watching Paladin and Gunsmoke if it were a Saturday night and the Ed Sullivan Show on Sundays. Joey was just a tot and didn't pick up much of the dialogue, but still sat in a trance just like his older brother, never taking his eyes off the snowy picture, even when grabbing a handful of popcorn from our bowl. He just groped and dug until he got enough to shove into his mouth to make himself look like a chipmunk.

And now back to the present, I followed Casey up to my old room which was now hers. She had insisted that I sleep in her bed, which actually was *my* old bed, so that she could rough it on the couch in the den and watch old movies on AMC until the wee morning hours. Joey and Cora were good with that if it was weekend or non-school night. Casey ignored my protests and began putting together her pillow and comforter to set up camp downstairs.

"Goodnight, Uncle Bruce. If you need a nightlight, there's one on the wall by the bathroom," she giggled.

"I'm a big boy now, Casey. I haven't needed a light on since ... well, since maybe a couple of years ago. And I don't wet the bed, either."

Now she was laughing. "That would be a *good* thing. Then I guess you don't want me to tuck you in or read you a story."

"Only if you want to."

"What will it be ... *Goldilocks* or *When Harry Did Sally?*"

"Get out of here, little miss, before I report you to your dad."

Casey was a McGowan, all right, with her zealous frivolity and lusty sense of humor. She grabbed an armful of comforter, formed her lips into a kiss and said, "Love, ya, Uncle Bruce. Sleep tight."

After she closed the door, I was thrown back to ten years ago and my own beautiful daughter. Although Caroline was always more serious than Casey when she was her age, there was still that same sweetness and winsome spirit that delighted me every moment I was with her. I shed my clothes, brushed, plopped onto my old bed and turned the switch on the bedside lamp. As the pale light of the half moon cast ghostly shadows of monster-like creatures on the wall, actually made by a gnarly oak outside the window, I realized a smile had broken out. I was twelve when Pops died and Dad moved us in here with Grandy. I saw similar figures on the same walls then and although I would never admit being afraid at that age to my parents or little brother, I refused to take my eyes off those abominable shadows until my heavy lids finally closed.

Lying in my old bed, I felt like John Boy Walton, returning once again to the home of his youth and to the remnants of his loving family. The house creaked and popped much as it did forty plus years ago as though it were saying to me, 'welcome home,' kid. I missed you.

Goodnight, Joey Boy.

Chapter 5

▼

I did need a place to stow away and remain inconspicuous. I also needed a plan, although it probably would amount to a lot of gumshoe work. Out of curiosity, I thought I would at least drive by Wolf Laurel and check it out. Thought it would also be good to see an old face which was very much a young one the last time I saw it.

I drove back across town, following Joey's directions, until I came to Seven Bridges Road (obviously renamed from something else after the group, the Eagles, made it famous) where I turned and took the second gravel driveway on the left. It was a charming house with more grace than grandeur, white with stylish lattice and millwork, cedar shake roofing, and a looming turret on the right side within what appeared to be a pentagonal room. The B&B was set down off the road about fifty yards and nestled under several large oaks and sycamores. Pink mountain laurel and feathered ferns graced either side of the wide veranda and lavender clematis climbed and intertwined along the banister.

I dropped down from the Suburban, tweeped my security system with the remote, and slung over my shoulder my tote which contained a toiletry bag, my Glock and other such essentials … just in case I decided to stay. Over the door was a historical marker bearing the B&B's original name and birth date: *The John Mason Wolf House, Circa 1869*. And on the right side of the door, a shiny brass marker read *Wolf Laurel, 1939*. A guy could enjoy such a place for a few days, I thought. But again, I may be coming and going a lot, and maybe I would be best suited to stay in some flea bag, considering what the place was going to cost. I doubted the Birdman would spring for this.

When I stepped up onto the veranda, a large Abyssinian came to greet me and began rubbing its tail on my pant leg. Cats generally avoid me, like I carry the scent of dog on me or something, but this one was obviously not going to be afraid of anyone or anything, weighing close to twenty five pounds. I reached down to pet the varmint which made it all the more amorous.

I opened the screen door that creaked and sang like one would expect and made my way to a high, rustic desk in the small lobby. My new friend zipped through the door with me. A dining room that would seat about eight people lay off to the left that also adjoined a small kitchen. Beyond the dining room was the hallway that appeared to have five guest rooms, three on the right, one immediately on the left and one at the end of the hall across from the last room. The place gave off a scent of cedar from the wood flooring which lay throughout, rough hewn but glossy smooth.

I dinged the bell which immediately brought out a very lovely thirty or early forties-something angel with silken, light brown hair pulled back behind two perfectly-shaped ears adorned with dangling diamond earrings, gorgeous eyes and a lovely smile emanating from somewhat full, pouty lips. She had on a sleeveless blouse with the name *Wolf Laurel* embroidered over the left of two very nicely-shaped breasts. Other than that, I didn't notice much about her. Whatever the cost, I thought, I would definitely be staying. But then I glanced at her left hand and, sadly, she was wearing a simple wedding band.

"Hi," I said in the sexiest Tom Selleck voice I could cough up. "Do you have a room for the weekend and maybe a couple of days longer?"

"I didn't until about a half hour ago," she replied in the same soft, sultry voice I would have expected. "We had a cancellation. Looks like you're in luck."

"I would definitely say that I am," I replied, then looked at her finger again. Maybe it was just a costume ring with some kind of stone that got turned around.

"I see you met Burt." She eyed the fur ball as he disappeared into the office behind the desk.

"Sure did. Friendly cuss."

"He's that way with everyone ... even with people who don't like cats. But they eventually come around and end up petting him."

Okay. Enough about Garfield. "Say, I used to know your proprietress several years ago. Would you know if Adrianna Randolph is around? I think she may have the last name Wolf, like the inn."

"Well, who might you be, just so she'll know who's asking?"

"Bruce. Bruce McGowan."

Cutie Pie looked at me a moment like she was undressing me with her eyes, and then stepped around the counter to my side. For the first time I got a glimpse of her legs under that clinging skirt. They fit the rest of her very well. Suddenly, she threw her arms around my neck and pulled me into the firm bulges on her upper torso. Somewhere in my sex-starved brain, which incidentally was enjoying every sweet second of the hug, I realized she must be Adrianna.

"Well, hello." That's all I could say.

She backed up at arm's length and held my hands in hers. "*I'm* Adrianna, Skip. God, you look good. I knew there was something familiar about those eyes. There may be a bit of snow on the rooftop, but I swear you're much the same."

There's also still fire in my furnace, sweetheart. Of course, you have no way of knowing that. At least, not yet.

"So you're Adrianna. The last time I saw you I think you were ten. You were a doll." I paused for dramatic effect. "Of course, I see you *still* are."

She flushed a little. Her blue eyes glistened from the tears of nostalgia that had formed. But the eyes were dazzling, moist or not. "You're sweet to say that. And you … you're as good looking as ever."

Now my turn to blush.

"My brother, Joey, told me you ran this place. He described you, but fell way short of doing you justice."

Remind me to kill the little rat for yet another of his practical jokes.

"Joe, yes. I've always liked him. A good looking guy, as well, but certainly not as handsome as you."

I nodded in agreement.

"I remember last seeing you the day I went away to the university. Do you remember what you said to me?"

"Mmmm, no," she replied. "Can't say that I do."

"That one day you were going to marry me."

She flushed again. Her lovely smile revealed a full set of white perfect teeth. I was glad to see she had all her teeth. One never knows in this good ol' state.

"I said that?"

"Uh huh."

"Oh, now I'm embarrassed. I did have quite a crush on you, but I guess it didn't take me long to get over it. I remember liking a boy in my fifth grade class. Liked him enough to end up marrying him. Mason Wolf."

"I've been pretty forgettable to a lot of women in my life. Why should you have been any different?"

She laughed and flicked an errant strand of hair back from her brow. I had only been talking to her for five minutes and already I regretted not coming back from college to marry her. Of course, I would have been twenty-two and she, *fourteen*. I didn't spend four years at WVU to come back and spend eight in jail.

"So you're staying here for a couple of days?"

"Maybe longer, now," I answered. She knew what I meant.

"Tell you what," she said. "We don't do dinner here at the inn, but if you'd like to join me at Tavern 1785 around seven, that would make my evening. I'd like to catch up on the last thirty-some years."

"Sounds great," I replied with the giddiness of a five year old. I didn't want to appear too anxious, so I forewent the cartwheels.

"Then seven it is," she said. "I have someone who stays at the office some evenings from six-thirty until ten or whenever I come back in from one of my usual exciting nights out." She rolled her eyes. "We can leave together from here after that, if you want."

"Okay. Looking forward to it."

I signed her book, went over the financial arrangements and took my key from her sweet little hand. I was staying in the Pine Room.

I still had about four hours to kill, so I dropped in on the State Police detachment outside Lewisburg. Mostly, I do not establish relationships with state and local police. First, they generally don't know what to make of me, and then, since I'm a card-carrying member of a terrorist exterminating organization, packing heat, they don't know whether to assist me in my investigations or investigate *me*.

The sergeant behind the desk looked to be six-seven and two-forty, sporting a Marine high-and-tight burr cut and a face like Herman Munster. This was a guy I wanted beside me the next time a bunch of thugs want to put holes in me. I could use him for a shield because slugs would bounce off this body like BBs.

"Can I help you, sir?" asked Herman.

"Yes, Sergeant. My name is Bruce McGowan and I work for an organization in the Department of State." I gave him my business card.

After studying my card like he was cramming for an exam, he said, "I see the State Department seal, but it doesn't give the name of your organization. What do you do for them?"

Here we go again. I'm in the extermination business, Herman. Nevertheless, I got out my ID to supplement the card and showed it to him. "I am part of a team that looks for foreign and domestic subversives." I put my finger to my lips.

"So that would be some kind of counter-terrorist organization. Is there something going on around here that involves terrorism?"

Did I mention the word *terrorist?*

"I'm just following up a lead, Sergeant ..." I looked at his metal nameplate. "... Storm." Well that sure as hell fits. "My brother owns McGowan Funeral Home and is also the assistant county coroner. He has an Arab John Doe on ice that got hit by a UPS truck about a week ago."

"Yeah, I heard about that. Down on Washington Street, it was. And you think he was a terrorist?"

"I have no idea what he is, Sergeant. I'm just checking him out. I do know he had no identification."

"Do you investigate every A-rab that ends up on a slab without an I.D?"

Obviously, Herman attended the same redneck school my brother went to.

"Naw. I'm actually taking a few days of vacation and just passing time. Anyway, do you have an investigator in the detachment I can speak with?"

"Lieutenant Harlan Williams is our uniformed detective. Right now he's at the Greenbrier Woman's Club giving a presentation about personal safety."

"Would you ask him to give me a call on my cell when he returns? I'll write my number on the card."

"Will do, Mr. McGowan." He eyed me like he still wasn't sure about me. I guess I have one of those faces. But nothing like his; that's for sure.

I got back to my room about five and settled in with a brewski from the Seven-Eleven. I had eyed the store clerk behind the counter with my ethnic-profiling baby blues. I told myself I was probably no different from every other white-bread, white man when it came to people of the Middle Eastern persuasion. Not that *I* thought they all looked alike.

The mattress on my bed was about ten feet high and required that I step on a stool at the bed rail to thrust myself up. I stretched out my hands behind my head and blinked a few times, realizing I still had a couple of hours before my date with cutie-pie Adrianna. With a frilly canopy overhead, tasteful Federal blue and white wallpaper, and an ancient drawer chest situated by a window with sixty year old distorted glass, the room boasted an elegance that was far too spiffy for the likes of me. Of course, at $155 per night, I felt I had every right to enjoy it. Birdman was going to drop a load when he reviewed the bill. Next time he would insist I stay in a place where they left the light on for me. And that would be a good thing seeing as how I'm still afraid of the dark.

I decided I would close my heavy lids for just a few minutes. Immediately the sweet face and petite body of Adrianna Wolf appeared like an angelic vision in my tired brain. Just a couple of winks and I would feel like a new man. But then similar to experiencing an electric shock, I jumped when my cell phone went off. I snatched it up, pushed *send* and a man on the other end identified himself as Lieutenant Harlan Williams, West Virginia State Police.

"Mr. McGowan, Sergeant Storm filled me in about you. Says you're investigating the Arab man over in your brother's mortuary. I'm actually the officer who happened to be on the scene when the guy got hit. We found no ID on him, and we still don't know where he's from or what he was doing around here. Are you investigating this man for the Feds?"

"For my organization, yes."

"I wasn't able to tell from your card what area of the government you work in."

"Personnel management," I replied with a dead-pan expression in my voice.

"I'll bet. Find 'em and fire 'em, huh?"

I prefer the word 'terminate', Lieutenant.

"Let's just leave it that I do State Department investigations."

"Locating possible terrorists, right?"

"Possible subversives, Lieutenant." I then changed the tenor of the conversation. "Did you know about the map he had on him?"

"Yeah, I saw it. It didn't make much sense and unsure it actually meant anything. It remained in the possession of the coroner along with other personal effects."

I sat up, now that my eyes were fully open. "Did you not think the situation warranted calling in the FBI?" I asked.

His hesitation to immediately respond fully reflected a defensiveness. I think he took issue with my tone of voice and insinuation of incompetence. I really didn't intend to suggest that; it was probably because he woke me up from my late-summer's nap.

"There just didn't seem to be enough substance to the sketch from my perspective to merit any federal investigation. But anyway, I did call someone I've known for a long time at FBI Headquarters in D.C."

"Who do you know up there?"

"A guy named Bob Tucker."

"Tuck. I know him well. We worked together on a terrorist case back in '99."

"You were FBI?"

"Twenty years."

"So that's what this is about. You think the Arab man was a terrorist?"

"We actually refer to them as extremists until we get to know them. You know, innocent until proven guilty."

"Okay then, suspected terrorists."

"Unfortunately, they're confirmed as terrorists when they blow people up. And it's my job to see they don't get to that phase of the plan." Since I had guessed this guy had now figured me out, I went along with his *terrorist hunter* theory about me.

"I take it that's when you blow *them* up. That's your real bag, isn't it?"

That's pretty perceptive, Detective.

"Some day I'll tell you in person."

"So be it. Why don't you come by my headquarters in an hour or so? We can talk more about it."

"Actually, that would be a little tight. I have a date this evening."

"You've been in the area one day and you already have a date?"

"I work quickly."

"You must. Well, how about tomorrow?"

"Tomorrow it is."

"Have a good time this evening."

Well, it appeared his nose was back in joint and he was now wishing me good hunting.

"Oh, but I intend to."

I hadn't accomplished much so far, so tomorrow I would devote my entire day to rubbing elbows with the town folk. First thing, the post office, then a couple of the motels, a counter lunch at Kaufmann's Drugs, some gas stations, and downtown shops. No need to look for Arabs in the bars or fast food places. Most Muslims are committed to a wholesome life-style and avoiding putting impurities in their bodies, which is criminal in itself.

It was getting late, so I would now be taking a chance catching the twenty winks. I may not wake up till four in the morning. I showered, shaved, primped and stared back at the handsome dude in the mirror. Adrianna was right; there *was* a good bit of salt in the pepper. Maybe tomorrow I'd rub in some Grecian Formula. Naw. Adrianna seemed to like the gray. Distinguished looking on men, you know.

After splashing on some Bvlgari, the cologne that is said makes a woman's nipples stand up like Vienna Sausages, I put on another Oxford. This time tan. I avoided the pink, because I was taking no chances in projecting my sexuality. The tan shirt with the dark green slacks creates that military macho look. Maybe on a future date, I'd show her my soft, more sensitive side and wear the pink Ralph Lauren.

At seven I slipped on my blazer and gave my tongue a shot of Binaca. At two minutes after, I heard the light rap on my door, wondering who that could be. I opened the door, finding a most stunning specimen of womanhood. She had on a tight black skirt with a slit up both sides, a white silk blouse cut to the cleavage and medium heeled pumps beneath tanned, hoseless legs that looked as though they belonged to a thirty year-old, although I knew she should probably be about forty-five or six. And she was also wearing that glamorous smile.

"Ready?"

Oh, yeah.

"Let's go. I'll drive," I said.

I opened the passenger side door and watched with great delight as Adrianna climbed onto the seat. "Thank you," she said. "Handsome and a gentleman to boot."

I can't remember anyone ever calling me that ... a gentleman, that is.

Although she didn't need me to, I helped engage the seatbelt, mostly because I wanted my hand to sweep over that tight waist of hers. *And* because I'm a gentleman.

When I pulled out onto Seven Bridges, my curiosity got the best of me, so I had to ask. "I assume there are seven bridges down this road, ergo the name.

"Yes, that's right."

"So, what body of water do they cross?"

"None."

"You've got seven bridges and no water?"

"That's right." I could see from the glint in her eyes she was playing with me. "Okay," she confessed. "My friends Ted and Scarlett Bridges live at the end of the road with their five children. Ted was instrumental in getting our road paved a few years ago, so the folks who live along here thought it would be fun to rename Magnolia Lane to Seven Bridges Road. Neat, huh?"

"Yeah, neat," I echoed, giving her a squint like that was all made up.

"Really. I'm telling you the truth," she grinned. "Would you like me to introduce you to them?"

I chuckled. "No, that's not necessary. I believe you."

Then like a blooming idiot, I started whistling the Eagles' song. And that made her laugh.

Chapter 6

We sat on the terrace at Tavern 1785 with a backdrop of late summer red roses weaving in and out of a trellis not three feet from our table. Twilight was suddenly upon us as the sun finally gave up on our day. We didn't order right away as neither of us seemed to be very hungry. I was sipping on my second glass of Merlot while Adrianna's marguerita glass was only half full. Or is that half empty?

There was a lot of small talk and then I asked her what she had been doing all these years. Her story didn't take long. She went off to college at Mary Baldwin in Staunton, married Mason Wolf after a long courtship and then they took over his family's business, Wolf Laurel, greeting guests for the next twenty-two years. The name 'Mason' had been handed down through several generations.

"We just lived a perfect life all that time," she said. "We loved one another, made a pretty good living and kept a piece of Greenbrier history going. And then he died." She dabbed a tear from her cheek. "It was a heart issue and it was quick. I closed Wolf Laurel for six months and went to Paris to live with my cousin, Yvette. She taught English at a girl's school during the day and French to me in the evenings. Paris was … c'est magnifique.

"These last two years have been tough for me, but I've had lots of encouragement from my parents and friends. And some really nice people have come to stay at the inn. I happen to be sitting with one of them right now." She smiled and patted my hand. I may never wash it again.

"I'm sorry about your husband and am sure he was a great guy." That sounded kind of lame, but I'm really not good at these tender moments. "I see you still wear your wedding ring."

"Yes." She turned it around on her finger a few times with her thumb, looking down at it with reflective eyes. "Okay, your turn. What have I missed all these years in the life of the man I was going to marry?"

"Well, as you know, I finished out at WVU with a major in Criminal Justice, and then there was that nasty little war called Vietnam. I got my diploma one day and draft notice the next. I ultimately went to Officer Candidate School, got a commission and joined the Special Forces."

"The Green Berets?"

"Yep. 'Fighting Soldiers from the Sky' and all that. I did my tour in Southeast Asia as an advisor to a Vietnamese Ranger battalion, came back and spent the remainder of my Army days in the exotic lands of Benning, Bragg and Belvoir."

"I don't think I've ever heard of those places."

"I'm just being silly. They aren't lands, they're penal colonies."

She looked confused. Most people are around me.

"I did have a nice tour in Germany for a couple of years. I got out after twelve to marry the lovely Darlene Eubanks who said she would not go down the aisle as an Army wife. So, I applied and was accepted into the FBI, chased bad guys, lived in places like Beirut, Nairobi and Detroit. Darlene didn't like the Bureau either and so I gave up on her. I got the feeling that it wasn't just me; she didn't like our government, either. No way I could stay married to a commie."

"I'm sure she wasn't a communist." She grinned. "And are you still with the FBI?"

"I retired nearly two years ago."

"Are you doing anything now?"

"I'm traveling a bit here and there at government expense."

"Yeah? Doing what?"

Well, I guess I needed to sugar-coat this a bit.

"I still work in law enforcement for the Department of State. I mostly do investigations, looking for immigration threats and subversives. Saving the world. Things like that."

Her eyes twinkled with amusement. "Interesting, Mr. Bond. How do you like your martinis? Shaken or stirred."

I laughed. Pretty. Smart. *And* a sense of humor. Well that does it. I'm looking for a Justice of the Peace tomorrow.

"It's not like that. I'm not a spy; nor is our New York department's assistant's name Moneypenny … although she thinks she is. I'm just dispatched by a special arm of the government to check out people with suspicious behaviors and may have designs on harming Americans."

"You're saying you hunt down suspected terrorists."

Very smart.

"Just illegals, that's all," I lied. "Actually, I think I've said a little too much. But you're very perceptive, not to mention inquisitive. Are you sure you weren't a government interrogator at one time, using the B&B proprietress as a cover?"

She giggled. "You're a card, Skip. Are you on some kind of mission here or just taking some time off? I would have thought you'd be staying with Joey and his family."

"Well, I guess I can tell you this; I will begin asking around tomorrow if anyone has seen any Middle Eastern-looking men in the area."

"Why Middle Eastern? Is there someone specific you're looking for?"

"Not sure." I began telling her about the Arab stiff in Joey's filing cabinet who was probably an illegal alien and that there may be others. I didn't want to alarm her about the sketch map of the factory, so I was selective about the information. Anyway, that was not for public knowledge. "I can start with you. Have *you* seen anyone around that looks Middle Eastern?"

"Well, there's Sayed at the Dunkin' Donuts."

I shook my head. "Donut shop? No. The cops would be all over that. Anyway, Sayed would probably be Pakistani or Indian. Slight difference in looks and color tone."

She smiled, then took on a contemplative expression. "There *are* two guys staying at Wolf Laurel that are definitely Middle Eastern, but I don't know anything about them. They just come and go and mind their own business, never saying anything. I think one must have left, though. I haven't seen him in about a week."

"What do they look like?"

"The one who I haven't seen lately is about five-nine, black hair of course and has a bunch of dark moles on his face."

That would be DAG. No wonder she hadn't seen him in a week. He had been hiding in a drawer at Joey's place.

"How about the guy who's still there?"

"He also has black hair, a little receding in places, light brown skin, clean cut and rather nice looking. He's probably twenty-five. I would say he's from the Gulf area … Iran or Iraq. Maybe Saudi Arabia."

Adrianna did seem to know her geography.

"What's his name?"

"I'd have to look it up."

"When did they check in?"

"Oh, about three weeks ago. It is a little strange. Most people don't stay more than two or three days. A week tops. The man staying there now did say he was a student at the community college. I know they started up Phase II of summer classes a couple of weeks ago. I'm not sure why they would be going to a little old community college here unless they were actually from around here."

"Are you sure you're not at least a private eye? You're mighty insightful."

"I guess in running an inn all these years, I've learned a lot about people and it has probably made me kind of nosy."

"Did it seem strange to you that students would be paying the kind of money to stay at Wolf Laurel just to go to a community college for a few weeks?"

"A little, but they'd still be paying $70 to $80 at other places."

"But a Super 8 or something similar would be half that and they could probably get a weekly or monthly rate."

"I guess they split the cost of the room and that would make it turn out the same. And I did agree to give them a break if they stayed a week."

"How much of a break?"

"$120 a day."

"And you're soaking me for $155?"

Adrianna smiled and winked. "I could cut you a deal if you stay longer."

"Sounds like a form of blackmail."

"Exactly."

I took another swig of the Merlot. "How long did they tell you they'd be staying?"

"Actually, I only talked to the one guy … the guy who's still there. He said they'd probably stay through the end of September, but would like to stay week to week. He pays at the beginning of each week in cash."

"That's still over $800 a week. By the end of September that will amount to about $6500. Pretty expensive board for a two month session at a community college."

"Yes, it is, now that you mention it."

I scooted out my chair. "Can you excuse me a moment? I'll be right back."

She fully expected me to hit the pisseria and appeared surprised when I went out to the street to my SUV. Retrieving my digital camera, I returned to the table.

"Take a look at this." I said, pushing the *ON* button and accessing my photo gallery. I showed her a couple of pictures of DAG. "Could this be the man who left a week ago?"

"I think so. It's hard to tell. He doesn't look too well. Like he got beat up."

"What he got was *dead*."

"Ew, yuck. What happened?"

"He tried to kiss a moving UPS truck. It happened about three blocks from here."

"I remember that. He stepped off the street and got hit."

"I think the word is *creamed*."

She studied the photos a little closer. "I'm pretty sure that's him, but it's hard to tell with his eyes closed. At least one of them."

"Well don't look for him back."

Then it came to me that I may no longer have needed to canvass the county tomorrow as planned. It was either coincidence or sheer dumb luck that I was staying at the very place that DAG and the other Arab cohort were bunking. *And* at a B&B owned by an old girlfriend. Of course, I didn't know ten year old Adrianna was my girlfriend at the time and that we were in love.

I realized I had shared more information with Adrianna about me and this mission, should I choose to accept it, than I had intended. That wasn't like me. But somehow I knew in my heart I could trust her to keep anything we discussed to herself. I really didn't want to use her as a pawn in my investigation, but she was going to be involved just by virtue of her proprietorship of the inn.

After I talked to the Birdman tomorrow, she may find herself unofficially partnered with me as I undertake the investigation of her Arab boarder. I was determined to find out whether a very real terrorist plot was being hatched right under her roof.

I thought it was time to change the subject, so I asked her about her friends.

"Well, I have a few close girl friends in my book club and a very special older friend in the Lewisburg Historical Society. Involvement in civic things keeps me sane, you know. Oh, I enjoy many of the people who come to stay at Wolf Laurel. It's interesting to learn where they're from, what they do, what they love and sometimes what they're running away from. But being the hostess of a B&B gets old and mundane seven days a week and I have to get away for a few hours to be with my buddies. Mostly, engaging in community projects. Good therapy for me."

I nodded, thinking at the same time that I needed some kind of therapy. Maybe she could help me with that. Therapy of the sensual kind.

She continued. "What about you. I guess with your travels, you have friends all over."

"Not really. Most of my life I haven't stayed in one place long enough to acquire any lasting friendships, although I do still hear from a few buddies from Special Forces and the FBI from time to time. But I did fall into some very meaningful (or was it meaning-*less*) friendships with some guys from Tennessee by the names of Jim Beam, George Dickel and Jack Daniels. Unfortunately, my brain stayed marinated half the time I was with them. Thank goodness I severed ties eventually with that bunch; but then I turned to the ladies … you know, Sara Lee, Little Debbie what's-her-name and Marie Calendar. And I allowed these women to do gross and sinful things to my body, many days leaving me feeling sapped and sluggish. So much for my addictive personality."

Adrianna smiled, but frowned with her eyes. "You're very strange, you know. Are you always joking around like this?"

"Joking? I don't understand."

She shook her head and smacked me playfully on my knee. I thought about returning the favor and going for *her* knee, but then thought the better of it. Maybe later.

It was now completely dark and I was getting hungry. I ordered steak and lobster, knowing full well that Birdman would end up paying for it. But Adrianna, who looked like she had eaten nothing but salads all her life, ordered of all things, a salad. What a surprise. There was even something sensual about the way she ate. She exuded sexuality and grace in every movement of her body, every engaging smile, every slow, dreamy blink of her blue eyes. Seductive blue eyes. In just a matter of hours Adrianna Randolph Wolf had gotten into my head. The wine helped put her there, as well. I knew, however, I needed to stay focused and not allow her to unwittingly distract me. And it wouldn't take much to subdue this love-starved heart.

We changed the subject again and talked about people we both once knew in the Greenbrier community. She told me more about Mason and I told her a couple of war stories, mild ones, both from Vietnam and the Bureau, to which she acted interested, but I could tell she was just being polite. So I stopped talking about myself.

After she worked through the last bites of her salad she laid her fork down, dotted her lips with her napkin, then looked at me and smiled. I smiled back, but *her* smile seemed to have a punctuation mark on it.

"Do you remember the summer my dad got beaned in the head by a 2 X 6 at the saw mill? You came over and cut our grass once a week. That may have been the last time I saw you."

"Yeah, I was just talking to Joey about that. It was the summer before I left for the university. How did your dad get, anyway?"

"For a year or so he could hardly stand on his feet. Besides having a concussion, he developed a blood clot, which eventually went away; but then a bad case of vertigo ensued. He healed up very well after that, but even today he has some balance problems."

"That's good … I mean the healing up part."

Her smile returned. It was one of those smiles that I knew something was rattling through her head … like she had just summoned up some kind of orgasmic memory. And I was right.

"I'm almost embarrassed to tell you this, but I will anyway." She giggled a little. "You would take off your shirt when you cut the grass and I would spy on you from my bedroom window. It would be hot and I could see the perspiration on your chest, gleaming in the sun, making you look like some bronzed god. You tanned very nicely. I kind of thought I was in love with you. But what does a ten or eleven year old know?" More giggles.

"Now you're embarrassing *me.*" How about taking *your* top off later, I said to myself? Turn about fair play, you know! "I guess I was some kind of exhibitionist back then."

She laughed and so did I. I couldn't remember when I had such a nice time with someone so fresh and unpretentious.

It was a beautiful night, in more ways than one. Rays of moonlight filtered through the leaves of tall trees and settled on the sweetest face I had seen in years. A slight breeze caught up the glorious scent of gardenias off the edge of the terrace, delighting our olfactory senses with their lavish perfume. Jumping off the branch of a nearby elm a hawk took flight, beating its wings against the indigo sky.

And then at the end of that most perfect night, I realized I owed Joey big time for telling me about her. Of course, I still needed to thump him on the head for storying about the weight, the hair and the big, ugly mole.

About ten-thirty we returned to Wolf Laurel where by the way she lived upstairs in the turret quarters. When we got to the lobby she walked me on down the hallway and to my door. I wanted most desperately to ask her in for a nightcap and steamy sex, but as she was already in my brain, I wasn't sure to what level I could afford to let myself go. We would just leave the night as two old acquaintances, reviewing old times and renewing old friendships. Obviously, she felt the same way as she squeezed my hand and gave me a quick kiss on the cheek. "I'm glad you showed up after all these years, Skip. Sleep well and I'll see you tomorrow." Then she turned and walked toward the stairs. I listened to her dainty feet on the steps all the way up and then along the upstairs hallway to her part of the house. And then I heard her door shut.

I had almost forgotten that my nickname was Skip when I was growing up. No one had called me that in years. I was always *Bruce* to my parents and Joey, but somewhere along the way the *Skip* handle started. I think it may have been when my gym teacher coach in the seventh grade began calling me Skippy from the way I drove to the basket when I played JV ball. I always felt he was making fun of me and that's why if you had to call me that, just shorten it to Skip. But the way Adrianna said my name made me not want to be Bruce anymore. And it made me feel eighteen once again. I knew one thing; she definitely made my equipment feel eighteen again.

And I have always been attracted to intelligent women, whether or not they were drop-dead gorgeous. Conversely, blonde, voluptuous-breasted, gum-chomping bimbos I avoid like the plague. I guess with me it's another one of those narcissistic deals where a guy with a cave man brain enjoys turning smart girls into his conquests. Psychological deviance? Probably.

Sitting at the antique secretary, by the light of the Tiffany style lamp I jotted down a few thoughts. DAG had moved in here with another man of the same ethnicity. Why were they students at the community college? Why not WVU, CCNY or USC? If they wanted to go to a small college because of the money, why not Glenville State or West Virginia Tech? Then again, if they had the money to stay in a place like Wolf Laurel on a longer-term basis, why couldn't they afford a real school? So many Middle Eastern men were wealthy. Some even were princes. But whether they had money or not, terrorists, often well-funded by extremist organizations such as Al-Qaeda or the Egyptian Islamic Jihad, were sometimes covertly placed in community and college settings to integrate themselves into society as America-loving immigrants.

And then I was wondering why 'roomy' didn't go by to claim his friend's body? Did he fear being exposed? Was it he that broke into McGowan and Sons looking for something? Maybe something incriminating he needed to get back? Like a hand-drawn map of a chemical factory?

I know I promised to share any findings with Jack, but again I wasn't totally straight up with him about that. Something called *turf protection.* Each time I found out something new, I would be compelled to call Birdman; then maybe I'd feed Jack some scraps. I generally didn't share my candy when I was a kid, nor did I play well with others. I'm much too old to start now, so Jack the G-Man would just have to be patient.

Coincidentally, bright and early the next morning, Jack called me before I called my boss.

"Like I told you yesterday, I thought I'd pay a visit to the funeral home today, Bruce. I *would* like to get a look at your friend before he is cremated."

My friend?

"Okay," I said. "When will you be here?"

"Can you meet me there, say around eleven? And maybe we can have lunch."

"Lunch at the mortuary, huh. Could you maybe pick a better place?"

I think I actually heard him chuckle. "A sandwich or something afterward."

"Fine. See you at eleven."

It was about eight-thirty and I figured by now that Birdman would be out of the rack and getting his family ready to go to Mass at St. Peters. I dialed his cell and after five rings, he laid his grumpy 'hello' on me. Maybe he *was* sleeping in.

"Okay, what's the score down there? I thought I'd hear from you yesterday."

"I think I've found a mate to the other sock … and right under my nose. Ironically, I'm staying at the same place dead guy was also staying before he … you know, checked out. And he had a roommate of the same persuasion who's still here. I can feel this one in my gut, Peregrine. There's an ill wind brewing here. Shall I stay with it for a few days?"

"I absolutely insist. I assume you spoke with the man in Charleston?"

"I did, "I said. "He appears to be on board and is meeting up with both me and the carcass today."

"Okay. You know the drill. Counterparts, big or small, get only what they need to know, when they need to know and not before."

"Gotcha."

"And let's make our conversations more frequent."

"For sure. Anything else?"

"That's it."

"Well, say hello to mother hen and the chicks for me."

There was that familiar click without a 'goodbye' or 'have a nice day.' Birdman needs to work on his telephone etiquette.

I called Joey and told him I'd be there in a couple of hours with the G-Man. He said he wouldn't have much time to spend with us as he was getting ready for the sixteen-year-old's funeral at one.

"How'd you find Adrianna, Brucie?"

"Like you said … obese, moles and warts, but actually has most of her teeth."

He laughed heartily. I guessed he needed that, considering what would be a very heart-*wrenching* day for everyone. I know I'd be a basket case where it came to children. I didn't know how he did it.

"I had a feeling you'd like what you found," he said.

"And that I did, little brother."

"Okay, gotta go. See you later."

I went to the Suburban to get more clothes. After woofing a breakfast bar, I donned a tee shirt that had a picture of Mickey on it, a pair of gym shorts and my Nikes, then went out to the veranda to stretch before my run. I was hoping Adrianna would be around to check out my Adonis body in these cute little shorts, but she had apparently already laid out the continental breakfast and retreated back to her quarters.

After the thighs and calves felt primed, I walked past the five vehicles in the parking lot to see which car likely belonged to the Arab boarder. Was he there today and would I be able to accidentally-on-purpose meet him somewhere on the premises? I would be Joe Tourist coming back home for a nostalgic visit and he would be Joe Terrorist, pretending to have a temporary visa and so blessed to be in this wonderful capitalist country of golden opportunity.

My SUV occupied one space. There was a Buick Electra, obviously owned by some older couple. Buicks are only owned by geezers and blue hairs, you know. The third vehicle, a mini-van, had a West Virginia tag and a sticker on the back from a local dealer in Lewisburg. That had to be Adrianna's van, although I would have taken her for a Porsche owner which would fit her sleek, sport-model body. Maybe she needed a van for hauling stuff in support of the B&B operation. A fourth vehicle was a Chevy pickup with an Alabama tag and a bumper sticker that read *I will only give up my gun when they pry it out of my cold, dead hand.* That was definitely a Bubba truck and I was set to wonder why he and his mama chose a rather expensive and classy place like this to stay in. Maybe it wasn't his wife with him and he was trying to impress her. It was pretty safe taking her to a fancy hideaway where he didn't know anyone rather than take her to a race at Talladega where he probably knew *everybody.* Anyway, he couldn't get into her underwear as easily around a grandstand full of good ol' boys all crammed in like that.

The car at the end of the parking lot was a ten year old Nissan Maxima with blacked-out glass. I continued my stretching routine behind the cars and made a mental note that the Nissan had a New Jersey tag, which didn't really mean anything. On the left side of the rear glass was a parking sticker from Valley Community College with a seven on it, indicating it would expire in July of the next year. This was obviously the Arab dude's car. Tomorrow I would get Birdman to run the tag.

I jogged out to the end of the parking lot and onto a farm road that twenty minutes later seemed to have no end. It had not taken long for the knees to start hurting and appeared to be time to turn around, which I did at a dilapidated barn. It was a beautiful lemon yellow Sunday morning, though. Birds were singing hymns, a church bell somewhere over the sweet, green-rich farm land was chiming and all was peaceful and holy. Wildflowers of blue, yellow and crimson dappled by sunlight graced the landscape in a distance meadow.

About a third of the way back to the inn a red vehicle approached from a distance … a van. Adrianna's van. When she saw me, she slowed to a stop. The window came down and there she was, smiling, obviously impressed with my athletic legs and tight butt.

"Hey, good lookin.' Want a ride?"

I was breathing rather laboriously and was afraid she would mistake that to mean I was out of shape. But I caught my breath and replied, "You're going the wrong way."

"No, I'm going the *right* way. To church."

"Oh."

"But I can take you back if you'd like. You look exhausted, not to mention sweaty."

Damn. I mean dang; this is Sunday. Now she *does* think I'm out of shape.

"Thanks, but I have to finish these five miles (actually three) and anyway, I'd ruin your seat as drenched as I am."

"Okay, then. Will I see you later?"

"You can count on it." There I go, sounding like an over-anxious puppy, with his tongue out and panting happily.

"Well, bye then." She winked and smiled, then pulled away.

I was then afraid that in the thirty seconds I had stopped, *rigor mortis* would be setting in; so I continued on at an even brisker pace. About ten-fifteen I chugged back into the parking lot and saw that the Nissan was gone. Missed him, dang it. There will be another time, Arab guy.

I then realized I only had forty-five minutes to shower and get to Joey's shop, so I zipped up the steps and down the hall to my room in anticipation of the hot, body-soothing shower.

Chapter 7

This was a courtesy meeting on my part with Jack. If I had blown him off, not only would he have been pissed, giving up a Sunday morning at church with his family, but he would think I was probably being rude and intentionally evasive. I still needed to keep him at arm's length in case the Bureau's services were needed, but otherwise, he would get very little out of me until Birdman gave me the green light. Again, it was also a case of not sharing my candy, being the self-absorbed guy that I am.

I arrived at McGowan and Sons a few minutes before eleven and found a government Crown Vic in a parking space in the front of the building. Jack had preceded me. Joey and sidekick Lester had already loaded the young girl's casket and flowers and were on the way to the church. I found Jack in the lobby gazing at some of the McGowan fine art accumulated through the years from Wal-Mart and Dollar General.

"Hello, Jack." I extended my hand.

"Good morning, Bruce. I didn't see anyone about and wondered why the place was left open, considering the break-in."

"My brother knew we'd be here at eleven and that you wanted to see the Arab corpse. Whatever the intruder wanted, he didn't find. I'm sure he won't be back."

He nodded. "Likely. I assume you know your way around here. You want to take me to the body?"

"The kitchen's this way." I led him back to the fridge room, eyed the dreaded embalming table and pulled out the Number Six drawer. DAG was still dead.

Jack looked over the body like he was some kind of forensic expert and knew what the hell he was looking for. But then again he was probably just curious about the dude and this was his way to get up close and personal to the situation. "I'm sure this guy wasn't a loner. Have you canvassed the area for others?"

"No, not really." I didn't lie. When DAG's roomy is staying thirty feet from my door, why burn shoe leather?

"Do you still plan to? I think it could prove meritorious."

"It's on my list of things to do."

His expression reflected that he was not sure of what to make of that comment … or me.

I quelled his concerns, however. "I'll be looking around starting tomorrow, Jack."

"Good. If you need Bureau assistance, we can have an agent from Southwest Virginia collaborate as appropriate.

*It's **not** appropriate, Jack, I almost said aloud. I don't want any Bureau noses up my backside.*

"We'll see how it goes, okay?"

He nodded. "By the way, we received this guy's prints from the coroner's office and ran them through our system as well as Interpol. No hits."

"He probably hadn't been in this country long enough to get himself arrested. Since he had no ID or prints on file, I'd say he also had no immigration status. Of course, 'illegal' is a status."

Jack continued. "I also ran a search on all known Middle Eastern visitors to West Virginia this year, especially from Iran, Iraq, Saudi Arabia, Libya and Yemen. There were only sixty-two such legals with visas in the entire state. There were none in Greenbrier County. We also secured data on all known extremists or radical groups on government lists and potentially operating in the state and came up with zero."

"It figures. West Virginia is not New York or Washington."

"Exactly," replied Jack. "As you know, the Jihad and Al-Qaeda have an immense hatred for moral decadence such as you would find in New York or other big cities. And as they accuse Washington of being anti-Islamic in its policies, allied with Israel, D.C. remains a primary target. I'm sure they don't consider a bunch of mountaineers with their earthy value systems as immoral or a threat to their agenda."

"But Jack, this state like many others is largely Christian and the radical Islamofascist sees Christianity as hedonistic, evil and anti-Muslim. Christians are *historically* targets of Islamic extremists. So why not target West Virginians and their industry? The good people of this state represent the very core of American values. By striking fear in the heart of Americans, attacking their factories and killing the innocent, the Islamic terrorist achieves his goal of demoralizing the good people in states like West Virginia. And you know as well that Muslims believe they're commanded by Allah and the prophet Mohammed to kill men, women and children, sparing none. This assures them life in Heaven and the more infidels they kill, the greater their rewards."

"Okay, I can't argue with that, Bruce, but so far, with what we have, I don't see any tangible evidence of a terrorist network here in West Virginia or any actual threat of a terrorist strike. Yes, the sketched map is certainly suspect, having been found on a dead Arab, but short of finding more of these guys, all we can do is speculate. I'm sure the security at the gates of the Charleston area factories will be stiffened. I would encourage you to go ahead and do your canvass. But I hope you're not wasting your time, my friend."

From Jack's attitude, I sensed his highers didn't think much about the schmuck in the drawer or his map, either. Jack appeared to be one of those cynical Doubting Thomas guys I hated working with who would wait for a grenade to be dropped down their shorts before saying "Houston, I think we may have a problem here." But he also appeared to be good with me doing the leg work, and just in case I did fall onto something solid, I would be good enough to go running to him and lay out all the bits and pieces on a silver platter. That will happen, Jack.

After taking another look at DAG, Jack pulled up his stakes. "Well, at least I got a look at the guy. Now I have a mental picture to file away in case something does materialize. About the map, I will do a Google Earth or GlobeXplorer on the computer and see if I can't start comparing the layout of some of these plants with the satellite image."

"I seem to remember that the Bureau has a more sophisticated interactive satellite system than the Google thing for you to bring up photos of the area factories."

"You're talking about SpyTrek. Actually, some of the private vendors have better quality than the agency program," Jack replied.

"Whatever. I *would* appreciate it though if you could give me a ring-i-ding if something matches up."

"You bet. And again, the same goes for you. By the way, are we still good for lunch?"

"Well, Jack, do you mind if I don't join you? I hate you drove two hours here to spend thirty minutes giving this non-terrorist the once over, but I need to get back and do some work." That was a lie, of course. I just didn't feel like having lunch with Jack today. I would actually be looking to have lunch someone else.

He sensed I was a little put out with his indifference on the matter. I really wasn't, because the less he pressed me about my investigation, the better. I didn't want him dogging me for information nor did I want some Bureau yahoo getting in my way. And I know first hand how they like to take over, making everyone else on the case feel subservient and stupid. I can be stupid without anybody's help.

I did promise again to inform him right away should something significant materialize and he did the same with me on the satellite search. I'll keep you on speed dial, Jack.

I pulled off Seven Bridges into the B&B parking lot and saw that the Nissan was still missing. Adrianna's van hadn't returned either. Church would be over and she was likely having Sunday dinner with a couple of her lady friends from White Sulphur she had mentioned last evening. I was famished and since I had passed up the Continental breakfast for a granola bar earlier, I turned around for Lewisburg and a hot dog at Jim's Drive-in. It was my hangout when I was a teenager and Route 60 was the strip. Wish I had that Z28 again.

The dog was as good as I remembered, so I had a second. I totally undid the three miles I had run earlier and what's worse, I needed a Pepcid.

On the way back I encountered the teenage girl's funeral parade on Highway 219. As was the custom in the earlier days, I dismounted and stood beside my vehicle as the grim procession passed. Joey threw up his hand as he went by with the hearse and I averted my eyes from the family car, dropping my head in respect. As the windows were blacked out, I wouldn't have been able to see the grieving parents anyway. Although I didn't count them, there appeared to be more than fifty cars in line. Most were classmates, I reckoned, in their pickups and pocket rockets. A few were driving nicer, later model cars, some riding with their parents.

My heart, heavy, I again thought about my sweet Caroline and what she was doing on a Sunday afternoon. Determined not to allow a mood to set in, I slid back onto the driver's seat and pressed the radio's *on* button. There was something soft and melodic playing and I didn't need *that,* either. So, I found a contemporary rock station, even though I hated the crap. And then that served to remind me that it was something the sixteen year old girl who was no longer with us would have been listening to and I shut off the box entirely.

I got back to my room, popped the antacid and grabbed a book from my bag. It would be a great afternoon to sit on the veranda, read, belch, and swig a couple of bottles of Evian. Also, I was hoping I would finally get to eyeball my Arab neighbor. And of course I was waiting for the Lady of the Inn who had somehow managed to get into my head. I read the first two chapters of the Grisham novel and as I started the third, I realized I had no earthly idea what the damn … dang thing was about. It was still Sunday.

At just before three I heard tires on gravel and looked up to see the Nissan pull in. To my surprise, behind it was a two door white Civic. I didn't want to act too interested so I glanced back down at the book, but watched them peripherally. A very nice looking olive-skinned man about twenty five, wearing a white shirt and dark pants got out of the Nissan, then waited at the rear of his car for the driver of the Honda to exit. Except, two people, both Middle Eastern as well, got out of the second car. The driver was a shorter fellow with a huge honker and a closed-cropped beard. The other was at least a half foot taller, somewhat older and thinning on top. In fact he was nearly bald. None of the three was over thirty.

One of the Honda men said something indiscernible and all three laughed. As I was still in running shorts, perhaps they had gotten a look at my legs. They looked harmless enough … even affable. But some of the deadliest serpents appear to be of the non-venomous persuasion. A coral snake can often be mistaken for a king snake.

As the three men trudged up the veranda stairs, my presence appeared to startle them. I guess they hadn't seen me *or* my legs.

I looked up. "Afternoon," I said. "Nice day, eh?"

Nissan man, who would be DAG's roommate, returned my greeting. "Yes. Yes, it is a fine day." I noted the thick Arab accent. Getting a closer look at him, I saw that he was indeed a good-looking kid with shiny jet-black hair, dark piercing eyes and a slight build. He glanced at the others who nodded to me, but said nothing. Then they went on inside to the lobby and made their way back to the Magnolia Room.

Three of them, now. Originally four. Still, none of the three had claimed the body. I waited until I thought they were in the room, then walked out to look at the rear tags on the two cars. The Civic had a Massachusetts plate and the Nissan, of course, New Jersey. There were Valley Community College stickers on the rear glasses of both cars. Either all three were genuine students from different states and had gotten to know one another because of their ethnicity or they were pretend students and the education was a ruse. If it was the latter, I smelled rats. I went quickly to the lobby, pulled a pen and scratch pad and returned to the cars to record the numbers.

When I turned to walk back toward the inn, I looked up to find Big Nose on the veranda watching me. At first, I didn't know if he saw me jotting down the numbers, but as I approached him, his icy glare told me he did. Either he had forgotten something from his car or he wasn't convinced I was just an innocent porch-sitter. I passed him without word and his incessant stare followed me until I was clear of him. I should have been more discreet and casual about my snooping. Obviously, I had been found out.

The man did go to his car and got out a backpack which he slung over his shoulder. While he was standing there, he eyed my Suburban. I could swear he was memorizing *my* tag. His lips were moving. I had returned to my rocker, retrieving the book, and when he mounted the veranda again, he intentionally diverted his eyes. It was all rather uncomfortable, if not unnerving.

I remained on the veranda pretending to be engrossed in Mr. Grisham. But the pages may as well have been blank. Runaway thoughts bounced off the corners of my brain until I thought I was getting a headache. If tell-tale eyes and expressions accounted for anything, I was becoming convinced there was something terribly wrong about these guys. Of course, I'm no psychologist, but from my training and experience I have learned a good bit about reading faces and assessing human behavior. That would be *behavioral profiling*, in government terms.

Some time after four-thirty Adrianna returned. She exited the van and upon seeing me in the rocker, she smiled. "Hi, there. Did you have a good day?" she asked.

"Pretty good. Mostly relaxed. How about you?"

"It was nice. I went to church … of course, you know that. Then I had lunch with a friend."

"Is she as pretty as you?"

She seemed to be uneasy with the question and then I found out why.

"Well, it was a *he* and I guess he's not bad looking." She paused before her confession, maybe because she was embarrassed to tell me or it could have been for effect. "I've sort of been seeing him. He's the high school coach, but it's all very innocent of course."

"Of course," I said coldly. I was a little hurt, but then I knew I had no right to be. Yesterday evening was nice, but it was just an evening. No real happenings.

She sat in the rocker beside me, then put her hand on mine. In a soft, almost apologetic voice she said, "He's just someone to talk to. I know he'd like us to develop into a couple, but I'm really not attracted to him."

Good.

"Adrianna, you don't have to explain anything to me. Hey, I've only really known you for twenty-four hours." I then smiled. "Actually, I've known you all my life."

"I know. But I did kind of feel something last night at dinner. I don't mind telling you that when I went up to my room, I thought about you lying down there all by yourself. I actually started to come down and knock on your door."

Now the birds were singing again and my heart was sailing on deep blue waters. I realized at that moment, she was not only inside my head, but she had also lassoed my big dumb old heart.

"I thought about you too last night," I responded like a fourteen year-old puppy dog wuss. Here I am, a government terrorist eradicator, but when it comes to the female species, I'm a joke. God help me if this woman ever offered her body to me. I'd probably retreat to a corner, suck my thumb and wet myself.

"Anyway," she continued. "I hope you stay around for more than a few days." She put her face close to mine and drilled me with her eyes. "I can use the rent money."

We laughed and I took the opportunity to ask her out for a cup of coffee.

"Let me check my messages and spruce up a bit. I'll be right back."

"I'll do the same and meet you out here, say about five? Heck, we may as well have dinner again."

"Okay. Don't tarry."

I practically skipped to my room, suddenly remembering why I got the nickname over forty years ago. As I was primping, the man in the mirror told me to slow this thing down and to keep my hormones in check. I certainly didn't need any distractions and I knew this was a huge one. But anyway, I would think about that tomorrow. I brushed my teeth, splashed some Bvlgari onto my nasty body and donned a golf shirt and shorts. Before going back to the porch, I called Birdman's number. He didn't answer. Must have something going with the family. No business was ever conducted when he was with his wife and kids. I admired him for that.

I did leave a message, however. "Eagle One, this is Bruce. You're probably barbecuing in the back yard. Hope you're enjoying the family. Call me sometime. Seriously, it's important. Chao."

We drove into town and climbed the hill on Route 60 until we reached the General Lewis Inn. It was a stately place all in white sitting back off the road with majestic eighteen foot columns on the front and a two-hundred year old highway coach in the front yard covered by an ornate port. I remember the place as a teen, having gone there to check out hundred year old relics hanging on the narrow hallway wall. The rooms were quaint, much like Adrianna's place, with beds so high off the floor that you might wake up with a nosebleed. Wooden floors creaked and groaned with every step and it all made for great ghost story material if you used your imagination.

Adrianna seemed to know the owner, Nan, and after a few pleasant words, we were directed through a rustic sitting room with a fireplace and into a small dining area. There was one other couple seated in the room by a window and we were positioned close by them at an adjacent table. Shortly, a kindly Black gentleman in a snappy, red bowtie and black vest presented himself to take our order.

"Coffee for now, thank you." I replied. "We haven't decided on dinner as of yet."

The couple by the window was elderly and still dressed in their church-going clothes. He was in a Matlock blue seersucker and she was wearing a stylish red hat. Stylish of course when Mamie Eisenhower was First Lady. She had the look of blue blood which would of course match the color of her hair.

I spoke soft and low so that the couple would not readily hear me, even though the man was wearing a hearing aid. But in my experience, a woman's hearing actually improves as she gets older. God apparently made them that way so that the art of gossip, which is actually a religion in some circles, would be perpetuated and handed down, generation to generation. My mom was a devout gossiper and her hearing was actually more acute than Superman's. It is a medical fact that in women the tongue's life support system is the ear.

I started right in with my conversation about the two Middle Eastern visitors and asked Adrianna if she had ever seen either of them or their Civic.

"I don't think so. And I believe Juanita, my maid, would have mentioned it if they had come through the lobby. Of course, we're all not always around. Is this something I need to be alarmed about?"

"I don't know. I will be focused this week on finding out who they are, where they're from and hopefully nail down their purpose in being here in Greenbrier County."

"I can tell my boarder that I can't give him another week ... that I have every suite promised the rest of the month. What's the purpose of you keeping an eye on him? Oh, I forgot; you're a government spy?"

"I check out immigration issues for the government, that's all. If it's alright with you I'd rather we kept him at bay where I can watch him. If something tangibly suspicious materializes, I will get my FBI acquaintance in Charleston to secure a court order to search his room. Unless you'd like to let me in there when he's gone." I smiled.

"I think I'd be in a lot of trouble if I did that. And I'm sure you would, too."

The server brought me a refill on my java and I dumped another pack of the blue stuff in it. The coffee was actually very good and I wondered why I had to doctor it up like that. A habit, I suppose. Looking over at the elderly couple again, I noticed that the little old lady had her dichotomous listening skills in full gear. Even though her husband was rattling on about some medicine he was taking, she cocked her head every once in a while in our direction to catch a word or two. She especially hung on words like 'FBI' and 'court order.' I thought about having some fun and making lewd and lascivious suggestions to Adrianna to see if I'd get a real rise out of the old lady, but I'd probably get Adrianna's full hand across my face, instead.

Speaking of my tablemate, I took notice how a ray of the evening sun, glinting off a water glass on the table by the window, highlighted her silken brown hair. She was radiant enough without the sunlight. And then her pretty face exuded a wholesomeness and honesty that I don't see much anymore in contemporary women.

But back to the conversation at hand. "You know I wouldn't do anything at all to put you in trouble with the law or place you in any danger. That was inappropriate to suggest." I paused to take a sip. "I *would* like you to do something for me, though."

She grinned. "Have I ever denied you anything?"

I really do like her.

"Do you trust that your night person and maid can maintain a level of confidence and discretion?"

"Absolutely."

"Would it be possible for you three to keep tabs on your boarder … when he comes and goes? And record when he has guests?"

"I think we can do that."

"By the way, did you remember the name he gave you?" I asked.

"Yes. I wrote it down for you." She opened her purse and after digging past her compact, cell phone, checkbook, tampon and keys, she found the slip of paper on which was written the name Assad Mohammed. Well, I was wrong again; I kept calling the *dead* guy Mohammed. At least now I had confirmed that these guys were Arabs and not Sicilians or Spaniards. And don't call me a profiler. Contrary to popular belief, I don't see all Mediterraneans, Arabs, Indians and other people of olive and brown complexion as look-alikes.

"And the other guy who apparently didn't stick around (DAG); did you happen to record his name?"

"You know, for some reason I never got his name. I think maybe it was because Mr. Mohammed paid the entire cost of the room."

"I see," I said. "I will be running Mohammed's name through my system, but since it may be like running the names Smith and Jones, we'll probably get thousands of hits. But now that I have a tag number *and* a name, I can narrow it down. Of course, he could have given you a bogus name, too." And then I remembered the student sticker on the car. "By the way, do you know anyone at the community college?"

"I know the Dean of Admissions, Paul LeMer."

"Good. The very guy I would be speaking with. If he'll cooperate, I should be able to secure all names, addresses, immigration statuses and et cetera."

"Do you want me to call him?"

"That may involve you more than I'd want. If somebody came in and tortured him for information, your name may be on his lips."

"There may be torturing?"

The old lady's ears did pick up on that question. I think I saw her scoot her chair a little closer to us. Whether she heard all of what we said or not, she diverted her attention back to the boring man that she had probably been married to for fifty years. He was still going on about his drug side effects.

We had been sitting and talking for a half hour or so when other folks started coming in for dinner. It was time to stop talking shop.

"How about some dinner?"

"I think I'm ready now," she responded.

"Won't be another salad, will it?"

"No, I'm up to here with salads these days." She whisked her hand across her lovely throat.

"Good. You look like you could use a hearty meal."

"You don't like my body?" She leaned into me and flashed that wanton smile.

I wanted to sweep the table off with my arm like you see in the movies and devour that body. But I thought that might draw a crowd, so instead, I leaned even closer to her face and replied, "There is absolutely nothing wrong with your body."

Expecting her to order something like prime rib, mashed potatoes and a hunk of pecan pie, she ordered a boneless chicken dinner.

"It's kind of sad, you know," I said.

"What is?"

"Where they come from."

"Where who comes from?"

"The chickens." I pointed to her plate.

"Okay, I give up. Where would they come from other than from chicken coops?"

"Why from Boneless Chicken Ranches, of course."

She stared at me with puzzled eyes. "What?"

"Yeah, if you ever went to one you'd remember it. It's actually pitiful watching them flop around, not having any backbones and all."

She started giggling again which re-attracted the attention of the blue hair. "You are nuts."

"I'd actually prefer that you'd think of me as funny."
"Funny *and* nuts," she remarked.

After dinner we drove the four miles back to Wolf Laurel. Upon pulling into the parking lot, I noticed the Nissan was gone again. I thought to myself, "now that I've seen you, boys, I *will* find out who you are and what you're up to."

We climbed the veranda steps and I asked her if she wanted to split a bottle of Merlot in my room. She said she really had to balance the books, as she had procrastinated the chore all day. Well, I don't call spending half the afternoon with the football coach, innocent or not, procrastination. But I left that alone.

I turned the key in the ancient lock and it clanked loudly. When I opened the door and turned to bid her *adieu* for the evening, she put both arms around my neck brought her lips within no greater than two inches from mine. She teased me with her eyes and parted her lips slightly, still not touching. I lifted her right hand with my left and placed my other hand to the small of her back.

"Wanna dance?" I asked.

She grinned, still tantalizing me with her ever so close lips. "There's no music."

"We can make our own."

"I'm very much out of practice."

"Doesn't really matter. I only remember a couple of steps, myself." I began swaying and then she started moving along with me.

"Another night, Mr. McGowan," she whispered. "You can count on it." Then she kissed me, gently. Her lips were like moist velvet ... lipstick flavored velvet.

When those ten seconds of pure bliss were over, I felt like having a cigarette. And I don't even smoke.

"You're killing me. You know that, don't you?" I panted.

"Uh huh." She gave me a peck on the lips this time. "I always wondered what that would feel like and thirty-five years later, now I know. You taste … delightful."

At that point, I was pretty much speechless. All I could do was stand there and nod like one of those little head bobbing dogs in the back window of a Mexican taxi.

She touched her fingertips to my lips this time, smiled and walked away. About halfway to the lobby, she turned and said, "Sleep well tonight, big boy."

Fat chance of that. But I knew I'd sleep hard.

Chapter 8

My head was still jammed up with Adrianna the next morning and then when I saw her helping to put out the Continental breakfast with her pinned back hair and wearing a tight, accentuating blouse, I just really had to get the hell out of there. I grabbed a pint of milk, box of granola, a plastic bowl and spoon and headed for the Suburban. It was seven-thirty five and I figured that if Assad Mohammed was indeed a student at Valley Community he would be coming out soon. Of course I had no idea as to his class schedule, so I may have a long wait.

It was already a celestial morning. As our Supreme Being, the Almighty, had already set the glowing red ball to rise to the occasion on the eastern horizon, a full Sturgeon moon was setting beautifully in the southwestern sky. But the sun was barely peaking over the distant trees, so it hadn't quite begun its mission of heating the atmosphere to its forecasted ninety degrees on this 28th day of August.

I finished off my cereal and sat for the next forty minutes reading my copy of the USA Today that every guest gets, until my cell phone went off. I could see it was Birdman. "Good morning, Preceptor, did you get my message?" I asked first thing.

"Yes. Sorry. I was grilling out in the back yard with my kids. I also had one of our old acquaintances from the Company over."

So, he *was* grilling. Why do I know these things? Either I'm psychic or have become able in the short time I've known this bird to read him like a book.

"Hope it was a nice evening for you. Say, can you run these two tag numbers? First one is on a 1990 or 91 Nissan Maxima with New Jersey plates NR 15773. See if it belongs to one Assad Mohammed. Got that one?"

"Yes."

"Good. The second one is Massachusetts 3492BG, a 1995 Honda Civic."

"Will do. Bad guys?"

"Unsure at this point. Could be a sleeper cell. I'll snap you some shots of the subjects when I see them again."

"How many?"

"Three that I know of. There was actually a fourth and he's the Arab stiff in cold storage, soon to be ashes. I'll send you his photos along with those of his cohorts. You may not be able to match him up with any Interpol photos. His mug has seen better days."

"Roger. I'll see what I can do. These people could be infiltrators, so you have the green light to continue your plans. Try to wrap this up in the next few days and see me here on the 1st with a complete report."

"Can't I e-mail it to you and just continue my vacation?"

"What vacation? Just be here on the 1st without fail."

"Yes, Mother Goose."

He didn't reply and I had the feeling he was about to click me again.

"Boss."

"Yes."

"Trust me. These guys are viruses. I can feel it in my bones."

"I understand. You have four days to prove it or you move on to something else."

"Wilco, out." I clicked *him* this time. It felt good.

I had my Nikon on the dash cocked to fire at such time Assad came out. That is if he ever did. I also felt that if I *was* about to uncover something heinous, it was good time to start carrying the Glock. I pulled it and the holster from the glove compartment and clipped it to my belt. The safari jacket I had on would cover the weapon, only if it did get stinky hot later, I would be uncomfortable. But it had to stay hidden so I would not be mistaken for a cop or a cowboy.

At eight forty-five Bama' the pickup owner came out with his concubine. I knew it had to be him because he was wearing a red baseball cap to match his neck, a tucked-in Dale Earnhart tee and a size 42 gut. What I could see of his belt buckle, it appeared to be bigger than his brain. His girl had mousy-brown hair and wouldn't have been bad looking had she had all her teeth. And then there were those two chins. Dressed in a pink Mickey Mouse sweatshirt and black, shiny tights, it was obvious she had consumed too many cheese pizzas. Even Spandex has its limits. Even so, the guy's hands were all over her as they walked to his truck; and because of that, I was now assured that she was *not* his wife. Maybe his sister.

No sooner had 'Bama and the bimbo pulled out, Assad stepped onto the veranda and trotted down the steps with a small olive drab backpack in hand. I nailed four close-ups with the telephoto before he reached his car. I waited till he backed out and headed south, then pulled out after him, allowing another vehicle to get in between us. We rode on Mountain View for a while and then the Nissan turned east. After two miles and a four-way stop, Assad went another 500 yards and turned into the campus parking lot at Valley Community College. Well, so far he appeared to be a student, but was this a smoke screen?

I gave him two minutes to disappear through the door at the main entrance, then I drove down every lane in the parking lot in search for the Civic. It was not there. Perhaps the two Honda men had classes at different hours or on other days, but I wouldn't think so. It was obvious that all these guys were friends and they either met in classes or came to Greenbrier County to converge and plot some type of mission ... like targeting a factory in the Kanawha Valley. While I continued to canvass the parking lot in case I missed the car, I saw the Civic pull off the highway. So that they would not spot my vehicle, I drove down the aisle to the rear of the campus and waited for them to park.

From a distance I watched the men dismount and walk to the same entrance Assad used. I waited another ten minutes, until ten o'clock, when I surmised their class would begin. At a few minutes past ten I entered the main door and stopped at the glass-encased wallboard to locate the office number for the Dean. I was vigilant to look out for any of the three suspects who may have been lollygagging in the hallway, then found my way to Room 140.

A large-set bleach-blonde about thirty sitting in a pod near the door asked, "Can I help you?" Obviously Joey was confused about his women and had described this gal as Adrianna Randolph. The sex of the two was the same, however, making it understandable how he could have gotten them mixed up.

"Is Dean LeMer in, please?"

"Yes, do you have an appointment?"

"No, I don't." I held up my State Department ID, which again, didn't tell you squat about me. But it did seem to impress the blonde. "I'm with the U.S. Department of State and need to speak with him about an important matter."

"I'll see if he is available." She continued to eye me curiously as she picked up the phone to buzz him. "Sir, there's a Mister ..."

"McGowan," I finished her sentence.

"... McGowan to see you. He's with the government." She paused. "Okay." Blondie hung up the receiver and said, "Would you have a seat, sir? He'll be out in a couple of minutes."

"Thank you, Joanne." That's what it said on her nameplate.

The community college was built in 1972 (I read that on a plaque when I came in) and it had developed that same musty smell that I remembered when I was going through my elementary and secondary schools. Even the halls and rooms at WVU had that odor. I used to hate the smell. It smelled like ... education. But then, sitting in the Dean's office, I felt a bit of nostalgia. It conjured up faces of teachers, long since departed, and school chums who went to the four winds and whom I will never see again.

"Mr. McGowan." The Dean startled me from my memory trance. All of a lumpy two hundred seventy-five pounds, LeMer appeared at first to be an imperious figure had it not been for his clownish face and horrible comb-over.

I stood and shook his hand. It was slimy and soft. No grip at all. Like he had just laid a cold, dead fish in my hand. And I knew right off he had never done a lick of manual labor in his life. "Bruce McGowan, sir. Thank you for seeing me."

I followed him past a half-dozen people crammed into pods, looking very frenzied and drowning in a sea of paperwork. We entered his office and at his beckon, I sat opposite his desk. A Kenmore fan wound up on its highest speed sat nearby on a credenza. Each time it rotated into LeMer's face, his comb-over flew straight up for a few seconds, then laid back down softly on the top of his forehead. I had momentarily lost my concentration, not to mention my composure. Slyly, I covered my grinning mouth, faking a cough.

Nonetheless, I finally got to the point. "Dean LeMer, here's my card and identification. I do research for the Department of State and by direction, locate individuals, such as illegals, subversives and other persons of interest. We have an interest in three of your students."

"Really? Who?"

"I only know one of their names and thought you could help me with the other two."

LeMer reflected a moment and moved forward in his over-stuffed wingback. He then leaned to one side and killed his breathing for a couple of seconds. Obviously, a silent one-cheek sneak. I wondered if I should clear the room. Then he breathed again and asked, "What organization did you say you worked for with the State Department?"

"I didn't say." Nor would I.

"McGowan, huh? I know of a Joe McGowan. Owns one of the funeral homes around here."

"Yes," I replied. "Joe's my younger brother."

"You don't say. Nice guy, Joe. I assume you don't live here, working for the government?"

"That's right. Now, Dean, can you help me with these students? I need information on Assad Mohammed and two or three of his friends." I had the feeling DAG would have been among them.

"You think they are involved with something ... I believe you said subversive."

Groan. "Yes. Possibly." This guy was starting to annoy me.

LeMer eyed me a moment as though he really should buzz the President ... both of the college *and* the United States, but then he pulled out several pieces of paper from his left hand drawer. "This is our current student roster." He looked over the first page, then the others, one by one. I'm sure they were alphabetical, so why didn't the bozo just zip through to the M's? "Yes, here's Mohammed's name."

"While you're looking at the roster, do you see any other students' names that appear to be Middle Eastern?"

He started counting, moving his lips. "Looks like an even dozen."

"Hmm. I didn't expect *that* many in a small college like this and in Greenbrier County. Do you mind if I look at the list?"

"No, no. These students are protected under the Privacy Act. There are addresses, phone numbers, social security numbers and other personal items on here. We have to maintain a confidentiality of this information. You would know that as well as anyone."

Don't try to school me on the law, Deano. I can have a court order slapped on your ass in less than an hour.

"Then perhaps you could just read me the names and leave the other stuff out," I replied, condescendingly.

"I think I can do that." He started reading the names of the twelve and I struck seven right away. These were obviously Black American students with Muslim names, for example, Jamal, Rashid and Kareem. The reason I knew this was because they had American last names like Washington and Johnson. LeMer wasn't exactly the genius he purported to be. I told him to forget about those.

The other five names had possibilities. "Let's try this, Dean. Of these five students, do any have Massachusetts addresses?"

He studied the names again. "Yes, two of them do."

"And can you give me their home *and* local addresses?"

"Mmm, no. Not without permission from the President, Dr.Stalnaker ... or a court order. You know that, too, Mr. McGowan." He gave me one of those condescending, schooling looks over his reading glasses.

I may just go ahead and slap you.

"Mr. LeMer, as an agent of the government I am authorized to at least secure addresses. This is not privileged information. Addresses can be secured in a number of ways. The phone book, for example. Addresses are not top secret."

"I don't know about that, sir."

Of course you don't, Einstein. Obviously that's why you're just an admissions Dean and not a bio-physics professor. But I could see we were getting nowhere. It's hard to match wits with an unarmed man.

"Can you not just jot down the five names for me?" *Before I come across that desk.*

"Let me talk to Dr. Stalnaker, first. I've probably let out too much. Students and their information need to be especially protected. I appreciate that you're from the government, but since you didn't produce a badge, I need a little more information about you, Mr. McGowan."

I came very close at that moment to putting him out of his misery. He obviously had to realize what a prodigious prick he was.

"Dean, would you mind if I zipped to the restroom before we finish this conversation? Morning coffee, you know. I'll be right back. In the interim, perhaps you can buzz your president for that talk."

"Of course, I'll do just that."

I did have to hit the whizzeria, so I made quick work of it. When I finished, I stopped back by the lovely Joanne's cube and leaned over her desk all official looking. I made sure my Glock was visible beneath my jacket. She saw it all right. I thought she was going to hyperventilate.

I took a chance. "Joanne. Dean LeMer told me to stop by here and have you print out the full student roster for me. Can you do that, Hon?"

"He said that?"

"Yes. Do you want to check with him?"

She glanced at the phone. "No, I guess not. He's on his line. I'll get it for you right away."

I watched her type in a password and hit 'enter.' The roster popped up on the screen.

She hit *print* and fifteen or so pages spit out of her printer. She then handed them to me and I folded them lengthwise in half and shoved them into my safari jacket pocket.

"You're a dear, Joanne," I said in my lowest, sexiest voice. "May I also remark how lovely that blouse is you're wearing? The color brings out the green in your eyes."

She blushed and I thought she was going to jump my bones right then and there. I winked and then ventured past the droids with the drained faces back to LeMer's office.

After dropping my body back in his chair, I let out an audible sigh. "Ah, what a relief. I was under pressure. That's one of the most under-rated pleasures of life."

The Dean looked confused. "What?"

"You know." Is he for real?

"Oh, the potty break." He grinned, revealed some very unattractive yellow teeth.

I hoped to hell he didn't use the word 'potty' with the students. If he did, he obviously ended up with signs taped to his back, like 'Kick me' and 'Yes, I'm a turd.'

"Well, Dean, what did your president say?"

"She wasn't at her desk, but I asked her secretary to have her call me. Then I'll let you know."

"That will be fine. I respect what you are required to do in these circumstances. I can see you're a pretty sharp fellow, knowing the law and everything."

He beamed like he had just out-maneuvered a big time government agent. Then he frowned a little. "Now knowing that there are three or four students who could be in trouble with the law, should we be concerned?"

"I'm not saying they're trouble or *in* trouble, but I will say this, Dean; if you notice any strange behaviors from any of the Middle Eastern students, you have my card. Call me."

"Strange in what way?"

"Any un-student behavior. You'll probably know when something's not right." *What kind of word is 'un-student?'*

"I will keep my eyes open."

Right, Paul. You don't have a clue.

Then he began some sort of soliloquy about how there had never been any trouble from students at the college. There were institutional standards of conduct, you know, and anyway, most of the kids in the area came from wonderful, nurturing family systems grounded in Christian values. I assumed he was also talking about the Islamic boys on the student roster from out of state. Paul prattled on in his nasal voice and my auditory system was remembering similarly annoying sounds such as teachers' chalk screeching on the blackboard and an old girlfriend that I had taken once to my bed who emitted shrill screams in her moments of climax. Again, that was *once*. My apartment neighbors asked me not to invite her back.

"… and as faculty and administrators we do enjoy such a warm and wonderful relationship here at Valley. Most of us have been here since the institution was founded …" Yada yada.

He had one of those voices that if I ever fell into the hands of the Red Chinese and was tied to a chair, forced to listen to a tape of him for more than thirty minutes, I'd spill every last bean. I tried to stifle a yawn, but embarrassed myself in letting out something audible from beneath my hand. "Hmm, yes. I'm sure," I said in my attempt to recover. But then I got up to leave and shook his hand. "Well, thanks, Paul. I appreciate your cooperation and will likely be in touch with you about things after you have a dialogue with your President."

I quickly released his moist, meaty paw, then tactfully shoved my hand into my pocket to wipe it off. He smiled and I turned to leave.

"Oh, one other thing, sir," I began, sounding much like Columbo. "Are you at liberty to tell me what classes these five or so gents are taking?"

"I think I can do that. Let me see." He went into his computer for the information. After studying the screen for a moment, he had a look of surprise on his face. "Only one class. One hour Monday through Wednesday, ten to eleven. The class is *Multicultural Issues in America.*"

Now that was a surprise to *me*. Not the class, but the fact that it was their *only* class.

"Again, thank you for your courtesy, Paul. I will look forward to hearing back from you after you talk to the Prez. I do need that information." *Not anymore, Mister Play-by-the-rules.* "And might I say you have a most accommodating staff. You should be very proud of them."

"Oh, I am, Mr. McGowan."

I left out, giving Joanne another wink as I passed by, and walked hurriedly to the front door. It was now ten forty-five and class would probably be out in five or ten minutes. I pulled my Suburban out of the visitor's spot and parked it in a row behind the Civic, sandwiching it between two other SUVs.

At three minutes before eleven according to my dash clock, the three Arab students left the building together. They stopped by the Nissan first to talk and then the two unknowns sauntered off toward their Civic. At the moment they were in proximity to their car I snapped a half dozen shots, getting both front and side views. They entered the vehicle, sat for a moment, and then when the Nissan passed by, they pulled out to follow.

I watched until they were off campus and back on the roadway, then followed at a distance of about a thousand feet. After making a few turns they entered Route 60 and headed down into Lewisburg. I thought at one point they were going to stop, but then I saw they were just slowing to allow a little old man with a cane to jaywalk in front of them at mid-block. That had to remind them how their friend got whacked the week before.

The Nissan and Civic then made right turns onto Jefferson, or Route 219, and pressed on toward the interstate. I kind of thought they'd take the expressway somewhere, but they continued on out of town past the country club. About a mile further they made a right turn onto the road leading into the Greenbrier Airport, a medium sized field that launched mostly Lears, puddle-jumpers and 727s. Why the hell were they going in there, I wondered? The airport did have a pretty good restaurant in it, according to Joey, and after parking their cars adjacent to the small terminal, that's exactly where they went.

I sat outside for a few moments contemplating whether I should go in for a bite and continue my surveillance up close and personal, but them knowing I was also a Wolf Laurel boarder and showing up for lunch in the same place they were would be too much of a coincidence. Especially considering I was seen scribbling something on a piece of paper behind their cars. I thought the better about going in and decided instead to grab a slider from a burger joint on the other side of I-64. It would take them longer to order and eat than it would take me to zip to Hardees, wolf down the burger and shake, return to the parking lot, and still have time to chew up a whole roll of Tums before they returned to their cars. I did just that, getting back to the airport right at noon. The cars were still there. It was getting a little warm, so I dropped the driver's and passenger's side glasses to get a little cross-ventilation going. The sweet Greenbrier air was intoxicating to the lungs and had it not been for the gut bomb I threw down, it would have been a most comfortable stake-out.

On the seat beside me I had laid *The Mountain Messenger*, a local weekend newspaper, and in flitting about here and there ... mostly there ... I had not read it. On page six was the Sports Section and the heading **Bobcats Look Good**. In reading further, it appeared that the AA team may even go all the way. A picture under the heading showed a player in practice nailing a tacking dummy under the watchful eyes of a coach. The coach was rather good-looking, tall and muscular, no gut, and poured into a pair of coaching shorts. I was suddenly very jealous, because this was the man who would be my competition. The caption under the photo read *Coach Dan Laramie looks on as defensive tackle Jason Matthews slams practice dummy.* So, this was the jock that had caught Adrianna's fancy, except of course she had told me he was just someone to talk with. I could readily see what she saw in him. I would be compelled to go for him myself, that is, if I went that way. Which I *don't*, okay? Well, anyway, I saw enough and hoped I wouldn't ever see the subject in person. That meant Adrianna would either be with him or with me when the other one of us sauntered along ... and somebody could get hurt.

Twelve-thirty and one o'clock came and went. The vehicles remained in place. I flipped through some stations, the few that they were, finally deciding on WRON. When I was a kid, this station played elevator music, which I'm glad they changed. But now today's Top Forty affects me like a dentist's drill. I tapped the radio off and checked my watch again. One forty-five. Either the suspects were yukking it up in the restaurant or they had given me the slip.

While killing more time, I took out the student roster and began scanning the names. Assad was there and so were four other Middle Eastern names. One kid's address was listed as Tel Aviv and a second was from Miami. The two from Massachusetts were named Fayz Al-Hazmi and Ahmed Omari. These were obviously Assad's friends. There was no local address indicated. The stiff at Joey's shop was still unaccounted for, but since I was sure he wasn't Israeli, I assumed he was the student from Miami. There was a status to the far right of his information ...'Dropped.' Actually he was dropped the hard way. It appeared that Joey's boarder was named Khalid Barem.

A couple of Lears took off and I watched a Cessna do several 'touch-and-goes.' Still no Arab boys. The churning in my gut passed after the last Tum went down and the fresh mountain air nearly turned out my lights. I slapped myself and checked my watch again. Two-twenty. I turned the ignition switch to 'accessory' and ran my windows up with the intent of going into the restaurant. But just as I opened my door, I caught sight of them coming out of the terminal. Assad was making flying gestures with his hand, gliding it up and then down. I figured that after their lunch they had gone to the observation area to watch the planes come in and take off. Long damn lunch!

Without tarry, they piled into their respective vehicles and began backing out. I watched through my blacked-out driver's glass as they passed my vehicle, and wondered in retrospect if they had recognized my Suburban. But as their windows were down, I could see they paid me no mind.

I had no sooner pulled onto the highway after them when my cell phone went off. The sharp voice on the other end hardly let me get my 'hello' out.

"Mr. McGowan, this is Lieutenant Williams."

"Yes. How are you doing today?"

"Well, I could be better. I just got my ear bent by a very upset Dean at the community college."

Uh, oh. Busted. I knew what was coming next. "Really? I just left there. What's the problem?"

"Mr. LeMer, I believe that's his name, said you hood-winked his assistant into giving you a copy of a confidential school document. A student roster."

"I'd say hood-winked is a little strong ..."

"No, I'd say it's not strong enough for what you pulled."

"Well, I asked politely."

"You know there are more appropriate ways to obtain information rather than deceitful tactics. Did you ever think to try them?"

"Not enough time to go through the red tape, Lieutenant. Anyway, there was no reason he couldn't provide me with the roster, given what was on it." I watched as the Nissan and Civic turned off 219 onto I-64 east and followed a quarter mile back. "I'm under a deadline to get as much information on someone who could be a person of interest before I leave for New York in a couple of days."

"You believe there is someone of interest at Valley Community? What kind of interest? You had mentioned you seek out suspected terrorist elements. Is that what this is about?"

"That's what I'm trying to nail down. There are several Middle Eastern names on the roster and they may somehow be connected to the dead guy in my brother's mortuary. If he hasn't gone to the oven yet."

"And how did you find out about these students ... that they go to Valley?"

"Long story, Lieutenant."

"Tell it to me sometime."

"I just need to do a lot more digging, but I assure you, you'll be the first to know. Maybe the second ... or third. But you're on the list."

"Can you meet with me on the matter before you leave town?"

"Do my best."

"Good. And for God's sake, do me and the community a favor; stay away from our institutions and especially LeMer. The guy's a putz."

"Don't I know it. Say, you're not from New York are you? Putz is one of their words."

"Hardly. But I do watch NYPD Blue. Probably heard it from Sipowitz."

I laughed. This guy was all right. "See you, Lieutenant. I'll contact you before I leave."

"Please do, Mr. McGowan."

I called Joey to see if he had cooked Assad's friend, Khalid. He said he was doing the barbecuing this afternoon. I really saw no reason to delay the party any longer.

"Can we do dinner afterwards?" I immediately thought how that sounded.

"Sure. Why don't you come by the house for supper?"

"Shouldn't you check with the wife first? I think she may feel I'm a bad influence on the girls, being the renegade that I am."

"She'd love to have you. And she doesn't think of you as a bad influence. A moron, maybe."

"She always was a good judge of character," I replied.

At the White Sulphur exit the cars slowed to turn onto Route 60. I allowed two cars and a septic tank truck to pull in front of me to help block the view of my big old SUV. A slogan on the back of the truck caused me to chuckle out loud … *We Are Yesterday's Meals on Wheels.* I guess they were proud to be Number One in the Number Two business.

About a mile east the Nissan turned left into the parking lot of the Jamestown Motel, followed closely by the Honda. I zipped on by, turned around at a street about five hundred feet away and pulled off the road where I could observe them from a distance. Actually the Jamestown was a series of a dozen or so rustic cabins, some of which were tucked in neatly directly behind the office and the remainder situated in a not so perfect alignment further back into the woods. I now assumed it was no accident that Assad and friends had purposely chosen out of the way places to stay so they could avoid a lot of people traffic. The men exited their cars and went directly to one of the 20 X 30 cabins behind and cattycornered to the office. It had a number 8 on the front.

After a few minutes, I decided I had spent enough of the day in surveillance and now that I knew where the other two suspects were bunking, I'd get on back to Wolf Laurel. I had just caught a glimpse of Adrianna earlier and hoped I would see a good bit more before the day was over. But when I pulled back into the inn parking lot about three-thirty, her van was gone.

For an hour or so I sat at my desk in the room going over what I had so far. I now knew the names of the three players and probably DAG as well. Each was keeping a low profile at hideaways in two different places and each, a community college student taking only one class, *Multicultural Issues*, which helped them learn enough about Americans to kill them. They were shelling out a good bit of cash each week just to take one class. The college scene was more than likely a way to integrate into the area without raising much suspicion. DAG (Khalid), had a map on him and obviously one or more of these guys broke into the funeral home to look for it. If they knew that Joey was also the assistant coroner in the county, it would be their guess that he had it along with Khalid's pocket contents. Of course, they had to figure the cops kept the map if it was recognized for what it was intended. If it *was* of strategic importance to them, they had to realize that the authorities would definitely be suspicious about it and the map had to be retrieved. Did each of the suspects have a copy of the map and for that matter, were there maps of other factories as well? Today they left class and spent over two and a half hours at the local airport. I wrote down the word 'why' in several places. These boys smelled. There was some kind of plot here involving the Charleston factory or I'm giving up this business to buy a bar in Aruba.

Chapter 9

"So, Big Brother, what have you been doing the last couple of days?"

"Thanks to you, spending a little time with Adrianna and looking for your dead guy's compadres. Is he a crispy critter yet?"

"He's done. Very well done. And what have you found out?"

As I mentioned before, I don't generally share information with anyone, except the Birdman. I did tell Adrianna just enough to enlist her into service and keep her vigilant. But since Joey found the map, got me here, and overheard conversations, I'd continue breaking my cardinal rule and fill him in. And anyway, I trusted my brother with my life and may have needed help from him before this was over. So I gave him just a little more information to satisfy his curiosity...except any knowledge about Assad's friends. For now, that is.

"Hmm. Interesting," Joey said. "It seems to me that the map is certainly the key and makes it pretty probable that there *is* a plot to blow up the factory."

I nodded. "Either that or the plan is to somehow get inside the plant and make off with something radioactive to put together a dirty bomb. Who knows what they're developing in factories right in the midst of population centers. Could be chemical, biological *or* radiological. The Kanawha Valley is still a viable target in a terrorist's playbook, just as it was in the Cold War. Remember, Eisenhower had the Bunker built under the Greenbrier for the Congress to be placed in the event of a Soviet strike. West Virginia may be just a minimally populated coal and tourist state, but few people realize how strategically important it is."

"So what's your next move?"

"I think I'll saddle up for Charleston tomorrow to scour the valley and determine which plant was featured in the sketch map. But enough about business. What's Cora having for dinner?"

"I think she said liver and onions. She knew you'd like that." He grinned and winked.

Of course, everyone I've ever known in my life knows I absolutely detest liver. I make it a point not to eat anything that used to be a filter. And then there's *escargot*. It's also my rule to never eat anything I would scrape off the bottom of my shoe.

"Liver, huh? Tell me Joey, did you put all of the Arab guy's parts back in after the autopsy?"
.
Joey's grin widened and then he licked his lips. "Would you like some fava beans and a nice Chianti with your liver, Bru-man?"

Well, it wasn't liver she was making. That was just more of Joey's sick humor. Actually, Cora had gone Italian, which by the way was my favorite, second only to hot dogs.

After dinner, I gave my compliments to the hostess, kissed the girls and zipped back to Wolf Laurel. Settling in with a bottle of Coors Light from my icebox, I picked up the remote and ran through the fifteen channels on my television. Twice.

I leaned back against the big, puffy pillow at the headboard and began jotting down some notes in my Day Planner about my findings. Slowly this was all unfolding in my head, but I was having a bit of trouble coming up with the story's climax. What these boys were planning would certainly have an explosive end. *When* and *how* were the questions.

And then behind me on the other side of the wall in the Cypress Room I heard the filtered voice of a woman. Except she wasn't talking. She was moaning. Not a painful moaning, although it *was* painful to my ears. She was the kind of bellowing and squealing where she was obviously engaged in something squalid. Momentarily, their bedposts began rhythmically bumping the wall and stomping the wood floor. I squinted at the thought of what was happening over there. What was worse was that our respectable little inn had suddenly become a sleazy motel, thanks to the likes of Bama and his wailing wench. I think that somewhere in the woman's salacious shrieking, unintelligible as it was, I heard her call out the name Bubba. And then it was quiet. Fortunately for me their redneck rodeo was over quicker than a nine second ride on a Brahma bull.

I hadn't noticed earlier, but the red light on my phone was blinking. No one should have been calling me on my land line as 95 % of the time I sent and received calls on my cell. After suddenly realizing who it might be, I jumped off the bed and snapped up the receiver. I touched the message button and listened to the invitation for a nightcap from the sultry voice on the other end.

I took a two minute shower, actually needing one after what I had audibly witnessed, then changed into a pair of Bermudas and a black V neck tee. After climbing the creaky stairs to the turret room, I rapped lightly on the door. In a few seconds, it opened. She greeted me with a tender smile and said, "I hoped you had gotten my message before I turned in. Did you eat yet?"

"I did ... at Joey's. You didn't fix dinner, did you?"

"No. But I was prepared to throw together a fresh salad if you hadn't."

Rabbit food. I was darn glad I had accepted Joey's invitation.

Her living area was warm and tasteful with bright colors in the couch and drapes. Although the inn's kitchen was downstairs, she had in her quarters a mini-kitchen with a stove, sink, refrigerator and a provincial style dining table under a hundred piece glass chandelier. A partially-visible third room was obviously her bedroom.

Adrianna had opened a bottle of White Zinfandel which I've always considered too light and sweet, but who am I to turn down anything alcoholic … or her?

"I just thought you could use some company, tonight" she said, "and Heaven knows I do. A person could go stir-crazy doing the same thing day and night without any meaningful conversation with anyone."

I wondered if that was what I was summoned for … meaningful conversation. My expectations were a little higher. "I know what you mean. Traveling like I do gets old, not to mention all the epicurean meals I have at McDonald's and Hardees's."

"I would have guessed you eat a lot healthier, considering you jog most every day and have a hard body."

I'll say. You should have checked me out last night, sweetheart.

"That's mostly why I *do* work out. And obviously you do as well," I remarked, licking my lips in my head.

"Yes, up and down these stairs fifty times a day."

I looked around the room, admiring her taste in furnishing and decorating. There were Monet and Renoir impressionistic reproductions here and there, which I would have expected in the home of a lady of such culture, and a couple of numbered prints. There were also ancient pictures of a man and woman around the turn of the 20th Century with cold, harsh faces, not smiling, but dignified. The faces reflected hard lives, and except for the man's facial hair, it would have been difficult to decipher who was which. If these people were Adrianna's ancestors, it was hard to imagine they evolved into someone who looked like her.

In the dining room stood a large china closet containing several ceramic what-nots, some pewter ware and pieces of fine crystal. I picked up a beautiful blue vase which had a Blenko label on the underside and nearly let it slip through my hands. Adrianna gave me one of those bull-in-the-china-closet looks. I quickly set it down and let out an inaudible 'whew.'

On an end table was a picture of a nice looking man in his early forties. That would be Mason, I reckoned. Beside him was another photograph of a boy, perhaps seven or eight, which I took to be a nephew or other family member. It was all very nice.

I'm not very good at small talk, being a man of action and directness. But I tried. "Beautiful place," I remarked. "And my guest room is well decorated, too. You've got a nice touch, Mrs. Wolf."

Her eyes darted about here and there and then she nodded. "It's been a works in progress all these years. I'm never fully satisfied with anything I do. You may even find *your* room completely redone by the time you leave."

We settled down in the living room with the wine. She sat on the divan opposite my love seat in a pair of loose shorts and one of those tops that when she made certain moves showed about 3 inches of mid-drift. A tight and youthful-looking mid-drift. Who cares what we talk about; I had a great view and could talk incessantly about absolutely nothing until the cows came home. I never understood that saying. Why not geese or hounds?

She shifted and uncrossed her tanned, perfect legs to re-cross them, this time the left over the right. I had a passing thought about that scene in Basic Instinct when Sharon Stone blew Michael Douglas' eyeballs out of his sockets when she methodically and teasingly shared with him the fact that she had on no underwear. With Adrianna, of course, the movement was swifter and more lady-like; although I thought I caught just a hint of black underwear with lace edges and the words 'Victoria's Secret.' But I couldn't be sure.

"So tell me, Skip, is there anybody currently in your life?"

"Like my daughter, my brother, my boss?" I knew where she was going.

"You know what I mean … a love interest."

That was pretty direct. But it did tell me she was interested, if last night's lip sucking episode didn't already give me a hint.

"I haven't been in any meaningful relationships I guess since my divorce."

"Wasn't that over twenty years ago?"

"At least. Oh, I've had a few friends along the way. Only one amounted to anything, but after she figured out how much the Bureau consumed of me, I guess she felt I had little left for her."

"That's too bad. What went wrong with your marriage?"

She *was* getting personal now.

"Well, I think the final straw was when she jumped on me about how much I was spending on booze and I threw back at her the $125 she had just spent on make-up. I asked her how come I had to give up my frivolities and she didn't. She said she bought the make-up so that she would look good to me. Then I told her *that* was why I bought the booze. I was pretty much toast at that point."

Adrianna laughed and smacked me on the knee. "You're bad."

"And how about you? This self-disclosure session is not going to be one-sided."

"I've been out with maybe two guys since my husband died."

"The coach being one of them."

"Yes, I guess you could include him in there."

"Hmm. You said he was just someone to talk with. Is he pressing for more?"

"He's pretty persistent. He'd be here every night if I didn't have the word 'no' in my vocabulary. We haven't been intimate, if that's what you're asking."

"No. Really, I wasn't. That would be too personal."

Adrianna smiled, but fidgeted a bit. "You know I make it a policy to never go out with anyone staying here. I don't mix business and my social life. I don't know why I made an exception with you. Maybe having something to do with old times."

"Or maybe my dashing good looks and charming personality."

She laughed and re-crossed her legs. She had no idea what that was doing to me.

"No, it's your humility." Then she laughed again. "I have just felt good about being around you these last few days. It's like I've known you all my life, which is partly true, give or take three decades." She paused. "So, tell me, Skip, have you ever been really head-over-heels, can't eat or sleep, hopelessly in love with anybody?"

I mulled that over for a few seconds, finally deciding on "Yes."

"With whom, an old girlfriend, your ex-wife or somebody since?"

"No." I rested my chin in my hand and looked away, staring reflectively out the window through the trees and deep into the days of yesteryear. "Her name was Emma."

"Emma," she echoed. "A nice name. Very Nineteenth Century. Maybe your first girlfriend?"

"No," I replied again. "Someone I worshipped from afar. She didn't even know I existed."

"Oh, that's sad. Who was she?"

"A British secret agent."

There was that puzzled look again. "What?"

"Her name was Emma Peel."

"Emma Peel. Now why does that name sound familiar?"

"Well, actually, that wasn't her real name. It was Diana Rigg, you know, the actress."

Adrianna arched her eyebrows and grinned, like what is it with this guy? "Okay. I think I remember there was a TV show ... a British thing …" She squinted as though that would help her remember the show.

"It was called *The Avengers*."

"Right. That *was* it."

I gave her my patented charming and tender gaze. "You know, you kind of remind me of her … wide, seductive eyes, sweet, full cheeks, lips that can be pouty one moment and break out into the prettiest smile God ever put on a woman the next. And then there was that jumpsuit that accentuated every tantalizing curve of her body and drove a generation of teenage boys like me bonkers. Ahhh, Mrs. Peel, as Steed called her."

"Are you for real?" she asked, arching the eyebrows again and shaking her head. I didn't know if it was because she pitied me or she couldn't believe what a nut I was.

"You don't have a jumpsuit, do you?"

"I don't even know what a jumpsuit is."

"It's a one-piece thing with pants … a zipper starts at the neck and goes south to the belly button … you get the picture."

"Do I *ever*. No, I don't nor ever did own one. I do remember seeing *The Avengers* in syndication once or twice on BBC. And I do remember her being attractive." She fluffed her hair. "You say I kind of look like Mrs. Peel, huh?"

"Well, not anymore. The woman has to be seventy-something now."

She laughed. It was an infectious laugh. Her face shone in the dim light with magnetic radiance. Small curved lines formed at the corners of her mouth. Her eyes danced and sparkled and I could still see a lot of ten year old Adrianna in them.

"Naw, seriously," I said. "I did have an early teenage fling of sorts with a girl from over in Alderson who went to the college … you know, the old Greenbrier College for Women … last two years of high school, first two years of college?"

"I remember. Most of the girls who went there though were from well-to-do families and from out of state."

"I was all of fifteen and Laura Lynn was probably seventeen, a senior. I fell hard. We both struck it up pretty good for a few months."

"What happened to her?"

"Well, at the time, I was still a sophomore at the military school, a townie as they called us, thinking I was pretty cool, dating an older woman. But in reality, I was gawky and klutzy, wore Hai Karate and Brylcreem … you know, the whole nerdy package. And then … well, I met her dad for the first time after she and I had been going out for seven or eight months. When I shook the man's hand and bowed my head sharply, my sunglasses slipped off my ears, likely because of all the hair grease, and landed on his shoes. He was one of those big business, society stuff-shirts who owned a high-end men's store and I was the product of a lowly mortician that people like him avoided like the plague. He later told her "You're not going out with any creepy undertaker's kid, especially somebody fresh out of kindergarten." And he said another reason she was not to see me was that it looked like she was getting all too serious. When she graduated from GCW, her parents sent her off to Sweetbrier for her last two years of college. And that, my dear, was the last I ever saw of her. I was crushed, of course."

"Are she and her family still around?"

"Well, when I was a junior at WVU her dad ironically ended up on *my* dad's creepy embalming table. Is that justice or what? I'm not sure where she is now. Someone told me she got married and pregnant not long after she left town, not necessarily in that order. But anyway, that was my first love and that's how we got broke up."

"Hmm." She shook her head. "Too bad. But you know what?" she replied. "I'll bet it wasn't her father that broke you up at all. She probably just told you those things."

"Why would you think that? If it wasn't her old man, then why would you think she dumped me?"

"It's obvious to me. The Hai Karate, of course."

"What?"

"Hai Karate was the most *un*cool, stomach-turning cologne a kid could wear. I'm surprised your girlfriend even went out with you a second time."

I smacked her hand playfully and she laughed. "Hey," I said, "I wore other stuff, too. English Leather, Canoe, Black Watch …" She laughed at those, as well; and as I thought back to those years, those bug juices, though still entrenched somewhere in my olfactory brain, *were* pretty lame.

I do believe later in our conversation I caught Adrianna sniffing in my direction to assure I wasn't still wearing any of those nauseous brands of kerosene.

We sat and talked for the next hour about life in the country when we were kids, even though we were a half generation apart. We knew many of the same people … school teachers in junior high, Manuel and his wife at the Court Restaurant and the Presbyterian minister at the Old Stone Church. The parson had been dead over twenty years, she said. She remembered sitting in the sanctuary there and looking up at the faces of us cadets in the balcony, wondering where we were all from. Of course she knew where I was from and she mostly had her eyes fixed on me. I would have been a junior or senior at the time and well over Laura. I sometimes thought about how a century or more ago those very balcony pews were occupied by slaves brought to church by their owners to receive a Christian education. And I shared with her the memory I had watching the Bond movies at the local theater in the sixties when Black kids had to sit in the balcony at the town theater.

Adrianna reached into the ice bucket to pull out the half empty bottle of Zinfandel and poured a little more into my glass. Then instead of going back to the couch, she slid onto the love seat beside me. Her perfume was light, but just the same, intoxicating. I got the impression we had been playing a game of Chess. There was strategy involved and we were studying each other's moves. Only, in the game of romance, we couldn't decide who would make the first move. Since she had bumped her piece up against mine, maybe it was my move.

"I gotta tell you," I began. "I haven't been kissed the way you kissed me last night in a hell of a long time. Maybe never."

"Is that so?" she replied, grinning and teasing me with her eyes.

"That *is* so."

"I can honestly say the same for me. I thought maybe I was a little out of practice."

"If you were, then you recaptured your skill in a hurry."

All we could do for a few moments was sit there and grin at each other. But then in our game of Chess I put her in check. I touched the nape of her neck up under the brown silk that lay on her blouse. Her hair smelled delightful with that freshly shampooed aroma ... something strawberry, I think. I kissed first her neck and her shoulder, finally moving onto her ear. She shivered as though I had touched my lips to her most vulnerable erogenous zone. She closed her eyes and began to breathe heavily. Her breath gave off the aroma of the sweet wine and I moved my mouth softy onto hers to taste its residual. Our tongues touched ever so slightly and she began to work over my lips, fervently, ravenously, like a starved animal. I could feel her hunger. She pulled back just a little to catch her breath. Then she parted her lips and moved them once again onto mine. I placed my hand inside her shorts and she moaned when I touched her. The nylon felt like warm silk to my fingertips. It was nigh time to satisfy our pent-up passion. I picked up her tiny body and carried her into the bedroom. All systems were *go*. Mrs. Peel, you're needed.

We were good together. Unselfish. Sometimes gentle. Sometimes like animals. It was amazing to me that after all this time, I was able to last more than four seconds. I couldn't believe the mind control and physical discipline I was maintaining to not only avoid sexual embarrassment, but having the ability to fulfill the desires of this supercharged little vixen. If I *had* disappointed her with a premature explosion of my single shot derringer, tomorrow and every other day I remained at Wolf Laurel, I would have to avoid eye contact. It wouldn't have been so much my system failure as it would have been a blow to my macho ego.

But as I lay motionless, spent and craving chocolate, which to me was like a smoker needing that after-sex cigarette, I watched her sleep. Her face only inches from mine was sweet and beautiful in the soft light. Her eyes pitched and roved beneath the lids. Dreaming probably. As she lay on her stomach making small wiffly noises when exhaling, I ran my hand gently up and down her spine from the base of her shapely neck to the small of her back, like a pianist running a glissando. In the calm after the fervent storm, it was as though years of bridled, unrequited passion, imprisoned much too long, had suddenly and violently been unleashed like the act itself had taken on a life of its own. I had no doubt that we could look at each other tomorrow, having no shame or regrets. But that look would be a different look, at least for me. The look of love.

I stayed with her for another hour, so as not to be charged as a hit-and-run driver, then slipped away. As I donned my shorts and tee, she woke and looked at the digital clock on the night stand, thinking it was time to get up and get breakfast started with Juanita. But then she looked at me in the dim light and smiled a sleepy smile. I took the smile to represent that I had indeed stayed with her to keep watch over her, and she liked that. It told her that I was a considerate lover and sex was more than just passion. She waved her fingers at me before drifting off again, and I quietly closed her bedroom door behind me.

I returned to my room, did my bathroom ditties and crashed onto my pillow. The black tee that I had on at Adrianna's I kept as my sleep shirt and it still smelled like her. I probably wouldn't wash it again until the aroma had fully dissipated. I smiled partly from revisiting every wonderful moment of the evening, but also from realizing what a nostalgic, sentimental wuss I was, which was in stark contrast to the calloused, calculating killer I had become from my years with the Army and the Bureau. If I had not loved those careers so much, I would have hated who I had become. One day I would leave it all behind me and settle into a sedentary life with someone like Adrianna. But as I lay there waiting to fade into unconsciousness, I knew there was no one I had ever met or would ever be with that was like her.

Chapter 10

▼

Lady of the morning
Love shines in your eyes
Sparkling, clear and lovely
You're my ... lady

—Styx

I arose early and looked out my window at a beautiful red sunrise, which of course meant there would be rain sometime later in the day. After jogging just over four miles, I showered and read my copy of *USA Today* all before eight. Then I actually took a seat in the dining room for breakfast. I thought this morning I would have something with a little more substance than the usual granola bar since I had worked up an appetite, both on my run and the night before. After an apple bran muffin, some skim milk and a cup of coffee as a chaser, I knew I shouldn't stray too far from my room for constitutional reasons, so I sat there a little longer.

Adrianna entered the room for a second time to greet a middle-aged couple that had come in the day before as well as a smartly-dressed, elderly Black lady with silver hair and glasses who looked to be a retired schoolteacher ... and then of course, there was *moi*. Assad did not partake of breakfast and as far as I could tell over the past few days, never had. I glanced out the window and saw that his car was still there.

The lady who tended me last night came by my table wearing a face as fresh and pretty as daffodils on an early spring morning. She whisked about the dining room visiting and serving each person, including me, like a spider spinning a web, precise and methodical.

A veritable fusion of energy. An errant ray of sunlight that pierced the room caught her brown hair, causing it to take on the color of chestnut. She looked a half-dozen years younger and ever more vibrant. *Did I do that?*

"Well, good morning, Mr. McGowan. Did you have a pleasant evening?"

"Mrs. Wolf, "I replied. "I believe I had the best night of my life right here in your beautiful inn." I was loud enough for the others to pick up their ears. Adrianna blushed. I continued. "The bed was … well let me say, erotically satisfying. And this breakfast muffin …" I kissed my fingers like the Frenchy guys do. "… superb. Obviously one of the most gratifying places I have ever stayed. I will come back again."

As she passed by on her way back to the kitchen, Adrianna gigged me in the ribs and whispered, "You are a bad boy."

Yes I am.

About nine I dropped my derrière into one of the front porch rockers and waited for Assad to come out. I wanted to see if he would acknowledge me and if I could get an impression whether he perceived me as just a tourist from Washington, D.C. (I'm sure he checked out *my* plates, too) who was beginning to wear out his welcome or someone who in fact was dogging him. Although I didn't think he and his friends had spotted my Suburban at the airport and in White Sulphur, it was possible. And if he did suspect I was there for reasons other than fraternizing with the beautiful proprietress of Wolf Laurel, perhaps his eyes would give him away.

It was a drab day. The air was thick, even swollen, and a soft, silvery drizzle began. But after a while the rain came down harder, beating a steady tattoo on the roof. The water poured from the roof and collected in the gutters, giving off a kind of clunky song as it rushed into the downspout near the veranda. I found it a refreshing change from the hot, sultry days of the past week. And considering I was feeling feisty and rejuvenated today, I wouldn't have cared if it snowed.

About nine-twenty the door behind me opened and out stepped Assad with the familiar backpack. I looked straight at him and said, "Good morning." I think it alarmed him as my greeting was not altogether expected. He turned slightly before stepping down from the veranda and returned the greeting with an obvious Middle Eastern accent. "Good morning, sir."

"Nice here, isn't it?" I was anxious to see where this would go.

"Yes. Yes it is quite nice." He seemed to eye me curiously. "I have seen you several times. Are you here long?"

His eagerness to engage in conversation surprised me. I figured he would continue on to his car and avoid any dialogue, especially if he was an American-hating terrorist plotting to annihilate infidels like me. But maybe this was his opportunity to satisfy any curiosity that he had about me and why I was looking at his and his friend's car. It could be he was wondering whether I was a Muslim-hating government agent plotting to kill Middle Eastern assholes like him. Or maybe I was just another nosy, self-absorbed tourist who had nothing worthwhile to do but pamper myself at a quaint country inn. He would be correct on both accounts.

"Yeah" I relied. "I thought I'd take a few days off from the wife and kids and come here to get the fog out of my head. Saw this place in the National Geographic and thought it would do the soul some good. By the way, friend, where are you from?" I tried to sound as folksy and common as I could. You know, just a good ol' American boy.

He paused a moment as though he didn't know whether to tell me he was from New Jersey or the fatherland, wherever that was. But he had to know I took a gander at his tag the other day. "I live in New Jersey, but I go to school here in West Virginia."

"You do? What made you decide on here?"

"I had a cousin who went to the college and he liked the area very much." Assad put his bag down to be further engaging, which surprised me even more. "What is your work?"

I was now standing to convey to him that I was a polite versus an ugly American and extended my hand. "Hey, where are my manners? I'm Skip. Skip ... White." There were only a half-dozen people in the area now that knew my real name: Adrianna, the two state cops, Paul LeMer and his accommodating assistant, and of course, Joey. There was no reason any of them would converse with him or his friends about me. As a check valve, I would tell Adrianna to refer to me as Mr. White from now on. He shook my hand and said his name was Assad. I knew that.

I continued. "I'm an architect and live in Georgetown. That's up in the D.C. area."

Assad smiled. "That is much a coincidence, Mr. White. My father is also an architect and lives in Washington. He is on the board for all architects practicing in that area."

Oops. Why the hell did I pick 'architect?' Why couldn't I have said 'salesman' or 'journalist'? "That *is* a coincidence. Is your father in commercial design or homes?"

"He builds very large buildings. Also many in New York and New Jersey. He would be sure to know you."

"Oh, I don't think so. I'm small potatoes and design houses. But I did have my fifteen minutes of fame. Maybe you've seen an article about me in Architectural Design? Frank Lloyd White. Of course my friends call me Skip."

Assad appeared to be digesting this load of horse hockey and replied, "No. I do not think so. But I do not read my father's magazines."

Good.

He added, "But my father is a contributing editor to that magazine and I'm sure he would have heard about you."

Not so good.

I had to get off the subject and *quick*. "What are you studying at the college?" If I were a lying sack of government waste and hot on his case, which I was on both accounts, he would know that I would find out.

"I am studying American culture, Mr. White. I have believed it important to know much about the country I live in. It is sometimes uncomfortable to live where people have different laws and customs from where I grew up."

"And where was that."

"Syria, Mr. White."

"I do understand what you're saying, Assad. You can go to different parts of the United States and find a difference in culture, even among Americans of the same race and ethnic background."

Well this conversation was certainly amiable enough. Of course he had been more truthful with me (except that he was plotting a terrorist act) than I with him. I hoped the counterfeit expression on my face was not giving me away. Then he said, "I have to go to my school now. I will see you again, Mr. White."

If I didn't know he was just being cordial, I would have taken that as a threat. Maybe it was.

"Call me Skip, Assad. It was good talking with you."

I watched him move at quick-time in the pouring rain all the way to his car. As he backed out and passed by me with the blacked-out windows up, I was sure he was looking my way and giving me the finger.

A moment later Adrianna came out to the veranda and nudged close to me. "Did I just see you talking with Assad?"

"Yes. And by the way, I am now Skip White from here on."

"White? Why?"

"As I am sure it was he and his friends that broke into the funeral home, I didn't want him to associate the name McGowan. I'm taking no chances on him targeting Joey and his family if he ever finds out that I'm onto him and his buds."

"Are you really onto him for that?"

"Maybe. We'll see."

"So, what are your plans today?"

"I'm going to Charleston, but should be back by six or seven."

"I'll be here," she said, pinching me on the butt at the very moment the little old schoolteacher lady opened the screen door behind her. Timing is everything.

I went to my room and punched in Jack's number on my cell. A woman who identified herself as Jane Myers and Jack's assistant, said she would buzz him.

Momentarily, Jack came on the line. "Good morning, Bruce. I have been wondering about your progress there in Greenbrier County."

"Got a few things going. Thought I would come your way today. Did you score with the satellite images?"

"Not sure. There are maybe three or four possibilities. The images aren't all that clear. I pulled up both government and private sites. I think you just about have to fly over all of them to get a true perspective."

"I guess for now I just need to drive around the area, take the map and canvass all the factories in the valley to see if anything matches up with the sketch."

"That will be a huge chore, Bruce, with the number of plants. I'm still not so sure there's credibility to the map and that we have a genuine threat here. Neither does Washington. By the way, I had an analyst do some research on each of the factories, what chemicals and propulsions are produced and whether any of them manufacture parts or products for the military. Although the Belle plant used to produce rocket fuel, there's nothing on the surface that would be of strategic or intelligence value and that would make any one of them a target for any reason. But the FMC plant still manufactures military vehicles and hardware. Could be some threat there."

"Is there a chance there is something Top Secret manufactured in any of these plants that you and I wouldn't know about?"

"Not sure, but I can check it out. I have a Top Secret clearance, as you know, and would think you still do as well. You and I would be privy to any such information we request. I can't imagine any terrorist network would have knowledge of something like that unless …"

"Unless there's someone on the inside who's feeding it to them or even drew the map."

"A possibility. But our sources will keep after this."

"Good," I said. "Do you have the time to ride around with me today? If I need to get inside any of the plants to talk with site managers, you have the credentials to get me in."

"I can't today. I'm leaving for a meeting in Washington in an hour."

"Hooverland. I'll be in D.C. tomorrow evening. Still live there, you know. I'll be stopping by Quantico to visit my daughter and then on to my condo for the night before driving on up to New York on Thursday."

"Will you be back?"

"I'm sure I will. The boss is intrigued about this sketch map and I hope to put the pieces of puzzle together soon. My experience, intuition and investigative nose tell me there is a plot here, and I'm not hinging it all on the map."

"What else have you uncovered that reinforces your suspicion?" he asked.

"Nothing really. Just a bad feeling, that's all." I didn't mention Assad and his companions, still thinking the better about sharing anything about them for two reasons: I needed to first report my findings to Birdman. After all, he pays my salary. Secondly, I *knew* guys like Jack … competent and effective, but aggressive climbers on the ladder to the top. If I clued him in, he'd have a team of Special Agents swarming like bees all over Greenbrier County and the suspects would be gone in a skinny minute. And although their plot may be foiled or abandoned, like a mess of Georgia fire ants, they would pop up in a mound somewhere else.

"Well, again, keep me informed if something tangible materializes."

"Okay, Jack. Have a good trip."

"You too."

In the uncertain shadows of my brain I was still bothered by the suspects' two and a half hour visit the day before to the airport just to eat lunch and watch planes take off and land, so before leaving for Charleston I decided to stop off at the airport office to inquire if anyone noticed their activities.

After entering the small terminal building, I noticed an information desk in the center of the lobby where I found a young man in a dark uniform with a plastic identification badge clipped to his shirt pocket. I identified myself, this time as Bruce McGowan, State Department agent extraordinaire, and asked him if he was on duty yesterday about noon.

"I was, sir. Is there something I can help you with?"

"I was wondering if you noticed any men of Middle Eastern background in the building?"

"If they're the men I'm thinking about, yes I did."

"What were they doing … Mike, is it?" I asked, looking closer at his ID.

"Taking flight lessons."

The surprises keep coming. "Flight lessons?"

"Yes. Over yonder at Ross Flight Academy." He pointed through some glass double doors, leading outside and to an adjacent building about two hundred yards toward the end of the airport campus.

This, I couldn't figure. These guys were students taking only one course at the community college and then they go to the flight school for instruction. As this was baffling to *me*, it would not raise the average cop's eyebrow. But I'm not the average cop. I've got enough conjecture and paranoia in me to suspect everybody as capable of doing anything at any time.

"Is the academy run by the airport?"

"No, sir. It's not connected at all. The school just rents its space from the county, but it has use of the runway."

I thanked Mike and made a beeline across the way to the academy office. Upon entering, I found a man, perhaps forty-five in a tan flight suit and a red ball cap sitting on the edge of a desk talking to a stern-looking woman with short-cropped blonde hair that had the texture of henna. She was thin and gangly, also wearing a jump suit, appearing somewhat masculine-looking and giving me the impression of a former Soviet Block Party member.

"May I help you?" asked Red Cap.

"I brought out my ID again and replied, "Bruce McGowan, Department of State. Are you the flight school proprietor?"

The man stood and held out his hand. "I'm Jed Ross, the owner. What can I do for you, sir?"

"There are three Middle Eastern men who I've learned are receiving flight lessons here."

"Oh, you must mean Assad, Ahmed and I can't remember the other guy's name."

"Probably Fayez."

"Yes, that's it. What about them."

"I'm just doing the standard background check that the FAA requires on foreign nationals. Just routine stuff. What can you tell me about them?"

"You know, that's strange. You're actually the first investigator I've ever had come by here to do any backgrounds on anyone."

Go figure.

"Well, anyway," he continued in an uninflected monotone which I found rather annoying. "They give me a hundred dollars a piece each time they take a lesson and Helena here and I take them up for the lessons."

"How many lessons have they had?"

He walked to a filing cabinet and pulled out a manila folder. "They've had ... let's see ... six, seven, eight lessons so far. Yesterday was the first day they actually took the controls."

"How did they do?"

"Okay. Each one of them seems to grasp the concepts well and I actually think they'll be qualified in a couple of weeks. You know, there were four of them initially. One of them apparently dropped."

Actually, dropped off the world.

"What kind of planes are they training on?"

"One of my planes is a Cessna Skyhawk and the other a Cessna 172."

"Ah, great little birds." Of course, I knew absolutely nothing about crappy little airplanes.

"Where do you take them?"

"Well, so far we've just flown around the county. As I said, yesterday was the first time they actually piloted the planes. We just did some touch-and-goes. They were nervous and made the usual mistakes with air speed and yawl. But after a while, they seemed to get the hang of it."

The blonde then spoke up. "Except the student I had kept bouncing the landing gear. I'm surprised the Skyhawk is not sitting on its fuselage right now." There was a gruffness in her voice much like I had expected would come out of her mouth. I'd hate to mix words with her.

"May I review their information packet? Just need the usual stuff, like the application, driver's license, et cetera. Better yet, can you make me a copy of all the documents?"

"I guess," replied Red Cap. "Who did you say you were with again?"

"State Department, Mr. Ross. Do I need to show you my ID again?"

"No, no. That's not necessary. Helena, can you make Mr. McGowan copies of the material?"

She glared at him like she could pull out her Saturday Night Special and nail him between the eyes. I'll bet she didn't get coffee, either.

Ross immediately realized the error of his ways and trotted to the filing cabinet to retrieve all the packets, then retreated to the copy machine.

Helena's eyes then turned to me. "You don't *look* like a government agent." The eyes were piercing and I considered running from the room.

"Don't let the fact that I am not in a black suit and tie deceive you, ma'am." Maybe it was my face that threw her. It certainly wasn't as mean and hard as the face she looked at in the mirror each morning.

Red Cap finished his copying and brought the folders to me. "Here you go, sir. Is there anything else you need to know about the students?"

"Mmm, yes. How much longer will their lessons last?"

"The flight program is set up for fifteen lessons or until I feel they're ready to be tested. Could be sooner or require more lessons. It's a 'pass or fail' course."

"So, if one of them took a nose dive into the side of a mountain, that would be a *fail*."

Neither Ross nor his Nazi sidekick thought that was funny. It was like a pall fell over the room.

"Well, I guess that's all I need," I said. "I appreciate your time. But I do need to tell you one thing. My background investigation is confidential and if divulged to anyone, especially the subjects, it is punishable by imprisonment for not less than one or more than three years and a $50,000 fine." Actually, I just made all that up. I just liked saying that stuff.

Ross replied, "We understand, sir. You were never here."

When I turned toward the door, a thought occurred to me. I was prepared to drive to the Kanawha Valley and try to somehow get a panoramic view of the nine factories from the road or bargain my way through the gates and compare map with buildings. But in a fraction of my time on the road and zipping around all the plants in the Charleston area, I could fly over and view layouts of the factories more accurately. It was suddenly obvious that this was what the map artist probably did as well, unless again he somehow gained information from within.

"Mr. Ross, did you or Helena happen to fly any of your students down over Charleston at any time?"

"No, sir. As I said, they've never been out of the Greenbrier Valley in my airplanes."

"Will your students be in here today for lessons?"

"No, the next lesson is tomorrow. I'm giving a lesson to our local Chamber of Commerce director this afternoon."

"Oh. I thought maybe I could get you to fly me over the Kanawha Valley today. I'd like to snap some photos of a couple of things from the air. A little project for my boss."

He didn't press me for what it was all about. "Well, I won't be able to, but Helena doesn't have anything going. She could take you."

Oh, great. I wondered if they had any parachutes to rent. "Sure, that will be fine." I looked at Helena who had obviously just finished eating a box of nails. She was still bearing down on me with her eyes. "What will it cost me for say three hours, Mr. Ross?"

"Normally that would be about $200, but for a government agent, gas money. How does $100 sound?"

"Sounds like you're singing my song."

Within a half hour I was in the air with the lovely Helena, headed west over the mountains. The sky had cleared out and it was becoming a pretty nice afternoon, weather-wise. Within another thirty minutes we were approaching the Kanawha Valley. All the factories around Charleston were within about ten linear miles, first to last, and I would be able to cover them fairly quickly. My pilot had not said a word until we hit the chemical valley, mainly because I was scared to death to ask her anything. Every once in a while I gave her a quick peripheral glance and the Ice Queen returned it with a look of her own that made the hair stand up on the back of my neck. Her mouth was half open and frozen in a scowl. Actually, the last time I saw a mouth like that, it had a hook in it.

Nonetheless, being the reckless risk-taker that I am, I decided to break the ice. "Are you from the Greenbrier area, Helena?"

"No."

I actually prefer that people elaborate a little more when they answer such an open-ended question.

"Then where *would* you be from?"

Her ice blues locked onto mine like an air-to-air missile. There went the neck hairs again.

"Is this an official question?"

"No, just making conversation." Sheesh.

She took about ten seconds to respond and I initially thought there would be none at all. "I live in Alderson, Mr. McGowan. But I grew up in Germany about fifteen years before that."

Well, there you have it.

I was just about out of small talk, but thought I'd keep it going. There was still the flight back and that forty-five minutes back to Lewisburg would seem double. "I hope you didn't mind taking me up today, Helena."

"No. I am always happy to help out the United States government," she replied abruptly.

I was glad she was happy. I'd hate to be on this bird if she was *un*happy and it was one of her bad PMS days.

We were snaking the Kanawha between two mountain ridges now at about five hundred feet, having just passed over the small burgs of East Bank and Cabin Creek, where again one of my Mountain State heroes, Jerry West lived and played ball. When we approached the DuPont plant at Belle, I asked her to slow the air speed and make a couple of passes. She looked at me curiously as to what our ride was all about, but said nothing. I pulled the sketch from my pocket and compared it to what I was seeing below. Although the map was roughly drawn, it still had enough detail for me to determine whether the buildings, storage tanks and overall layout matched up. I also took a couple of shots out of my window. After reviewing what I had, it seemed fairly clear that the first of the factories that lay between Route 60 and the Kanawha was not the one in the sketch.

I then asked Eva Braun to fly further down river to the Union Carbide plant in South Charleston. Again, I could readily see that Carbide's overall layout was not congruent with the map nor was it on the Route 60 side of the Kanawha. I waved her on.

That left FMC, which had five, not *two* storage tanks, a couple of factories in Nitro, Union Carbide in Institute and the Monsanto and AmeriCan plants further west. As we flew over AmeriCan, the factory layout seemed strangely familiar. After having studied the sketch map for four days, its image had become burned in my brain. The adrenaline began to pump through my arteries as I compared map to plant. If I had traced the hand-drawn map onto transparencies, it would have overlaid what I was seeing below verbatim. The two buildings indicated on the map with radioactive symbols were situated on the ground exactly as drawn. Each was connected by a series of pipes and conduits to two large storage tanks. The railroad distribution point and two large depots by the river, perpendicularly placed, were exactly to scale as well. It was clear that the map found on the Arab John Doe was not only of AmeriCan, but had been drawn from aerial observation.

"Helena, can you get me a little closer to this plant without raising the suspicions of everyone down there?"

"May I ask now what this is all about, Mr. McGowan?"

I fully expected that if I did not tell her something, she would next fly me to some desolate air strip in New Mexico, bind me with duct tape, and stake me out in four directions with rawhide, pour honey over me and let the ants have a picnic. I looked closely to see if the insignia she was wearing on her jumpsuit was aviator wings or an iron cross.

"I'm on a *couple* of missions here, Helena. The series of background investigations is just one of them. I'm also doing a study for the State Department on factory pollution in the Kanawha Valley. As an example, see the liquid pouring from that culvert there into the river? And notice the smoky haze laying like yellow fog throughout the valley. People have to breathe that stuff. Did you know that the incidences of lung cancer and silicosis in this part of the state are twice as high as any other chemical area in the country?" I was even beginning to impress *myself* with this load of horse hockey and wondered where all this crap I make up comes from?

"And you are now a government scientist working with the EPA?" The scowl was now actually more of a sneer.

Well, it was obvious Helena knew I had thrown her a line. She glared at me, then banked the plane around to the right, dipping my side to where my face was stuck to the passenger's side glass and I was looking at the ground. At that moment, I really wanted to be just about anywhere but in a flimsy contraption, hundreds of feet up with Frau Helena. But I was pretty damned sure I could take her. And there was no way in hell my ass was getting dumped out of that airplane.

After I had clicked off a few shots of AmeriCan, we winged our way back to the east. We touched down at the Greenbrier strip about four-thirty and my underarms were soaked. With as many near misses I had had from errant RPG rockets and AK-47 rounds while doing recons and combat assaults in Hueys back in Vietnam, for the first real time after landing, I felt like kissing the good old Greenbrier earth.

"Thanks, Helena. Might I say you are an excellent pilot. I've flown with a number of aviators in the bush and in hostile environments. They were good, but I believe you're the best." I was so glad to be down, I could have told her anything. "Here, don't tell your boss, but please accept this." I placed a $100 bill in her hand.

"But you already paid for the trip," she said. The scowl was strangely gone now.

"I know, but this is something extra for *you*."

It was like the sun had come out from behind the clouds. She smiled and it was actually a pretty smile. I thought her face would shatter in a thousand pieces.

"You should do that more often, Helena."

"What?"
"Smile, of course."
And there it was again.

Chapter 11

▼

And I found out a long time ago
What a woman can do to your soul...

—*Eagles*

Back at Wolf Laurel, I sat at my secretary reviewing the photos I had taken of AmeriCan on the three-an-a-half inch screen of my digital Nikon. I had clicked off about a dozen shots of the factory from different angles as Helena was dipping and banking the Cessna, turning my stomach inside out. The pictures served to reinforce my earlier convictions, that I had located the probable terrorist target. If indeed there *was* a plot. And I was increasingly sure there was one. On the way back to the B&B, I had seen a One Hour Photo sign at the Walgreen's on Taylor, so I lit out again and deposited the film card at the store. While it was in process, I grabbed a cup of coffee and a newspaper at a Seven Eleven next door, returning to my Suburban to catch up on what was happening in the world. Same tragedies and heart breaks going on, whether you were in the Middle East or in Hollywood.

When I pulled back into the lot at Wolf Laurel, I noticed Adrianna's van was not there. I hadn't seen it earlier, either. But I did hope she would be back soon so that we could have dinner, starved that I was. I zipped through the shower, threw on a pair of khakis and a golf shirt and went out to the veranda to plop into my favorite rocker. As the rain had stopped hours earlier, it was still rather cool and damp. Shrill tree frogs were going nuts in all of the still-wet landscape. Twenty years from now I could see myself porch-sitting like this with a shawl wrapped around me and eating vanilla pudding.

Off to the left side of the porch a hummingbird whirred in one spot for several minutes making love with its beak to a rhododendron bloom. I thought how amazing that was for the tiny critter to stay suspended for that long, beating its wings several hundred times in a mere five seconds. I also thought about one other of God's amazing creatures, Adrianna. It was nearly six and she had yet to return.

About ten after six, the little schoolteacher lady, who had arrived at the B & B the day before, stepped out onto the porch, smiled at me and sat down in the rocker to my left. She had on a black, loose hanging dress, black hose and short-heeled dress shoes. Looking very sweet and proper. As she appeared to be in her early seventies, I took to wonder how many years she might have taught school and again how many children's lives had been changed from studying under her.

"Hi, I'm Skip." I stood to take her hand.

"Well, good evening, Skip. My name is Lottie. Lottie Throckmorton. Fine evening, isn't it?"

I took a deep breath and exhaled. "I love evenings after the rain. So fresh and exhilarating to the lungs."

"You sound like a poet, Skip. Are you a writer?"

"No, ma'am, although I have written the equivalent of a half dozen books in memorandums and correspondence over the years. I've worked for the government all my life." I hoped Assad wasn't listening on the other side of the screen and I knew Mrs. Throckmorton had no reason to spill the beans about me to anyone. I needed to get her disinterested in *me* and put the focus of our conversation on *her*. "Are you still working or retired? You remind me of a schoolteacher I once had.

"Well, I've never taught school, although I wanted to at one time. I retired last summer after twenty four years as a New York congresswoman."

Sometimes I scare myself as to how accurate I am in guessing peoples' professions. Schoolteacher … congresswoman. I was pretty close.

"That's very impressive, Mrs. Throckmorton. I'm sure you represented your district well."

"Call me Lottie, Skip. Yes, I guess I did all right. A lot of people even wrote in my name on the ballot last fall, but I was tired and needed a permanent vacation."

"Are you here on part of that vacation?"

"Well, yes. My staff went together when I retired and gave me two weeks at Wolf Laurel. Jackie, my personal assistant had stayed here a few days a couple of years ago and loved it. But I don't know what I'll do for two whole weeks. I don't have a car to go anywhere and don't need one; I only eat breakfast and then just have snacks for lunch…and anyway, I have no desire to gad about town. But I do like to read and this place is very conducive for that. I had told my staff I needed to go to some out-of-the-way place to catch up on all my reading. Guess they took it to heart. It's so relaxing and beautiful here."

The place did indeed have some lovely amenities. And one of them was missing. Where *was* Adrianna, anyway?

"It *is* pretty here." I settled back in the rocker and sighed. "A guy could get used to a place like this."

"Yes." She nodded and settled back as well. As she rocked and hummed some old song, the wood creaked beneath the runners of her chair.

I liked Lottie. She seemed genuine and straight-up … obviously, a complete paradox to the typical politician. We talked a while about really nothing and then the light of day began to fail. She pulled her sweater tightly into her bosom, excused herself and stood to go back inside. I stood to show my politeness and thanked her for a pleasant conversation.

Burt joined me for a while. After I scratched him a couple of times behind his ears, he jumped into my lap. I hadn't been much for cats, but this guy had a unique personality. "So, where's your mistress, old boy? Looks like we both got abandoned today." He answered with a mew and cranked up his motor. After a couple of turns in my lap he settled down for an apparent nap.

The sun had long gone. The dark, colorless leaves of the large maples allowed just enough of the waning twilight to peer through. But within minutes, the day finally gave up the ghost and the grounds were totally dark with the exception of the mellow light cast by a gas coach lantern at the end of the walkway. I rocked a while, feeling a bit like a geriatric porch-sitter, listening to the crick-crack of the runners, wood on wood. The crickets and tree frogs were making music together. A kind of *night* symphony. There was a bullfrog somewhere close by being answered by the female, which is sometimes called a cow. It all made for a pretty night, the cool air, the critter sounds, Burt's warmth on my lap. But I was getting a little sleepy, not to mention bored.

At eight forty-five I gave up on the mistress of Wolf Laurel, dumped Burt and went on to my room. I had no sooner pottied and turned on the TV when I heard soft footsteps in the hallway. I immediately recognized them to be hers. They stopped at my door and then I heard the gentle knocking.

I opened the door and started my routine. "Well, I'd say it's about *time* you came home," I chided, looking at my watch. "Your mother and I have been worried sick that you were in an accident, but more-so worried that you may not have clean underwear on. I may just have to punish you."

She smiled and pushed her way by me. "Does that mean you have to spank me?"

I shut the door. "I'm afraid so." My smile was more like a diabolical grin.

She sat on the edge of my bed, kicked her shoes off and laid back. "Did you eat?"

I sat spread eagle and in reverse on the desk chair within a few feet of the bed. "No. Nothing since breakfast. I thought we would be having dinner together."

She sat up. "I'm sorry, Skip, but we didn't talk about that or else I would have."

"I just assumed we would. Oh, well. No big deal. Where'd you go?"

"Well, my friend, Dan, called me this afternoon and asked me to go to the team's first scrimmage with Beckley. Then after the game, which by the way the Bobcats won, I had a bite with him."

I took a moment with this. "A bite," I repeated rather sardonically.

"Yes, and that's all." She was suddenly very defensive. "That doesn't bother you, does it Skip?"

A pain shot through my chest. I knew it wasn't cardiac arrest. More like cardio-jealousy.

"A little."

She swung her legs off the bed and leaned into me. "Skip, listen. Last night was … absolutely wonderful. Since you have been here, every cell in my body and every facet of my soul have been fulfilled. But my point is, we've only been together a few days. I've just gotten to know you again, but I still have friends I've known for years. I do have a life outside of the inn … and that of my guests."

Well, that just about did it. I had been reduced to a 'guest.' What a difference twenty-four hours make. Last night may have been the most passionate night of my life. But tonight? The only passion I was feeling was something between anger and resentment. But being the trooper that I am, I swallowed hard and bit the bullet. "Okay, I'm sorry. I'm just feeling a little jealous, that's all. And I don't have the right."

She jumped down from the high mattress and stood at the rear of the chair, pressing her tight lower belly against my hands. She then leaned down and kissed me on the forehead. "That's sweet. *You're* sweet."

I didn't want to be *sweet*. I wanted to be mad as hell. I guess I'm still in the fifth grade when it comes to my continuing education in Women 101.

Standing up, I took her hands in mine. "Well, I suppose this is goodnight and goodbye for a while. I'm leaving for D.C. early in the morning tomorrow and will be in New York on Friday."

"Oh," she responded, looking not only surprised, but a bit pained.

I *felt* like saying, "Now you can spend all the time you want with Mr. Macho Jock. So I'm just going to go away and may not even come back, nanny nanny boo boo." But that would be my five year old child coming out. To save myself a great deal of embarrassment and maintain my dignity as well, I thought the better of it.

"You *are* coming back, aren't you? I had blocked out your room for as long as you needed it, thinking you would be staying a while longer. At least until you were through with your investigation. Are you done with it?"

I get it, now. It's all about keeping the rooms rented out. I began to boil under my collar again. In a low enough voice so that Assad would not hear me, I said "No. There's still work to be done. I'm still focusing on your Arab boarder down the hall and what he is up to."

"So you *are* coming back here?"

"Either here or I'll stay at Joey's."

She appeared very vexed about my answer. "Well, I would like to know for sure. The Labor Day weekend is in great demand and I have at least two couples on stand-by for your room."

"Then perhaps you should go ahead and give it to one of them."

As all this was escalating well beyond our levels of comfort, we both knew that this was really about Dandy Dan. She stood looking at me with disappointed eyes. There was a degree of hurt in them as well.

I wasn't about to let this go any further, so I took her hands and said "I do plan to come back on Sunday. Go ahead and rent out my room; I don't mind. I'll just stay over at Joey's. Anyway, Assad thought I was just here for a few days of R&R. If I show back up after leaving, he may get suspicious."

Her eyes softened. I knew my terse tone of voice had indeed hurt her. She was trying to keep them from spilling tears down her cheeks.

"You can stay with me when you come back," she said in a near whisper, trying to keep her voice from cracking.

I pulled her into me and crisscrossed my hands around her back. "That, my dear, is very tempting, but I should go ahead and bunk with Joey and family. I think they felt slighted because I didn't stay with them. And my staying with you would not only draw attention, but would probably not be a good Public Relations scenario for Wolf Laurel."

"Okay," she replied. "But I'd like you to spend Labor Day with me if you can. A bunch of my friends and business associates are having our annual picnic at the State Forest. There'll be people from the community college and the high school who will be setting up venues and games to help generate scholarship money for the county's underprivileged kids. It'll be fun. So how about it?"

"I'm not sure, but will think about it." So I did for a couple of seconds. "Oh, hell. Why not?"

"Good. Now that that's settled, would you like to come up for a glass of wine or cup of coffee?"

"No. I'd better not. I have to throw my things together and hit the sack. I'll be leaving out around five thirty." Anyway, I was still pouting about how the evening had turned out, the knuckle dragger that I am.

She caught my expression. "Are we okay here?"

"I'm okay. How about you?"

"You just seem a little distant, that's all."

"I don't mean to be," I replied, taking her in my arms. "You'll have to forgive me. I'm … just a very complex human being."

She put her lips on mine. "You don't taste complex."

"Well, that's not my complex flavor. That's my licentious flavor."

She laughed. "Guess that's it for tonight, huh?"

"I guess. Gotta pack and clean out my room."

"Then I'll see you Sunday." She capped off our rather doleful evening with a wet, sucking kiss. She definitely did not fight fair.

I was greeted by the first light of the golden sun just as I reached the crest of a long mountain grade near the exit that turned off to Goshen. Adrianna had pierced my brain more than a dozen times in that first hour and I was soon regretting my episode of juvenile jealousy the night before. I felt like turning around and going back to Wolf Laurel to spend just five minutes with her to assure that we were indeed okay. And I was not happy with myself for another reason: I had let her inside me and she was unwittingly causing me to lose my focus. It was just as well that I would be away from her for a few days. Perhaps now I would be less flaccid and weak-minded and return to my old impervious, despicable self. Just thinking about it, I was already feeling heathenish.

Going a full twenty-four hours without food and totally famished, I had breakfast in Lexington with an old Vietnam buddy. We whiled away a couple of hours reminiscing and swapping war stories. As many times as we had coughed up these old tales, it was sometimes difficult to separate fact from fiction. There was one story we left alone, however. It had haunted my dreams so often, I had no desire to revisit it while still conscious.

After a bit of manly embracing, I moved on to Richmond and then up to Fredericksburg where I pulled over to call yet another friend, John Esposito, a former Bureau partner I had served with in Phoenix for a couple of years. He was now teaching at the FBI Academy and one of my daughter's instructors. As it was not yet the weekend and Caroline, along with her candidate peers, had no life outside the academy until Friday evening, I had to perform a little hook and crook with good old Johnny to get a dinner date with my little girl. There was also a bottle of Scotch in it for him.

I went on to my apartment in Georgetown to look at my mail and clean up for the evening. I did have a couple of hours to kill before I joined the I-95 South parking lot. Caroline's training would end at 1800 (that's 6 PM to civilians) and she would be ready about seven.

I called for the boss and got his assistant. "Virginia, is His Spyness in?"

"He's on the phone, darling."

"Then I guess I'll make love to *you* for a while. How's my favorite sex symbol?"

"Still waiting for you to ask me out, big boy."

"I'll be there Friday. Where do you want to go?"

"How about my place," she replied. "I could make you a candlelight dinner of pasta and wine, and then you and I could sit by the fire in something skimpy and see where the night takes us. Twenty minutes with me, Brucie, and you'd never look at another woman."

"You're a tease, Virg. You know Tom would never go for that."

"I don't mind if Tom watches; do you?"

"I don't think his heart would take it. You'd better give up on that idea."

"Well, okay then. But five minutes after he's planted, your bones are mine, lover."

At sixty-two, Virginia de Hussey (yep, that's her real name) was the only live wire among an otherwise anal New York CTT group and the glue that kept everything together. And she was neither shy about what she said or how much of her voluptuous bosom she revealed. I know she drove Birdman nuts, not because she was still a well-preserved, histrionic middle-aged woman, but largely because she was often disruptive to office decorum. But she was very good at what she did. Left over from the Cold War, she had been the personal assistant to two CIA Directors and knew enough about foreign affairs to be an invaluable resource to the boss and the team. The Bureau wanted her and the Company wanted her *back*. But she liked working for people with integrity and moral soundness … and that was Birdman.

We finally ended the telephonic foreplay when the boss got off his call. In a moment, his raspy voice was on the line. "What do you have, Bruce?"

He was always to the point, not 'Hello, how's it hanging' or 'I missed you, big guy.'

"I've got some names and addresses for you." After spelling the names phonetically, I began filling the boss in on the suspects' activities. I added, "I also need for you to find out everything you can on AmeriCan, a factory west of Charleston."

"I assume you matched up the sketch map with the plant."

"Building for building. Even the dimensions were accurate."

He took a moment to write down the information. "So what's the deal with the flight lessons?"

"Beats me," I replied. "Either they intend to continue reconnaissance of the factory or drop something nasty on it. Or maybe they just want to learn to fly airplanes like some people want to sky dive or bunji jump."

"I don't think it's the latter, Bruce. You're doing good work. We'll of course talk more about this when we meet up. You *are* planning to be here Friday?"

"I'm halfway there now. I'm having dinner with Caroline tonight and will drive up tomorrow afternoon."

"Good. Tell her I wish her good luck in getting through her training. I know she'll make a splendid agent. She's the kind of personality I'd like to see on our team one day. Maybe replace you, old man."

"Not even funny, Hawk. I want her to have a nice long career behind a desk bagging dirty accountants and CEOs, only drawing her gun once a year to qualify."

"I don't blame you, Bruce. Give Caroline my best."

"Will do. I'll be at the Dorsett tomorrow evening if you want to have dinner."

"See you Friday, Bruce."

I had on my pink Polo again, mainly because Caroline likes me in it. I'm not really a GQ kind of guy, but Ralph (Lauren, that is) and I have been pals for years. He should be paying me for all the advertising I do for him. I've got to admit I look pretty good in his stuff. Caroline said it's a preppy paradox to my tanned, rugged looks.

We met at *Steverino's*, a restaurant and bar where Steve Allen played eons ago when he started out. The guy at the piano even looked like Steve, big funky glasses and all. He was actually pretty good and if you didn't know Steverino was dead, you'd think for sure it was him.

Caroline was there before me at a table set off by itself on a kind of balcony over-looking a second level of tables. She stood and hugged me and I noticed that she was a bit thinner than the last time I saw her … about three weeks ago. Her beautiful brown hair was now cropped short.

"Are they not feeding you, Sweetheart?"

"I'm eating well; they're just working it off me."

"I remember when I went through your training, ten years older than you are now. I thought being thirty-three and out of Special Forces, all the physical crap was long behind me."

"So, what kind of physical requirement is there for what you do now?"

"Being able to drag my sorry butt out of the rack in the morning and maintaining a normal heart rhythm after two cups of coffee."

She laughed her little girl laugh, something I missed terribly. "If I know you, you're still religious about your five miles every day."

"Religious is a good word. By the end of the third mile I'm praying there won't be a myocardial infarction at the end of my run."

Caroline smiled. Funny, I hadn't really noticed before, but her big brown eyes had a hint of warm honey in them. Maybe it was the light. "You look good, Dad. You must be doing *something* right."

I winked and smiled back. At five-five and a hundred fifteen pounds, I wondered how she was able to compete with her male peers. But since she was my only child, I raised her to respond like a girl *or* a boy, depending on what life threw at her. Actually, I've got to give her mother credit for the girl part. The beauty and brains may have come from her mom, but by Gawd when she was with me, I taught her to prepare herself for the real world … the dangerous world. By age ten she had a black belt in Tai Kwon Do and on the firing range could match me shot for shot with a 9 mm. Her mother hated me running interference into her plans for Caroline to become Miss America and a concert pianist. Although I didn't discourage her undertaking these things, I felt they were distractions in the real game of life. More recently, however, in realizing that Caroline would ultimately be facing danger in the vocation I practically pushed her into, I knew that if something bad ever happened to her, I would not only have to face the wrath of her mother, but the face in my mirror each morning.

I ordered a carafe of Merlot, but as Caroline was concentrating on keeping her head and body sharp, she asked only for water. After each of us had a salad, then my New York Strip, medium well, and her scallops would follow whenever. Stevie was singing and playing Chevalier's *Thank Heaven for Little Girls*, which was ironically the very thing that was on my heart tonight.

I noticed that an older, conservative looking couple at the next closest table would look at Caroline and me and then work their lips. Obviously, they thought the young chick at my table was out with her Sugar Daddy. I leaned down toward their table and offered an unsolicited explanation, pointing at Caroline, "My daughter ... *really*." The woman turned her head quickly back to her husband, exhibiting both a degree of disdain and embarrassment.

"Dad! Behave."

"Yes, sweetheart."

"Are you seeing anyone these days?"

"Not exactly. Who has the time for a social life when I'm gallivanting from here to God knows where? Actually, I don't even know why I keep an apartment."

"Isn't it time for you to settle down into a nine-to-five gig, get married and join the Elks?"

"In other words, you want them to find where I left my bones after I jumped off a cliff in some remote area of Idaho."

"Don't you think it's time, Dad? You're fifty-four years old and been running too long."

"Who says I'm running? This is what I do. This is all I know. As long as I'm healthy enough to still knock down bad guys and remain in complete control of my life and faculties, I'm doing okay, Kiddo."

"Sure you are," she said, sardonically. "I still worry about you."

"As I do you. And how about you, Missy. Is there a love in *your* life?"

"Right now it's the Bureau, I guess. But rest assured, Father Dear, one day you will have some grandbabies to bounce on your knee."

"I will definitely be looking forward to that."

The dinner arrived and I started digging. Two days in a row I had missed lunch, and then dinner the night before, but I wasn't telling Caroline. She would worry about me and a lecture would follow.

"How are Uncle Joe and his family?"

"Good. The girls are beautiful. I don't guess you've seen Casey and Molly in over five years. You wouldn't know them."

"I guess not. Love to see them. Have you been taking a few days off or working?

Between bites I filled her in on the Middle Eastern boys and their suspicious activities. She agreed the whole deal appeared stinky. Of course, I left out my sexcapade with Adrianna.

"So how's your mom?"

"I guess okay. She had never had any meaningful relationships since you guys divorced ... except now for Ned."

"Of course, where would she find anyone as wonderful as me again?"

Caroline shook her head slowly, like one does out of pity. "Still the same old dad ... narcissistic, egotistical and self-absorbed."

"You left out handsome, hunky and humble."

"No wonder Mom gave up on you. There wasn't room for anyone else in your life but yourself."

"You're being pretty critical of your old man, aren't you? You have no earthly idea what kind of ill-tempered nag your mom was when we were married. And when it came to the wedding vows ... love, honor and obey ... she totally ignored the last one."

I knew it was wrong when it came out of my mouth. Caroline laid down her fork and fired a laser beam with her green eyes. I recognized that look. It was one her mother used to wear. One that could melt the chrome off a trailer hitch. I really must be an absolute Dodo, managing to piss off two women in as many nights.

"Don't malign Mom like that," she retorted sharply.

"Sorry, sweetheart. You're right. Maybe you should add 'stupid and insensitive' in describing me as well."

I thought the smile would come back, but no such luck. Although we still had about a half hour left in our father-daughter rendezvous, I wondered if I had enough time to surgically remove my size ten Weejun from the inside of my mouth. I pushed back my half-eaten steak and drained the last drop of Merlot from my glass. There were no words exchanged for a while, then I broke the ice and smiled at her. It was my apologetic smile.

She heaved a sigh. "I'm sorry too, Dad. I just want you to realize that Mom's had a tough time and she's a really good and sweet person."

"I know she is. Probably *too* good for the likes of me. I'll say one thing: you've got her integrity and stamina. And did I also mention 'feistiness'? Those make for a good cop."

"Like you," she said.

I shook my head ever so slightly. "*You* be the good cop in this family and make up for all your old man's shortfalls. I'd be proud as a peacock to see you one day becoming the Bureau's first female Director."

The smile finally came back. That let me know she was no longer P.O.'d at me, although I'm sure she still thought I was a derogating egomaniac. Obviously, the *one* good thing she inherited from me was her keen and accurate perception.

I pulled out from Steverino's parking lot and took a slight detour off the main highway onto a secondary road that would not only still take me out to I-85 North, but also by Darlene's house near Woodbridge. The road was narrow and a bit twisty, but a good deal less traveled.

Darlene had married a guy named Ned who looked and sounded about as nerdy as his name. He was also as bald as a cue ball with a forehead that belonged on a Neanderthal. But who am I to be critical? I don't think she latched onto him because he had a lot of money and owned a twenty-some acre farm off the road, but she certainly didn't marry him for his looks. I suppose he was a nice enough guy and treated her well. And maybe after me as a husband, he was the kind of fellow she needed … someone who would dote on her and give her the time and attention she deserved.

After coming to a stop at the end of their driveway I pulled off the road into a small turn-around area. Although it was purely dark, with the aid of their yard security light I could still make out the details of their huge, looming farmhouse perhaps fifty meters back from the road sitting majestically on a small hill.

"You finally did all right for yourself, Darlene," I whispered to no one. "And I'm okay with that."

What I wasn't okay with was my Austin Healey sitting unloved on the gravel driveway off to the right side at the garage. At least Ned had the compassion to put a car cover on it. He probably had a Ferrari in the garage and there would be no way he would allow Darlene's ex-husband's sports car to share floor space with his ride. The bastard.

They had a nice spread and I had every right to feel envious. But I didn't. Places like that required a lot of money and work. Even if I *could* afford it, I wouldn't be home more than twenty-five days a year to enjoy it.

My driver's side window down, I sucked in the cool night air. It was very peaceful, way out there in the Virginia countryside. The full moon stunned the northeast horizon, rising blood orange against a blackboard sky and spreading its haunting glow softly across the pasture. Harvested bales of hay, dark and colorless, were scattered irregularly over the dimly lit field, appearing as centurions, sleeping, even dead. It all made me feel damn lonely and suddenly I realized these feelings were all about missing Adrianna, desperately and painfully. I sat there hating myself for having pursued her in the first place. I was feeling that same old gnawing pain of love that I probably hadn't felt since I was sixteen and when Laura Lynn's old man made her dump me. I already had enough physical pain going on in my body, like in my knees and my chest, to have this achy love thing going on as well. It was like having a kind of sweet poison running through my arteries.

After a while and another look at the lonely little 3000 sitting under wraps, I shook my head, dropped the shifter into *drive* and accelerated slowly from the side of the road. My unpretentious little apartment awaited me.

Chapter 12

Late Thursday morning I was fighting the Battle of the Potomac on my way to Reagan National. Somebody was changing a tire on the shoulder on the Beltway and as thousands of rubbernecking drivers had never before seen such a phenomenon, I was stalled. My frustration soon eased when my cell phone rang. It was Adrianna.

"Well, good morning," I answered.

"Did you have a good evening with your daughter?"

"It was very nice. And I did my best to improve her knowledge."

"About FBI stuff?"

"About her father being a complete jerk."

She didn't laugh, not because she didn't think it was funny; she probably knew Caroline was a good judge of character.

"Oh," she replied. "Well, I'm sure you loved seeing her again." She paused. "I missed you yesterday."

"You missed seeing me before I left or you actually *missed* me?"

Another pause.

"I miss you."

Those three words sent a shot of adrenaline through my arteries. "I miss you, too," I echoed in my best eighth grade schoolboy voice.

"Where are you now?"

"On the Beltway headed for the airport. My plane arrives in New York at two this afternoon … that is, if I can ever get out of this parking lot. Wish I were there with you instead." The Saccharin tone in my dialogue was beginning to make me sick.

"Me too. Another rainy day here and they always make me blue. By the way, you asked me to take note of anything having to do with Assad's activities. Besides the two Arab men who have been hanging out with him, there was another, older gentleman here yesterday evening."

"He was Middle Eastern as well?"

"Yes. A little more dark-complected and older … maybe 45 to 50."

"Hmm." Definitely a network of some kind, I thought. An older man wouldn't be a student. Why would they have any association with him? "Were they engaged in any unusual activity?"

"No. I heard them talking loudly in the parking lot and again as they passed by the desk. I couldn't understand what they were saying. It wasn't English they were speaking. The older man was angry about something."

"What kind of car did he have? Were you able to get the tag number?"

"I didn't go out to get the tag, but I think he was driving some kind of van. It looked a lot like mine. I don't mind telling you, this all seems to be rather unnerving."

"Adrianna, I'd like you to just go ahead about your business and not record any other activities. I don't want you to feel uncomfortable about this and I certainly don't want them to get suspicious. Tell your maid to stop her mental notes as well. I shouldn't have asked either one of you to do that."

"I'd feel a lot better if Assad would just go ahead and leave. But I can't ask him to leave without cause. And he's already paid for next week."

"Yeah, booting him will definitely raise his antenna."

"He has refused maid service ever since he came here. He just asks for fresh towels when he stops by the desk each day. Juanita, my maid, has never been in his room."

"That's probably a good indication there are things in his room he doesn't want anyone to see."

She was silent for a moment. "When is it you're coming back?"

"Probably Sunday night. Like I said, I'll be going to Joey's."

"Did you decide for sure if you're going with me to the Labor Day picnic at Greenbrier State Forest?"

"Only if you bring some fried chicken."

"I'll be sure to make some."

"And chocolate cake?"

"That too."

"I'll bring a bottle of Merlot."

"I don't think they allow alcoholic beverages in the park."

"You're kidding, of course."

"No. Those are the rules and the event committee reinforced that in bold letters on the flyer."

"Communists."

"Maybe I'll clink glasses with you Monday evening here at my place if you'd like."

"I'd like."

"Be careful in your travels."

"Okay, sweetie. See you in a few days."

"Bye, Skip. I …" She didn't finish.

I thought maybe she was about to say the 'L' word. I wished she had. It would certainly hold me over until I saw her again.

My plane landed in Newark just after two and I got a taxi to the Dorsett in Manhattan. The hotel was ancient, but grand. Not the same grand as one would find at the Wardoff Astoria, but quaint and nostalgic 1940s grand. It was especially nostalgic to me, because nearly twenty-four years ago one Caroline Ann McGowan was conceived there in Room 240 on my wedding night. And it was also a time when I was in love with Caroline's mom. But that was then and Adrianna was now.

The Birdman knew I would be staying there *and* in Room 240, as he had already left me a message. "Just wanted to remind you ... nine o'clock sharp, tomorrow. Don't be late."

I saluted the red flashing light on the phone and deleted the message. He could have just as easily called my cell, but I think he just enjoyed being anal and let me know he could anticipate my every move and routine. I was determined not only to piss him off, but let him know his dictatorial powers didn't work on me. I'd show *him*. I'd be in his office at 9:05.

When I stepped off the elevator onto Birdman's floor, I bumped into Abu Narziz, our Arabic translator. I had met him on a couple of occasions within the past year ... once in a meeting at Zulu Headquarters and then again at Ft. Bragg two months after. The reason for the second meet-up at Bragg was to suck out the brain of a man known as Khallad, the architect of the U.S.S. Cole attack. The Yemenis had arrested Khallad for the bombing and after President Clinton, the CIA, CTC and NSA had tried diplomatically and 'otherwise' to take custody of the terrorist, Zulu moved in and appropriated him through less than diplomatic means. Delta Force had a little to do with it as well.

Abu, an Iranian army commander, who Khomeini called the Hero of Sousangerd, when he successfully repelled an Iraqi attack sending Saddam Hussein's forces back across the border, was later imprisoned by the Ayatollah for refusing to employ chemical weapons in answer to Saddam's own chemical use. Abu, who was exiled in the sixth year of the eight year war, ultimately escaped and sought asylum in the United States. Immediately establishing his loyalty and trustworthiness, he became an invaluable asset to the CIA as an Arabic translator. When Birdman was tasked by Washington to start up CTT, he brought Abu with him.

"My friend Bruce," he said, embracing me about the shoulders and kissing me on each cheek. I didn't know we were that close.

"My friend Abu," I echoed. "Great to see you."

I took a moment to fill him in on Assad and the others.

He lowered his voice into a near whisper. "Ah. You may be onto something there in West Virginia. This man, Assad, may be just a student, but I do not think so. I take him to be an Islamic idealist like many who have come here, but he could also be one of the Jihadist young lions of which there appear to be many in this country now. As you have learned, some are in the universities, but others have gone to work in the factories, the airports and the financial institutions, each of the venues being significant targets for terrorists."

"You know about the AmeriCan possibility?"

"Yes. Preceptor told me you had done a reconnaissance of the factory."

"There could very well be a lion on the inside."

"Yes, perhaps. That is often the plan. Someone on the inside will feed information about security weaknesses to those who plot from the outside. The insider may work there for months, even years. They are very patient. The subversives plan and wait … wait for the day and time. Then the orders will come down."

"Years?"

"These are all people who dream, Bruce … dream of achieving glory as martyrs. They begin as young boys receiving their indoctrination in schools, mosques and especially their family systems … learning to hate, training to kill. It is all very sad." Abu's face took on a somberness that I did not see in our previous meetings. I suspected that he knew first hand what Jihadist poisons were injected into the brains of young Arab children concerning the Great Satan. "Our enemies are all around us, Bruce," he added. "Our eyes and ears must always be open."

And then his pager went off. Abu checked the number and said, "I must go, now. I will be interested to see what will happen with your case, Bruce. *Assalamu alaikum*, my friend."

What little Arabic I knew, I did remember 'peace be unto you.'

"Wa barakatuhu," I returned the blessing.

At precisely 9:05 I stopped by Virginia's desk. I didn't have a hat to throw on the rack, but in keeping up my Bond image, I humored her with the Moneypenny handle. And as this always tickled her, she would respond by referring to me as 007.

Today Moneypenny had on a plunging blouse that revealed unusually perfect cleavage for an older gal and I stuck around a couple more minutes to appreciate the royal magnificence. And as if on cue she said, "Go on in, 007," then winked.

I reciprocated with a quick double eyebrow raise.

I tapped first on his door and then entered.

"Come on in, Bruce, and have a seat at the conference table. You're late."

Lionel Byrd sat engrossed in something on his desktop monitor, but when I approached his desk, he stood like the gentleman he was and extended his hand. Did I mention that it was actually *me* who coined all the bird code names? It just sounded Ian Fleming-ish and the 'Byrd' name made for good fun. Byrd, always dapper-looking in his three piece gray suit made of a faint, light wool herringbone and characteristic unlit pipe in hand, did look like an M. Only he looked a bit older today and that would make him a P or a Q. Birdman was one of the good guys I had known in all of this law enforcement business. Not an ounce of pretentiousness or obliquity.

But there was a carriage of pride in his demeanor, devoid of arrogance and conceit.

"Good trip?"

"So-so."

"Did you give Caroline my regards?"

"Of course." Not. I had forgotten.

"She's a beauty," he said. "Favors her mother." I caught the sarcasm. *My good looks are in there somewhere too, Birdman.*

Byrd decided after thirty seconds of small talk to cut through the chase. "Okay, lay this all out for me. What's new about the suspects since we talked?"

"Before I begin, what did you find out about AmeriCan?"

"Well, it's a plant of strategic value that produces several toxic chemicals, including GB, Chlorine and Hydrogen Cyanide gases. The GB is an isopropyl agent, Sarin, that would be used as a last resort by the U.S. military. Naturally, our government's *official* position is that there is *no* use of chemical or biological agents in the event of war."

"Naturally. I do remember most of my NBC education and training from Special Ops days. GB and other nerve agents, once released into the air, cause immediate constriction and secretion of mucous from the mouth. Then there are the convulsions, the paralysis of the nervous system and death in a matter of minutes. Nasty shit."

Byrd nodded. "GB has been around for decades, but only recently reproduced in uncertain quantities for stockpile, and only to be used in retaliation of a chemical strike on the battlefield. Of course this is Top Secret information and even at my level, the State Department didn't want to release that to me. I'm only passing this on since you have the same clearance."

"Don't worry, I won't tell more than two or three people."

Birdman eyed me sternly.

He continued. "AmeriCan is owned by U.S. and Canadian companies, ergo the name. And here's the clincher: it's also partnered with an Israeli organization. That's why we can indeed speculate at this point that the factory is a very real target by your little nest of Middle Easterners, given the detail of the sketch. My boss is very interested in this now and wants you to stay the course."

"And your boss would be who?"

"Sorry. I can't tell you that, Bruce."

"Okay then, let's say you get knocked off. Would my paycheck suddenly stop? And furthermore, who would I have my silly little conversations with?"

"Let's say I *do* get knocked off, as you so eloquently put it. You would be contacted by my replacement."

"Who is?"

He gave me that look again without responding. Now I really *was* starting to worry about future paychecks. I'd have to make sure Byrd stayed alive.

I laid out the photos I had taken of DAG, the three suspects and AmeriCan. I had ordered 8X10s of the factory.

Yes," began Byrd. "These will be most helpful. I'll run these faces through Interpol and the FBI database to see if there are any hits. Perhaps we'll find them among our compiled list of subversives in the Muslim Student's Association, which is a very radical student group, well indoctrinated and propagandized. One of their goals is to establish an order of caliphates by grooming these young Muslim men for a kind of Islamic priesthood. A dollar to a donut that's who these boys are." He spread out *all* the photos and studied them a little more in depth. "You did well, Bruce. It's astounding that the sketch map looks like an overlay to this photo here. They have identified these two buildings and tanks where the gases would be stored. I agree the map had to be drawn from the air, so obviously either one or more of these men flew over the factory or someone else did and supplied them with the sketch."

"Likely someone on the inside," I added. "How else would the average terrorist schmuck know about what a strategic type of factory like AmeriCan would produce?"

"Indeed," he replied, reflectively, stroking his chin. "Your brother did right to call you about this. I trust he will maintain a high degree of confidentiality."

"Joey? Of course. Undertakers are sworn to secrecy by the National Mortician's Board."

"Are you making that up?"

"Yeah," I grinned. "But think about it. Sometimes they find out things on dead people that family and friends would never suspect. They're held to standards and codes like any other profession, and in some ways, such responsibilities are even more fiduciary in nature. That's when families are the most vulnerable. Dead men tell no tales and neither does my brother."

"Okay."

"What did the auto tags turn up?"

"The Nissan is registered to Assad Mohammed. No surprise there. The Honda's owner is one Afain Shareq. That name is nowhere close to either of the two men's names you provided. Could either belong to one of their fathers or a friend."

I nodded. "There's another interesting item. I talked to the owner of the Bed and Breakfast where I've been staying and she said a man between 45 and 50 visited Assad Mohammed two days ago. The man was having an animated conversation with the three younger suspects in the parking lot. Could be he is running the show and I wouldn't be surprised he was upset about the missing map. Either they need it for whatever raid is being planned or the man fears it has fallen in the hands of the authorities. I'm pretty damned sure that was what the break-in at the funeral home was all about."

"Then you need to find this man." He crunched on the pipe stem and bore down on me with trenchant eyes. "This B&B owner … is she the woman with whom you have struck a special friendship?"

How the hell does he know about her?

"Special friendship?"

"How much does she know about you and what you do?"

Well, somehow and for some reason the greatest currently living spy man in the world has kept private tabs on little old me. He apparently knows my moves, both business-wise *and* social-wise. This was going to rattle me. I knew he trusted me and was complimentary of my work; so was he still required to know my activity every moment? And who required that of him? I didn't readily respond to him.

He continued. "It's my business to know everything about you, Bruce, even when it involves acquired relationships."

"So you think I have a relationship?"

"If it's not one, you missed your chance. Now for the answer, Bruce."

"I have engaged Ms. Wolf as an informant, given her capacity as the inn's proprietress. She only knows I work for the government and some kind of investigator."

"As she is not a professional, you can trust her to be discreet?"

"She has no reason not to be, boss."

"But things could slip out."

"Not with her."

"You must be careful about this, Bruce. The suspects can't pick up on her. Cease any activity on her part to watch the men."

"I already have."

"Good. So, go ahead and get on back to the inn to continue the surveillance. Your intuitions have been dead on. Get the goods on them any way you can."

"So, you now want me to continue staying there."

"Actually, it has always been okay for you to stay there. I'm also glad you rekindled an old friendship with Adrianna."

"You know her name and about our friendship years ago?"

"There's nothing I don't know, Bruce."

"Oh yes there is."

"Oh no there isn't." He paused for effect. "Just be careful not to mumble in your sleep." His eyes had a more patriarchal tone now.

Birdman was good … and obviously sneaky. Now I was *embarrassed*. I wondered if there was some external video or listening device in proximity to the inn. Maybe in my locator chip. And I now assumed he had been privy to our secret interlude. *Damn!*

I broke away from that subject, quickly. "You don't care about the bill there?"

"How much is it per night?"

"I thought you knew everything."

"For some reason, not that."

"$300."

"*What?* That's not going to fly."

"Well, would you approve half that? $150."

"That sounds more in line."

"Good. I'll negotiate for that or press for a special Government rate. Anyway, she's a special friend, remember?" I figured if I told him up front the place was $150 per night, he'd blow a gasket and insist I stay at a $40 a night Motel 6.

"So, tell me again what she knows about you?"

"Again, not much. She thinks I'm some kind of immigration cop," I lied. He probably knew I was lying since he knew everything else.

"Okay. Keep it that way."

"How long should I stay on this?"

"Right now? As long as it takes. I have a feeling something's on the move and hopefully you'll be in position to out-wait them."

"When will you expect the profiles from Interpol on these faces?" I asked.

"This is Friday and it's tough to secure information over the weekend, especially holiday weekends."

"So I return there and wait."

He nodded. "Hopefully there will be increased and significant activity that you can monitor and evaluate. It would also be good to get a look inside both the B&B suspect's room and the bungalow where the other two are staying. There would be no way, however, without a court order, but we don't want to go that route. Understand?"

"I understand," which meant I would use my own discretion and means. "Anyway, getting a court order would make them disappear in a hurry."

An immediate problem was that I was no longer staying at Wolf Laurel and I sure as hell couldn't take a room at the Jamestown Motel. That would be a dead giveaway I was on their trail.

I continued. "Don't we need to get AmeriCan alerted for a possible terrorist attack?"

"Your phone call the other day was enough to get the ball rolling. They've increased security on the gates and there will be observers in strategic locations outside of the factory as well."

"And the airspace around Charleston?"

"Covered. The West Virginia National Guard will be patrolling the skies in that area. Every small plane in the area will be monitored and if there's one up there without a flight plan, it will be shot down. Of course, I don't know how long this vigilance can be kept up. It may be weeks or months before any plan they have is executed."

"In Charleston, every Labor Day weekend, the city puts on their Stern Wheel Regatta at the Landing. They bring in a couple of big names, block off the boulevard and let the beer flow. They even have a New Orleans-style funeral parade. There may be as many as two hundred thousand there over the weekend. A prime venue for a dirty bomb." I shook my head. "Don't even want to think about it."

"I know all about that, Bruce."

"Of course you do," I said to the man with all the answers. "Looks like as always you've done your homework, boss. What then do we do about the Bureau? The Charleston agent is pressing for any new and continuing information."

"The Bureau, the Company, CTC. They're all looking for a piece of the pie … and all the credit," he replied. Byrd swiveled around and looked at me glumly. "Jack Fuentes and his post have been alerted to anticipate an attack on AmeriCan or somewhere in the Kanawha Valley, but we have not given them everything. You know the area and your one face is better than five Bureau faces out there beating the bushes. I agree with you. We don't need a bunch of hot shot agents running amuck without a plan rounding these people up. Just have some random dialogue with Charleston and keep their number on your speed-dial in case you need to engage them. And don't hesitate to bring in the locals as necessary. Stay close to the suspects, Bruce, but not *too* close as to garner suspicion."

"Roger that. These maggots will spook and run at the first sight of a Crown Vic."

Byrd nodded, then swiveled in his chair facing the window. As he bit on his pipe and scanned the rooftops of commerce below him on Wall Street, he was silent and reflective. After a few moments he spoke. "We're vulnerable, Bruce. You know, I look out over this city some days and think how easy it would be for just one hatemonger with a suitcase device to wreak havoc, bring down buildings and kill thousands of people. Islamic radical factions thrive on hate. They don't believe hate is a bad thing ... that it is necessary and is justified by the Koran. Any people who are outside of the Dar al Islam or House of Submission are infidels, and violence is the only resource."

I didn't respond. I have always been struck by this man's philosophical and spiritual nature, not to mention his intellect, political and otherwise. Any attempt on my part to have an engaging dialogue with Lionel Byrd would be like a seventh grade Civics student conversing with a Harvard Political Science professor.

He continued. "These radicals also instill in their youth a hatred of the West, a degrading of women, and a belief that the one true path to Heaven is to lose their lives by killing as many Americans as possible. It is the necessary combination that will lead to Muslim unity. They literally follow the words of Muhammad and Imam Muslim: *The gates of Paradise are under the shadows of the swords.* As a Muslim's deeds are on a balance scale, his good is measured against the bad, and although they wait until the Day of Judgment for the final tally, they believe that Allah does guarantee he will admit the true Jihad into Paradise for giving up his own life to kill infidels.

"The Jihadis are like Nazis in Kaffiyahs. They are a radical form of Wahhabi Islam, undergoing a kind of inquisition, who want to finish the Holocaust and destroy not only Israel, but Jews everywhere. They ultimately want to control all of the Middle East, to include OPEC and the entire world's economy."

I nodded like if he hadn't offered up these profound observations, I would have. Byrd was indeed a scholar on this stuff and it was always an education for me just to be around him. But I had to add some of my own reflections to show him I was not a *total* ignoramus on the topic. "And then there is that obsessed hatred of Western depravity. Islamic ideology mandates that immoral secularism must be eradicated. To do that, all of America and its entire population of men, women and children, the epitome of immorality, must ultimately be exterminated. These people are not just ruthless, but they have no value of human life. To the Jihad, if you are not Muslim, you may as well be a piss-ant mashed on the sole of one of their sandals."

Birdman sat a while longer, fingers formed prayer-like under his chin, and gazing from his window beyond the clutter of skyscrapers toward the Hudson. He was quiet for the longest time. I thought he had fallen asleep after I had begun to chime in with my observations. But then he slowly whirled his chair back around and affixed his eyes on mine. "We need more tangible information on this nest, Bruce, to find out for sure whether they are Al-Qaeda, Hezbollah, Aden-Abyan Islamic Army or even Jaish-e-Mohammed. You know what to do and how to gather it."

"Okay," I replied, like I knew what the hell all these Islamic organizations were. I would definitely need to do some Googling.

"Remember what I said about your friend. I hope you can keep her out of danger. She's a very pretty lady, Bruce."

Okay now, that *did* it. How the hell would he know what she looked like? How was he doing this and what kind of toys did he have at his disposal? I felt at that moment like I was in the room with a reincarnated Ian Fleming and J. Edgar, all wrapped up in one.

"Yes, she is," I agreed. "So are we done, Boss?"

"We're done," he replied, maintaining his reflection.

"Lunch?"

"No."

As usual, Birdman was short on his goodbyes. He pretty much punctuated the end to all conversations with one or two words, leaving his fellow converser hanging like a dangling participle.

So I had lunch with Moneypenny. We had a nice conversation, but I had trouble making eye contact with her since breasts don't have eyes.

Chapter 13

After getting back into Georgetown at two thirty on Friday afternoon, I took a nap, then dined at my favorite Italian haunt, Mariano's. As I had enjoyed Georgetown this past year, complete with its university flavor, nifty shops and riverfront restaurants, for some reason I again felt very alone. Although I had tried all evening to expel the feeling, it was all about missing Adrianna. Just in one week, this woman had inadvertently caused me some very real interpersonal distress. I thought I actually enjoyed being me, having a very focused and uncomplicated life; but just as I had realized the other night on the road outside Darlene's house, I was a very lonely person with no real future in sight … at least a happy one.

I sat by myself listening to a pretty young thing at the piano bar singing some ballad in her awful beauty pageant voice, strained, cracked and loaded with false vibrato. Then images of another lovely woman and her soft, Southern voice penetrated my brain. I guess I had always thought I would one day meet someone that I felt good about … good enough to marry. But I still had contributions to make to our country. And as I was still in pretty good shape and healthy enough to continue doing the work of law enforcement, helping to keep our country safe and free from those bent on destroying it, I didn't need the responsibilities and distractions of a relationship. But, of course, I hadn't counted on Adrianna coming into my life. If she expected more from me, I knew I would end up hurting her and feeling sorry for the both of us.

After dinner, I stopped off at *The Cat's Meow*, a nifty knick-knack shop down the street, and found a most lovely crystal vase which I thought would look nice on Adrianna's dining table. I shelled out $250 after whittling the little lady behind the counter down from $300, although I was sure it cost her something like $49.95; but for some stupid reason I felt I had made a great deal. As I walked out of the store, I caught the reflection in the storefront window of some poor, lonely and sentimental shmuck who had allowed a little time and distance away from his girlfriend to develop a mushy mass in his brain and at the same time lighten his wallet. If they saw my moony eyes now, both my old Special Forces buds and new Zulu pards would be laughing their asses off.

I went on back to my apartment and dipped into some Merlot, feeling even sorrier for myself than before. I thought a lot about how and why Byrd was keeping tabs on me. I knew it was nothing personal and there was no lack of trust. Was everyone in his peep sight? How about the couple sleeping in the Lincoln bedroom? I suddenly felt very naked, not to mention paranoid. But after catching a little of the tube, sleep came over me just after nine-thirty and put me out of my misery.

The TV that had partnered with the wine in knocking me out woke me up the next morning with the early edition of Fox News. I was still slumped in the over-stuffed sofa chair where I had passed out and my neck hurt. A car bomb had gone off in a Tel Aviv marketplace, killing more than twenty people. A PLO extremist group had already taken credit and the face of Arafat, looking more like Willie Nelson than Willie did, was all over the tube half-heartedly condemning the blast. It would not be long until the Israeli government would retaliate with a raid on some known terrorist stronghold, vindicating the deaths. Wonderful, I thought.

Saturday morning I ran the Mall from where I parked my car near the Capitol building to the Lincoln Memorial and back. My shadowy twin running along side kept perfect pace with me. I did catch a breather and some water at the Vietnam Memorial where I ran my fingers across the names of four of my Special Forces compadres. It had become a ritual of mine each time I ran. I knew precisely where each name was as I had visited them scores of times since the emplacement of the wall.

Back at the ranch I did a week's worth of laundry, showered and went again to Mariano's for supper. Strangely enough, the beauty queen sounded better than the night before. It may have had something to do with the carafe of wine I gulped. But then later when she started singing that one song that at least one contestant always did in every pageant ever held, *I Feel Pretty*, I knew at that very moment my life sucked.

I couldn't wait for the light to hit my eyes around 6:15 on Sunday morning, so having awakened at five, I swung out of bed, showered, grabbed my bag and suitcase and hauled ass for West Virginia. This time I went west to pick up I-81 and the northern neck of the beautiful Shenandoah. If God ever decided to come back to earth and take up residence, I was sure He would settle somewhere in that part of Virginia. There's a good thing about having a job where you set your own hours and get to travel. You can take your time getting from one place to another and zip off the highway to see anything you want. And I did just that. I first visited the site where the VMI cadets fought a battle with Yankee troops at New Market and then I exited at Staunton for a superb country lunch at Rowe's.

Further down the pike I stopped at the Washington and Lee campus to visit the Lee Chapel. If there was ever a place that gave me such hallowing serenity and peace, it was here. Sitting in the front pew, I gazed for several minutes upon the magnificent marble statue of Robert E. Lee lying in repose on the battlefield. The sanctuary was deafeningly quiet as I was the church's only visitor. After a while I closed my eyes, blocking everything from my mind, including Adrianna, Arab terrorists, arthritic knees and other annoyances. I listened for a message from God, but I had been such a heathen over the years, He probably wanted to take me out to the woodshed instead of giving me His valuable time. But He finally showed up, showering me with a sudden spear of sunlight through the leaded glass window. I looked up at the sun-dappled cross above the General and it was purely the first time I remembered having such a religious moment since I was a kid. That is, except for last Monday night at Wolf Laurel.

Driving long hours on the interstate opens up the brain to thousands of thoughts that interweave and run onto one other, often making no sense. But ultimately they will all dissipate which will in turn allow me to settle onto one of them. In the process, I will sometimes dwell on some pressing matter or some regret, like my divorce, or maybe on Caroline. And sometimes it may be a gnawing, even fearful thought that will engross me to a point where I don't remember passing an exit or a town, then suddenly finding myself two counties away.

Sometimes I may even begin second-guessing myself on theories I had earlier solidified. I was convinced that the Arab vermin were planning to somehow attack AmeriCan. Then I began thinking if this was all just speculation on my part ... that I had made too much of the map and the boys' behavior. But I always trust my instincts and they usually don't disappoint me. Again, what if I was wrong and we took this too far and I took out an innocent Arab student? You see, those are the kind of fearful flip-flopping thoughts I can have. I guess I just think too damn much.

But then, there was that compelling picture in my brain of a car driven by a young Islamic terrorist with a Russian-manufactured suitcase bomb on the seat beside him crashing through a barricade and taking out the AmeriCan factory. Although these compact weapons of mass destruction that the Kremlin had intended to be detonated in American cities during the cold war weigh less than 40 pounds, they could easily cause damage equal to the bombs dropped on Hiroshima and Nagasaki. Even a suitcase bomb could create a fireball reaching 10 million degrees. A bomb exploded within a factory that manufactured hydrogen chlorine gas would be devastating enough, but with a nuclear device, there were sure to be few survivors in the entire Kanawha Valley. Anyone not immediately consumed by the fireball and shock wave would still expire within three days from radiation poisoning.

I shut off my festering brain, turned on a classical music station and listened to something by Mozart, I think. I pressed harder on the accelerator as though it would help me expel horrendous images in my head of people screaming and dying. No, goddammit, I would *not* second-guess my instincts about these bastards. I was right. I was *definitely* right about them. And I would stop them.

I called Joey just east of Clifton Forge and told him to expect me somewhere around four. He said he saw Adrianna at church as she was coming out. He was going in to set up for a one o'clock funeral and asked her if she'd like to come to the house later for dinner, knowing of course I would be coming back. She said she'd like that, but her assistant was off and there was a new couple coming to Wolf Laurel between five and seven. She'd take a rain check.

At ten minutes till four I turned north onto South Ivy Road and then down the lane that led to the old McGowan place. Hearing the unmistakable drone of a small plane, I looked to see a small red-and-white Cessna buzzing the landscape about a thousand feet up. It circled the farm once and then disappeared over the tree line. I wondered if it was Assad out for a Sunday drive.

Cora had prepared yet another wonderful dinner and I made sure to compliment her. Joey couldn't begin to realize how good life was for him. A pretty wife who could actually cook, two sweet girls who adored him and a business that ... well, two out of three ain't bad. After stuffing my gills with the heavy spaghetti supper, I slipped out to the porch and called Adrianna on my cell.

"Hi, stranger." She looked absolutely stunning over the phone. I could tell that from her voice.

"Hi yourself," I replied, trying not to sound too anticipatory about seeing her tomorrow, which I'm sure would be a fabulous day, and which at day's end, if I was lucky, may conclude with a nocturnal rhapsody. "Did you miss me?"

"Yes," she said.

"I'm anxious to see you."

"And I'm anxious to see you. Breathlessly so." She then changed gears. "Did you accomplish everything you set out to do?"

"Been busy, all right. I've kept my nose to the grindstone, shoulder to the wheel and ear to the ground; but baby, I only have eyes for you."

She laughed. "Seriously, what all did you do?"

"Well, in all my time away, I only spent three hours with my daughter, three hours with the boss, and the rest of the time either on the road or doing my laundry or in bed."

"By yourself, of course."

"You mean while I was on the road or doing my laundry?"

"You know what I mean, silly. In *bed*."

"And what did *you* do these last few days?"

"Behaved myself," she replied.

"Will you behave tomorrow?"

"It depends."

"On what?"

"On you. If you give me anymore trouble, like a few nights ago, I may have to punish you." She let out a soft giggle.

"You mean spank me?" *My* turn to say that.

Now she laughed. "Only if you're naughty. And I hope you are."

"You can count on it."

"Pick me up about eleven?"

"I'll be there. I don't mean to change the subject, but have you seen Assad today? Not that you're supposed to keep tabs on him now."

"He left out yesterday morning, but I don't think for good. He only had his knapsack with him. The older guy in the van came by and Assad followed him in his car. I happened to be snipping some roses for the vase in the lobby. Assad has always greeted me when we pass one another, but yesterday he just gave me a cold look and didn't say a word. It kind of gave me the willies."

"So his car is still gone?"

"Yes."

"Who do you have staying there now?"

"Well, besides Assad, Lottie Throckmorton is still here; she has another week or so. I also took in a nice middle-aged couple from upstate New York and there's a younger couple from Virginia Beach now in your old room."

"How *dare* they!"

"You're funny."

"You're cute." Starting to make myself sick again.

"See you tomorrow, Skip. Kiss. Kiss."

"Bang. Bang."

I took a little walk to melt some of the calories away. The fresh evening air electrified my lungs and re-vitalized my tired brain. It was now seven-fifty and the sun had begun to fade. The remnants of its orange glow still filtered through the trees on the far horizon. When I returned to the house, Joey was standing on the front porch with a half-smoked stogie.

"Beautiful evening. I think I worked up a hankering for that pie now."

"Better hurry, Brewster. There may be one piece left and if you don't snag it, I will."

"Why don't you go ahead. I've got to go out anyway. Don't wait up."

"It didn't take you long, big brother."

"What?"

"To hook back up with the Lady of the Inn."

I faked the kind of sheepish smile like when one is found out. "Who said I was going out to see *her*?"

He just shook his head and waved me off. "I'll leave the light on for you, Casanova. Don't wake me when you're slippin' back in about three o'clock."

I nodded, still smiling. The thing was, I would *not* be seeing Adrianna where I was going. At least I hoped not.

I changed into my black cargo pants and black tee, donned a black baseball style cap and left the house in my black Suburban in the black of night. Obviously, I was going for concealment when I parked my SUV along the road behind some trees adjacent to Wolf Laurel. The Nissan was still gone, but in the driveway there was a Buick (the older couple), a Mustang (the younger couple) and Adrianna's van. I remembered Lottie didn't have a vehicle. It was just after ten and the lights were already off in Adrianna's room. There was a light on in one of the two front rooms. I scanned the grounds for any movement and waited for my purple vision to set in.

After about ten minutes, I snapped my Glock in its holster, shoved my black metal flashlight in *its* holster and moved carefully around to the back of the house. Assad's suite, the Magnolia Room, at the far end of the house had windows at the side and back. I wondered why he got the Magnolia Room and I only rated the Pine. Through the blinds I could see there was no light on in the room. I had to assume he was still not there.

Assuring that all was quiet inside, I entered the dimly lit lobby after unlocking the front door. Adrianna had not asked me for my room key when I left and this same key also worked in the front door lock. With as much stealth as I could manage, I crept down the creaky hall floor and located the door to the Magnolia Room. I checked the door for a wire that may have been connected to something that would go off and mess up my handsome face. It appeared there was none. From my belt I then took out my handy-dandy burglar kit and with the two picks, worked my magic on the lock. After a few seconds the deadbolt clicked open. The lock below the ancient doorknob was a piece of cake. Slowly, I pushed open the door and listened with my eyes tightly shut for a click or a boom. Finally satisfied the entrance was not booby trapped, I entered the room.

I switched on the flashlight and first shined the beam onto both beds to assure they were unoccupied, then quickly scanned the main room and bathroom to reaffirm there was no one about. It was time to go to work.

The room smelled like a mixture of curry and incense, which was pretty damned nauseous. At least it didn't smell like B.O. or dirty socks. Carefully and methodically, so as not to disturb the turf, and still being cautious to look for explosives, I began checking out Assad's closet. I rifled the pockets of his clothes and sifted through several plastic bags. One of the plastic bags contained only dirty clothes and another, some cans and boxes of food, the labels of which were printed in bold Arabic. A nice pair of Mediterranean-looking roach killers caught my eye and I shook them out.

In two dresser drawers were a half-dozen folded shirts and rolled socks. The guy was a neatnik; I gave him that. Maybe even obsessive-compulsive. A copy of the Qu'ran laid dead center on the desk, beside of which was an 8X10 notebook and pen. His textbook, *Multicultural Issues in America* was to the left of the Qu'ran. The drawers to the desk were for the most part empty. The left drawer contained an Innkeeper's Guide like the one I had in my room (or used to have) and in which was a picture and description of Wolf Laurel in the West Virginia section. In the center drawer were two more pens and some B&B stationery with an image of the inn at the top left.

I checked between the mattresses and under the beds, as well as the bathroom medicine cabinet, finding nothing. A rolled-up mat was in a chair by the door which I unfurled and inspected. It appeared to be Assad's prayer blanket.

After five minutes in the room, I was convinced that if he had anything of suspicious nature in his possession, it had to be in the backpack he was never seen without. The man traveled light, likely didn't eat much, and probably spent his time in the room reading and praying.

I put the beam of light back on the notebook and opened it. Counting seven pages of neatly penned hieroglyphics, which appeared to be Arabic, I pulled from my pocket my digital, set it for flash and photographed each page. I then opened the Qu'ran, finding a loose sheet of paper behind the front cover on which was written four paragraphs, at the end of which were numbers, some kind of message I took to be scriptural verses. Also in the book was a picture of a young, beautiful Middle Eastern girl who was perhaps his sweetheart or sister.

Making sure the two texts and notebook were aligned on the desk top just as I found them, I made another sweep of the room in case I missed something. I apparently didn't. Just as I reached for the doorknob to leave, I heard the front door to the inn shut and footsteps in the lobby. It was just one set of footsteps, so I figured it wasn't the newer boarders. Switching the flashlight to *off*, I turned the deadbolt lock to the right and the doorknob to its locked position. The footsteps were now in the hallway and I knew it must be Assad returning at a most inopportune time. How rude is that?

Quickly, I slid under the near bed and unsnapped my holster. If it was Assad and he decided to check under the bed for vermin (like me), I'd have to plug him. The footsteps stopped at the door. For a moment there was no sound at all from the other side. I wondered if he had heard me. Just in case, I pulled out the Glock and screwed in the silencer. Finally, I heard the deadbolt click, followed by the second lock. After Assad pushed the door open, the room illuminated. He then shut the door and the locks clicked again. I watched his sandals pass by the bed a couple of times and then disappear to the closet. It was a stroke of luck that I chose to hide under the bed; my first inclination was the closet. Of course, that was also *his* good fortune. He could at this very moment been lying on Adrianna's floor with a nasty hole in his head, changing the color of her rug.

The sound of a bag unzipping and the rattle of a plastic bag told me he was transferring something from his canvas tote into one of the two Hefty's … maybe more dirty clothes. I then watched the sandals approach the bed again where he stopped. He was so close to my face I could see the toe with the ingrown toenail sticking out of the sandal. Go ahead and look under the bed, Assad, I thought. There's a boogeyman under here. Your worse nightmare, as a matter of fact. But he didn't. He only stopped to drop the backpack on the mattress. Then, as I hoped he would, he trotted off to the bathroom.

I heard the commode seat clatter against the tank and then the audible urination, right in the center of the water. It was certainly loud enough to drown out any noise I would be making crawling out from under the bed and scrambling for the door. I prayed for his sake his bladder was full as I quickly turned the locks, opened the door to step out and re-closed it gingerly. I continued my escape softly down the hallway, thinking that by this time, his lizard was fully drained. In the morning, when he left his room, he would discover the unlocked door and wonder why it was so.

On the way to my car I checked for anyone lurking about who may have seen me, then slipped away from the parking lot to my vehicle. My work is often a matter of luck. And I was lucky I had not stopped the unfolding plot before I could figure out its particulars. Not to mention having to kill Assad Mohammed prematurely.

Chapter 14

▼

A lazy fog hung over the green hills and fields early Monday morning, the 3rd, as I ran along South Ivy on my second mile. Pockets of the cottony mist lay like hosts of ghosts left over from the night, refusing to go away until chased by the sun which had not yet peeked over the far tree line. White farmhouses and ancient barns of chestnut plank filtered by the fog appeared opaque in the morning twilight. The air was fresh and cool and the warm vapor from my lungs spewed like cigarette smoke, which incidentally had never passed through my lips. As it was quiet and seemed that nothing in the world was stirring on this Labor Day morning, it tended to magnify the steady pound-pounding of my Nikes on the pavement.

This Greenbrier morning, like many others early on in my life, created in my soul a religious, even holy experience, mollifying my spirit, and seemingly defying the evil that lurked in the shadows of our liberties … an evil whose mission it was to infiltrate and violate our beautiful land. Images of radical Islamofascists wreaking tragedy upon this state's people and industry, demoralizing and horrifying the innocent, angered me, shattering the peace that had abided in me when I began the morning. I ran harder as though the physical act itself was a way to unleash my anger upon the malignancy that sought to destroy America. I was now more determined than ever to find out if a real threat existed, as I was sure it did, the scope and depth of that threat, and at all costs choke it off. Was I kidding myself that I could do it without engaging the FBI? Maybe. But if and when I did get the goods on these guys, I knew all I had to do was press 2 on my speed-dial. Birdman would have Zulu on site in a flash if needed. It's good working for an organization that provides same day service.

Cora had a country breakfast waiting for me when I returned from my run. Today's granola bar would lay in my bag yet another day. The aroma of flapjacks on the griddle, bacon and rich, black coffee brought back sweet, nostalgic memories of life in the 1960's at the McGowan Homestead. I loved the old place. The house *and* the funeral business had been left equally to Joey and me; but I didn't want either, much to both Joey's *and* my ex-wife's protests. But I did reluctantly accept a share of the life insurance proceeds and Dad's 30.06 as my inheritance. The money went to a college fund for Caroline, which I later found was only a drop in the bucket. Thank God for the student loan program.

Dad taught Joey and me to shoot … rifles, shotguns, pistols … even the bow. He was an avid hunter of anything that crawled, moved on four legs or flew. Although Joey and I never really took an interest in hunting, we allowed Dad to drag us into the woods during quail, duck and deer seasons. I learned that it wasn't enough to go out in the wild when it was just plain *deer* season; there was a separate *doe* season as well. I asked him one time if there was a *Bambi* season and the man of a million cornpone mortuary jokes didn't think that was a *bit* funny. Hunting was serious business.

Nonetheless, every year in mid-December when the leaves were all gone, he'd take Joey and me out to the woods behind our house and direct us to shoot clumps of mistletoe out of the trees. We collected the shot-up foliage and then Dad gave it to Mom who hung it on the overhead door facing between the parlor and dining room.

Before long they were standing under it doing suck face. I never understood why two people got romantic under a clump of fungus that was formed from bird crap. I also never understood why Dad was the one that got smooched from this deal and all I got was a raspberry on my shoulder from the recoil of the twelve gauge.

But those were great times … innocent times. I sometimes wonder why and how I turned out to be me. I was a nice kid growing up, meek and timid, wouldn't hurt a fly, a respecter of all people. How did I go from an undefiled, inoffensive little kid to a smart-tongued, imperious, sometimes bigoted, heat-packing exterminator? I *have* been analyzed by Army, FBI and private practice psychologists along the way and always checked out okay. It sure as hell didn't say much for their assessment skills.

I know Dad favored Joey, anyway, as he knew his younger son would ultimately take over the business. I was the squeamish one, remember. When Dad took us out there to hunt, I couldn't pull the trigger on a deer. I still can't. *Human* vermin? Now that's another story. Perhaps it was all a matter of preserving the innocent. And maybe I also felt there was no challenge in hunting down four-legged critters that threatened no one and couldn't shoot back. Anyway, I think it all came together for me when I joined Special Forces and went to Sniper School. There I found my niche. Contrary to popular belief, I was neither indoctrinated nor brainwashed. I just learned from that experience who I was destined to become: a purveyor of the good and an exterminator of the evil.

Anyway, this was the morning of wonderful smells: the intoxicating aroma of a Cora McGowan breakfast, and yes, even the pungent stench of cow piss and manure in the countryside, which by the way to me is nature's perfume.

We finished breakfast about eight thirty and I showed my appreciation to Cora by planting a kiss on her forehead. Joey told me to watch that stuff and I retorted with some noise about stealing her away one day. After the playfulness, I excused myself and went to the den to call Adrianna about the day's events.

She seemed a bit upset when I answered. "It's been a most interesting morning around here. Not long after Juanita arrived she came to me in tears. It seems Mr. Mohammed accused her of being in his room. He said that things had been disturbed and he found his door unlocked this morning. She told me he was screaming in her face and mixing 'American and foreign' words, as she put it."

"No kidding," I remarked in forced amazement. Actually, I *was* a little amazed that he found anything disturbed. I thought I did a good job putting everything back. That's an obsessive-compulsive for you. "Did he say anything to you?"

"Well, I was getting ready to go down and ask him why he jumped on her, when he came up and started banging on *my* door. As soon as I opened it, he started on me about invading his privacy and violating his space. Says he now doesn't feel safe, because either someone was in his room over the weekend or tried to get in with a key while he was sleeping."

"What did he say was disturbed?"

"He didn't. He just said things were not in the same order they were when he left on Saturday morning."

Hmm. *I* thought things were in good order. I must have left a hair under the bed or the commode seat up.

"Gee. Sounds like your boarder is the sensitive type. Makes one suspicious about him, doesn't it?"

"I assured him no one was in his room as I was emphatic that he had gotten no maid service, respecting his privacy. He still ranted and raved and threatened to move out."

"We don't want him to do that. I *have* to keep an eye on him."

"How are you going to do that staying at Joey's?"

"Well, I could move back in, but you booted me and gave away my room."

"I did not. You left, remember?"

"I just took a vacation from my vacation, remember?"

She was silent for a moment.

"Skip, you didn't by chance …"

"Break into his room?"

"Well …"

"I thought that was what you were going for. Look, I've been a law enforcement officer for over twenty years. What do *you* think?"

"I'm sorry. I didn't mean to insinuate … anyway, you were in Washington and New York until last night and I know you went to your brother's."

"Right." I hated lying to her. Actually, I didn't. Sometimes impressions are perceived as lies, however. And I make impressions on everyone I meet.

"I guess I'll just have to keep an eye on his room so he doesn't have a reason to pop like that again."

Lucky for him I was in a good mood last night. *He* was the one who nearly got popped.

"Be careful about watching him and his room too closely. He may misconstrue your intent."

"I just wish he *would* go away."

"Just hang with him as a boarder for a while and keep your distance. See you in a couple of hours."

I had stepped out on the porch with some coffee to take a deep drink of the still cool morning air. Joey joined me.

"I forgot to ask you how Caroline was."

"Good. Sends her love."

"And back *to* her." He came over and plopped his butt on the banister. "Do you have any more information on the dead guy?"

"Neither his DNA or photo set off any alarms with the Bureau. I'm running his mug through Interpol. And I did find that the map you secured was a near perfect overlay for a plant in Charleston."

He slammed his hand down on the banister. "Damn! I knew it meant something. Do you think he may have planned to blow it up?"

"Who knows? We may never know."

"You think there are more A-rabs out there?"

"Could be, Joe. That's one reason I'm back and sticking around for a few days."

I still didn't want to clue him in on *everything*. I wasn't worried he would let anything slip out, but for his and his family's safety, he didn't need to know.

"And another reason would be Adrianna, I take it."

I didn't answer, but took a sip of my coffee and just smiled. I wondered if Birdman would know that I had added my brother to my list of confidants. The boss now obviously suspected that his star agent just can't keep a secret. I talked into my locator chip and said, "Only a couple of people know about all this. Really."

"What?" responded Joey.

"Sorry, Joey. Just talking to myself."

He shook his head and went back inside.

What happened later that morning was what I feared might happen. The very moment I pulled into the parking lot at Wolf Laurel and stepped out of my vehicle, Assad appeared on the veranda. We would be passing one another again. He knew I had left, so why was I back if my vacation was over? Obviously, he would now think I was more than just a tourist. Maybe I was the guy who broke into his room.

As I reached the steps, I forced a fake smile and greeted him with a "Good morning."

There was no return smile. He just nodded, gave me a cold look and passed on by.

Hmm. Something I said? Something I did? I started to ask "What the hell's your problem, you Islamic fascist prick?" But it's not like me to be sarcastic. And anyway, I wanted to be in a good mood for the day. I didn't want to go to Adrianna's picnic upset that I had to pop someone. He gave me a parting shot with his eyes, then ducked into his Nissan. I guessed that we were now on an even keel. I suspected *him* and he suspected *me*. The difference was that I was a world-class burglar and he was a world-class terrorist asshole.

After we both discreetly said *Aloha* in sign language with our middle fingers, he pulled away. I went on up to Adrianna's suite to help her carry down the picnic items. She opened the door to me, gave me some wonderful lip service, and dragged me inside for seconds. "Missed you," she panted.

"Me too." That wasn't quite the response she was looking for, but that's the patented male answer to many amorous declarations, such as "I love you." Maybe I should be more specific and say something like, "Yeah, what *you* said."

I placed my gift in her hands which had been wrapped in white, slicky paper and garnished with a dainty pink bow.

"For me?" she said. "How thoughtful." I nodded in agreement.

She took the box to the dining table and began gingerly separating the scotch tape from the paper, careful not to rip it. I shuddered to think she would be saving the wrapping and some day I would get it back on my birthday or at Christmas. She finally opened it and placed her hands over her breasts, exclaiming "I love it! I love crystal." She then turned and gave me a powerful hug and another peck on the lips.

I was kind of waiting for more, but she quickly let go and said, "We have to load the car and get on out to the State Forest. Things will be cranking up soon."

After a couple of trips up and down the stairs, I wondered if in fact we were picnicking for the afternoon or camping out for a week. It would be tight, but the rear of my SUV may just be able to hold the picnic basket, quilt, table cloth, yard umbrella, king sized cooler, ice tea cooler, four plastic bags of chips, cookies, condiments, a chocolate cake, container of fried chicken and a badminton set. I can just see me out there batting around a shuttlecock like some big fruit.

As we loaded the last of the inventory, I gave Adrianna the once over … maybe the twice over … as she walked around to the passenger's side to get in. She was wearing a black sleeveless top tied in a knot at the waist, revealing two soft, shapely shoulders, two firm, tantalizingly pointed breasts and two tight, slightly muscular biceps that had obviously been conditioned at a gym. And the gams? Such a treat for *my* sore eyes. Perfect all the way up to her Gloria Vanderbilt shorts.

Fifteen minutes later we entered the Greenbrier Forest and drove along a winding park road into a large, grassy picnic site. A family shelter constructed of redwood and a tin roof was already filled up as were a dozen or so benches scattered throughout. We pulled in between two walnut trees and began to unload Adrianna's stuff. She found a shady spot near a huge sweeping willow and spread out her quilt. We sat down and then I leaned back with my hands folded behind my neck and gazed into the swaying tree tops as they met the blue sky. Adrianna cast off her tennies and low-cut socks, working her toes into the cool grass. May I say they were lovely toes with perfectly manicured nails painted with blood red polish.

I scanned the arena, estimating about a hundred people so far. She was expecting over three hundred. "And who all is it that's supposed to be here today?"

"Mostly, it's just a community thing," she replied. "It's sponsored by the Chamber of Commerce, the Osteopathic School, Valley Community, and several clubs and organizations. The theme is "Labor for Youth." A lot of kids will be here today, many of which won't be able to afford college."

"Kids. Oh, great."

"Most of the kids will be from the high school, but a few from the college as well. There'll be venues set up by local businesses with brochures and information about them."

"Like a job fair."

"Sort of. Only there won't be any interviews going on. The vendors will give the kids insight about what they do. As you can see, *The Greenbrier* is set up here along with the Sheriff's Department, Zanzadyne Pharmaceuticals and others. Over there in that booth is Valley Community."

I looked across the open grassy area where she was pointing and sure as hell, there was Paul LeMer. So let me get this straight. Not only was I going to spend my day avoiding ants and kids, but Paul the Putz as well. Since I had committed the 'mother of all faux pas' in his office the other day and made him look silly, I doubted very much if he wanted to be my badminton partner. So, being the master of disguise that I am, I put on my black ball cap with the Special Forces logo and flight glasses. I think Adrianna liked the look.

A clown came by juggling some balls, followed by a pasty-faced mime, imitating a mechanical man. He was definitely annoying. It set me to wonder that if you shoot a mime, do you use a silencer?

Adrianna put out the fried chicken and trimmings, then poured us some ice tea. I no sooner stripped a leg when a glum-faced, well-built jock about forty-two or three sauntered up to our blanket with such determination, I thought he was intending to plop down with us. He was a nice-looking chap with a Marine haircut, which unfortunately for him accentuated two huge ears that stuck out from his head, resembling a taxi-cab coming at us with its doors open.

"Hi, Dan," greeted Adrianna. She gave him one of those finger waves.

He in turn gave *me* a penetrating look that would make a lesser man seize like an epileptic and wet his pants. Obviously, he was none too happy to find his squeeze sharing bed covers with the likes of me, handsome as I was.

"Hello Adrianna. I *thought* that was you across the field. I actually hoped you would be here. Who's the *old* guy?" He stood with hands on hips looking rather ominous, not to mention, pissed.

Although a bit indignant about the 'old guy' slam, I stood and thrust out my hand. "Name's Bruce, sonny." That's about all I had in me for the guy.

Dan was not going to let this go, much less shake my hand. He gave Adrianna a cold look. "I kind of thought *we* would be spending the day together."

She tried to disarm him with a smile. "We never talked about that, Dan."

"Well, I thought it was pretty much understood." Now he looked *hurt* and pissed.

"I'm sorry, Dan. We don't have that kind of relationship where one of us assumes ..."

He interrupted her. "That we have something going between us? Well, I certainly believed so."

I thought I'd try to clear up the confusion. "Well, Dan, let me explain how things are ..."

Now he interrupted *me*. "Uh ... I wasn't talking to you, sir."

Adrianna was now beyond embarrassed. "Dan, that wasn't necessary." It was like we were all in the ninth grade and she was a cute little cheerleader sandwiched between two jealous jocks, vying for her attention.

"Yeah, Dan," I added.

Adrianna shot me a poisonous dart. "Skip, please."

Dan stared me down for a couple of seconds like he could mop the blanket with me. But I glared back with one of those laser-fired, penetrating beams that could burn through the hull of the Queen Mary. *Okay, Danny Boy, the pipes are calling. Now get lost.* He stood for a few moments in silence with his Popeye arms folded across his chest. He must have been reading my mind because he then put up one hand as if to say, "forget it," turned heel and strode away.

"*That* went well," I remarked.

"He didn't have to act that way," she said, dolefully. "I've never given him the impression that we are an item. All we've done is have an occasional dinner and talk."

"Have you kissed him?"

"Okay, dinner and a one time kiss. Well, maybe two. But nothing beyond that."

"Nothing carnal?"

"Absolutely not," she replied indignantly.

"Sorry. Can we eat now?"

She sighed and shook her head. I wasn't sure if it was me or good ol' Dan that ruined her day. But anyway, she went ahead and refilled my tea tumbler which was a good sign it wasn't me.

About a half hour later Danny Boy, who had been watching us from a distance, trekked back across the field to our blanket with considerably less piss and vinegar and with his wounded ego obviously shoved up into where the sun don't shine.

"Hey, Adrianna … Bruce. I really have to apologize for my behavior earlier." He grinned a cheesy grin. "You know how we boys are sometimes, right Brucie?"

No. I pride myself in being rational and mature in such scenarios. Not like you, schmuck. Watch the Brucie shit. But to be polite, I nodded in agreement.

He continued. "Say, if you two are interested, we have a Labor Day tradition of getting a bunch of guys and gals together for a friendly game of flag football. About a dozen players from my senior squad are here and it would be great if you all join us in a few minutes."

Well that sounded a heck of a sight more interesting than badminton. However, I replied, "To tell you the truth, Dan, I was never that much of a jock…"

Adrianna jumped in. "Hey, that's okay, Skip. I don't know the first thing about football, but I used to like playing 'touch' with the guys when I was younger. Come on. It'll be fun."

And I used to play 'touch' with the *girls* when I was younger. As a matter of fact, I still do.

"I don't know," I replied reluctantly. "I probably wouldn't last three plays."

"We'll take it easy on you, old sport," offered Dan.

*Should I just go ahead and punch **you**, old sport?*

Adrianna stood and reached out her hand to pull me up from the blanket. "I'll protect you out there, sweetie. If you get a boo-boo, I'll play nurse later."

I thought Dan was going to burst a blood vessel. And after what Adrianna just said, I was left feeling like a complete wuss.

"Oh, all right," I said, rising. "You shamed me into it." Actually, she did.

Well, here I was, lined up with Adrianna on my right, a three hundred pound heart attack waiting to happen on my left, and a mixed bag of volunteer boys and girls, aged twelve to eighteen on my team. Opposite us weenies were Coach Dan, six of his players from the varsity squad and two girls from the school soccer team. I think a junior high team playing the Dallas Cowboys would have been a fairer fight. And then there was the taunting and jeering from Danny's boys across the line of scrimmage. Like *that* was going to intimidate me.

Our center pitched the ball to our twelve year old quarterback, who after seeing Dick Butkus barreling toward him, panicked and fumbled. I scrambled to recover it about the same time Coach Dan and his two hundred-ten pound frame plastered me from the side and drove my chin into the grass.

"Whoa!" I yelled. "I thought this was flag football, not a Tough Man contest." Dan stood over me like Thor while I laid there checking to see if I still had all my teeth.

"Sorry, Skippy."

I detected a bit of sarcasm there.

I got up and brushed myself off, taking both my banged-up pride and tailbone back to the huddle. I had lied to Dan. Bad knees and all, one thing I could do was run. And I not only knew enough about football to be coaching the Steelers, I was an all-conference running back my senior year at the military academy.

This time I called the play and lined up behind the quarterback, telling him to just turn around and give the ball to me. I'd handle the rest. After the handoff, which was clean this time, I started left which drew in the entire defense like a magnet, spun and zipped right. I got behind Adrianna, thinking no one would dare crunch her, being Coach's girl and all, took a couple of stutter steps to avoid a flying defender and sailed un-deflagged past the marker for a touchdown. The kid had tried to stay with me, but I smoked him like a cheap cigar. When I turned around to bask in the glory, I saw an angry Dan standing with hands on hips and sporting a scowl. He then put a finger in the face of three of his All Stars.

It was Dallas' turn on offense. On the first play, Dan's quarterback faked an end around and short of crossing the line of scrimmage, he fired a bullet to the tight end just about the time I got there. As we both went up for the ball, we collided and knocked ourselves out of bounds. The kid sprawled onto the turf, but Murphy's Law which had followed me around all my life, caused me to cream an innocent bystander on the sidelines. Paul LeMer.

Bruised and highly irritated, he crawled out from under my frame. I think I hit him so hard, his mama felt it. As I reached out my hand to help him up, he then saw for the first time who it was that had ruptured his spleen. "You!" he yelled.

"Are you okay?" I asked, helping him up.

"Yes, but ..."

"See ya," I said, scooting back to the game. I glanced back in his direction. He was holding his head and yelling something unintelligible.

On the next play, I was attempting to run down a very fast kid who was firmly cradling the ball like Coach taught him, and just as I reached for his flag, I was blind-sided again by my new friend Dan. This time it was my eyeballs that hurt.

I was getting pretty beat up about now and began to second-guess myself about the noble game of badminton, played by kings and other royalty. About the time the birds in my head stopped chirping, on the next play another golden boy started a run up the middle with Dan ahead of him, poised to give me another shot. I faked a head-on counter-block, then at the last second threw a roll block that upended Dan, tossing him on his head. Adding insult to injury, I yanked the flag off the runner.

Out of the corner of my eye I saw Dan coming at me, yelling something about a cheap shot. He actually pushed me like the sore loser he was. So I pushed him back. He didn't much like that and threw a round-house punch, which I blocked with my left, then cocked and fired a straight punch that caught him on the bridge of his nose. He dropped like a rock. Stunned, he stumbled to his feet about the time Adrianna stepped in between us. The squad gathered around their humiliated coach to check him out, then the grumbling started. I think I may have heard the word 'kill' in there somewhere. One of the heroes brushed her aside and stuck his face in mine. The lip ring was all I saw. There were expletives spewing from this kid's mouth that I had never even heard at a Special Forces reunion.

I stuck my pinky finger through the ring and pulled the kid to his knees by his lower lip. "There are ladies present, Sissy Boy. Now lose the language or lose the lip. Your choice." The boy threw up his hand as if to say 'uncle.' I helped him up and after a perforating glare, he walked away nursing the lip.

Meanwhile, Adrianna the referee sent me to my corner and pulled a hanky from the pocket of her shorts to stop the blood flow from Dan's nose. I actually didn't mind her tending him as it served to humiliate the prick even more. Anyway, I needed to retreat to my blankie to nurse my own wounds from Dan's body shots. When I plopped down, I looked around and then started talking into my chip in my forearm, "How'd you like that, boss?"

In a while, Adrianna came back to our picnic spot and sat quietly on the blanket beside me. "And are *you* all right?" There was definitely some snottiness in the question. She wasn't just cool; she was downright frosty.

"I'm sorry, Adrianna. I guess my competitive nature got the best of me."

"It had nothing to do with game, Skip. It was about me, and I don't like it one bit."

"But he started it," I replied, sounding very much like a six year-old being scolded by his mama.

Adrianna wanted to be angry, but as I nuzzled her neck, she couldn't quite quell the smile that broke out. She turned her head so I couldn't see it.

I put my face up to hers and said, "I fought for you."

The smile turned into a grin. "No, you idiot, you fought for your stupid ego."

Chapter 15

To keep *rigor* from setting in, I stood up to move around and then walked through several of the venues. Large and small business owners from Lewisburg and White Sulphur had the ear of teenagers and young adults alike. Four community colleges from a two county area, including Valley, had administrative personnel and counselors set up in booths talking with high school juniors and seniors about life after graduation. A few kids were hanging out at the Greenbrier County Sheriff's display asking bright questions like 'what kind of gun is that?' and 'did you ever shoot anybody?' And there was even something for *me* at the end of a long series of booths … a coffee stand.

I stood at some distance eyeing the big and lumpy Paul LeMer with his comb-over flapping in the warm breeze. Beside him were a man and a woman. The lady looked to be a senior administrator of sorts, perhaps even Valley's president, and Paul was sucking up to her shamelessly. The man was about forty-five, with a dark olive complexion, slightly balding and sporting a neatly-trimmed black beard. I couldn't tell from the distance what nationality he was, but he was definitely Middle Eastern. I wondered if he was on staff and if he had any relationship with the Arab students. Perhaps he would be worth checking out, although I was not happy with myself for profiling the guy. For all I knew, he could be an Israeli-American patriot or a respected, long time professor in the West Virginia Educational System. But stereotyping or not, it was my job to be suspicious. I turned a moment to pay for the coffee and when I looked up again the man was gone.

Adrianna waltzed back to where I was standing, accompanied by a pretty, petite blonde with shoulder-length hair and eyes the color of golden brandy. She and her friend were jabbering on about the woman's recent divorce, but when they got in closer proximity to me, the volume went down.

But then the blonde eyed my hunkiness and nudged Adrianna's arm. "Are you going to introduce me?"

"Oh, I'm sorry. Skip, this is Lisa."

Well, I obviously looked a sight, like I had been playing a blood-letting game of rugby.

But maybe she liked that sweaty, dirty, banged up look. When I held out my hand, she cocked her head to one side, smiled wantonly and took it. If I read the body language correctly, she would be asking for my phone number the moment Adrianna was out of sight. But Adrianna read the signals, too, and sent her a subtle message by slipping her hand into my freed-up hand. So there I was, both of my hands clamped on to the hands of two honeys.

"Hello. Good to meet you," I said to Lisa rather matter-of-factly, in turn reading *Adrianna's* body language. Lisa finally released her grip.

"And good to meet *you*," she replied, eyes dancing and lips smiling.

Adrianna seemed to notice how honey-dipped her friend's voice had become, so she jumped in. "Lisa and I have been friends for eons; of course, she was a few years ahead of me in school."

Of course. Rather catty comment, I thought. Jealousy can do that to even the sweetest and most consecrated of souls.

The blonde kept her eyes on me, anyway. "You don't remember me, do you, Skip?"

"Should I?" I grinned like a Cheshire cat.

"I used to be Lisa Ramsay. We went out once or twice when you were home from college."

Then the light bulb finally came on. "Oh yeah … Lisa!"

"Remember that time we were driving around and your car quit on you? You said you were out of gas and I thought 'can't this guy get more original than to try that line on me?' But then I found out you really *were* out of gas and we walked for nearly two miles looking for a station."

"Hey, I *do* remember that."

I guess Adrianna was taking no chances on me getting re-enamored with my former squeeze. She edged even closer to me to make it perfectly clear that Lisa was definitely not welcome to renew our old friendship. It felt good to see that old jealous shoe on the other foot for a change.

Lisa got the picture, all right. She checked her watch and feigned as though she had something else going. "Well, anyway, Skip, nice seeing you again after what … thirty years?"

"Must be. Great seeing you again, too."

With that, she shook my hand again, this time rather business-like and without that extra little squeeze. Waving bye-bye to Adrianna, she sashayed off. I hoped the little messages given off did not put a dent in the two women's friendship. But I knew they'd be all right with each other … that is, just as soon as I left the state.

Adrianna and I walked arm in arm back to the blanket. I took notice of her smile … a rather sardonic smile at that.

"*Well*, Romeo, you *did* get around in those days, didn't you? Any other old girlfriends I should know about?"

"Mmm, no, but if you'll wait right here, I can go check around."

She didn't respond; but she did pinch me on my left buttock.

We packed up the Suburban about three and headed back to the inn. It took another fifteen minutes to unload all the cargo, most of which we didn't use ... including the badminton game. Once settled inside, Adrianna went to take a shower. I grabbed a cold brewski from her fridge and plopped my sore bones in her leather recliner.

The steam filtered out of the shower and rose like a ghostly wisp from beneath the bathroom door, then dissipated when it hit the coolness of the living room. I listened to her humming and heard the clunk against the shower floor when she dropped the soap ... and then dropped it a second time. I wanted in the worst way to be in there with her. And then I thought, 'just as well.' As beat up as I was, I wasn't sure I could muster up anything ... including my body from the chair.

I was just getting comfortable, remote in hand and ready to click, when she called from the bathroom. "Skip, can you come here for a minute?"

My body protested, but at the possibility of seeing her naked, I managed to coax it out of the chair. I bargained with it by telling it that if it cooperated, it might be richly rewarded. It didn't care. But the brain, the largest sex organ in the body, won out.

I peeked gingerly into the bathroom and said loudly above the beating of the shower spray against the stall, "Okay, I'm here!"

She stuck her head out and said, "Can you do my back?"

"I can do anything you want, my dear."

She laughed. "You may want to take your clothes off; otherwise, you'll get soaked."

The tee, the shorts, the underwear and socks came off in just under three seconds, a new world record. Gradually, the bathroom was becoming even more humid and steamy as though a dense fog had settled in, making it difficult to see. But I had no trouble finding the shower since King Richard had his radar out and happily pointed the way. I opened the shower door and slipped in behind her. She handed me the soap and I lathered her up. Working with both hands, beginning at the nape of the neck just under her pent-up hair, I gently caressed and massaged her shoulders and then her beautiful back as it cascaded down, down, down. Slowly, lovingly, I worked over nearly every inch of her skin. She moaned and writhed, backing into me, grinding, even dancing, until we were enjoying the mind-numbing passion of sexual love. Obviously, she had forgiven me for my adolescent behavior at the Super Bowl today.

After our twenty minute shower we looked like two albino prunes, she the more succulent prune. We dried off with large, thirsty towels and she handed me her over-sized terry bathrobe to put on, which still didn't quite close in the front.

"Why don't you relax in the living room while I throw our clothes into the washer? Can you pour me a glass of Chablis?"

I was feeling pretty salubrious about now. The hot shower and furious ardor did much to soothe my wounds and the soft bathrobe made me feel like a newborn babe again. All I needed was a little massage with some baby oil. Aside from getting knocked around a few hours before, I was having the best Labor Day of my life. I was in the company of a woman, feeling after all these years something deep and penetrating to the soul. If it *was* love, I wasn't sure I wanted it to be; but it surely felt like it. I was actually feeling sorry for poor dumb old Dan who was probably still sitting somewhere with ice on his nose, trying to stop the bleeding, not to mention the bleeding going on in his heart. Maybe I was just relishing the fact that today was a day I won for a change. I won the game, I won the fight and I won the girl.

About seven-thirty as the red-orange sun finally dipped over the horizon, its last rays fading on the living room wall, Adrianna brought out some cheese, crackers and summer sausage. We shared a new bottle of Chablis and she turned on the tube. CNN was broadcasting a special on the Taliban in Afghanistan and its continuing threats against the United States and Israel. The most dangerous man in the world was not Putin or Arafat, but a man resembling a Twelfth Century tribesman, Osama Bin Laden. He had taken responsibility for a myriad of terrorist acts in the past few years, resulting in the loss of American lives, all in the name of Allah.

Not thirty seconds into the broadcast, Adrianna switched channels. "Enough of that. It frightens me to even think there may be terrorists in this country and right under our noses. You've even got me scared about my boarder. The more I think about Assad and the way he blew up, I want him out. He may *be* just another Middle Eastern man who wants to assimilate in our society and take advantage of the quality of life in America, but he doesn't act like it. He's defensive and reclusive. So, before he pays another week, I'm giving him notice."

"If you can just hang with the guy a little longer, I need a bit more time to determine if he is an immigration concern. Don't worry. Now that he knows I'm back around, I will purposely make myself more visible. Hopefully, it will make him force his hand and expose anything he may be up to." I came very close to spilling all the beans about him, but I didn't want to alarm her; neither did I want him to be tossed out ... out of my sight.

Ultimately, I knew the wolf would leave the lair, bare his teeth and position for some kind of attack. And I knew what it was and where it was; I just didn't know when. I would do my damnedest to be there when he made his move.

"By the way, do you have a room coming back open for me?"

"Your old room will be available Wednesday for you if you want it."

"And I'll take it. I can remain at Joey's until then."

"Except tonight?"

"Is that an offer to stay here?"

"You can stay here as long as you want. You know you don't need to rent the room."

I pulled her down onto my lap. "Thanks. Maybe I'll stay with you tonight, but for the sake of your guests and because of the surveillance and other work I need to do, I will start bunking downstairs. I wonder, though, what your guests may imagine about me."

"I'm not worried about the guests. Mrs. Throckmorton knows about us."

"Knows about what?"

"That we've been … together."

"You told her?"

"No, silly. She didn't become a congresswoman without having acquired good perception skills. She sees the way we look at each other and says we make a cute couple."

"Hmm. Maybe *you*. But *cute* doesn't quite fit *me*."

Adrianna gave me a warm, wet wine-flavored kiss. "*I* think it does."

"Hey," I said. "Can I use your computer tomorrow? I need to send something to my boss."

"Sure."

I reached for my cell and called Joey. I told him I was staying back at Wolf Laurel for the night, to which he replied, "You *dog*."

"But I'll be back over some time tomorrow."

"Great. Come for breakfast?"

"No thanks, little bro. I've got some early things to do, but will catch up to you later after you leave the shop."

"Then supper?"

"You bet."
"Tell Adrianna she's welcome, too."
"I will."

When I finally stirred, Adrianna was already up and in the downstairs kitchen putting out the sweet rolls from Clingman's Diner. There were muscles and ligaments that hurt I didn't even know I had. No run this morning. After the bathroom chores I settled down in the leather recliner in my freshly laundered tee and BVDs with Adrianna's laptop on my knees. I inserted the disc from my digital camera and down loaded the photos of the notebook entry Assad so graciously provided. I sent them as an attachment to the following e-mail:

Dear Condor,

A friend of mine wrote the attached, but I'm unable to decipher much of it. Can you have it translated? Will anticipate your call.

Merci

At nine-thirty I joined Adrianna in the dining room for some coffee and toast. Either the other boarders had eaten earlier or weren't interested. If I had known I'd be alone, I could have just stayed in my briefs. I was on my second cup when I heard the sound of footsteps in the hallway. It was Assad. Our eyes met briefly, but as he continued past me, he looked away. I couldn't let this moment pass. It was time to engage him and this time it would not be casual conversation.

"Assad," I called. He froze in position at the door, then turned slowly around.

"Yes?" he replied coolly.

"Good morning."

I thought for a moment he wouldn't return the greeting. His eyes, resolute and steady, never blinked. Then with a response as icy as his stare, he said, "Yes, good morning."

"You're off to school, huh?"

He paused a moment, then in a very unfriendly tone, said, "So, you have returned. It was my understanding you were going back to Georgetown and your job."

"Well, I liked it here so much, I thought I'd take a few more days."

"It must be very nice to have a job where you can work whenever you choose." There was snottiness in his delivery.

"I have a very understanding boss … me."

He moved closer to my table, which surprised me a little. I got the impression he was trying to intimidate me with his deliberate stare, and if he was, he'd better go back to Terrorist School. "Why do I not believe you are who you say, Mr. White? Tell me again about your business."

Adrianna glanced at me and shifted uneasily.

I wanted to be sure I gave him the same vocation as the other day, so I had to hit my recall button. "I design homes. Why would you say such a thing, Assad?"

"It is very strange considering that architects are a small and very close group of professionals. Neither my father nor his friends have heard of you. My father is on the Virginia Board of Architects and has data on all people in the business in the Northern Virginia area. He does not know your name. He would know about you if you are who you say you are, big fish or small fish."

Busted. The bastard actually checked up on me, so obviously he had his suspicions.

"Is that so, Assad?"

"Yes, it is so."

"Don't I look like an architect?"

He was back to the penetrating stare. "I do not believe you are an architect."

"What's the deal, Assad? Why are you questioning my integrity?"

"I do not like people who tell lies. *That* is the deal, Mr. White, or whatever your real name is." I could swear Assad's English was getting better.

"If I'm not who I say I am, then who the hell am I?"

By this time, Adrianna, showing considerable apprehension, was apparently afraid the conversation would deteriorate further, and said "Excuse me." She removed herself to the kitchen. But twenty feet away, she would still be able to hear the tête-à-tête.

Assad turned his attention back to me when she left. "I do not know who you are, but you seem most interested in me. I have seen your vehicle at places I have been. That is too much of a coincidence."

"Really? Like where?"

"At my school, at the airport, and in the next town toward Virginia."

"I don't know what to say, Assad." I really didn't. "I thought we had a nice conversation last week and can't imagine why you would be telling me these things."

"Because you are … I believe the word is … deceptive. I want to know at this moment why you checked my car and my friend's car … and why you follow me."

Maybe I'm just your typical bigot and hate all camel jockey assholes who come to this country to kill Americans.

"If you believe that is the case, you tell *me*." Obviously, I had underestimated his perceptiveness.

"I think for some reason you and that woman seem to make me and my friends your business. I believe she has invaded my privacy and gone into my room to look for things. Either her or the Spanish woman."

No, that was me, dingleberry.

"I can't imagine that either of those women would have done that. Let me say this. If you don't believe I'm an architect and merely extending my vacation in this beautiful Bed and Breakfast, then you and I have a problem, Assad."

"I have no problem, but if I find that you are following me again, *you* will."

I settled back in my chair and dropped the half piece of cold toast I had been holding onto my plate, rather defiantly. I thought about smacking the boy around and re-designing his face, the architect that I was. But I let him have his say, making him think he was intimidating me. If I acted like a tough guy or otherwise gave him the impression I was a cop or government agent on his trail, he would walk out that door, gather up his friends and find another nest deeper in the hills until he was poised to execute his plot. Maybe he would anyway. I wouldn't push the envelope. Not this time.

"Sorry you feel that way, Assad. I thought I was being friendly. I hate that you think I'm a phony and a snoop."

He didn't respond, but slung his knapsack over his shoulder, warning me again with a cold, pendant stare. Whatever it was I needed to connect him and the target, AmeriCan, I suspected was in that bag. But he always had it with him and getting a look inside was not going to be easy.

As soon as he had shut the door behind him, Adrianna came back to the dining room and sat down. "That made me very nervous, Skip. Do you think he's onto you about being immigration?"

"No, I don't think so. He knows I'm not an architect, but maybe he thinks I'm just some poor lying American slob trying to impress somebody. Of course, he *has* seen my Suburban at places he's been and he's trying to figure that one out. Maybe he thought if he pushed my buttons a little, I'd get pissed and slip up. I know he'll be more vigilant now and make it a point to know what *I'm* doing. I'll have to stay two steps ahead of him. Assad is calculating. Conniving. But you know what? So am I."

"Tell me again, Skip. Why are you spending so much time and government money checking out this guy? Is it solely because Assad is Middle Eastern? I mentioned the word *terrorist* last night and it seemed you were taken aback a little. Is there more to him and his friends than merely being suspected illegal aliens?"

"All I can say is there could be. Any illegal from the Middle East could be a subversive. I hate to say it that way. I'm not in the profiling business, Adrianna. There are a great number of very respectable Arab people of the Muslim faith who are here on visas and have even become naturalized citizens. They love their new country and are respecters of America's mainstream culture and religions. But from day one, *this* guy has bothered me. You see how defensive he is. Innocent people with nothing to hide don't go around vehemently accusing their proprietors of going into their rooms. *And* refusing free maid service. He is beyond just being a very private person. Subversive or not, he bears watching."

"Just be careful, Skip. I saw the look in his eyes. It was the same look I saw when he confronted me. Can I now give him notice?"

I picked up her hand and kissed it. "Again, please give me a couple more days, okay? Not to worry. I'll watch my backside. And I'll be watching yours, too." I did my Groucho imitation by raising my eyebrows a couple of times.

After my little chat with Assad, I went back upstairs to Adrianna's computer and Googled information about AmeriCan. There was no reference to its Canadian or Israeli ties, perhaps for political purposes. Neither did the information go into any great detail about its products. Obviously, from its chemists right down to the snuffy on the line, many of the employees would have government clearances. It was certainly not public knowledge that highly toxic gases were being produced at the plant. Fears that some kind of chemical accident could happen would result in a massive public outcry, considering the nuclear disasters at Three Mile Island and Chernobyl. And now *I* knew that the erupting of any one of their tanks would send up a gas cloud that would exterminate 100,000 people in a short matter of time. For all any Joe Citizen knew, AmeriCan produced run-of-the-mill household chemicals like ammonia, boric acid and hydrogen peroxide. But how would four terrorist lads know this or that the great Zionist whore was partnered with the Great Satan in the AmeriCan enterprise? The knowledge had to come from the inside or from a much underestimated Al-Qaeda Intel system.

Adrianna came back up and told me that Juanita was readying my quarters. The Virginia Beach couple had departed a day early. Maybe she told me that because I was wearing out my welcome, sitting around in my boxers, banging on the computer and making like Freddie the Freeloader. I thanked her for her hospitality, grabbed a beer from her fridge to put in my icebox for later, and went on down to my room.

Juanita had just laid a chocolate on my pillow when I walked in. By her side and always underfoot, was her pet Chihuahua, Garcia, looking much like a nervous little rat. Adrianna's cat, Burt, made it his career to terrorize the little bastard unmercifully, and I was sure that one day he would have Garcia for breakfast. The pooch wasn't too sure about *me*, either, as he sat staring at me with those huge glassy eyes and baring his little rodent teeth.

I tried striking up a conversation with him. "Yo quero Taco Bell?"

Juanita giggled. "He's a good little dog and keeps me company while I'm cleaning the rooms."

"He doesn't leave any brown jelly beans in any of the rooms, does he?"

"Jelly beans?"

"I'm sorry, Juanita. Just a little attempt at humor."

"Oh," she laughed, although she had not the slightest understanding of what I was talking about. But I did quickly scan the corners of my room just in case Garcia left me a package.

"I hope your stay has been good here and look forward to serving you again, Senor Skip. Any time you need fresh towels and sheets, you call me, okay?" Her accent was as thick as molasses and so was her body. She was certainly a jovial, accommodating sort, not to mention a very hard worker.

I shoved twenty bucks in her hand. She smiled widely and gave me a slight curtsy. "Gracias, Senor."

"And thank *you*, Juanita. I looked down the hall to assure Assad the Arab Asshole was not lurking around, then softened my voice. "Say, I caught wind of the tongue lashing the gentleman in the Magnolia Room gave you. I'm sorry you experienced that."

"I don know why he say those things. I do not go into his room. I respect his wishes."

"Don't worry about it. He's a jerk."

She then moved closer to me and whispered, "I did as Ms. Adrianna ask. I see him come and go and make notes. She put it in her book. I am not sure why she want me to check on him, but I ask no questions."

I whispered back. "It was I who asked Adrianna to do that, but I also told her not to do that anymore."

"Are you police?"

"No, but I do work for an organization that tracks illegals and foreign nationals who act suspicious." I put my finger to my lips so that she would keep it under her hat, not that she would tell Assad. She may not ever even speak to him again.

Juanita displayed a bit of apprehension. "I do have a green card, Senor."

I put a reassuring hand on her shoulder and smiled. "I know, Juanita. Please don't think that was reflected on you. It's the man down the hall I'm concerned about."

She nodded. "He is very strange, that one. I don't know about your job, but am glad you stay here."

"I should be here for a while longer. You come to me anytime you see something he does that concerns you or if he gives you any more trouble."

"I will, Senor Skip. Thank you for the money." She placed it in her apron pocket and closed the door behind her on her way out.

Joey called and said Cora wasn't feeling well. She had been prone to migraines over the years and this was one of her bad days. She begged off for dinner and asked if Adrianna and I could make it either tomorrow or the next evening. I told him I'd check to see if that was all right with Adrianna and get back to him. As neither of us had pressing agendas in the evenings, we should be okay for any night. Unless of course, Dandy Dan needed Adrianna to help heal his fractured ego. I smiled, wondering what size his honker was today.

Adrianna and I had a casual dinner at a new rib joint about seven and then returned to the ranch. Being the good B&B hostess that she was, she saw me to my door, kissed me goodnight and climbed the stairs to her pad. I suppose both of us thought about a little 'nocturnal delight' before lights out, but as we all know, sometimes a little time and distance between interludes makes the next encounter all the sweeter. And it was just as well; neither my mind nor my body was focused in that direction. I was a bit tired, even though I had not done squat all day. Could be I was still feeling Dan's shots from the day before. I hoped he was still feeling mine.

Chapter 16

▼

I was flying over the Mekong in the first Huey as Command and Control of the first assault wave on the village of Phan Le, a known Vietcong stronghold. We were taking pretty heavy AK-47 fire and two RPG rounds zipped within ten and twenty yards of the blade and skids, respectively. The chopper to my right took a direct hit in the tail rotor, causing it to go into an uncontrolled spin and explode into a sandbar on the south edge of the village. The blade continued to spin and whip violently until the riverbed killed it.

The helicopter company consisting of twelve Hueys and three Cobras enveloped the village, firing twenty millimeter rockets and a steady 7.62 barrage from the M60s. Like ants the VC scurried from hooch to hooch, but since many of the thatched roofs were set afire by tracers, which accounted for one in five rounds, the enemy was resigned to gather their families and disappear into the jungle.

As we circled back around the river's edge, the door gunners cut down the few remaining holdouts, allowing my A Team to dismount and begin a sweep of the burning huts. From two spider holes we began to take AK-47 fire which wasted three members of my team. We immediately returned fire and the snipers were quickly neutralized. My light weapons NCO dropped a grenade into both holes just in case there were more rats further down.

At my two o'clock I detected a glint off metal inside one of the hooches. I grabbed the M79 off my RTO and shotgunned the 40 mm grenade through the open window. A brilliant flash accompanied the expected *whumph* and grey smoke from the explosion began to pour from the doorway. A few seconds later a girl child about six or seven stumbled through the door and down the ramp. She was bleeding profusely from the head, waving a stump which a few seconds before was her left arm. As she stood frozen for a moment, I saw the pain and horror reflecting in her eyes. And then she fell face down in the mud. Her blood gradually began to turn the water in the mud hole a bright red. I ran to administer to her, but she was already dead. As I fell backwards from my haunches and sat down in the red mud, the monsoon rain which began to pour harder added insult to my emotional pain and misery. I stood and then stepped onto the ramp that led to the door and was greeted by the faces of Assad Mohammed and his friends, Fayz Al-Hazmi and Ahmed Omari.

I blinked open my eyes to the flute of morning sun that had pierced the opening between the blind and window sill. It was a dream that I had had a hundred times in the past thirty years. It was always the same. It was a haunt that I could not shake from my unconscious ... a reliving in my dreams of the one horrific event in my mental scrapbook that had stayed with me since the Phan Le incident. I had gone into the hooch after killing the child and found the shattered body of her mother. At the end of my dreams she was there, just as I found her. But over the years the final scene in the dream had changed. While wading into that often predictable stream of unconsciousness different faces sometimes emerged. I would find in place of the mother the faces of old friends, my ex-wife or a boss at the Bureau. Some would still be alive while others were as dead and as bloodied as the child's mother. Now in this new dream there were three new faces. Faces of my prey. I was surprised to wake up and actually remember the names of Assad's cohorts.

As I lay there, drained and drenched in sweat from my fitful night of dreams, I realized I had over-slept by an hour … the hour in which I was used to rising. The digital clock on the nightstand read seven-forty. After bargaining with my body, we decided this again was not a day I would go on a morning run.

I allowed the stinging spray of the hot shower to beat upon my head and shoulders for a full five minutes. After shaving and dressing in a pair of khaki slacks and a blue and gold Mountaineers golf shirt, I sat at the desk to call Birdman. It was after eight and he would probably have been at his desk for over an hour. I had a 'missed call' from him on my cell while I was in the shower.

"What do you have, Boss? Were you able to get the material translated?"

"Do you have access to a secure fax machine?"

"Yes, at my brother's business."

"The funeral home?"

"Yes."

"Do you have the number?"

"I think it's on his card in my wallet. Wait one." I found it and gave it to him.

"I want you to be at the fax machine when I send it. For your eyes only. When can you get there?"

"I was going to slide by the funeral home about four. Then I think I may be having dinner at his house later."

"Make it sooner. I'm leaving right at four."

"Banker's hours?"

"We need to talk."

"Okay. What's wrong with right now?"

"I want you to read the translation first. Why don't you go on to your brother's place now?"

"Okay. Can you give me a preview of coming attractions?"

"I'd rather not." He paused. "All I can say is, it may be time to send in the assets."

"Which assets?"

"You know which assets."

And I did. He wanted to dispatch Zulu.

"It's not time yet, Preceptor. I've got a bit more leg work to do and we need to know for sure about these guys."

"Go now, Bruce. You need to read the fax. This is now officially a matter of national security."

"All right. Give me an hour. I will be at my brother's place at exactly nine-thirty. Let's 'sympathize' our watches." I guess he and a hundred others were getting sick of my play on the 'synchronize' word.

"Nine-thirty," he reiterated. My phone then lost the signal. He had hung up on me yet again without saying 'bye.' I will still have to work on his telephone etiquette one day.

I went to the breakfast room and said 'good morning' to Adrianna who was whisking about helping Juanita put out more sticky buns and fruit. All I wanted was a cup of coffee. Lottie was having oatmeal and no one was touching the buns. So that Adrianna would not be offended, I broke down and had one.

"Good morning, Skip," greeted Lottie. "I haven't seen you in a few days and didn't know whether you were still here or not."

"I had to go back to Washington on business. But here I am again, like a bad penny. How long is it you are going to stay?"

"Another week. I'd like to stay forever, but I need to get on back to South Carolina and my little place in Ninety Six."

"I remember passing through Ninety Six one time years ago," I said. "I stopped off at a souvenir shop on the main street and bought a piece of jewelry for my wife … now ex-wife. It was a necklace with a nicely made pendant with a colorful stone in it. I thought it was pretty unique, but when she quizzed me about what the stone was made of, I came clean."

"What was it, Skip?"

"It contained quail droppings."

"Oh, yes. I know about that. Quails make very colorful … droppings, and someone made a bundle back in the '70s enclosing them in glass or plastic, making earrings, necklaces and the like out of them. Haven't seen any of them lately, though. It was only a fad, you know. So, what did she think about the necklace?"

"She actually liked it until I told her what it was. She said she as much expected something like that from me. It wasn't enough that I *treated* her like crap; now I wanted her to *wear* it."

Lottie smiled. "I'm sure she didn't mean it like that."

I nodded. "I'm sure that's the case, too." But … she really did mean it. I changed the subject. "Well, Lottie, do you miss serving in congress now?"

"Sometimes. It's like I wake up some mornings thinking I'm playing hooky; but then I go to my kitchen, get some coffee, and go out to the garden to tend my roses. Then the *missing* part is over. And I get to see my grandbabies a lot more. No, I don't miss it, Skip."

"Well, I imagine your constituents miss *you* and were fortunate to have you represent them."

She took my hand in one of her brown, long-weathered hands. "You're a sweet boy, Skip. Nice of you to say that. I'd like to think they do."

I let her go back to her oatmeal and walked out to the veranda. Adrianna followed and slipped one of her hands in mine.

"Hmm, nice morning," she remarked.

I nodded. The air *was* fresh and pure. We both stood for a while and allowed the morning sun to warm our faces. It was all very electric.

"I see Assad is already gone this morning," I finally said.

"He probably didn't want to run into *you.*"

"With good reason."

"Where are you off to today?"

"I'm going out to the funeral home to see Joey and then ... who knows.

I'll check with him to see if we're back on for dinner tonight."

"I hope Cora is better."

"Me too. Well, see ya." I leaned down and kissed her lips. It was like kissing warm honey made right in God Almighty's own beehive.

I pulled into McGowan and Sons about nine-twenty. I wondered when Joey was going to drop the 'Sons.' I also wondered when I was growing up why they called it a funeral *home*. Who the hell would ever want to *live* there? It wasn't even a home for the dead. It was sort of like a motel, a very expensive motel, where they stayed a couple of nights till they went to live in the City of Stones. Oh, well. Who was I to question these things? I went AWOL from the business eons ago.

As soon as I closed the front door, Joey thought it was a customer and came out to greet me. "Hey, this is a surprise. Figured I'd be seeing you this evening."

"Are we on for dinner? I was wondering how Cora was."

"So far so good today."

"Say, Joey, can I use your fax machine? My boss is sending something over?"

"Sure thing. In my office."

At precisely nine-thirty Birdman rang my cell. "Fax is on the way. Call me." Click. I wish he didn't go on and on like that in his conversations.

In a few moments, the fax machine began spitting out paper. Apparently, Assad had been in some kind of meeting with the other players after which he penned the material. Although no names were mentioned, I understood immediately that someone important was directing that meeting. The six pages in Arabic had been condensed to two. There also appeared to have been some paraphrasing by Abu, our translator.

"Our leader gives us hope today that the soft under belly of America will soon be cut open by the mighty sword of Allah. May he be praised. Bear witness there is no god but Allah, and Mohammed is his messenger. The blood of Americans will give us vindication because the Great Satan and its infidels have shed Islamic blood for over a century.

Allah has surely blessed us. The Qur'an and the fatwa give us our spiritual nourishment and make us strong against the infidel oppressors. We have learned from our training at Imam Ali how to integrate into the infidel society and wage war on them. To know them we must pretend to fall into sin and become like them. But Allah knows our hearts and our mission as he has set us on course. He will forgive our sins because we only take them on to fool the infidels to make them trust us.

Our leader is also Allah's messenger. He established himself among the Americans many years ago to do the will of Allah. He has been like the ant who moves obstacles many times its size and weight for long periods of times, over miles of ground, to prepare for the big mission. As the ant's mission is to survive when the cold approaches, it prepares cleverly for that mission. Our leader is strong and stalwart."

Assad Mohammed continued his praise of Allah and went into great detail about the content of his morning prayers alone and those at sunset with his friends. "... *my brothers give me the support and sustenance which also comes from Allah himself...*"

"*Our leader has educated us about the devices and the missile. He himself is all wise and understands the principles of the devices. The explosions will devastate the city of the Great Satan. There will be many cities affected and other brothers commanded by Allah will carry out similar missions. Our devices will only be the catalyst that will set in motion the secondary explosions. From those explosions a greater horror will be realized by the infidels. By the wings of man, we will achieve martyrdom. We will sacrifice our blood to spill the blood of the infidels. By the wings of Allah we will then enter heaven. I swear before God I will do what I must to assure the massive death of all infidels. We will shake the Roman Throne. They will die in the thousands and the world will see the power of our God, Allah the Almighty.*

"*God is great. He is my refuge. He is my strength. The God of Abraham and Moses and the great messenger Mohammed gives me many blessings. He will reward me when our battle is won. The battle is soon.*"

He stopped there as though he was interrupted or perhaps tired. I dissected the document and underlined words and metaphors that directly or passively referred to the explosions. The devices were obviously bombs, maybe dirty bombs. There was also reference to a missile or missiles and attacks on several cities. I knew that Bin Laden had purchased as many as forty bombs from the Chechen Mafia for $30,000,000 and several tons of heroin. None of the bombs had turned up to this day. Assad and his friends were obviously lieutenants dispatched by Bin Laden or people like him. They had become Jihad or students of Islam waging their holy war. They had trained in Tehran in the terrorist training camp, Imam Ali. I learned about the camp from some of the radical Muslim extremists we detained and erased after the World Trade Center bombing.

The secondary explosions would be the erupted tanks of chlorine gas and cyanide and these gases would be propelled throughout the Kanawha Valley annihilating literally thousands of innocent, God-fearing West Virginians. It was unthinkable to even speculate how horrible the devastation would be. The bomb or bombs would not need to have radioactive components, but I expected they would anyway. I wasn't sure what the missile or missiles would be used for, unless they couldn't get the bombs into the plant. A shoulder fired missile from the high ground to either side of the river would give the gunner a visible target within AmeriCan. It could alternatively knock airplanes out of the sky, especially Air National Guard aircraft patrolling the skies.

There also had to be someone on the inside. Time would be of the essence to pinpoint who he or they were and in what area the person or persons worked. And when plant officials were notified of our suspicions about such insiders, all employees and their cars would be searched by security for suitcase bombs, explosives or other devices. FBI agents would also rove the grounds outside the plant as well as inside.

Now we had two important documents: the map and the proof of a plan to attack AmeriCan. But if they had bombs, how would they be delivered? Would the terrorist element drop them from planes, set them off after crashing the gate or would the insiders try to smuggle them in? Then again, would some type of system be fired from a missile off an adjacent hillside? And finally ... when would it happen?

I knew that Assad and company hadn't ventured far on any given day, except perhaps the weekend I was gone, and I expected his leader was within the county or a few miles across the border in the backwoods of Virginia. I was sure it had to be a local Middle Easterner and not Bin Laden or one of his immediate subordinates. The tone of the document alluded to meetings which just about had to be local as I suspected none of the men had been out of the country recently. I was hoping Byrd, the Bureau and Interpol could confirm that.

I leaned back in Joey's plush leather desk chair and allowed a hundred thoughts to zip through my brain like a meteor shower. Byrd was ready to bring the Zulu team in to take these guys out. In doing so, however, we may only choke out a few of the weeds. It was obvious they were only a small part of a vast terrorist network. I wondered if all the elements within that network had planned to stage a series of attacks all at the same time or over a series of days or weeks. It seemed more logical that given the element of surprise, they would be on the same day. After a singular major attack, the country and all its factories, infrastructure and government buildings would be shut down and thereafter maintain high standards of alert. Zulu would be effective, but I was convinced that the terrorists would not be taken alive to be tortured into confession. As disciplined and committed these local terrorists were to their religion, they were prepared to die. DAG's cyanide capsule was proof of that. Given the terrorists' deaths, we would have only slowed down the entire network. But one way or another, it would be up to Zulu to take down this element.

The longer I stewed about whether it was actually time to bring in Zulu, the more I became convinced Birdman was right. At least we would stop the AmeriCan mission. I had worked with a military version of Zulu when I was in Vietnam. It was an elite, but deadly faction of Special Ops called the Provincial Reconnaissance Unit, only there was very little recon to it. It was made up of a Vietnamese Dirty Dozen type element with the sole mission of true counter-terrorism, which in fact *was* terrorism. The mission, whether covert or overt, was assassination. It got the job done ... and cleanly. The targets were known or suspected Vietcong to include key officials, dirty village chiefs and the like. Bad guys just disappeared without leaving a hair. It was like they never existed.

But whether Zulu was engaged or not, the Bureau needed to be apprised. If we didn't give them a piece of this, the Director would not only have a good case of the red-ass, but on a strategic level the FBI would never again cooperate with or trust us.

I studied the message in depth, finding most of it pretty straight forward. The reference to 'shaking the Roman Throne' I had heard before and knew that it meant killing Christians whom the radical Muslims perceived not only heathenistic, but a threat to the very tenets of their religion.

I got the boss back on the phone. Although I knew he was ready to send the boys, was he willing to partner with the FBI? Again, not only did I believe we were compelled to do so, I felt an allegiance to an organization from which I was drawing retirement.

"Before we chat, Scorpion, we need to invoke Krypton. I'm sure my line is secure, but am not sure about your cell or any land line in your area. People now have new, sophisticated eavesdropping devices that can compromise both mediums."

This was Byrd's notice to me that our dialogue had to be in cryptographic format. In other words, nothing could be said in the open and we had to talk in metaphors. I always liked playing this game. I was always Scorpion. He had asked me to pick a code name under these circumstances and I thought 'Scorpion' made me sound dangerous.

"First of all, do you think there's any way you've been breached?" (that means *found out*).

"No. I don't think so." I replied; although Assad knew I was no architect. And that's for *damn* sure. All I can draw are stick people, stick houses, stick dogs …

"So what's your take on the thesis?"

"Well, it's obvious now that the bull's eye is what we thought it was and the big bang is no longer a theory. I agree we need to order take-out."

"Who's the kingpin?"

"Don't know. Could be someone local; could be Public Enemy Number One ... you know, from the Old Country." (Bin Laden)

"My money's on the latter."

"Maybe. But the tone of the manuscript indicates an ongoing relationship with someone local."

"Okay, whatever. We still need to kill the weeds. I'm sending in the Roundup team."

"More will spring up elsewhere, you know."

"But the chore is to stop the growth where *you* are. We'll deal with the new pop-ups."

I love this spy code stuff.

"We need to inform Fabulous Boys Incorporated," I replied. I made that one up, meaning of course the FBI.

"Not sure I follow that one, Scorpion."

"Think phonetic alphabet; only substitute new and improved letters."

"I get it, now," said Birdman. "I don't want them bumping into the Roundup folks. But you're right. I will work on setting up the Tango Foxtrot."

"Okay, but it may take more time than we have to unite all the egos. We know where the weeds are, but we need to corral them and snuff them all out at once."

"I can have everyone at your location by Saturday morning. You will be their contact and make yourself accessible to receive Pest Control at coordinates Mike Delta 37964451. Refer of course to your guide book." He meant my Cryptographic Super Duper Spy Handbook.

I checked September's pocket Signal Operating Instructions, having just shredded August, and we were to meet and greet … let's see … somewhere near the Greenbrier Hotel in White Sulphur. I wondered if he was actually going to put these guys up at the Greenbrier. I liked where I was staying, but I'd be more than pissed if they got to stay in five star lap of luxury.

"Did anything turn up from the major landscaper (meaning Interpol, I think) on the weeds?"

"Nothing. Either they are all new crabgrass with no history or they've been very careful to blend into the lawn. There *has* been some activity in the old country (meaning Great Britain). A couple of cells were uncovered recently by the Big Bobs (MI5)."

"Did you check out the subject's daddy? (Meaning Assad's father)"

"Affirmative. He's clean."

I figured as much. Assad was one of Al-Qaeda's young lions. Older, Middle-Eastern professionals who had been in this country for many years were enjoying the fruits of capitalism and not trying to blow up their potential clients. "Should I go ahead and contact my new friend in the big city?"

"Your Fabulous Boy counterpart?"

Hey, that code name was mine. Get your own, Turkey.

"Yes," I replied.

"No. Not right away."

"Professional courtesy, Condor. I promised to share."

"Then give him my number. If his location wants in, my rules apply. Turf protection, you know. They need to concern themselves with the lawn; we'll take care of the weeds. I'll be having a dialogue with their CEO."

About that time I was getting a little tired of the daffy dialogue and suspected we wouldn't be fooling anybody anyway with all the hooey.

"I'll see him first thing in the morning and will plan to meet your boys Saturday. In the meantime, I will be looking at the personal effects of the other two where they live."

"Good. I will be looking for heavy take-down. Stand by for further tomorrow." He clicked me again before I could click him.

I had an idea. "Joey, can I borrow your car this morning. Maybe one of the family cars?"

"What for?"

"I'm too visible in mine."

"Oh, I see. Sneaky peek stuff, huh?"

"Something like that."

"Okay, take the Lincoln. But no bullet holes," he warned, pointing his finger at me. "And be careful. I've gotten all the business I need this month."

"I'll get it back to you this afternoon. Looking forward to dinner. What's cooking?"

"I don't know. But you know Cora. She'll be puttin' on the Ritz."

I left McGowan's Pickup and Layaway and drove out to the Greenbrier Airport to see if the suspects were still on routine ... the one hour class at Valley followed by the two plus hours of flight lessons at the flight academy. It was eleven-fifteen and I figured the time was about right for them to be driving in. But when I arrived, I found both the Maxima and the Civic were already there, side by side between the restaurant and the entrance to the small terminal.

I had the goods on Assad and although I was 95% sure Ahmed and Fayz were in the conspiracy as well, I like all the pieces to fall into place without any doubts before people are terminated. So, getting a look at the stuff inside their cabin while they were flying the friendly skies may prove even further enlightening as to their roles in the AmeriCan plot. I may even find that there were others in the equation. Nonetheless, I had just over two days to set things right in my mind and complete the puzzle before Zulu swept in.

The Lincoln was nice and I thought to myself maybe I ought to get rid of my big black box and start styling and profiling in something like that. The windows were also tinted black smoke, and as I could see out, no one could see me inside clicking off shots with the Nikon or picking my nose at a traffic light. It's a proven statistic that seven of ten guys explore the nasal cavity on a regular basis while they're behind the wheel, digging and burying up to and including the second knuckle.

After trekking the ten miles out to White Sulphur, I pulled the family car into one of the parking spaces to the rear of the office at Jamestown and eyed Cabin Eight for any activity. After about five minutes I tucked my Glock in the back of my pants, grabbed my digital, looked around for any snoops, then got out. Just in case one of the boys had stayed back, I rapped on the door, at the same time eyeing the lock system. There was no answer or bumping around inside and the door did have a dead bolt. For the second time in less than a week I was committing the crime of B&E. Of course, I could have waited until people came home, hoping they would let me in to look at their stuff and then they would naturally admit to me they were Amim Ali trained terrorists up to no good. That would put a bow on it for me, and then I could ask them to wait there a couple of days until their new Zulu friends came by to kill them.

I pulled from my pocket my handy little kit and fiddled with the tumbler, all the while checking over both shoulders for nosy people. I heard the click and immediately tried the doorknob. Fortunately, for time's sake, there was no lock on the knob and the door creaked open. After quickly closing the door behind me, I pulled my Glock to sweep the room.

The cabin was probably 20 X 30 with twin beds on the right, separated by an eight foot armoire. A blue velvet couch and two sofa chairs were in a sitting area on the left. A TV hung on the wall adjacent to the bathroom door. It was a kind of cheesy place and even smelled like cheese ... limburger. Not quite the pristine quaintness of Wolf Laurel. Obviously, either Assad's bankroll exceeded that of Fayz and Ahmed or he was higher up in the food chain and rated a nicer place.

I began my search of the usual places, the armoire, a small closet which housed three pairs of pointy-toed Arab roach killers, two rolled up prayer blankets and some clothing which I frisked. Then I performed thorough searches of the bed linen, the couch and chairs and the bathroom. Inside of the medicine cabinet were the usual toiletries and a prescription for Benadryl with Ahmed's name on it. The pharmacy was in Binghamton, Massachusetts, which fit. A small desk with two drawers on either side sat under the TV.

On the desk were two books ... again as in Assad's pad, the Qur'an and an Arab-English dictionary. A myriad of ash and trash lay in the two drawers: pens, pencils, Certs (for the limburger breath) and some Lance crackers, among other items. In the bottom left drawer was some sort of device with a crank and two wires connected to a timer. It didn't take a genius to figure out it was the catalyst to an explosive device. After placing it on the desk and snapping several shots, I put it back in the drawer.

I then looked under the bed. You always check under beds for stuff ... monsters, dust bunnies, bombs, people hiding and the like. A backpack similar to the one Assad had surgically attached to his shoulder was shoved about a foot back. I checked the pockets first, finding a paperback in Arabic, a folding pocket knife and a tri-fold transparency containing pictures of Big Nose and Baldy, looking a little younger, somewhere in a desert scenario and holding AK-47s. In the background of the photos were burning oil wells and I wondered now if these guys were Iraqi and the pictures were from Desert Storm. There were also photos of young Middle Eastern women in burkhas.

In the main compartment was a notebook containing several pieces of loose paper, two magazines, *Alneda* and *Waaqiah,* Azzam pro-Taliban publications by a press in Saudi Arabia, and to my alarm, a Department of Defense field manual on Chemical, Biological and Radiological effects and dispersion. Among the loose papers was an identical copy of the AmeriCan map. On a second sheet was a diagram with numbers reflecting distance from Point A to Point B and a series of inner circles or fans from the targets depicting radiuses of speculative, probable and actual collateral damage. On the left side of the page was an X from which there was a line to the target reflecting trajectory and it was obvious this would be a shoulder-fired missile situated on high ground.

This was the icing on our cake. I laid out all the material on the floor and took more photos, being careful to return everything to its proper compartment. As this was an illegal search and nothing I had found could be used as evidence in a court of law, it would still be fruitful to a tribunal. Illegals or combatives in this country plotting terrorist activities are not subject to the U.S. Court system nor would be considered enemy soldiers protected by the Geneva Convention. So, this illegal search didn't really matter when it came to disposing of these guys. And why the hell would vermin like this be protected under the Constitution? Anyway, my job is more about protecting the American people than preserving the Constitution. Especially where it comes to abominable subversives. We would be sure to do our work swiftly and efficiently when it came down. There would be no opportunity for the press, the Congress or ACLU lawyers to catch even the slightest breeze about this going down.

Just in case the boys came home early, I peered through the Venetian blind to scan the parking lot. Satisfied there was no one about, I opened the door, snapped the lock and stepped out onto the gravel walkway. Suddenly, my eyes caught what appeared to be a young Middle Eastern woman in a blue maid's uniform with towels in her hand closing the door to the cabin next to Cabin Eight. Had she seen me actually leaving the cabin? As I continued walking, our eyes met briefly, but we did not acknowledge one another. The less engagement, the better. I made my way back to the Lincoln, feeling the woman's eyes on the back of my neck. I wondered whether she was allowed to clean the men's quarters or did they also refuse maid service like Assad.

After sliding under the wheel of the Lincoln, I saw that the maid was still looking suspiciously in my direction. Perhaps she had become acquainted with the Cabin Eight occupants and was maybe even collaborating with them. I figured if that was the case, she would only be their pawn to keep a watchful eye on the place. In their culture, a woman would not be partnered with men on any venture, much less a terrorist plot. Women were the subservient gender, having not the role, the intellect or the capacity to partner with men. Anyway, my question to myself regarding her license to clean Cabin Eight was answered. She inserted her key in the lock and went inside.

I really didn't have anything else to do until it was time to pick up Adrianna for din-din at Joey's, so I decided to sit for a while. When the boys returned, they should not be suspicious about the Lincoln and would likely pay it no mind. At least they wouldn't associate it with me. If the Jamestown men were still on routine, they would either accompany Assad to Wolf Laurel or come back here. It was a 50-50 shot and I decided to take this one. I also wanted to see if the maid would say anything to them. And here I was again missing lunch. I'd be starved by suppertime.

The maid came out of number eight after about a half hour, carrying a bundle of soiled towels, which she threw into the laundry basket still sitting outside the door. She cast another glance at the Lincoln, then moved on down to Cabin Five further back in the trees. I called Birdman to let him know what I had done and my findings, being careful to send the information in my clever code that even 007 would have trouble deciphering. I also called Jack Fuentes to alert him that some information was coming down though his channels of major significance that involved the subject of our previous conversations. He asked pretty please if I would come to see him Thursday morning. We could also do lunch. I told him it was a date.

I knew once the scenario was laid on the Bureau, that would generate a great deal of political infighting about who should take out the terrorists and who should get all the kudos. Fabulous Boys International would just have to take a back seat on this one, if Byrd was as powerful as I thought he was. And although Birdman had refused to divulge the name of his boss, I knew it was none other than the President himself. I had figured that out on one of Byrd's weekly trips down to Washington when on the tube the next day I saw a press photo taken in the Oval Office of Mr. Bush with Mr. Byrd and the directors of the FBI and CIA. I had heard that Birdman was angry that his mug had been photographed, the super secret spy that he was.

At two-thirty, as I had hoped, both the Honda and Nissan rolled into the parking lot in front of Cabin Eight. This time not only the driver's door of the Nissan opened, but the passenger side door as well. The passenger was a man about forty-five and had a dark beard. *It was the same man I had seen with Paul LeMer at the Labor Day picnic.* My instincts rarely fail me. There was now officially a fourth figure and I would have two days to find out who he was.

That meant I would have to re-establish my friendship with the good Mr. LeMer.

I snatched my professional Nikon off the seat, dialed in the telephoto and zapped a half-dozen shots of the man. Then I continued my watch as all four players stood outside of the door conversing. The three younger men were positioned together, standing erect, almost at attention, listening respectfully to the older man. His manner appeared instructive and he punctuated his dialogue with animated gestures. I wondered if this was *Fearless Leader* indicated in Assad's treatise. It seemed that *Multicultural Issues* was not the only class these kids were taking. I had no doubt this was a session of yet another, more important class to them called *Terrorism in America 101*. I wish I had learned to read lips somewhere along the way.

The pow wow seemed to be breaking up and the band of confederates went inside the bungalow. I sat there for a few more minutes and about the time I reached down to turn on the ignition, the maid came out of Number Five, looked in the direction of the Lincoln, then went to the door of Number Eight. I saw her knuckles rap twice, after which the door opened and she went on in as though she were expected. Within ten seconds the door opened just a crack and I knew then that someone was checking out the Lincoln. I also saw the blind move at the window. I began backing out slowly past the office and toward the road, being careful not to let them see the license plate. They wouldn't be able to tell that the Continental was a funeral home family car, but I didn't want to take a chance they would connect Joey with the break-in and surveillance, putting him and his family in jeopardy.

And now they knew for sure that someone or some government entity was onto them. After backing onto the highway, I headed back to McGowan and Sons to get my vehicle. As I was taking no chances the suspects would break for one of their cars and follow me, I put the pedal to the metal and began straightening out the curves on old U.S. 60.

CHAPTER 17

I dropped off the Lincoln and told Joey I'd see him in a couple of hours. Back at Wolf Laurel, I saw that Assad hadn't returned. Adrianna's car was there and that meant she was not somewhere with Dan nursing his wounds from Monday's fracas on the gridiron. I had the feeling Dan was not interested in going out with either one of us again.

Anyway, I grabbed a shower, a Diet Coke and a pack of nabs to tie me over. Juanita stopped by to bring me fresh towels and another bar of soap. I think she had become enamored with me as she stayed a while to tell me about her mother in El Salvador and that more than half of her wages went to support her and three siblings. Maybe she was just trying to get me to warm up to her in case I was really INS. As she was leaving my room, we heard someone enter the hallway and saw that it was Assad returning from his bombing rehearsal. Although we were clearly within a couple of feet from him, he looked straight ahead, avoiding eye contact. He looked pissed about something. I'm sure the Jamestown maid gave him and the element a full description of me. Or maybe he thought I was doing Juanita and that supported his notion that I was a lying, whoremongering infidel. Being the religious zealot that he was, he probably thought I was servicing *all* the ladies. I heard his door shut and Juanita made a face that included eye-rolling. Obviously, that was an international expression practiced by all women.

Jack called me just after five, probing for any new information I may have. I asked if he was available tomorrow instead for the sit-down and he said he was. We'd meet at nine.

Just before six-thirty I knocked lightly on Adrianna's door, which she quickly opened. I could get used to being greeted with that sweet smile at the end of my nine-to-five workday. "I'll be ready in a second," she said, giving me a succulent kiss on the lips. "Need some lipstick."

"Good. I like the taste of lipstick. I'll take seconds when you come back, if you don't mind."

She smiled again and retreated to the bathroom. Be careful what you ask for. She returned with the appetizer, only it tasted more like dessert. She looked mah-velous in her white 'skorts', pink shimmering blouse and white sandals with three inch heels that accentuated her perfectly-shaped size six feet with the pink-coated toenails. But again, who's noticing?

We didn't share much about how each of us spent our day as we zipped to the other side of town. Hers was the same old routine at the B&B and mine, I couldn't tell her about. She'd think I was some kind of low-life burglar, and I didn't want a little thing like my criminal activity to taint her fond impression of me.

"That's my church there," she said, pointing to a small, white building with a steeple that looked straight out of a Norman Rockwell print. It was set back off the road among four or five gigantic willows that metaphorically served as a vanguard against all that is evil and which would threaten its parishioners. As I cruised by the church with my window down I heard the little congregation from the Wednesday night prayer meeting belting out *"O victory in Jesus..."* Their voices rang and reverberated throughout the grove and into the adjacent meadow as though a choir of angels had descended upon the valley called Greenbrier. I reminded myself that there were people plotting at that moment to destroy this perfect peace, this simple and beautiful picture of Americana, and I would be damned if I let that happen.

"You haven't said much since we left. Is anything bothering you, Skip?"

I turned my head and gave her a half-hearted smile. "Naw. I was just trying to remember. I think I went to a couple of funerals there when I was a kid. Not that I knew any of the deceased; but Dad used to drag me to most every funeral."

"I guess that had to have an affect on a kid, to always be around the dead and the grieving. And then the cemeteries ..." She shook her head.

I winked and broadened my smile. "That's largely what made me the psycho I am today. I probably lived the macabre life Stephen King writes about."

"Oh, come on. You're not a psycho. You're sweet and funny, and maybe sometimes a little serious. But you seem perfectly well-adjusted."

"Defense mechanisms, my dear. What you see on the outside ain't necessarily what lies deep in the dark recesses of the soul."

She took her fingertips and placed them between the buttons on my shirt and made tender circles over my chest hair at the heart. "I know what's in there and it is nothing but good and right. I also know you're a tough-guy, hardened by experiences that the average person would never ever realize. And I'm sure that if you ever had to be violent, it would be because you are protecting someone or something you love from a terrible happening."

"Like when I punched out Dan?"

"Let's not go there, you bad boy."

"Now I'm *bad*. I was *good* a minute ago."

She gave me a playful punch in the arm, then leaned into me, placing her arms around my waist the rest of the way.

When we arrived at Joey's, we were greeted at the door by Cora. "Adrianna, hi. We have both lived in this area all our lives and have yet to run into one another. I'm glad it's finally happening." They hugged.

"Me too. It's funny. We've probably passed each other a hundred times somewhere in Lewisburg."

"Well, anyway. It's wonderful to finally meet you," Cora said. "Joey has mentioned you on occasion … more lately than in the past." She looked in my direction and smiled.

There was a lot of pre-dinner small talk, mostly about who knew who and who's doing what now. We sat down at the table and the family joined hands for the blessing. As Joey was speaking to God, I again was made to realize I hadn't talked much to the Creator over the years or showed Him the appreciation He was due. He had certainly gotten me out of a hell of a lot of scrapes in my lifetime. Sorry about the *hell* word, God.

It was a superb dinner as usual … pork loin with gravy, mashed potatoes, green beans, hot, buttered rolls, and peach pie for dessert. I should go to this restaurant more often.

After supper, the women cleared the table, loaded the dishwasher and retired to the living room for coffee and more talk. The adult women carried on like old friends, and after a while, Molly and Casey disappeared with their cell phones, one by one, into their rooms for more meaningful conversations with their friends.

Joey and I took our usual places on the front porch. He sucked on a Dominican and I sucked in the cool evening air.

"What's going on now, Bruce? Not that I want you to leave, but you're sticking around a long time on this dead A-rab case. I know it's not just because of Adrianna, unless you're thinking about retiring for good and settling down. Don't you have a job to get back to?"

"My job is not just in Washington, Joey. Anyway, I'm still officially on vacation, thanks to my boss."

"Okay, be that way," he said, exhaling a three second stream of blue-grey smoke. "But I know different. I know *you*. Don't get me wrong; I'm sure there are things you can't discuss. Top Secret things." He paused for a drag. "You did tell me about AmeriCan in Charleston and shared a couple of things with me that you told the FBI guy. If there's more you can't tell me, no problem. But you know I won't go out and blab to anyone."

"You're putting me in a tough spot, little brother." I turned my head away and gazed out over the meadow for several moments. Then I looked back at him and smiled. "Okay. Maybe a smidgen. Before this is all over, you'll probably know, anyway. Your stiff led me to three, maybe four more of his kind. I found out they all have the same map in their possession. And don't ask me how I know that. One of these guys is actually staying at Wolf Laurel, and if I have to stay there as long as he does, I will. The others are bunking at a location in White Sulphur Springs."

"Ha! I *knew* there were more of them. And I wager they're planning some kind of suicide mission on AmeriCan. I'm right, aren't I?"

"Can't go any further with this, Joey."

He looked away and shook his head.

"What would make people like that want to blow themselves up, Bruce?"

"Well, put yourself in one of these guy's shoes, little brother. You have no Jesus, no Christmas, no TV, no football, no Dallas Cowboy Cheerleaders, no Wal-Mart, no hot dogs or beer. You wear rags for clothes and towels for hats. You can't shave. Your wife can't shave and by the way, she smells like your camel. Do you really want to live any longer?"

That fueled a bit of laughter. "I see your point."

We were silent for a while and then he pressed me a little more. "So, how're you planning to stop them?"

I didn't answer.

"Come on, Bruce. What's your plan?"

I looked at him, thoughtfully, then leaned over the banister and spat onto the ground below. "Let's just say we've got people lined up to make this all go away in the next few days."

"Will my business suddenly pick up?"

I shrugged.

Joey stuck his finger into my chest and with succinct articulation said, "Just make sure *you* don't become my business, Brucie. If these men are as dangerous as you make out … just be careful, that's all."

We locked eyes. Serious eyes. Then I nodded. "Let's go back to the girls," I said.

We all sat in the parlor chatting for a few minutes more, balancing our peach pie and cups of coffee on our knees. One custom both Joey and I picked up from the old man was pouring the hot coffee from the pot into our cups and allowing it to overflow into the saucer. Our first sip of the java was always *from* the saucer. As the spilled-over liquid would have cooled nicely, the roofs of our mouths would not get scorched. Adrianna watched us both suck out the saucers and smiled. She loved folksy traditions.

On the way back to the inn, Adrianna put her hand on my thigh and squeezed it. "Nice people, Joey's family. I loved the girls … so cute and perky."

And then it happened. I wish to God I had never asked my next question ... that one, probing, evening-ending question. "So why is it that you and Mason never had any kids?"

There was no response. I thought at first she didn't hear me. Then she released her hand from my thigh and turned toward the door.

"We did," she replied softly.

"Oh." I was afraid to go further, sensing that somewhere inside her was an old wound. I suspected perhaps she had miscarried.

But she continued. "We had a son. His name was Johnny ... John Mason, to be specific." There was a long pause. "He lived to be nine." Then the sobbing came. I quickly pulled off into a school parking lot.

"God. I'm sorry." I placed my hand on hers and squeezed sympathetically.

"It was leukemia. We tried everything ... transfusions, treatments, even the Mayo Clinic. He was gone in only eight months after the diagnosis. But even though it's been five years now, every day I think about him. Some days are better than others."

And now that I had reopened that wound, today was one of the worst.

"I ... had no idea, Adrianna."

She turned her face toward me, and even in the dim light, I could see that her beautiful, glistening eyes were full of pain.

"Didn't Joey ever tell you?"

"No," I answered softly."

"It was he who buried Johnny in the little cemetery behind the church."

I couldn't respond from welling up myself and all I could think to do was pick up her hand and kiss it. Now tears were streaming down both of our cheeks.

I suppose out of respect for Adrianna, Joey decided not to tell me about her Johnny. He learned to be tight-lipped from the old man. When the dead is buried and gone, perhaps for their own emotional health, undertakers choose to talk about the living, not the dead. And I am sure that knowing I was establishing a very nice relationship with Adrianna, he did not want me to go into it with pity.

There was little more said as we continued back to the inn. I took her to her door, held her for a minute, tightly and lovingly; then she went inside and closed the door behind her.

I was determined not to go to bed depressed, so I slumped into the Queen Anne chair that sat in a corner of the room and picked up my copy of *The Far Side*. Soon I was yukking away and feeling a hell of a sight better about myself and my big, freaking mouth. I got through the paperback in fifteen or twenty minutes and tossed it on the end table. Not being the least bit drowsy, likely due to three spilled-over cups of caffeine, I turned on the TV. Two or three times I ran the remote up and down, trying to find something palatable besides the half dozen mindless sitcoms violating my brain. Where were the sophisticated comedies of yesteryear like *The Beverly Hillbillies, F-Troop* and *Gilligan's Island?* I clicked on ESPN and it was re-running the 1997 Tyson-Holyfield fight where they showed Iron Mike munching on Evander's ear. I wondered if Mikey had also gotten Van Gogh. And then they put on a ringside interview of Don King … the perfect example of what you get when you mix Rogaine and Viagra.

Anyway, my attention was suddenly diverted by the sound of tromping feet on the wooden hallway floor outside my door. I counted three sets. The voices were muffled and indiscernible, but I could tell they belonged to my Arab neighbor and his comrades. In a few moments their noise dissipated inside Assad's room.

Leaving the TV blaring, I grabbed my keys, slipped out of my quarters and crept stealthily outside to my Suburban. Both the Honda and Nissan were in the parking lot, serving to confirm that the boys with Assad were not two new and different terrorists. I glanced up to Adrianna's turret room and saw that she was still there. The ghostly motion of her shadow passing in front of the window was apparent through the blind. From my cargo compartment I took out my latest spy gadget, a portable parabolic dish. It was a handheld listening device with a pistol grip on one end and a bell-shaped amplifier on the other resembling a miniature satellite dish. To accessorize my snoop toy the manufacturer, *Nostradamos*, had built in a mini tape recorder with earphones. *Nosy*, for short, had a listening range from operator to target of up to fifty yards. Now if it could only see through walls ...

I moved through the flower garden and positioned myself by a large tree in the dark shadows approximately fifty feet from Assad's room. Blinds on the east and south windows were room-darkening and positioned tightly against the facing. As I did not see crack one, there was no opportunity to peer in anywhere. When I turned Nosy on, Arabic speaking voices immediately faded in.

My Arabic is weak at best. I'm not that good in learning other languages, which often makes me wonder why I was selected for this type of business in the first place. I took a year of German in military school and a second at the university. I thought I had nailed it down pretty well until I started a flirtatious conversation one evening with a pretty German lass serving drinks at the Infantry Bar at Ft. Benning. Although I had no idea what she was saying, I rattled off a few words from memory. Unfortunately, I must have mispronounced something that came out sounding like the German word for 'slut.' Not only did I get an earful of Bavarian brimstone, but a face full of the scotch she was about to serve me.

Anyway, I was deciphering only a word or two from the boys in the room. I thought I recognized the Arabic words for prayer, Heaven, fire and fight (or struggle). And then there was *insha'allah* or 'God willing.' After a few moments of trying to talk over one another, they got quiet. One of them then began a chant which I took to be a kind of prayer. And then there was silence. I thought at first they may have skedaddled; but since I did not hear them shuffling around or a door closing, it came to me they were probably kneeling on their prayer blankets facing Mecca. Whichever direction that was. I wondered if my hand-held listening device was interfering with their prayer signal. But whatever they were asking for, I was determined they wouldn't get it.

I remained at the tree line for perhaps another fifteen minutes and then their dialogue started up again. Funny, I didn't hear anybody say Amen. There was some noisy scurrying and then a door shut. I took it that Ahmed and Fayez were now leaving, so I zipped around to the front corner of the inn to observe them to assure they were returning to their car. They were. When they pulled out I checked the veranda to see whether Assad was waving bye-bye to his buds or had stayed in his room. Satisfied he was nowhere in sight, I returned Nosy to the Suburban and sauntered back to my room. Tomorrow I would overnight the tape to Byrd and Abu.

As I lay in bed that Wednesday night, I pushed Assad and the other terrorists well back into some obscure corner of my brain, returning my thoughts instead to Adrianna. There had been enough loss and sorrow in her life these past few years to last a lifetime. And although on many days I'm sure she wrapped herself in that cloak of grief, she somehow managed to generate enough emotional strength to carry on life and business while wearing a face filled with joy and happiness.

I hardly saw it coming. I had let this woman inside my head at a point in my life where it was more important than ever to keep it clear ... and all the while she was running mission interference. It was the one thing for over twenty years in law enforcement I said I would never let happen. And it was my own fault. I had let my defenses down and fallen in love. Well there it is; I finally said it to myself.

Sometime after midnight I ultimately lost consciousness. From out of the dark and troubled recesses of my brain, I had the dream again. Same village ... same hooch. This time the bloodied child stumbling from the doorway was little Johnny Wolf. I knew it was him somehow. It was the face of the boy in the picture on Adrianna's end table. When I went inside the hut, I found the body of a dying Adrianna. The horror of my dream awakened me with a jolt. With blurry eyes I looked over at the clock on the night stand. Two-fifty. Again, as was the case so many nights in the last thirty years, I did not get back to sleep.

My morning, which really began at three, actively began at six when I showered, donned a polo shirt, jeans and my Tony Lamas, then locked the door behind me, all in a half hour. At a quarter till seven I hit the drive-through at Hardees's for coffee and a biscuit and set out on I-64 west to Charleston. Within the two hours it took to get there, Jack Fuentes would already have had his coffee, kissed his beauty queen wife, dropped the young'ns at school and be dutifully sitting at his desk. I should be his first customer.

It was a cool morning, feeling almost like October, but the fresh mountain air whipping through my open glass was invigorating. I needed it to keep my dopey brain awake. But the brain was too busy to sign off anyway. For one thing, Adrianna's sad eyes kept flashing through it. I wondered if the night was good to her ... if she slept or if the sadness that she had so carefully camouflaged, up until I opened my mouth, consumed her night.

But as much as I was beating myself up, I really couldn't keep blaming myself. How could I have known?

My cell rang as I left the toll booth on the turnpike just east of Cabin Creek. It was Adrianna. I took a deep breath and answered. "Well, good morning," I said as cheerfully as I could fake it.

"Where are you?" Her voice seemed a bit shaky.

"Almost to Charleston. I'll be at the Bureau in about twenty minutes. Anything wrong?"

"I've got a little problem here, Skip."

"What? What is it?"

"Someone broke into my office last night … probably when we were at Joey's. But it could have been during the night."

"That's doubtful. I'm a light sleeper and my room of course is only a dozen feet away. Was anything taken?"

"The place was ransacked. Drawers spilled out and papers strewn about. The only thing that appears to be missing is my ledger, which has the names and addresses of all my guests."

"*That's* not good."

"No. The last two years of guest information are in that book. I used it as a mailing list *and* I have to have it in case I'm ever audited."

"I'll give you one guess who took it and what he wanted with it."

"You mean Assad."

"Assad," I repeated. "Now he has matched up my *real* name with the room and will also have my address in Georgetown. I'm also afraid he will now associate the name McGowan with the funeral home he broke into. This may well have put Joey and his family in danger. You did list me as Bruce McGowan, didn't you?"

"Yes, I'm sorry."

"Why be sorry? It wasn't your fault. You were just keeping records as you're supposed to do."

"Why would you think Joey and his family could be in danger from learning your name?" she asked.

"Like I said, I don't trust Assad. Who knows what ulterior motives he has?"

"The strange thing is, I had a money box with about eight hundred dollars in it. I saw where someone opened it, but left the money."

"It was Assad, all right. In his warped value system, he's not a common thief, but he would not blink an eye but to cut the throat of an infidel American."

"Skip, that's horrible," she responded in a frightened tone. "Why would you say that?"

I ignored her question as I already had said too much. "Did you call the police?"

"They're here now. A couple of deputies from the sheriff's department. They're dusting for prints."

"They're wasting their time."

"I don't mind telling you I'm a little scared, Skip."

"I'll be back later this afternoon. Maybe you should go somewhere for a few hours."

"I don't want to leave the place without anybody here. When Juanita found out about this, she went home. The poor soul was frightened to death."

"Okay, then. Is Lottie still there?"

"Yes. I guess she's in her room."

"Go ask her to have some tea with you and engage in some lengthy conversation. Tell her what happened and that you need some company. Is Assad there?"

"No. His vehicle is gone. I haven't seen him all morning. He was gone when I came downstairs at seven."

"Okay. Just be careful today."
"Come back soon."
"I will. Call me if you need me."

Jack Fuentes opened the door to his office and came out to greet me, hand extended. "Come in, Bruce."

I followed him in, closed the door behind me and plopped into the chair facing his desk. He lowered himself into his leather chair and sat with hands folded. People who sit behind desks tend to think of themselves as in situational control, holding the cards, several rungs higher than the lowly serf in the straight-back chair. Except *I* was the guy holding the cards today.

"I guess we do need to talk about all this, Bruce. I had a conversation with Washington which had earlier been talking with *your* organization. Sounds like you've been a busy guy. You found three more suspects connected to the dead Arab, and even know their names, addresses and routines. When were you planning to tell me all this?"

"Today."

"And I understand your guys have organized a task force to capture and as necessary neutralize the threat."

That surprised me. I didn't realize CTT, meaning Byrd, had let the cat out of the bag. I would have to counsel with him about being so loose-lipped.

"If that's the information you got. Has your office been tasked anywhere in the equation?"

"We're focusing on AmeriCan. We have a Task Force profile team on the inside looking around and checking out employees from the plant manager right on down to the guys who sweep up. Uniformed and private security has been doubled, and there are roving guards on the perimeter."

"Do you have the south hill area covered that overlooks the plant?"

"No, why?"

"I have cultivated some new information that they may be planning to shoot a shoulder fired missile into the plant, probably to take out one of the storage tanks if a bombing or other attack fails."

"And how did you *cultivate* that information?"

I smiled and did my Groucho eyebrow thing.

"You didn't."

"I did what I had to do."

"And without a court order, I presume. I guess that was the way you conducted business when you were with the Bureau. I have heard about the old days and you guys who bent the rules to the breaking point."

Don't be anal, J. Edgar.

"No. You've got the wrong guy here, Jack. But it does frustrate the hell out of me to have in my possession probable cause only to be refused a warrant by some liberal judge."

Jack spun a half-right and looked out his window. "Whose abode did you burglarize."

"Everyone's"

"Wonderful," he said sarcastically. "Okay, I'll bite. Why do you think there may be a missile involved?"

"I found what appears to be a trajectory and dispersion diagram. The trajectory begins at a point that looks like high ground in the sketch and ends at the target … the factory." I took the card from my digital Nikon. "Can you do me a favor and have this printed out?"

Jack buzzed his assistant who promptly materialized. I like well-trained assistants. My last one made *me* get *her* coffee.

"Any idea from your 'investigation' when a strike may take place?"

"No, but I've got to believe soon. The Arab staying at the place I'm staying is planning to leave October 1st. Either these guys will just hit-and-run or disappear for good when they blow themselves up."

"Suicide bombing. What do you think … car bomb crashing the gate or missile?"

"You need to prepare for both."

Jack reflected a bit, stroking his chin. "When is your team arriving?"

"Saturday morning, 0900 at or near the Greenbrier."

"The Greenbrier?"

"Go figure. Nothing's too good for *our* boys. Actually, they're driving down earlier in the unit van and will call me for a meeting place."

"And the mission?"

"The usual. Capture and interrogate. If they resist capture … total erasure. They never existed."

"You know these people vow never to be taken alive."

"And I respect people with those vows. As a matter of fact, I would do anything in my power to help them *keep* their vows. Anyway, if we take them alive and hold them for prosecution, they will lawyer-up and some ACLU prick will complain that the poor immigrants had their civil rights violated. But I'm less concerned with that right now; we have to stop them from getting to AmeriCan. When AmeriCan is safe, the good people of Charleston live."

Jack looked at the pictures of his family on his credenza. I knew this all rattled him and he would do everything he could to support us on this mission, even if it meant the Bureau would take a back seat. His assistant came in with the prints and Jack studied them intently. He nodded, but said nothing.

I placed my hand on Jack's shoulder and smiled at him. "One way or another, we'll take them down, Jack. I promise you that."

It had become personal with him, now, given the fact that he, Diane and the kids were Charlestonians and would be among the victims of any deadly chemical cloud. And it chilled me to the bone to imagine a scene where possibly a hundred thousand people would suddenly begin choking and convulsing, where every failing breath was petrified, people would be crashing their cars or littering the sidewalks with their corpses ... like something out of a 50's sci-fi movie.

I asked Jack to send the scanned photos of the older man I took the day before to our office in New York, giving him Byrd's e-mail. I knew that Interpol had to have something on the man who appeared to be the terrorists' leader. I also asked him to overnight Nosy's tape. Tomorrow I would find out the older man's identity from Paul LeMer.

Jack and I had lunch at a dive on Quarrier Street famous for its fried chicken and black-eyed peas, but definitely not its atmosphere. The walls were a dirty white, the tables and chairs were circa 1950s and the cook was of your greasy spoon version ... tee shirt, tattoos and obviously ate at his own restaurant ... every bit of 300 pounds. I couldn't make him out clearly where he was in the back, but either he had a moustache or a half-smoked unlit cigar in his mouth.

A very large waitress with fiery dust mop hair, plopped a plate down in front of me containing two pieces of glistening chicken, a volcano of mashed potatoes with red-eye gravy and corn bread with a slab of unmelted, artery closing butter sitting on top. For whatever reason, I had actually let Jack talk me into eating at the Cardiac Café. But since I was a runner and in pretty good shape, I could handle garbage like this. Jack, however, was choking down country-fried steak and milk gravy; and given his sedentary lifestyle and cute little pouch he was developing above his belt, I feared for his life.

I finished the breast and after gnawing on the thigh for a few seconds, I laid it down in what was left of the potato mush.

"Don't you like the lunch, Bruce? You look a little green."

"It's okay. But I think I now have *ticker* shock. You don't happen to have a fibrillator in your car, do you?"

He laughed. "Hey, the body needs a little grease like this every once in a while for system regulation."

"I hope to hell you don't make this place a regular pit stop."

"Of course not, Bruce. I'm fortunate to even get out of the office for lunch once or twice a month."

Almost on cue, Miss America, whose Jungle Gardenia perfume made me even more nauseous, came back to our table to deposit the check. Jack snatched it up quickly, the gentleman that he was.

"How about some dessert, Jack?" she asked. "Your usual or would you like to try some of our lemon chess pie?"

I had just sucked in a swig of coffee and nearly spewed it all over the waitress. And Jack, the big liar, appeared to be right embarrassed. He smiled sheepishly. "Okay, maybe more than twice a month."

The waitress shrugged when Jack didn't order dessert and sashayed away.

"You know, Jack, I remember a grill in the Bronx a few years back and getting served at the counter by a gal in a tank top built a lot like this one. I had ordered a hot dog and some fries, and the guy on the stool next to me ordered a double cheeseburger. The waitress then took two frozen beef patties out of the freezer and slapped each one of them up into her armpits to thaw them out. I sat there with my mouth open for a few moments and then the alarm went off. 'Oh, Miss,' I said. 'Cancel the hot dog, will you?'"

Jack *wanted* to laugh, I could tell; but his dignity got in the way. After pursing his lips together to regain his composure, he said, "I'm gagging here, Bruce. Not a good story to tell at lunch."

I was sure he couldn't wait to tell my joke around the water cooler when he got back to the office. And I was also glad to see a more relaxed, even human side of this uptight kid.

Jack cleared the bill and I thanked him very much. I told him I was stopping by the AmeriCan factory on the way back to talk with the plant superintendent. I was mainly interested in finding out if there were any Middle Eastern types working there in some capacity who could in fact be 'insiders.' It may be a long shot, but still worth checking out.

"I need you to go with me, Jack. Without credentials, I may not be able to even get past the gate, much less get in the see 'the man.'"

"I have a ton of things ahead of me today, Bruce. How about doing this some other time?"

"I may not *have* another day for this. Can't you spare a couple of hours?"

I must have been wearing my beggar face. He sighed and shook his head. "All right. Let me make a couple of calls. Are you always this convincing, Bruce?"

"Always. Not to mention charismatic."

He gave me one of those looks ... you know, like I was something between a knucklehead and a nuisance. But I could tell he liked me, bad jokes and all. He pulled out his cell, called the office, and after a couple of *okays*, he nodded to me and clamped the phone shut. *Atta boy, Jack.*

With his badge and ID and my captivating good looks, we made it through the female guard on the gate. She gave us a site map which took us to the administration building. At the information desk we were directed to the superintendent's office. Carl Hamner, the boss, came out to greet us. He was a nice enough guy and once we got acquainted, he wanted to know the purpose of our visit.

"Have you been contacted in the past few days by anyone from the government?" asked Jack.

"Well, we've had government people *all over* the place lately. I got clued in there's some kind of threat in the area, although no one really wanted to go into specifics. Said they're combing all the plants for possible security breaches."

That's what he was supposed to think. Obviously, the FBI was keeping a tight lip about any *specific* threat at AmeriCan.

Hamner continued. "But I did have a peculiar conversation with a gentleman with the State Department in New York by the name of Leon … no, Lionel Byrd." He then looked at my card again. "Hey, *you're* with the State Department. Is he your boss?"

"One and the same."

"He asked me several questions, mostly about what we manufacture here, how our products are used, et cetera. I'm afraid I wasn't too informative. I'm not used to talking with people on the phone about such matters without being sure they're who they say they are."

"Yeah," I replied. "For all you know, the guy could have been a telemarketer or Jehovah's Witness."

Jack gave me another one of those looks. So did Hamner, and he didn't even know me.

"Ahem … yes. Well, anyway, I made sure I didn't tell him anything that wasn't common knowledge."

Jack's turn. "I'm going to ask you a question, Mr. Hamner, which may sound a bit irregular. How many Middle Eastern employees do you have here?"

"Your government guys have already addressed that with me, too, Mr. Fuentes. They've been through all their personnel files. We have several employed here. Most are from Israel, though … Tel Aviv, to be exact. But I take it you all are interested in other nationalities. So, why should I be concerned about an employee's ethnic background?"

"There are subversives aloof in the area and we're afraid they have infiltrated various facets of our society, sir," Jack replied.

"So that's why you government guys have been swarming all over the plant. You think there could be some type of terrorist infiltration here at AmeriCan?"

"Perhaps, Mr. Hamner. Please keep that confidential. Remember, you have a secret clearance yourself."

The plant manager settled back in his chair and folded his arms. "I'm not surprised at your theory considering what we manufacture. But everyone here has had a thorough background check done on them. Most have some type of security clearance. But, yes, we do have several *Arab* gentlemen working here … three of which are from India and Pakistan, I think. Chemical engineers, gentlemen; not subversives."

"You know that for sure? How many is *several*?" I asked.

"Four, to be exact. Look, they don't hire just anyone at AmeriCan or any other strategic plant, especially those contracted with the government. I'm very confident about the men. Anyway, before hiring these people, as part of the background check, the FBI performed an exhaustive investigation on them and turned up nothing. Two of the engineers were working for the government in Washington before they came here and another began his career with a sister factory in Nepal. Same parent company and ownership."

Hamner did allow Jack and I to review each of the four personnel shields and although we were not permitted to make copies, I took notes. On the surface the men did appear clean. Two of the four graduated from M.I.T. Another, a Jordanian, had been educated in England at Oxford. There were no immediate red flags, unless we chose to look at the men through profiling eyes. I would have Byrd run their names, descriptions and histories through Interpol and both the FBI and CIA intelligence systems.

But who knows what the face of a terrorist looks like these days? I remember as an American advisor to ARVN and Peoples Self Defense Forces in Vietnam, some of the same smiling faces of the villagers whom I trained and trusted during the day, turned up as dead Viet Cong infiltrators at night, killed when they attempted to propagandize or terrorize the people of other villages.

Hamner offered us a tour of AmeriCan which we happily accepted. Jack and I donned hardhats and goggles and followed the superintendent along the factory streets past buildings where machinists, scientists, equipment operators and millwrights labored. Over twenty-five hundred employees went in and out of the plant every day. Obviously, Hamner and company had been wary of the employees with Middle Eastern background as he had come up with their names immediately. I would call that ethnic profiling at its best. Did he also know the other twenty-four hundred and change by name as well? He explained that he made it a point to know who the plant's key scientists were. Of course, there were over *four hundred* chemical engineers working there. *Nice try, Hamner. I'll bet you don't know all **their** names. You're just like the rest of us WASPS.*

We strolled past the two large storage units which I already knew contained the hydrogen chlorine and cyanide gases. Hamner, however, never divulged their content. And just as most all the factories up and down the Kanawha reeked with either the gagging rotten egg smell or that pungent, noxious odor that nearly takes one's breath away, I wondered how much of the pollution pouring out of the smokestacks at AmeriCan had just the tiniest bit of escaping poison. The kind that would stop your breath entirely. And like it would do some good, I capped my hand over my mouth and nose as I walked along.

Hamner, amused by my discomfort, remarked "It's all very safe, you know. In the past year we have had zero accidents and illnesses stemming from any incidents here." I wondered if that meant *before* last year there were people dropping like flies because something bad had sprung from one of those tanks.

The tour was over in about twenty minutes and not a second too soon for me. It wasn't necessarily that revealing, but it *was* educational. I gained a hell of a respect for the plant's men and women and what they did. Of course, I wondered what their life expectancy was. I reminded myself to check out the obituary in the Gazette before I left town. If a great number of the dead were listed as having worked at AmeriCan or another plant, expiring at forty-five or fifty from silicosis or lung cancer, I would not be back. I may not even cross the Alleghenies again. Either that or I would stop off at an Army Surplus and buy an M1A1 protective mask.

When Jack and I returned to his office, I asked him if there happened to be any decontamination showers in the building. He said *no* as I expected he would. I did fax from his machine the names of the four Arab engineers to Byrd, asking him to run them through his Intel sources. We then bid *adieu* and I lit out. Once departing the Kanawha Valley and reaching the safe side of the Alleghenies, I lowered my window to suck in the fresh, uncontaminated mountain air. My mouth wide open, I hung my head out of the window like a dog and to passing traffic I'm sure I resembled a gasping guppy that had just plopped out of its bowl.

Chapter 18

Just before pulling off the interstate at Lewisburg I called Joey, telling him not to be alarmed, but it appeared Assad Mohammed was the primary suspect in the break-in of Adrianna's office. It wasn't enough that he knew I was dogging him, but if it was he who stole the ledger, he could easily associate the McGowan name. I suggested that to Joey that he keep a close eye on his girls and otherwise stay vigilant. I hated the fact that because of me, he and his family may be in danger. Joey understood, but although I could hear the concern in his voice, he said not to worry; he would take the necessary precautions. And Cora knew how to use the home security service … Smith & Wesson.

I beat it back to Wolf Laurel, arriving about four-thirty and catching Adrianna at her desk in the office. She stood and thrust her arms around my neck as soon as I appeared in the doorway. It had been a tough night *and* morning for her, considering she had conjured up the sad memories of her son and her office was rifled, both because of me.

"I'm so glad to see you …" she whispered in my ear. It wasn't a romantic whisper. More so one of relief and release.

"So, the ledger is all that's missing? Nothing else?'

"I think that's it. God, Skip, he could have broken into my residence. I'm glad I have a second deadbolt on my door."

I looked at the office door and obviously the perp wasn't as neat and professional a burglar as me. The door frame around the lock was chewed up as though an angry crow bar had been at work. The lock was old and had given away easily. One thing I noted and wondered if the sheriff department had as well: the lock on the front door of the B&B had not been jimmied or broken, which meant someone entered with a key and only boarders had keys. Only Lottie, Assad and I were the current boarders; so there you are. Of course, any previous guest could have made a duplicate key before leaving and come back to rifle the office. But I wouldn't think so.

"It's obvious that your burglar knew you were out yesterday evening and likely saw us leave. Like I said on the phone, I'm sure it didn't happen during the night. I definitely would have heard wood splitting." And I *knew* it didn't happen while I was listening in on them. "Did the deputies say they'd look for Assad?"

"They said they would question him here and I'm to call them when he returns. They did talk to Lottie. She said she had gotten a cab and went out to dinner the same time we were gone."

"Well, if no one was here for a couple of hours, it wouldn't have mattered how much noise he made breaking in. Obviously, he was watching when we all left. I'd sure like to have a go at Assad, but he'd jack rabbit and we'd never see him again. I wonder if he knew he'd be under suspicion and has already flown the coop. I still need him to be here just another day or two."

"For what?"

"Just ... surveillance at this point. I'm still working up a profile on him."

"What's specifically going on with Assad that you can't tell me, Skip?"

If I told her everything, she would want him out in the street the moment he came back. A terrorist living at Wolf Laurel? Not only would she boot him immediately, she'd toss me right along with him.

"It's an immigration matter, like I said before. Look, I've got it under control. I *will* know where he is from now on at all times. Maybe we ought to check his room."

"No, Skip. You know how he blew up the other day when he thought someone had been in there. Of course, nobody did."

"Of course."

"And anyway, with instructions never to go in his room, he could have the Better Business Bureau or Association of Country Inns down on me."

"We wouldn't want that. But what if there would be an emergency ... like a fire or Martian attack?"

"I'd just rather leave his room alone, Skip. Okay?"

"Okay." I put up my hand in resignation.

She sighed and sat down at the dining table. "I just don't like what's going on here. This has always been a place where we didn't even used to lock the front door. The guests were trustworthy and brought in no problems. This is the first real time I haven't felt safe. I guess there'll be another night without sleep."

"You'll sleep tonight," I said. "That is if you'll invite me to stay with you."

The anxiety seemed to leave her face almost immediately. "I think that's a good idea. I'll make us some dinner this evening."

It was a light dinner and portions were small. Of course that's the way she ate, and that's why she wears a hundred-ten pound frame. Considering the last thing I had in my mouth was lunch's fried chicken and potatoes, it was like having an hors d'oeuvre supper. But the fact that I didn't jog at daybreak balanced things out. Still, I knew I'd be raiding the fridge by midnight.

We sat up for a while watching TV. There was this stupid sitcom, which I had always hated, but after my second glass of Chablis, I thought it was hysterically funny. I let out a few guffaws and Adrianna just stared at me like I was some kind of bleeping goofball in a fraternity house. By ten-thirty I had settled down, finding again both my dignity and suave demeanor.

But jocularity then turned to conversation of the more serious persuasion when she said, "You know, I've been wondering ever since we had our first conversation; why did you all those years ago decide on a life of danger and violence? First the Special Forces, then the FBI and now whatever mysterious thing you're doing. Couldn't you have gone into insurance or something?"

"Insurance? Me?" I laughed. "Now that *would* be dangerous to me. I'd be dead inside two years. Of boredom."

"But do any of these things you've done make you apprehensive about facing death?"

"Ohh-kay, kiddo. What gives? What's with the morbid talk?"

Her green eyes then took on a more melancholy hue. "Nothing really. I'm just a kind of a worrier, that's all."

Then it became clear to me that having lost a husband and a son in a matter of five years, the subject of death and the possibility of losing someone like me, her new squeeze, was really preying on her. And to me that was bitter-sweet. On one hand she made me feel as though I was in the same company of love as Mason and Johnny, yet it was obvious that their deaths would continue to haunt her.

I patted her hand and smiled. "Hey. Not to worry. I *do* look after myself; but yes, I think about death sometimes. I just don't dwell on it. I'm not like these people I hunt who are more than willing to take their celestial dirt nap at twenty-five or thirty just to gain the favor of Allah. They actually love *death* more than we love *life*. And they give up their lives with smiles on their faces, so sure of where they will be going when they cross over. I'm not giving up my life with a smile and sure as hell am not taking innocent people with me. They may *think* the place they're going is Heaven, but in my opinion their new abode will make Death Valley feel like Alaska."

"It sounds like you're talking about Islamic terrorists … the kind I've been reading about. Is that what you think Assad is? A terrorist? Was that what you meant about … you know … the throat-cutting of Americans?"

That caught me flat-footed. I guess in mentioning 'these people' in my little soliloquy, I slipped and inadvertently alluded to the fact that 'these people' (obviously describing Islamic terrorists) were 'the people I hunt.'

"Beats me," I replied. "But from Assad's erratic behavior, he does bear watching." That's as good as I could do and not spill all the beans. "Anyway, why did we get on the subject of death and the afterlife?"

"I think about it sometimes, that's all," she replied. "Do you?"

"Do I what?"

"Think about it much."

I could tell she really needed to talk about death and this life after death business, maybe as a catharsis or perhaps she was looking to see where I was in my spirituality. I think it may have been the latter, 'cause if I turned out to be a Darwinist or agnostic, being the spiritual person that she was, she would be wasting her time with me.

But I kept the heavy topic going. "Well, I *have* had occasions to think about it. Death is so … final …" As soon as I said that I realized how stupid and redundant it sounded. But I continued, "… like one moment I am breathing, talking, enjoying my state of consciousness and awareness, and then I get taken out of this life, suddenly and so rudely the next. I have to admit I've wondered at times if it will all just fade to black and I cease to exist. If that is so, then what was my purpose in being born and living a life in the first place? And I think, since I am a being of higher intelligence, why should I be cast into the same state of nothingness as a dog or a cockroach?"

She added, "How anyone could ever think we all just hatched from some piece of matter that formed on a rock is beyond me. Each of us was born with a purpose in life." Her eyes now had that faraway look. "Even when life is over all too soon."

But then again, all this caused me to think about something that happened in my mom's life a very long time ago. As I paused and allowed my eyes to wander around the room in obvious contemplation, she took my hand and said, "A penny for your thoughts."

"You want to hear something bizarre? I haven't thought about this in years. When I was four and Joey was born, something happened to Mom. She had a very difficult delivery. It seems that right after my little brother popped out, Mom started bleeding. Something about a placenta abruption. Her blood pressure suddenly dropped and then her heart stopped. The doctors worked on her more than two minutes, but her body didn't respond. The last paddle shock and cc of adrenaline administered, the doctors shot glances at one another, shook their heads and began pulling off the gloves. But suddenly there was one beep on the monitor, then two and then a series of irregular beats. After a while her heart was beating rhythmically. They said it was amazing and had never seen anything like it.

"I was too young to realize what was going on, except I remember Dad bringing Joey home from the hospital without Mom. Even though Dad told me she was coming home, she didn't for the longest time. I just kept thinking she wouldn't be back and that it wasn't a very good trade Dad had made ... a pukey little bald-headed guy that cried all the time in exchange for Mom. But after about ten days, several units of blood and restored blood pressure, Mom came back to us."

Adrianna's eyes were attentive, even inquisitive. "Amazing. Two minutes without oxygen … I can't imagine. I assume she had no brain injury as a result?" She then paused for a moment. "But how does that relate to what we've been talking about … you know, life after death?"

"I was getting to that. I think I was about ten when I overheard Mom telling another woman over a cup of tea in the parlor about those two minutes she was, well, legally dead. She said about the time her heart stopped she felt herself rising from her body and floating up to the ceiling. She actually looked down on her pale body and although she knew she was probably dead, she was really okay with that. She said there was such a wonderful peace about the experience. She watched over her body for a while longer, then felt herself smile as she passed through a dark tunnel, drifting silently and softly toward a brilliant light that seemed to be drawing her to it. The light was warm and reassuring. She said she felt like an angel she had seen in a picture show, all in white, glowing, flowing.

"And then another woman who had been dead for five years appeared before her, holding out her hand. 'Mom!' my mother called. Her mom then put up her hand like a cop at an intersection. She was smiling and shaking her head. 'Go back, sweetheart,' she said. 'It's not your time. You have a new baby to care for. Bruce needs you, too.'"

I suddenly felt moisture on my cheeks, not even realizing my tear ducts had been leaking. Adrianna took my hand again and squeezed it.

I continued. "And then my mom said she saw herself rejoining her body. She heard the joy and celebration erupting in the operating room and opened her eyes to a host of smiling doctors and nurses."

"Wow," Adrianna exclaimed. "What a deep and wonderful story. But did you ever think that was all a dream?"

"While she was clinically dead? I wouldn't think so. As far as I know, dead people don't dream."

She turned her head slightly and squinted her eyes at me. "Smart alec."

And then suddenly she became quiet. Her eyes moved from mine to the floor and back again. She was reflecting, I thought. About something. All I knew was … it was something sad. And then my suspicions proved correct.

"I had a similarly strange experience the night Johnny lay dying. He had lapsed into a coma and as I was sitting by his bed holding his hand, a kind of vision of him appeared on the opposite side. It was crazy … scary even. Here he was lying nearly lifeless and yet he stood beside himself, smiling and mouthing the word 'mom.' He nodded a kind of reassuring nod and suddenly the monitor stopped beating … along with his heart. Then the vision was gone. And I knew right then and there that he had gone to Heaven. All that remained was me. And that horrible flat line sound."

She swallowed hard to fight back the tears. "I didn't even summon the nurse. Somehow I knew it would be useless. I just sat there holding his hand.

"I dream about him so often. He is standing there just like that vision I saw of him, saying 'mom … mom.' I always feel so helpless. I can't save him in my *dreams*, either."

I nodded and kept my eyes fixed to hers. "Yeah. I know about such dreams."

We said nothing further to one another. I guess we had poured out enough melancholy between us to last a year. At least I had.

After the heavy conversation, she settled in close beside me. We sat for a while and it started to storm. It was quiet in the house, which magnified the sound of the blowing rain against the clapboard siding and the thunder that clapped sharply and rolled throughout the valley. I had just shared with her my mother's religious moment, just as Adrianna had shared hers with me. And now sitting with this very beautiful woman, feeling her soft breath on my face, I was having one myself. It had been good to reminisce and philosophize about things. And in conjuring all this up again … well, I was feeling especially good about God, family and the lovely Adrianna Wolf, all whom I loved. In a while we walked sleepily to her bedroom. I don't know whether my lights went out before hers, but the next thing I remember, a brilliant shaft of the September sun through the window drilled my eyes open. It was ten past eight.

Immediately, before taking on any other thoughts of the morning, my mind compelled me to recall the nightmare I had only minutes before I awakened. When I dream, it's like experiencing a Hollywood production in vivid Technicolor, complete with complex plot, spectacular cinematography and surround sound. Some parts of the dream I find have already escaped back into crevices of my unconscious, but I'm generally able to retain the more significant, sometimes horrific pieces that will haunt me the rest of the day.

I was ten years old again and riding shotgun with my dad in an ambulance down Capitol Street in Charleston. People were bustling about, in and out of the *Diamond* and *Stone and Thomas*, jaywalking at intersections and brushing by one another without making eye contact having determined agendas in their brains. Suddenly, a woman grabs at her throat and falls face down on the sidewalk. The child holding her hand goes down with her, then convulses. A man in a fedora stumbles into our car and falls over the hood. His face is painfully drawn and milky saliva spews from his mouth onto the windshield. He tries to form the word 'help,' but nothing comes out. He falls off the hood and onto the street by the car. When I look back, bodies are lying everywhere, their faces silent and ashen white. Suddenly a hand forms over my nose and mouth. My dad is trying to keep what is in the air from consuming me, but I then see that he begins to seize as well. Blood pours from his nose and ears and then the car careens onto the sidewalk and into a building.

This is the kind of nightmare that should have awakened me at its climax and I was surprised my brain allowed me to actually finish it out. Except I didn't stick around to see myself croak. Since Assad and company were clearly planning to achieve this catastrophic scenario, that was obviously the reason for my dream. After I finally awoke I lay in gooseflesh with my arms locked behind my head and under the pillow for several reflective moments, then sighed, and swung my legs off the mattress. At least it was a different nightmare for a change, but one of proportionately greater tragedy. And as I had been responsible for some of the deaths of the people I usually dreamed about, I was determined not be responsible for failing to stop the deaths of a hundred thousand or more people as depicted in this new dream.

Adrianna had been up for a couple of hours and was already downstairs preparing the breakfast. She hadn't been putting much of it out the last few days, considering Lottie ate like a bird, I wasn't around half the time to eat it and Assad never partook of *iftar* (breakfast). I hit the potty, dragged myself down the stairs past the dining room where Adrianna and Lottie sat talking and drinking coffee. They both smiled, for different reasons, and I gave them a wave on the way to my room.

I had fully expected Assad would have returned the favor and break into *my* room last night, especially if they knew I was keeping the lovely Adrianna Wolf company. But everything was intact. Since he now knew who I was, I was sure he would go through my stuff trying to find out more about me. Except there would have been nothing to find. My weapons, cameras, notes and *life* were in the Suburban and all someone had to do was sneeze while passing by it and the bells and whistles would wake the town of Lewisburg four miles away.

I looked out and his car was still not there. It wasn't there all night, either. I suspected that he somehow knew the cops wanted to interview him about the break-in and intentionally stayed away.

I changed into my cute gym shorts and parka and began pounding the pavement past the rows of white fencing, fields of stacked hay and bold, stately farmhouses set back off the road. The sun was warm on my face even though the cool morning breeze made the hairs on my legs stand up.

As I do a hell of a lot of thinking when I jog, I wondered if one day soon I could really hang everything up and come back home to spend my waning years with someone like Adrianna. God wasn't playing fair, tempting me with mornings like this.

From behind me I heard the whine of tires on asphalt and at first, didn't pay much attention to it. The vehicle then slowed. I assumed that it was because the driver was coming up on a jogger, although I was on the proper side of the road; but then I saw who it was. It was a black Nissan Maxima with blacked-out windows. A sudden surge of danger hit me as the car slowed to a near stop when it came even with me. I didn't know whether to expect the Nissan to suddenly swerve and bounce me into the meadow or if the left side windows would drop down after which a hail of bullets would rip my carcass apart like you'd see in old Eliot Ness TV shows. The car stayed with my steady eight mile an hour pace for a few seconds and then it finally moved on. It was obvious that Assad was making a statement. He knew from my routine I'd be jogging and could get to me any time, especially when I was the most vulnerable … without my Glock. But his day was coming and that day was tomorrow.

When I got back to the B&B it was just after nine. A thought came over me and before I returned to my room for a shower, I stopped to visit with Adrianna. I felt we needed some time together away from the inn. Tomorrow would be a difficult day and the mission could go down in several ways. It may be the last time we would have a day to just kick around. Juanita was back and had apparently realized a day's pay would help her cough up a degree of courage. She could manage things at Wolf Laurel till we got back.

I pulled Adrianna off to the side. "Say, how about you and I taking off for a few hours and going to Joey's cabin by the river. We can pick up some KFC or something and make an afternoon of it."

"Oh, I can't do that. I've got to look after this place today. And under the circumstances, I don't want to leave Juanita by herself. She'll be spooked all day."

"Juanita overheard our conversation. "No, please. Go ahead. I can take care of things here. You should take a day for yourself. If anything happens, I have the deputy's card and he will be here quickly."

"I don't know," Adrianna said. It was one of those 'I want to, but I shouldn't' replies.

"Sure you do," I coaxed. "Look, I'm going to get a shower and will be ready in half an hour." I pushed her forward to the door.

"You'll be okay, Juanita?"

"Yes. Yes. Please go and have a good day."

"You call me on my cell and let me know how things are going. Promise?"

"I promise."

Adrianna discarded her apron. "Maybe it'll be fun. See you in the lobby in a few minutes."

I noticed that Assad's car was still not in the parking lot when we left. It wasn't there when I went for my jog either, which told me he definitely anticipated my morning run and waited from a concealed position for me to get on the road.

"Do you mind if I stop first at Valley Community?" I asked. "I need to talk with Dean Le Mer."

"No problem. I'd like to chat with him myself."

I wanted to chat with LeMer alone, but she would get suspicious if I told her to wait in the SUV.

I skimmed the parking lot for the Nissan and Honda in their usual parking spots, but they weren't there. I couldn't remember if they had class on Friday or not. It was ten-ten and they should have been in class.

When I approached Joanne, LeMer's blond assistant, did *I* ever get the cold shoulder? I was the guy who obviously got her in trouble last week. But I was glad to see she didn't lose her job over it.

"Is he expecting you?" she snipped.

"No. But if you tell him Ms. Wolf is here to see him, I'm sure he'll come right out."

Joanne told him and he did. Of course, he wasn't expecting me and the sight of me nearly stopped him in his tracks.

"Ah, there's *His Immenseness* now," I said. Adrianna gigged me in the ribs with her elbow.

"Paul," she greeted, approaching him with an outstretched hand. He took it and smiled at her. Then he looked at me and scowled.

"What's *he* doing here? Or should I say, what are you doing with him?"

Adrianna gave me a puzzled look. "I don't understand. Is there something not right between you two?"

"I think you should ask Mr. McGowan who seems to have no respect for institutional regulations."

"Skip?" She turned to me.

I shrugged like I was completely in the dark.

"Well, anyway, Paul, I need to ask you something."

"Go ahead, my dear. I will certainly listen to *you*."

Good ol' Paul. Always the gentleman.

"Lisa Ramsay, an old friend who is a supporting patron of the county library, is doing a book drive and is looking for any textbooks and books of both fiction and non-fiction to increase their inventory. Do you all have books from time-to-time you discard? I'm helping to make contacts with schools and private citizens who'd like to donate."

"For you, Adrianna, I will check with our librarian to see what we have. I will also make a few calls to peers at other two and four year colleges in the state. We're all good about helping one another out."

Whoop-T-do.

"Thank you, Paul. I'll call you in a week or so to see what you've been able to gather."

"Wonderful, my dear." He picked up her hand and kissed it. The Frenchy do that a lot. Makes you sick. "Now, Mr. McGowan, do you have a question for me?" He pushed back his nerdy glasses and peered through them with two beady little eyes.

"May I speak with you in your office?"

"I suppose so." He then turned to Joanne and tried to make a joke. "If I'm not back in five minutes, I've probably been taken hostage by this man and you can call 911."

And I think she'd do it, too.

Adrianna stepped into the hall as I followed LeMer back to his office. His clothing smelled sour from underarm perspiration and cheap cologne. I actually started feeling sorry for the big lug. He couldn't help it that he didn't have anything going for him. But then, ashamed of my cynical attitude, I thought it was high time I was nice to him.

"What is it, Mr. McGowan? Do you have more deceptions for me today?"

"Look, Dean, I apologize for the shenanigans the other day. The government really did need the information I appropriated, and believe me, it is very grateful. If the investigation we're doing is successful, there may even be a commendation for you for making it all come together."

"Really?"

"And your United States Government needs something else from you."

"What is that?"

"This time its information on someone else. Someone you may know. We're looking for an older Middle Eastern man about forty-five or fifty, slightly balding, but with a beard. He may even be a teacher here."

"We do have a visiting professor here from Saudi Arabia who teaches a couple of classes."

"And his name would be?"

"Navab Abouzar, I believe how you pronounce it."

"Thank you, Paul. Do you have his address?"

"It's a Crows, Virginia address, as I remember. Let me see." He accessed the faculty information on his computer. "You can get his Bio on line, you know, by accessing the school's web site. Yes, here it is ... Star Route 58, Crows. That's all it has. Funny, there's no box number."

"What classes does he teach?"

"He teaches Physics and a class called *Multicultural Issues in America.*"

Bingo.

"How long has he been on staff?"

"I'd say about a year."

"Paul, we may need to subpoena his personnel file. You have one don't you?"

"Of course. Has this man done anything wrong?'

"Not that I know of. An immigration investigation, that's all."

"I see." He allowed his black glasses frames to slide down his greasy nose again as he appeared to be digesting the information. I knew he wouldn't give the man's personnel file up without the subpoena and me doing a B&E on a state institution? Well, I just wasn't about to go there.

"Is Mr. Abouzar here today?"

"Let me see. No, he doesn't teach on Fridays."

"And logically, there is no *Multicultural* class today."

"Correct."

"The professor will be here Monday, I assume."

"Yes, he will."

"Well, my five minutes are up. Paul, I do thank you for the information. Again, I will give your name to my highers in Washington, so one day, expect to see a plaque or something with your name on it signed by our State Department Director."

I thought Paul was going to pee his pants. "That would be wonderful. I have just the place for it on that wall."

I was certainly leaving the Dean's office on better terms than I thought. Paul would relish the idea of getting some kind of recognition from the government and I would remain in his good graces, until one day months or years from now when the space on his wall was still empty, he would figure out once again that he had been duped.

Adrianna was still hanging out in the hallway talking to a few girls whose parents she knew. "Did you get what you needed from Paul?"

"Sure did."

"What was going on between you two when we came in?"

"You know how these liberal college commies are. They hate everybody that works in government."

She had that confused look on her face which she wore a lot when she was around me.

Joey's camp was not much to look at. A rustic, flimsy cabin house, poopy brown in color and needing a new roof and porch, it listed a little to one side. On several occasions after torrential rains, the Greenbrier River had gotten up to the front porch, threatening to turn the cabin into Noah's Ark. But it had somehow stayed the course over the years and hopefully would stay the day while we were in it.

The river's bank was littered with fallen trees, resembling decaying wooden giants. Barren branches, extending into the water and catching a variety of natural and manmade deposits, served as a feeding haven for redeye bass and trout.

Adrianna was quite the angler. She, her husband and little Johnny had fished the Greenbrier often, but after she lost both of her men, she sold the boat. However, she still had Mason's gear. I was down-right impressed that she had no problem cutting up bloodworms or handling crickets and could cast out and drop her line within three feet of her intended target. I was still trying to get past the bloodworms.

But there was nothing like spending the day in God's woods to take one's mind off of things. Everything that was bad seemed so far away and what would happen tomorrow … well, that was tomorrow. I watched her with admiring eyes as she worked the rod and reel. Her face had that determined look, but there was also a smile, frozen, intense-like. She was like the water … fluid, energetic, constant, full of history and life. Never ceasing. A light breeze kicked up, catching her hair and making her appear even more goddess-like than she was. I smiled and she returned it.

"It's beautiful out here," she said.

My smile deepened. "It sure is." She knew what I meant.

Another cast and the sinker plopped about forty feet out just beyond a large branch. She was like a surgeon with the rod.

"If you could conjure up one, what would be your perfect day?"

"Well," I replied. "This would be one of them."

She nodded. "But besides today, just to get away on a vacation to relax, letting go, making every care in the world disappear. Where would that be?"

"Oh, I don't know. Maybe I'd be sitting in an Adirondack on a beach white as sugar, looking over pristine blue-green waters, smelling the salt air, drawing the sea breeze into my lungs, listening to the screeching gulls as they circle an electric blue sky, and sucking down cold, cold Heinekens." I paused for effect. "Of course, you'd be in the picture. You'd be with me on that perfect day."

"Mmm, nice. Take me there tomorrow."

I turned my head away, reflecting solemnly in advance on 'tomorrow' and what it would bring. "Wish I could, my dear."

Reality checked back in and I watched as Adrianna continued to work her magic in the waters. I was impressed how the fish jumped on her bait within only minutes after she dropped in on them. And after she had reeled in several good-sized trout, she cleaned them, fried them up in some butter, olive oil and paprika, and added some sliced potatoes and onions in the old iron skillet we found beneath the stove. They went down nicely with a couple of cold Coors.

It wasn't long and I was ready to kick back on the rickety porch in one of the well-worn rattans and watch the gentle Greenbrier flow by. Its crystal waters sparkled and gleamed like thousands of little diamonds in the five-thirty sun. In short order, I found that Adrianna had other things on her mind. She knelt at my legs, ran her fingers over my knees and locked her dreamy eyes on mine. Obviously, she was over the fear and sadness she had experienced the past couple of days. I hoped Joey had changed the sheets in his last two or three trips to the cabin.

Just after seven, the sun was casting the last of its golden rays through the oaks and sycamores. A whippoorwill chanted a repetitive version of *September Song* and after our own song, *Afternoon Delight*, and a nap, we agreed it was time to pack up. It had been a good day and we both certainly needed it.

CHAPTER 19

▼

I arose early Saturday morning, skipped the run, but stepped out to see if Assad's car was there. It actually was and that was a surprise. Considering what would go down during the day, I did want him there ... and everyone else out. And I hoped that the cops were not still interested in questioning him about the office break-in. That would throw a monkey wrench in our plan.

I went through an equipment check, then drove out to partake of a light breakfast at the Shoney's breakfast bar. After the winding nine mile drive on Route 60 to White Sulphur Springs, Old White, as the Greenbrier had been known for a couple of centuries, came into view. I compared the map coordinates with the topography and discovered it wasn't the Greenbrier where Zulu was staying; it was The Roche Motel just down the hill. Sorry, boys. From the looks of it, it should have been called The Roach Motel. Rather than talking Roundup, we should have been talking Raid.

I pulled into the parking lot about eight. As it was too early to expect the team, I cast off my Glock and shoulder holster and walked back up the hill approximately five-hundred yards to the famous resort with its spectacular gardens. It was right damn peaceful there. I took a seat in the gazebo, leaned back on the bench and allowed the sun now peeking around a huge magnolia to warm my face. A couple of morning joggers, a middle-aged man and a much younger woman, greeted me with nods as they negotiated the meandering path. The man was puffing a little, attempting to stay even with his gazelle girlfriend. She obviously wasn't his wife as he was desperately trying to impress her.

After I took a twenty minute stroll down a pathway flanked by hydrangeas and brilliant chrysanthemums, I ended up back at La Cucaracha just in time to see the team's Ford Expedition pull in. All four doors opened and out came what looked to be two guys resembling X-men in black SWAT attire and two others that looked like Wesley Snipes and the Rock. I had no doubt they could engage a battalion of Red Chinese, kill half of them and send the remainder back across the Great Wall screaming for their mommies.

Two of the goons I recognized right away. The Wesley Snipes character was Chuck Robinson, code name *Viper,* who was also ex-Bureau and on a team with me when we took down Manny the Mouse Carbone that day in South Manhattan. Another one of the X-men was Ty Marshall who worked out of the CTT office in Washington. I hadn't gotten to know him very well. In the year-and-a half I had been with CTT we had been on separate assignments, off to the four winds ninety percent of the time. Anyway, Ty was a very private, sometimes distant son-of-a-gun and hard to get to know. The other two guys were Jeff Palmer, a Brit who as I remembered would rather golf than eat, and Burt Candellera or Candy for short. I knew Palmer would like to go ahead and get this thing underway, take down the scum buckets, and be on the first tee at the Greenbrier by noon. And then there was Candy, lean and chiseled, sporting a buzz haircut, and still moving with ramrod exactness, just like the Marine captain he was in Desert Storm.

We all shook hands like a bunch of guys at a college frat reunion. They went by the motel lobby for their keys and then we piled into Chuck's room for the strategy session. His elegant quarters quickly became a mini situation room. The boys then went right to work. I was hoping we'd have a couple of donuts, tell a few war stories and get slap-happy, but these guys wanted to get down and dirty immediately.

Chuck, being the Zulu commander on this gig, kicked off the meeting. I began my briefing, starting from when DAG, who I believed to be Khalid Al-Barem, as deduced from the student roster, was discovered. I filled them in on my surveillance as well as what I found in their rooms. They already had a transcribed, translated copy of Assad's notes, my photos and my report to Byrd. They did not have the more recent photos I had snapped of the missile diagram and trigger device. Neither did they know of my tête-à-tête with Assad when he accused me of being a fabricator.

Chuck, however, had something for me to see. Last evening, Byrd had faxed to him a transcript of the tape Nosy and I recorded from outside Assad's window of the chatter going on inside. Our interpreter-translator, Abu Narziz, had quickly converted the Arabic dialogue to English script.

One huge revelation surfaced that reinforced my earlier suspicion about the burglary of Adrianna's office. The perp was indeed our favorite Arab boarder. And he knew my name. I took the script from Chuck and began reading:

Subject One: *My friends, I have new information for you. While the hostess had gone off with the man called White, I went into her office. There were notes about each of us recorded by her and the Spanish woman. It was obviously the man who engaged them. From the guestbook I learned the man's name is McGowan, not White. He must be a policeman as we suspected.*

Subject Two: *Then he must know who we are and what we plan.*

Subject One: *No. I only think he **suspects** things about us. I do not believe he knows anything for sure or we would be arrested by now. It had to be him who came into my room, but there was nothing here for him to find. The short time we remain, I will be sure to watch him.*

Subject Three: *Does our leader know we are being watched?*

Subject One: *I told him. I asked if I should kill McGowan. I see him out running on the roadways and I could erase him at any time. But he said that would bring others to investigate and the death of this man is not our mission.*

Subject Two: *McGowan makes me fearful the way he always appears where we are. He has to know something* (the man's voice becomes anxious, almost argumentative). *I say we kill him now!*

Subject One: *Please calm yourself, my friend. We will not move against McGowan. We must not allow him to distract us. We must remain focused.*

Subject Three: *Assad is correct, Fayez. Be patient. In only days we will become immortal. I have long dreamed of this. We are lions from the desert crouched for the fight.*

Subject One: *I too had a dream three nights ago. I saw the explosions clearly and our spirits rose above the fire and smoke. I saw many people fall. Even the trees seemed to wilt and the mountains quaked and tumbled, signaling the greatness of Allah.*

My friends, what we will do is not about emotions; we are driven by our strong Islam belief and we have faith in the Judgment Day. I am sickened with the Americans. They are spoiled, lazy and fat. But most of all they are ignorant. They place their faith in the material things of this world and in false gods. There is only one true God.

(The sound of chanting by all three subjects)

Pray with me, my friends, for it is written that we should worship God and his messenger Mohammed. We must struggle for jihad for the cause of Allah with our very persons and he will forgive our sins. Admit us into the Heavenly Gardens, Allah, where there are flowing streams and allow us to enter the pleasant Garden of Eternity. Oh, Allah, we will not be afraid to give up our lives. Our faith in you defies our fear. Our cause goes beyond jihad. We welcome quital and will trade our lives for the hereafter.

(There is now silence and the subjects appear to be engaged in silent prayer for a period of time).

We stood stoically, looking at one another with staid eyes, fully convinced that the terrorists' mission was not only substantive, but tentative as well. We knew our raid was going down none too soon.

"Well, we know *what* and *where*," I began, "but *how* and *when* are the questions. They make it very clear they will kill themselves in executing their mission. Do they plan to break through the gate at AmeriCan and explode a device into one of the storage tanks or drop devices on the plant by aircraft and in doing so, blow themselves up?"

Chuck responded. "Probably the latter. I guess that's why they're taking the flying lessons? But why the missile, Bruce ... that is if they have one?"

"Well first, in regards to the planes, I'm pretty damned sure these guys have not been taking lessons for recreational purposes. Some time earlier they likely flew with someone over AmeriCan to do a recon and map out the plant. They didn't fly on their own because the flight instructor at the academy said their training had been limited to the county. I agree with you, Chuck. They've been learning to fly with the intention of chartering planes and dropping explosives onto the plant. They'd have to fly low in order to shove the bombs out onto their target with some degree of accuracy. The targets would be Buildings A and B here (I pointed them out on the sketch map) and the adjacent storage tanks of cyanide and chlorine gases." And then I thought for a moment. "Maybe they even plan to fly the planes *into* the tanks, I don't know. These people don't mind killing themselves and I suspect their mission includes suicide. Even if they did shove the bombs out of the aircraft, the explosions below would knock the planes out of the sky.

"Now as to the missile, that could be a check-valve if the bombing attack fails. Someone could be positioned on the hillside above AmeriCan to either fire on the target or knock down any fighters that may try intercepting the planes."

Candy added. "They could also be targeting a commercial airliner either on approach or leaving Yeager to make some kind of statement."

"Possibly," I replied. "But a missile bringing down a 747 or a military aircraft in a more metropolitan area like New York or L.A. would be more impactive and kill a hell of a lot more people. Now *that* would be a statement."

"We seem to have most of the puzzle pieces laid out, but there's no way to connect them for a complete picture without knowing for sure what means they'll use in their attack," said Palmer, checking his watch.

"Hopefully, we'll find that out at capture. So how do we do this, Chuck?" I asked.

"We'll leave here in two vehicles. Bruce, you and Candy will go back to where you're staying and take Assad Mohammed into custody. Ty, Jeff and I will raid the Jamestown lair and nail the others. We'll blindfold them and then take them to the Wolf Laurel location for preliminary Q&A … Bruce, you need to clear everyone out of there. Then we bring in our chopper to the local airport to transport them down to Ft. Bragg and on to Guantanamo Bay by C-130 from Pope for a more intensive interrogation."

"Of course they'll not go down easily," I remarked. "I'm sure they've been extremely vigilant, expecting me or the FBI to make a move on them. It's obvious now that Assad Mohammed has been watching me as much as I have him, especially the last couple of days."

"Well if they won't go down friendly-like," replied Chuck, "then we'll take them *out*, no questions asked. A disposal unit will then be dispatched. Of course, the value of this operation is to gain knowledge of not only their plans, when and how, but about other elements that are part of a larger scenario. Merely wasting these guys won't get it done for Byrd."

I nodded, but added, "You know that hardcore Islamic militants will definitely not give of up *anything*, even under extreme duress. These creeps are suicidal and whether it's part their plan or not, they will blow themselves up along with their targets. The more infidels killed, the greater the favor from Allah. And whether they die by their own hands or by ours, they will be dying for their God."

Chuck smiled. "Then we'll hasten their meeting with Allah, if it comes to that. But I wonder if they believe that being killed by an infidel will send them to the furnace in disgrace."

"And I wonder if instead of harps, like they give you in Heaven, you get accordions in Hell?" I replied. The Zulu boys actually laughed at that.

The smile then quickly vanished from Chuck's face. "Okay, any questions?"

I raised my hand. "When's kickoff?"

"1100 hours, which is in …" he looked at his watch. "… nine minutes. Any other questions?"

The guys shook their heads, but I asked one more. "Where're we doing lunch afterwards?"

Chuck seemed a bit irked with my trifling. "Just watch out for collaterals," he added, which meant 'don't let any friendlies get in the way.' I would be sure that didn't happen at Wolf Laurel.

At one minute till the hour Chuck's cell went off. It was Byrd.

"Viper, are you set?"

"We are."

"Begin deactivation in six-zero seconds."

"Wilco."

"I want a SITREP (situation report) as soon as this goes down."

"Roger."

I gave Chuck the directions to the Jamestown venue and after performing a radio check with our high-tech Dick Tracy walkie-talkie ear and wrist pieces, we lit out promptly at 1100.

I then called Adrianna enroute to Wolf Laurel. "Why were you gone at the crack of dawn again?" she asked. "I thought maybe we could have breakfast together."

The nerve of her. She was beginning to sound like somebody's wife.

I blew off the question. "Are Juanita and Lottie there this morning?"

"Yes, why?"

"Did any other guests come in yesterday or today?"

"No, but tomorrow there's a couple coming in from Missouri for four days. Why all the questions?"

"Listen carefully. This is important. I want you to quietly get Juanita and Lottie out of the inn. You all go somewhere and stay until after three."

"You're scaring me, Skip. What's going on?"

"No questions. Just do as I ask, okay?"

"Does this have to do with Assad?"

"Yes. Is he still there?"

"I think so. His car is here."

"Okay. Go now!"

"You're not going to shoot up my house, are you?"

"Go!" I repeated.

Within ten minutes, Candy and I were pulling into the gravel lot at Wolf Laurel. I checked to see if Adrianna's van was still there. It wasn't. But there *was* a figure leaving the last step of the veranda. Assad had come out of the inn with a large duffle bag slung over his shoulder and was walking toward his car. What happened then seemed in retrospect as a choreographed slow motion whirr right out of an old Six Million Dollar Man scene. Just as Candy stepped out of my Suburban, Assad was within five feet of getting into the Nissan. Apparently, he saw Candy's black uniform-looking non-uniform, complete with gun belt, and panicked. As Candy stepped toward Assad's car, gun drawn, Assad jumped in, cranked the engine and gunned his vehicle toward Candy, throwing gravel forty feet behind him. Unfortunately for Candellera, he didn't jump out of the way fast enough and the front bumper of the car bowled X-man ex-Marine over.

I had already exited the driver's side, but as Assad sped by me, nearly clipping my door, I too had to jump out of the way. I drew my Glock and fired three shots through the back glass of the Nissan, one of which apparently struck Assad somewhere other than the head. I could see the outline of his body jolt when the round hit him. The car cut erratically to the right and plowed into a grove of scrub pines. After taking out several saplings, Assad accelerated back onto Seven Bridges and headed north.

I keyed my mike. "Agent down! Agent down!"

Chuck immediately responded. "What's happening, Scorpion?"

"Candy Man is hit. The suspect saw us coming and ran him down with his car. I need to tend to him. Send the paramedics and get the locals on your freak. Tell them to intercept a black Nissan Maxima with a shattered back glass heading north on Seven Bridges within two miles of Highway 60."

"I copy. Is Candy all right?"

"I'm seeing to him now," I said, running toward him. Candy was not moving and I observed that one leg was badly mangled. Blood was now pouring from his nose and mouth, and he was choking on it. I carefully turned his head to the side and let the blood drain into the gravel.

"Candy, can you hear me?"

He nodded.

"Don't move. I'll be right back."

While running to the Suburban to retrieve my first aid kit, I summoned Chuck again. "He's alive, but he has facial lacerations and what appears to be a comminuted fracture of his right leg."

"Goddammit! What else will go wrong?"

"Why? What's going on there?"

"Nada, man. The Jamestown targets had already abandoned ship. Their cabin is cleaned out and the manager says he doesn't know when they left. They were here last night and that's the last he saw of them."

"All right, then look for the Middle Eastern maid I told you about. She's a player and unless she skipped with the boys, she's around somewhere."

I went back to Candellera and applied a compress to his head. The blood had stopped, but although he was tougher than a two dollar steak, I could see the pain in his eyes. His face, however, refused to show it.

The paramedics were on the scene within minutes and once Candy was addressed and loaded, I accompanied him to County General.

What began as a slick, well-planned operation ended with three terrorists missing in action, a G-man in the hospital and serious wounds to the rest of our egos. As I was sure Assad took a bullet, I alerted the staff in the ER to look out for an Arab man with a big hole in him.

The extent of Candellera's injuries was as I expected, a badly displaced fracture of the lower leg, a concussion and of course the deep facial wounds. The good news was that he would survive and to a rough-and-tumble guy like him, they were just flesh wounds. As soon as I was allowed, I paid him a visit in ICU.

I stood at the foot of his bed and picked up the clipboard that contained his chart. Like I could actually read the physician's hen-scratching.

I must have startled Candy from a good dream brought on by the morphine, as his body jolted. He opened his eyes and in a guttural voice said, "What the hell are you doing?"

"Oh, nothing," I replied. "Just checking to see if you were going to die."

He closed his eyes again for a moment. "You're a shit head, McGowan."

"That's what they tell me, marine. Hey, you looked good out there today. Do you plan to take your act to the circus?"

Candy didn't appear to be amused. "I heard your shots after I went down. Did you nail the bastard?"

"I'm pretty sure I did, but he got away."

He brought his fist down hard on the mattress. *"Son of a bitch!"* I could tell he was not happy about the deal. "I thought you Special Ops guys were supposed to be crack shots."

"I thought you marines were supposed to be quick and agile."

Candellera shook his head, dismissively. "How about the other targets?"

"Gone before Chuck and crew got there."

"Well if that ain't a fine crock of monkey shit."

"Exactly."

Candy raised himself up on the pillow and apparently knocked off one of his EKG hookups. The machine let out a high-pitched signal and the monitor flat lined. A gaggle of nurses suddenly flew into the room and converged on the bed, thinking his ticker had stopped. When they discovered the problem, they re-hooked him, then turned and gave me dirty looks.

"*I* didn't touch a thing. I swear."

The head nurse who closely resembled Ernest Borgnine in drag jammed her finger into my chest and pushed me out the door. "And do not come back in here, sir."

Not on *her* shift, I wouldn't.

I went down to the cantina for a bottle of water and sat mulling over the fiasco. Blaming myself as much as anyone, I knew I could have handled the thing a hell of a sight better than I did. I wondered where the little prick went. For that matter, where did they all go? Hoping they didn't reorganize at Wolf Laurel, I called Adrianna on her cell, telling her to remain away. I would still meet her there at three. She again wanted to know why and I said I would explain later.

The next call I made was to Jack. His office said he had just left. His normal schedule was to work only half days on Saturdays. I did reach him on his cell and from our conversation, I got the impression he was laughing his ass off. I'm sure he was thinking that if it had been an all Bureau operation, it would have gone silky smooth. The terrorists would have all been where they were supposed to be, given up peacefully and sang their hearts out about their plans to blow up AmeriCan.

As I was still talking to Jack, Harlan Williams from the State Police showed up. The look on his face did not reflect a pleasure in seeing mine. I signed off and stood up to greet the lieutenant.

"Okay, Mr. McGowan, what the hell do you Feds think you're doing coming into this area taking on such a mission, putting the civilian populace in danger, and keeping every state and local authority in the dark about it? Have you people not ever heard of professional courtesy, not to mention law enforcement decorum?"

Well, I guess not. That's a new one on me.

"Look, Lieutenant, this mission was classified. Besides the President, the State Department and Attorney General, no one except this task force knew the particulars." I didn't tell him I had clued Jack in on the deal. But Jack needed to know so that he could set about protecting AmeriCan, the citizens of Charleston and Diane.

"Uh *huh*. I think that's a pile of horseshit. When were you planning telling us what's going on?"

"Well, you did get a call didn't you? We asked you to run down our escaping terrorist."

"I see. You botch your operation, let three suspects escape and then you call us to help you find them. Like we're the Lost and Found department."

Well it just seems all crazy when you say it like that, Harlan.

"Okay. Maybe it *didn't* go so well; but now is not the time to mix words. So, is there any luck finding the Nissan?"

Williams looked at me derisively and sighed. He then took two quarters from his pocket and dropped them in the vending machine for a cup of coffee. "Nothing yet. We have the APB out. I understand you may have winged the guy."

"I'm pretty sure of it. I alerted the ER here. Can you do the same with clinics and doctor's offices as well? Also, we'll be looking for a Valley Community professor named Navab Abouzar. We believe he's tied in with these guys if not their leader."

"You'll have to spell that for me. Do you have his address?"

"Just somewhere in Crows. We have a route number, but no box number. Perhaps you can check with the Virginia State Police."

"Okay," replied Williams. "But you see how this works? You tell me things; I help you catch bad guys."

I *got* it, Harlan. Don't be so condescending.

Chuck, Jeff and Ty and I sat on the veranda at Wolf Laurel licking our wounds and lamenting our failures. Our morale had been quelled, our confidence defeated. With the team listening in, I took the opportunity to break the news to Byrd. As gingerly as I could, sugar-coating my capsule of the events with words like 'unfortunate' and 'unexpected,' I dropped it all on him. The score was terrorists-3 and Zulu-0. Actually, we were minus one, considering Candy was in the hospital. I thought I actually heard the gears grinding in Byrd's head, but suspect it was only the sound of his teeth chewing on that old pipe of his.

"I had hoped this would have gone down cleanly and successfully, Bruce," he said. "I suppose you now realize these people will remain underground until their planned day of attack. We had our opportunity here; now you tell *me* what we could have done differently." Byrd was never a man to berate or to point a finger of blame when exercises failed to achieve results; but his well-minced words and intonation had a way of making one feel lower than snake poop. And we did, anyway.

"I have no excuses, sir." That was the response I learned years ago in the Army after I had screwed something up. "Timing is everything. We probably should have raided the nests a couple of days ago. Obviously, they were onto me, and as I knew they *would* do, they jumped ship. Assad Mohammed had apparently loaded up and was on his way out to leave for good when we intercepted him. His room is cleaned out."

"Lovely."

"Another thing, boss, airplanes will be used somehow in the terrorist attack. I'm convinced of that, given the lessons. Suggest the FAA and FBI be alerted so that all airports and private operations are placed on notice to watch for these guys."

"Done." He paused for a moment. "Find them, Bruce. Engage all counterparts and turn over all the stones. This thing got away from us in a hurry. My boss will not be happy about it. The team will go to the capital city to hook up with friend Jack by 1700 tomorrow if the element does not materialize in your area. Keep this tightly wound and tell the locals to not engage the media. We don't want an epidemic of panic. Call me with your results ASAP. Got it?"

"I copy." I would've said 'Have a nice day, boss,' but he was already gone. I closed my cell phone and looked at the other three who had taken on the appearance of statues while I was getting reamed by Birdman. "We need to get out and beat the bushes, guys. If we don't find them by tomorrow evening at 1700, you all are to dispatch to Charleston to collaborate with the Bureau and wait for further from Byrd."

"Where do you think they went, Bruce?" asked Chuck.

"I have a feeling they're in some kind of staging area with this professor guy. They could be back in the woods somewhere or on their way to Charleston. Every cop in the state is now looking for them and their cars. I think we need to start combing the Crows area to look for any evidence of a residing Mr. Abouzar. It's possible that with the cursory address he gave the school, he may not even live around there. But they're all somewhere they can hide their vehicles, such as a barn or residence with a garage. Chuck, we need a chopper in here to recon the entire county as necessary. Look for a white and a black car together and check out any vehicles under tarps. We may be wasting our time in Crows, but suggest we go house-to-house first and ask around. I'll check the White Sulphur post office to see if he has rented a box. I'll also get back with the college Dean and perhaps Valley's President to see if I can gather more information about him."

"I'll go on ahead with Jeff and Ty," replied Chuck. "Suggest we meet up back at my room at 1900 and then we'll do this again tomorrow. Bruce, I guess you'll stay in touch with your Bureau and State counterparts for their updates."

Team Zulu dejectedly set out for White Sulphur Springs and a rendezvous point to meet the chopper which was dispatched out of Washington at 1345 hours. I stayed at the inn and called Paul LeMer to obtain contact information on the President, Dr. Angela Stalnaker. His information was short and sweet. Mostly short.

Upon securing the address, I drove immediately out to the President's house, finding it to be a large, grand Victorian set high on a hill off of Route 60 in Lewisburg. I introduced myself and told her up front that Professor Abouzar was a suspect in a police matter. She seemed surprised at hearing that, but said unfortunately she knew very little about him. She did say that he was a very bright and pleasant man, passionately committed to the education of his students, but otherwise very private, socially. He had a Doctorate in International Studies and the kind of credentials that would allow him to teach in most any major university. Immediately before coming to the community college he was on the faculty at Seton Hall. I wondered if he had had previous contact with the New Jersey boys and arranged not only for bringing them to the area but their admission to Valley as well. He would see to their continuing education in Terrorism 101.

Dr. Stalnaker gigged me for a little more information about why I was after the professor, but I side-stepped her questions with questions of my own. I could see the concern about Abouzar in her face. She asked if she should go on to the college, pull his personnel shield and see if there was any other information of significance. Of course, I already *had* his information. All she knew was that he lived in the Crows, Virginia area, but didn't know where. Shaking her head she added, "He seems like a very passionate and precipitate man ... working one-on-one on his own time with students outside the classroom, especially those teetering on a failing grade. He even helped us out in our booth at the Labor Day picnic."

"Do you ever monitor any of his classes to ... you know ... review the content of his teaching? A course like *Multicultural Issues* opens up a myriad of possibilities when it comes to filling young people's heads."

"Is that what this is about, Mr. McGowan? Is our government afraid he may be poisoning our students' minds with some kind of political or Islamic propaganda?"

I dodged the question and fired another. "Is he required to teach in harmony with a specific syllabus and curriculum?"

Obviously I was being rude in not responding to her question as she shot me a glare. "Yes, we provide the text and generic syllabus for all instruction and require adherence. And no, I personally have not sat in on any of his classes." I could tell she was getting a little testy with me, so I needed go in a different direction to keep our dialogue flowing.

"Doctor, these are just questions that will enable me to learn a bit more about the man. Do you know anything about his life outside of the college?"

"As I said, Professor Abouzar is a very private man, Mr. McGowan. He teaches his classes and goes over-and-above with some of his kids *after* those classes; but then he leaves the campus. I guess he goes home like every other brain that's been picked and drained by our students. I don't know much else about him." She paused a moment. "May I ask again why you are looking for Dr. Abouzar?"

She was not about to give up on her inquisition.

"It's a matter of about a hundred unpaid parking tickets, ma'am." I lied.

"What? But you said you work for the State Department. Why is the Federal government interested in parking tickets?"

A good question indeed. Now if I could just think of a good answer.

"Interstate flight to avoid prosecution, which is an even more serious offense for a foreign national. It will affect his visa status, you know."

She reflected on that. "Oh." Her eyes took on a bit of a frown while digesting the information. "I suppose that could be a big deal; but now you have me fearful there may be more to him than meets the eye."

Very perceptive, Madam President.

I really thought at that time I needed to bring our little conversation to a close before I started running out of fabrications *and* credibility.

"I understand your concerns, ma'am, but I don't believe he'll be back to finish out his classes."

"How do you know that?"

"He knows we're after him and keeps on the move."

"To avoid prosecution for parking tickets?"

"Sounds ridiculous, doesn't it?" And it did. I was surprised someone with her education was swallowing this pony poop.

If for some reason he does materialize, I will ask that you call me right away. And be careful, Dr. Stalnaker." I reached into my pocket. "Here's my card."

She nodded. A renewed look of worry clouded her face. "Thanks, Mr. McGowan; I will." Then she mumbled, "I must say, this is all very confusing, not to mention disconcerting ..."

It was *more* than disconcerting to me. *Exasperating* would be a more appropriate word. But there was no question; we had to pull out all stops to find this guy.

I met Adrianna back at Wolf Laurel on the veranda at three as planned and she had Lottie Throckmorton with her. There were looks of fear and apprehension on both of their faces. I was still dressed in my SWAT looking garb and both women stared at the Glock in my shoulder harness. I'm sure to them it was like they were looking at a different person than they had gotten to know ... like the old Skip had died and come back as the Terminator.

"Okay, what's going on, Skip? You have scared us half to death." She quickly checked over her place as if to look for bullet holes.

"Please, ladies. Have a seat. I do need to explain to you what came down this morning."

Adrianna and Lottie did as asked and took up two adjacent rockers. I pulled up a straight-back chair and sat backwards in it, facing them.

"First of all, I need to come clean with you all about some things. I do work for the government, but I am a counter-terrorist agent, working in the Department of State. Adrianna, I did tell you that I investigate possible subversives, but my job actually goes beyond that. I not only hunt down terrorists, but I *bring* them down as well ... anyway I can. I've been watching the Arab man who occupied the room down the hall from you, Lottie. We suspected from the onset he was a terrorist and I have been attempting for the past week or so to gain information on him as regards a possible plot against the American people. I just hope this hasn't upset you ladies."

Then I specifically looked at Adrianna. "There are some things you really don't need to know. But I *will* tell you this. A team of my folks came here today to take Assad Mohammed into custody along with the other two, and maybe a fourth, who are, or were, in a motel in White Sulphur. Unfortunately, they were a step ahead of us and cleared out before we could get to them. But another agent and I did drive upon Assad as he was leaving here. He struck my partner with his vehicle and put him in the hospital. The good thing for you all is that Assad is gone and apparently so is the danger."

Adrianna sat without word and stared at me. I couldn't tell at first whether she was angry or just disappointed with me, but she was certainly stunned. She knew pretty much about what I had been doing, but I'm sure she thought I was just gathering enough information on Assad to get him deported … if in fact I found out that he *was* a bad guy. I knew she didn't like the idea of a possible raid on her place, but mostly, I think it was both my deceptiveness and the scope and depth of my position with the Department of State that surprised her. She pulled on her lower lip and looked away from me.

"I'm sorry, Adrianna. I didn't intend to put you all in danger, but this thing just developed as I went along. I really didn't know how it would turn out … whether I would find nothing or whether we'd find that he was in fact a terrorist."

"Fine, Skip," she replied with a soft but biting tone. "I guess you were just doing your job." She then paused. "Was I just part of that job, too? A means to your end? You convince me to keep him here so that you would gain enough time to set something like this up? I don't like being a pawn on your State Department chess board."

The questions stunned me a little. "If you're thinking that way, Adrianna, then you've got it wrong. I didn't stay here to get to know you as a means or convenience just so I could get the goods on Assad and this sleeper cell. It was purely incidental that I chose to stay here. And then you … we … happened. You have to know I really do care about you, Adrianna … I think even more than you may realize." I picked up her hand and held it tightly. "I hope we're still good here."

Lottie spoke up. "Of course you are, dear. Adrianna, I know the way this man looks at you. And you, him. He's doin' his job, that's all. And you, my dear, are in no way part of his job."

I looked back at Adrianna and smiled, devilishly. "Yeah. What *she* said."

She looked away for about ten seconds, then back to me. "I'm not okay with this by a long shot, Mr. McGowan. You have a lot of making up to do, you know. But I guess we can talk about this later. That is, unless you intend to remain … how shall I put this … less than forthcoming?"

I gave her a reassuring smile and then turned back to Lottie. "Sorry you were exposed to all this, too, Lottie."

"Don't you worry none about me, Skip. I'm just glad you found out about this man. I hope you eventually hunt him down and bring him to justice. And the rest of them, too."

I think Adrianna *was* okay with it all … or at least *would* be once she thought about it. I told her I had to get out and continue my search for the suspects, but would be back later. One thing I had to do was get her out of my head for a while. She was in there enough as it was. I didn't need to add her displeasure with me to the list.

From the look of Assad's room, it was obvious he was prepared to leave anyway. I think he and the others had actually planned to vacate about the same time. The room had been cleaned and was spotless. His soiled linens and towels had been neatly stacked on the floor by the bed. When he left out, whether or not he had affirmed that I was moving in on him, obviously seeing Candellera spooked him and that's when he reacted. The question was ... did each of the suspects leave to consolidate in a staging area? The attack on AmeriCan could go down over the weekend or perhaps early the next week. I knew the Air National Guard would be scanning the skies over Charleston. The FBI would have AmeriCan covered and the State Police would be patrolling the roadways in the Kanawha Valley looking for the terrorists' vehicles.

LT Williams called me back about six and told me that Abouzar's vehicle was registered in Virginia and was a 1999 Dodge Caravan, blue in color, tag number TAY-513. His address was again listed generically as the star route with no house or box number. I called Chuck and gave him Abouzar's vehicle information. They were still canvassing on Highway 202 also known as Star Route 58, going house to house and now looking for the van as well. No one knew of anyone with the professor's description living along the route or on any of the intersecting county roads. Chuck said he and the boys would give it up at dark and begin again on Sunday morning. I begged off on meeting them later at the Roche.

I swung back by the hospital to check on Candellera. He looked pitiful, bruised and battered, and his right leg suspended by a pulley and cable. But he was in a hell of a sight better spirits, all things considering. Ernest Borgnine was off shift, so I knew I would live yet another day. I filled Candy in on our canvassing activity. And then I told him that Byrd was going to have him airlifted to Walter Reed on Tuesday, providing he was able to be moved. He wasn't too happy with that. I guess he thought his leg and head would heal overnight and he'd be joining us for a power breakfast in the morning before we took down the terrorists.

After driving around aimlessly, looking for the three vehicles, I returned to my quarters at a little after seven. I think Adrianna had been worried about me, because when she heard my Suburban pull into the parking lot, she came out to meet me. I threw off my shoulder harness and carried it and the weapon in my left hand. I then took hold of Adrianna's dainty pinkies with my right. She eyed the Glock again and since she hadn't seen me with it before today, I'm sure it was all very strange and uncomfortable for her. Her image of me had obviously changed. I was no longer the frivolous, good-natured romantic interest wearing the slightly older face of a long-departed hometown boy. Of course, I wasn't around her when I was with the Bureau. She would have understood then that because of what I did, I had a badge and a gun and she would have taken me for what I was. But I had projected myself quite differently over the past ten days and she obviously didn't know what to make of me.

I accompanied Adrianna to her room and as she went to the fridge to get me a beer, I slipped in behind her and placed my arms around her waist.

"Why do you do this, Skip? Why this kind of work?"

I sighed and pulled her tightly against me. "Because ... I'm only one of a few who *can* do this."

She didn't respond.

"Look, sweetheart, whatever or whoever you think I am now, I'm still the same person I was. And I'm still crazy about you."

She gently leaned her head back into my chest and I kissed her hair. It smelled freshly shampooed. She then turned around in my arms and kissed me tenderly, playfully, and gently bit my lower lip. Her body was warm and I began to heat up; but the cold air from the still open refrigerator provided a counterbalance.

"And you, sir, are all I think about these days. Why does the guy I'm falling for have to be some kind of government spy?"

"You're falling for me?"

"Maybe," she replied, smiling and teasing with her eyes.

"Well, maybe I can say the same for me."

She giggled. "Do we sound like a couple of high schoolers?"

"Hey, I'm still a high schooler inside, you know."

"I know. Especially inside here." She thumped me on my noggin. "And here." Then she pressed her lower body into my stiffening loins. We were compelled to take the conversation down the hall. In our close encounter of the blissful kind, I found her immensely satisfying considering this had been a most *un*satisfying day.

"Well, so much for the dessert," she said, smiling. "How about some supper?"

I rolled over and checked out the clock on her night stand. "Eight-thirty? Where did the evening go?"

She pulled me back into her and said, "If you don't remember, I will just have to show you the instant replay."

"Oh, yeah. Now it's coming back to me."

A little after nine and craving chocolate for some strange reason, I asked Adrianna if she had a Hershey bar or a Snickers.

"Not up here, but I keep candy bars behind the counter downstairs for kids sometimes." She jumped out of bed. "Let's go get one."

We threw on our clothes and went to the lobby where we found Lottie in the dining room munching on some apple slices.

"Hi, kids," she said. "Hope you don't mind, Adrianna, I got an apple from the Frigidaire. I got a little hungry a while ago."

"Not at all," she said. "We're a little hungry, too. Both of us missed supper."

"But," I added. "We had dessert."

Adrianna gave me her *don't go there* look.

"Why don't I grill us up some pancakes? I like breakfast sometimes for supper."

"Oh, that sounds good, "Lottie replied. "Of course, that will lay heavy on my stomach for hours."

"No problem. We'll just all sit up together and talk."

That's easy for you to say, Adrianna, I thought. I'm the one here that needs beauty sleep.

I actually did sit up talking with Adrianna and Lottie until well after eleven-thirty. We talked some about the events of the day, but I soon changed the subject. I don't pick at old scabs. I was more interested in Lottie's history. She grew up in Prince Edward County, Virginia, and the year after the schools were integrated in 1954, the county suspended all public education. She was a junior in high school when that happened and was not able to finish out her education. All the White kids had opportunities to continue their education at Prince Edward Academy at a very reasonable cost. Blacks were not invited to apply nor were approved when they did. For five years, until the Federal government stepped in, an entire generation of Black children went uneducated. One of those who escaped was Lottie Nelson. Her church was able to make arrangements to have her placed with a Quaker family in Iowa who saw to her education.

Years later, Lottie had become an advocate for civil rights and was photographed with President Johnson just after the passing of the Civil Rights Act of 1964. Shortly thereafter she moved to New York, became a councilwoman and was ultimately elected to a New York congressional seat. As she had told me a few days ago, she relocated to Ninety Six, South Carolina to be close to her grandbabies.

"So, Skip, do you intend to be with the government the rest of your working life?"

"Not sure, Lottie. I'm getting tired of being a government man. I've actually been one in some capacity since I was twenty-two years old. I'm thinking I'd like to only work a couple more years and then chuck it all. What I'd like to do is maybe something completely away from government work, like hiring on as a swimsuit model photographer for *Sports Illustrated*."

She laughed. "Can't quite picture you doing anything like that. But I'm sure whatever you finally retire doing, you'll be doing something worthwhile. You've got a lot of work years left, so you'll figure it out. I remember a quote by George Eliot: "It's never too late to be who you might have been.""

"Unless you're a *has been* like yours truly. But you, Lottie … you have lived a significant life. You have fought nobly and selflessly for people of color."

"I have worked so hard in doing my part to assure that *every* American enjoys every freedom that the Constitution guarantees its people and that we can live without fear and persecution. And I tell you one thing, Skip. I may not be as strong and influential as I once was, but I'll be damned if I will condone any son-of-a-bitch to come into this country and threaten the freedom and safety of U.S. citizens. I would fight like I have never fought before to keep that from happening. You find these bastards, Skip, and you stop them from hurting even one American."

My heart was exploding with admiration for this woman, the beacon of freedom that she was. And then I couldn't help but smile, hearing all that profanity spouting from the sweet little woman. For the first … no, second time today, I felt good … not to mention *full* from the hot pancakes. But it was the warm conversation I had with Lottie that allowed this day of 'unfortunate events' to end on a high note.

I stayed the night again with Adrianna. Now neither of us cared how it looked; and certainly Lottie didn't. If Birdman knew he was paying for a room I wasn't occupying, my next lodging on the road would be the rear compartment of my Suburban. But we laid together talking, holding and caressing one another for an hour or so. And then after she was quiet awhile, from out of the blue came a subject that had ended abruptly a few nights before.

"He was a wonderful child, Skip. Sweet, always happy, loved puzzles and could solve the Rubik's Cube in five minutes. He wasn't athletic, which somewhat disappointed his dad, but he made up for it as a brilliant student."

She went on about Johnny, this time without the tears, and as I held her, I almost felt the catharsis in her body. She said that Mason was never right after their son died and although the official cause of her husband's death was a heart dissection stemming from rheumatic fever when he was a child, she almost knew he had died from a broken heart instead. She had been alone since Mason died. Within weeks of his funeral, her parents moved to St. Petersburg.

"I had a beautiful life once ... like a lovely and colorful stained-glass window. But then it got shattered. I've tried piecing together all the broken fragments and making some kind of mosaic out of them to fill up the big, gaping hole in my life. I really don't have very much to do that with. I have my friends and I have Wolf Laurel. Somehow that's not enough." She paused. "But I do still have all the beautiful pieces in here somewhere ..." She tapped her heart.

All I could do was nod. Any words of consolation I had would only sound trite and empty anyway.

After a moment she continued. "Our minister said that it was God who chose the time for Johnny to go. Why would God do that? Why a child ... a sweet and precious little boy who had an entire life to live? Why couldn't God wait until he was old and I was long gone?"

For a long while, as we lay face to face, scarcely a foot apart, I kept my eyes steadfastly on hers, still silent. And then when my words finally came, my voice seemed to crack a little. "I used to listen from another room in the funeral home the breaking of people's hearts as they spilled out their grief onto one another … and onto Dad. They wondered 'why', too. Some of the people who had died were younger … husbands, wives, adult children … although I can't recall if there was ever a child. I would have remembered that."

Her eyes remained stoic and glistening in the wanly light, but she didn't reply.

I went on. "Maybe … God just loved Johnny so much, He wanted him to go and be with Him. I guess that's His choice, although we can't understand it."

"I'd say that was rather selfish of Him, if that's the case. He gave our son to us and then, just like that (she snapped her fingers), He decides He doesn't want us to have him any longer. How cruel is *that*?"

She turned her face away. "Every morning I get up asking Him that. Every Sunday I go to His *house* and ask Him that."

I searched her eyes again, allowing her vexations a moment to digest. I had no more words. It was as though someone or something had crept inside my throat and stolen my voice. With the backs of my fingers I brushed her silken hair, following it down to the point where it lay on the pillow.

Adrianna smiled, weakly. "Okay, McGowan, enough of this sad stuff. I go there too much as it is." She then rose up and reached for her bathrobe, wrapping it quickly around her as though the baring of her soul had made her feel self-conscious.

She went to the bathroom for a few moments and then returned and sat back down on the edge of the bed.

"Thanks, Skip," she said in a low voice.

"For what," I whispered back.

"I guess for just being here … for coming back into my life once again. You spending these few days with me … it's been like a fresh breath of air. Things that I have shared with you I haven't even talked about with most of my girlfriends. You make it so easy for me to let out things that have lain on my heart these years."

I smiled at her. In a strange way, I didn't mind exposing my seldom seen soft side and serving as a special 'girlfriend.' I thought at that moment I had never felt so close to anyone as I was her. I pulled her back down beside me and scooted my body up against hers.

We were both silent, but still holding one another, watching the soft moonlight through the window create a beautiful and sensual ambiance especially for us. Then after a while as she slept deeply I watched her chest swell and retract. Her lips were slightly parted and her warm breath smelled sweet, feeling much like a light tropical breeze on my cheek. If this wasn't love, I would never in my life know what it felt like.

Chapter 20

Lieutenant Williams called mid-morning on Sunday just after Adrianna left for church. He volunteered there had been no sightings of any of the three vehicles and we both agreed they were probably parked under a canopy of trees back in the woods or in someone's garage. The APB hit all wires and there were pullovers everywhere from Lewisburg to Charleston. What few Arabs there were in the adjacent counties had unfortunately been profiled and stopped by law enforcement; some of the people were found to be Hispanic and even Native Americans. The word as to why Middle Easterners were being sought was not explained to law enforcement, much to their frustration; but I was pleased that Harlan Williams was true to *his* word that information about the probable terrorist plot was not being revealed.

Chuck and boys did spend the day covering the White Sulphur-Crows area by chopper as planned and I combed Lewisburg and Western Greenbrier in my Suburban. Still nothing. Not a trace. It was as though the terrorists had dissipated into the atmosphere.

I had suggested earlier to Adrianna that she get a locksmith in to change both the lock on the front door and on the Magnolia room. Assad had neglected to turn in his key before he left out, the bozo. He didn't even have the courtesy to tell his hostess how much he enjoyed his stay.

At four the Zulu team met one last time on the veranda at Wolf Laurel. Needless to say, we were not sitting around with joined hands singing *Kumbaya*. We were all a bit solemn and for the umpteenth time we rehashed what we had, but mostly what we *didn't* have. It was like a replay of the old TV show *Where Are They Now?* But more like *Where Were **We** Now?* After a while we were reduced to talking over old times at the FBI. We sounded like a bunch of old VFW bench warmers telling war stories. Chuck then announced that he had had enough and after they would swing by to check on Candy at the hospital and draw little hearts on his cast, they would take off for Charleston.

It was time to give Byrd an update. He wasn't going to like our Day Two results. Again.

"You want to call him or shall I?" Chuck said.

"You have to get your marching orders before lighting out for Charleston, you know, so why don't *you?*" I replied.

"Yeah, but you have a way with words; and anyway, he likes you better than me."

Why did I suddenly think it was 1960 again and my little brother and I were trying to agree who would own up to our dad for something we both did? In this case, what we didn't do ... locate the targets.

"All right. *I'll* call Dad," I said.

"What?"

"Never mind." I speed-dialed Byrd's number and he answered, gruffly.

"No luck, Boss. They've all but disappeared."

"That's not good news, Bruce."

I assumed we could now talk in the clear without metaphors as the mission got declassified in a hurry. "You know, I've been thinking. I believe it was their plan all along to leave their quarters yesterday morning and reconsolidate in hiding to gear up for their strike.

They may already be in the Charleston area, but somehow I don't think so. Unfortunately, Eastern West Virginia is so rural, mountainous and covered with triple canopy foliage, an army couldn't find these guys. And did I mention Greenbrier County has more caves than any other area of the state? Of course, a cave may make them feel right at home."

"Seems there's really nothing more you can do there. I can't allow you to remain there forever, you know. Who knows what their timetable is. It could be six months before they strike. These guys may also have set up a rural training base to rehearse their plan as they generally do over and over. If they can't be found, then our best recourse is a good defense. The Southern West Virginia Bureau has the Kanawha Valley covered and more specifically, AmeriCan. They will pick up the hunt. Plan to pack it in on Tuesday, Bruce. I want you here for a full brief at 0900 on Wednesday. Is Chuck there with you?"

"Yes, he is."

I switched the phone over to Chuck and after a few seconds he replied. "Yes, sir. Yes, sir. We're leaving right now." He then pushed the phone to me.

"Should I not go to Charleston, as well?" I asked Mr. Byrd.

"No. Chuck and team have it covered. If the targets aren't found by the weekend, I'm sending them back to Washington. You, I need to see."

"Okay, I'll get back to Georgetown Tuesday and take a red eye out first thing Wednesday for your location."

He was silent for a while. I could hear the disappointment in his breathing. "Bruce, you do good work. Sorry you folks were not able to get a slam dunk on this."

"No sorrier than me, Boss."

I lost the call and knew he had hung up. I didn't even mind it this time. I hate failure and whether this was all or partially my fault or not, I did not like telling that man I couldn't get closure on the mission.

We all stood and after a group hug, the Zulu guys piled into their SUV.

"Stay in touch," said Chuck. He formed a gun with his thumb and index finger and made a clicking sound with his mouth. I returned fire with mine. As soon as their trailing dust rose and dissipated, I went back inside to my room to brood some more.

Monday I visited Candellera again and then drove around without design, hitting the community college parking lot, the airport and other places I had seen them frequent, but knowing they wouldn't be stupid enough to risk being anywhere near them. It would be a stroke of needed luck if I even saw one of their vehicles. I wondered how badly Assad was hit and who had treated him. The wound was probably not that serious or he wouldn't have been able to zip down Seven Bridges and out of sight.

Knowing that I would be leaving for Washington the next morning, I asked Adrianna out to dinner at Tavern 1785, where we had gone on our first date. It was there I told her that I'd be leaving in the A.M. She was quiet the rest of the evening ... not a pissed quiet, but a sad quiet. It was like it was the last day for us on campus and we would be going our separate ways after graduation. We went back to her place and after a nightcap, turned in. Neither of us wanted me to sleep in the room I had abandoned a few nights before. We made love again, but it was bitter-sweet love. And neither of us seemed to be into it.

She was so quiet and still, I thought she was asleep. Her face was faintly illuminated by the waning moon, but it was still light enough for me to see that her cheeks were moist. I kissed them and told her I *would* be back, somehow, someway. She turned over away from me without response and in only a couple of minutes she *was* asleep, breathing deeply and peacefully. It took me a while to get to sleep, and then at some point in the early morning hours I had the dream again. This time I saw that the child who stumbled out of the hooch was not a child at all. It was difficult at first to see the face through the smoke and fire. But gradually, as the face took form, I heard a helpless cry escape from its lips. It was the horrified face of Lionel Byrd.

Tuesday morning dawned cool and clear. I took a pre-breakfast jog around seven-thirty, showered, packed, and then joined Adrianna and Lottie for a bun and some coffee at the dining room table. As I would be leaving in a few minutes and Lottie would check out tomorrow, a mood of melancholy hung over the room like a pall. Adrianna was still quiet, but she did mention that a couple would be coming in later in the afternoon and she would place them in the Gardenia Room. As of Wednesday, her two favorite guests *ever* would be gone. Lottie patted her hand and said she *would* be back one day, and may even bring her grandkids with her. I would miss Lottie too. I felt we had struck up a special friendship as there were few people I had met in my life who were so genuine and humble. Of course, that was largely due to the circle I was used to running in,

But I knew that five minutes after I was on the road to Washington, I would be missing the beautiful mistress of Wolf Laurel. By the time I hit Georgetown, I would be ready to turn right around and come back. And the next day, when I was sitting in Mr. Byrd's office, likely receiving new marching orders, I would be thinking seriously about chucking it all and coming back to Greenbrier County to love and family and maybe some cushy security job. On the way out of town, though, I would stop by to see Joey and promise to make my visits more frequent. And that I would, primarily because of one Adrianna Wolf.

While we were sitting and talking, Lionel Byrd called me on the cell to fill me in on the most recent Interpol report he received. It seems one of the AmeriCan employees' names that I supplied him *was* on the hit list. Mouri Abasi, a chemical engineer and M.I.T. grad, happened to also be a graduate of the Dar al Islam 'school of terrorism' at the Beit Jalla Palestinian training camp in 1996. Obviously, this is one background check that had slipped through the crack. He was arrested the day before and in process of being interrogated in Guantanamo Bay. There were no documents or other information found on him or at his residence in Charleston's grand South Hills to connect him with any of *my* subjects. Whether he had repented of his sins since working at the plant remained to be determined. I suspected, however, his co-workers would not see him again. Maybe nobody would.

Seven days a week, the television on the wall in the dining room brought a dose of Fox News to the guests partaking of breakfast from as early as 6:30 until Adrianna shut it down sometime just after nine-thirty. We were actually paying little attention to the tube as its volume was down and the commentators, two men and a lone woman, appeared engaged in some friendly bantering. Adrianna was asking me about Caroline and perhaps when she finished her training, I could bring her back with me some time so that she could meet her. I glanced back at the screen and was alarmed to see smoke pouring from one of the World Trade Center towers.

"Hey, look at that," I said. "Looks like there's a fire at the World Trade Center."

Adrianna went over to the TV to turn it up and about the time she touched the volume button, I was stunned to hear from the commentators that a commercial aircraft had struck the tower. "Holy shit!" I exclaimed. "Did you hear that?"

Both women gasped. "Is that for real or a movie?" said Adrianna.

I couldn't respond, because I knew it was real. Then the female network anchor confirmed again our worst fears. "Oh, my God, people," she exclaimed. "An airliner has just slammed into one of the World Trade Center towers. We can only speculate that it was either due to pilot error or mechanical problems. There has to have been significant loss of life in both the airplane and the building."

"Those poor people," lamented Lottie. "I always feared a plane would some day go down in a highly populated area like New York."

But as we watched the tragic scenario unfold, suddenly we saw the second plane strike the other tower. The massive fireball carried completely through the depth of the building and out the other side. My brain initially refused to accept the fact that this was actually happening. And our faces frozen solid in horror reflected that denial.

It took me about three more seconds for it all to register. "God Almighty, it's a terrorist attack!" And three more seconds later, the last puzzle piece finally fell into place. I jumped to my feet and ran to my room for my Glock. Hustling back through, I tore past the women and yelled, "You all stay here and lock up. I'll be back when I can."

"Why? Where are you going?!" Adrianna exclaimed.

I didn't answer, but ran out the front door to the Suburban. Snatching the .308 from the rear compartment, I laid it on the passenger seat and spun out onto Seven Bridges. My first thought after digesting the New York tragedy was that Assad and the others had de-assed the area on Saturday for a major airport, boarded two commercial jets and took control of the cockpits to crash the aircraft into the towers. Yet, would they be able to assume control of 747s when they only trained on Cessnas? That's why on second thought I believed that the hijackers in New York were not them. But as it was all too clear that AmeriCan was going to be a target today, likely along with several other targets, I couldn't think of any place to go but to the Greenbrier County Airport.

I figured that Assad and his confederates were smaller fish, piranhas if you will, partnered with the school of sharks that attacked New York. But instead of *bombing* AmeriCan or crashing through the gate to explode their bomb, it was even more apparent that they had planned all along to fly the Cessnas *into* the deadly storage tanks, sending them and 100,000 Charlestonians into eternity. I didn't know why my gut sent me to the airport, but somehow I knew something would be happening there. If it wasn't already too late.

As my breakneck speed carried me there in less than ten minutes, Assad's words recorded in his journal nagged at me from the periphery of my brain. I had wondered about the significance of one sentence ... a sentence I earlier thought was pure metaphor ... *"By the wings of man we will achieve martyrdom ..."* Now the meaning was all too clear. Why in the hell I had not interpreted these words was already haunting me. If the terrorists did reach Charleston and carry out this catastrophic mission, these mere haunts would eventually dump me into a state of permanent abasement.

I slid into the parking lot and across the field directly to the flight academy. Holstering my Glock to my belt, I also grabbed the .308 from the seat and ran to the door. Given my warning to the FBI and FAA through Byrd, I thought there would have been guards or officers posted outside of the academy, but they were probably somewhere in the airport terminal.

With the .308 cradled in my right hand, I threw open the door to the academy with my left. The first thing I saw was a trail of blood which appeared to have been created by the dragging of a body through the back room doorway. Kicking open that door, I found a man dressed in security guard uniform. He was older, perhaps 65 or 70 with a crew cut and looked like he could have been a former Marine. The man's throat had been cut and blood still drained from the nasty gash at his jugular. His eyes were frozen open, reflecting the horror of the last moment of his life.

I then ran to the academy office where I found the bodies of both Ross and Helena. The brutal scene sickened me. Their throats had also been sliced. Helena's wound was so severe, she had been nearly decapitated. Her head remained attached to her neck by only a strand of muscle. I would have guessed that she put up one hell of a fight. I hated the grisly scene before me, but I hated these goddamned terrorists even more. I deduced from the still gushing blood that the butchery could not have occurred more than a couple of minutes before. My stomach turned over and my brain was suddenly rendered impotent. The immense adrenaline hit my heart with a burning flush, causing it to pound vehemently and my blood to thunder in my ears.

Tearing through the back door that led to the tarmac, I caught sight of two men, one making his way toward one of the Cessnas approximately two hundred yards away and the second already entering the cockpit of another plane. And that second man was Assad. He looked in my direction before closing the plane's door and signaled the man still walking. The second man appeared to be the one I referred to as Big Nose. Suddenly, as he spun around in my direction, he pulled a pistol from his belt. I quickly raised the .308 and fired a single round that caught the man squarely in the throat. Flesh and blood exploded violently between his jaw line and chest and he dropped like a brick.

Meanwhile, as Assad had already engaged the starter, the prop began buzzing. I fired one round through the Cessna's right door and then as it began to move away from me, I fired again, striking the tail section. I ran by Big Nose, not pausing to see if he was dead. I knew where my bullet had struck and didn't need to further inspect my handiwork.

Spying something resembling an open golf cart that pulled a train of baggage units, I jumped in, hit the starter and sped away at neck-jerking ten miles an hour across the tarmac to the runway where the Cessna would set up for take off. Rather than following it to the end of the strip, I drove in the opposite direction to intercept it as it took off. I was able to make the middle of the runway just as the Cessna started its takeoff run. When the wheels lifted off, the bird blasted across the eastern margin of the field, its noisy prop shredding the still air. I fired the first of two rounds into the engine compartment. After the second one hit, the plane immediately spat black smoke and sputtered. It was going nowhere. Assad was able to glide the plane off the end of the runway where it crashed into some scrub brush and flipped over.

My little cart was doing all it could as I pressed on in the direction of the wounded plane. When I was within a hundred yards, one of three bullets struck the cart, each arriving a split second before I heard three distant reports from what appeared to be a handgun. I swerved right and then left to make myself a more difficult target, and then caught sight of Assad running into the woods toward the highway. I stopped and fired several shots that I heard ricocheting into the oaks, unsure whether I nailed any part of him at all.

I figured he would be making a break for the road, so I shanked the cart off to the right across a small field, suddenly finding myself on the state highway and in the path of an oncoming semi. Pucker time. I swerved and the semi swerved after laying on his locomotive horn. It was a good miss. The truck went on, still blaring its horn and I rode further down the road looking to see if Assad had come out. About the same time a white Buick approached fifty or more yards to my front, Assad busted out of the tree line into the path of the car. The Buick skid to a stop and Assad brandished his handgun in the face of the driver, a woman. He quickly opened the driver's door and tossed the elderly woman onto the asphalt. Quickly he slid behind the wheel and gunned the car in my direction.

As I knew he was coming for me, I brought up the .308 and fired two rounds through the windshield. His head well below the steering wheel, my rounds zipped harmlessly by. As he was still bearing down on me, I grasped the rifle tightly and jumped out of the cart into a ditch, a split second before the car slammed into my ride. The impact catapulted the cart over me within inches of my head. By the time I crawled back out, the Buick was gone.

And then Farmer Brown came along in his '84 Dodge pickup. After he slowed cautiously to a stop to see what the commotion was, I ran to the driver's side of the truck and shoved my ID in his face. "Sir, I need your truck. There's a fugitive on the loose about a quarter mile ahead."

"But … I can't give you my truck. I don't keer if you are the law …"

I didn't have time to argue. "Get the hell out of the truck, sir!" I opened the door, grabbed him by his bib overalls and politely sat his ass on the road.

"You can't …" That's the last thing I heard from the man as I tromped the accelerator, laying rubber for fifteen feet.

After setting sail to the west on 219, I saw the rear end of the Buick exiting onto I-64 toward Charleston. I pulled my cell from its holster and dialed 911. A female operator answered promptly.

"Ma'am, please either 'patch me through to the West Virginia State Police or give me the number for the Lewisburg detachment."

"Sir, would you please identify yourself?"

"I'm a government agent, Bruce McGowan, and need that contact right away."

"And for the record, is there anything you need to report?"

"Yes, I will report your *ass* if you don't get them on the line and NOW!"

A wounded pause. "One moment, sir."

After a few moments I heard the voice of Herman Munster on the line. "Sergeant Storm here; how can I help you?"

"Damn, finally," I said. "Sergeant Storm, this is Bruce McGowan, the State Department agent from a couple of weeks ago. Do you recall?"

"Yes, sir, I do. What can I do for you?"

"I am in pursuit of a confirmed Arab terrorist who commandeered a white Buick Century traveling at a high rate of speed on I-64. I am in a blue Dodge pickup about a half mile back approximately five miles west of the Lewisburg exit heading west. You need to intercept the Buick and suggest you set up a roadblock near the Alta or Sam Black Church exits. The terrorist is enroute to Charleston, possibly carrying a bomb."

"Does this have anything to do with what happened at the World Trade Center and Pentagon today?"

"The Pentagon?"

"Yes. You didn't hear? Terrorists flew a plane into the building killing a great number of people."

"*Son-of-a bitch!*" I screamed. But after a moment I calmed down a bit and replied. "I didn't know that, Sergeant. I've been busy chasing *this* asshole. Yeah, I think there *is* a connection. You will find three DOAs out at the Ross Flight Academy at the Greenbrier Airport and a terrorist on the tarmac with my bullet in his throat. You need to get people out there to secure the scene. And get the roadblock set ASAP, please."

"Roger, sir. I'll dispatch units to intercept."

"Tell them he's armed, but to watch out for an explosive device also. He may set it off if he gets cornered."

"Got it. Out."

The old pickup was doing all it could, but the Buick was not a Vette either, so I managed to stay with him at just over a hundred miles an hour.

My cell phone rang and it was Chuck. He was calling from Jack's office in Charleston. "Bruce, I assume you've been following the WTC event?"

"I just saw it earlier and took off to the Greenbrier Airport, Chuck. I got there in time to stop two Cessnas from taking off. One bad guy is KIA and I'm chasing the other one. The locals are setting up a roadblock west of Lewisburg on I-64."

"Bruce. Byrd would have been in the World Trade Center north tower."

"Oh, Jesus. I didn't even think about that." I let it sink in a moment. "Since his office was on the fifteenth floor, maybe he got out."

"Knowing him, he probably stayed to help people out and went down with the building."

"What do you mean 'went down?'"

"Both buildings collapsed, Bruce. Thousands were burned or crushed. Al-Qaeda has already taken the credit for the thing."

I felt at that moment I couldn't get my breath and found myself sobbing.

"Bruce?"

Suddenly at the Sam Black Church exit Assad must have spotted the stopped cars in advance of the roadblock. He swerved onto the shoulder, passed the cars, struck a State Police cruiser on the exit lane and continued west on Route 60 toward Big Sewell. I snapped my cell shut and gave pursuit past the damaged patrol car and onto the two-lane behind him.

I flipped open my cell and got Storm on the line again. "Sergeant, I'm still in pursuit. He blasted past your roadblock and is going west on Route 60 toward Rupert. He's determined by hook or crook to get to Charleston. Need to set a new roadblock before he gets into the more congested areas in these small towns. Set up somewhere before Rupert."

"I copy."

About a mile further west, as we approached a hill, the Buick slowed behind a coal truck going about thirty-five which allowed me to close the gap. Each time Assad attempted to pass him, he found a curve and an on-coming car. Thank God for West Virginia mountain roads. I felt this was the time to make my move. Now within two car lengths, I waited until his vehicle entered a left hand curve again and plowed into the left rear corner of the Buick, sending it into a spin and carrying it down an embankment off the right side of the road. The car then T-boned a large oak on the passenger side, expelling Assad through the open back glass that had been shattered when my rounds I had fired earlier into the windshield had gone on through. The remaining shards of glass lacerated his body in a dozen places. He first landed onto the trunk lid, and then slid off onto the ground, leaning partially against the rear wheel.

I stopped the pickup on the shoulder of the road and with Glock drawn, moved cautiously down the thirty foot embankment. Assad lay writhing in pain, partially covered by a clump of weeds. His white shirt was torn half off, revealing a large section of gauze taped to his left shoulder. I *knew* I had bagged him at Wolf Laurel.

Around his waist was what appeared to be an explosive device strapped onto him with duct tape. On his left side was a triggering mechanism similar to the one I had found in his compadres' cabin. He was also laden down with C-4. Seeing that he had in his right hand a Beretta, I commanded, "Lose the gun, Assad!"

Weakly, he raised the gun and swung it in my direction, but I fired a round into his *right* shoulder, causing the Beretta to drop from his hand. Blood immediately spurted from the wound and I suspected I had hit an artery. He grimaced in pain and grit his teeth together. Then he began to drill me out with his steely, hateful eyes. It was a battle of stone-cold stares for a few moments. And for some reason there was a strange anticipatory stillness in the air.

Now bleeding profusely from the cuts on his face as well as from the .40 caliber round in his shoulder, Assad spoke in a feeble, garbled voice. "You are a filthy bastard, McGowan, and I will see that you are in Hell, just like the New York infidels are this very day."

"Hell may be waiting for me, prick, but I will guarantee that you *and* your chieftain, Bin Laden, the Son of Satan himself, will get there long before I do." Blood from Assad's right shoulder wound was now pooling beside him. "Where's your leader, the professor, and the other asshole."

"I would die before I tell you anything, infidel."

"I can arrange that at any time. Tell me where they are, Assad. You're running out of time *and* out of blood. I can save your life with just a couple of words."

"I am not afraid to die. Allah has many rewards for me."

"Like those 72 virgins? Tsk, Tsk, Assad. Have *you* ever been fed a load of camel shit. There's a very good reason they're all still virgins, you know. They're ugly as hell and covered with boils. Your Allah has a hell of a sense of humor."

"You blaspheme the name of Allah by the very opening of your mouth." With that, he lifted his left hand in the direction of the triggering device.

"Don't do it, Assad, or in two seconds you will be riding your horse straight *into* the gates of Hell. You failed in your plot to kill thousands of innocent people, so no reward for you. No Jesus, no Allah. But, when you stand before the one true God, you will *damn* sure get what's coming to you."

"Brave words for a dead man," he replied. His face wreaked of pain as he continued the hand across his body. But before he could place his fingers on the device, I pumped two rounds into his heart just inches above the C-4 body wrap. His torso flinched with each thud and his hand dropped harmlessly back to his side. I heard him exhale one long, sighing breath and then he was still.

"Ma'assalama, Assad," I said, maintaining my stance and aim for a few seconds. Then I moved toward his body to assure he had not been wearing a bullet-proof vest that may have stopped my slugs. Bright scarlet plumes of blood gushed from the tight shot group right at the heart. He was dead, all right, and likely catching his first whiff of sulphur.

The coal truck driver, who in his side mirror had seen Assad's vehicle plunge down the embankment and had obviously later heard the report of my two shots, stood at the top of the hill. He called to me, "What's going on down there?"

"Don't worry about it, sir," I replied, holstering my Glock. "Just dumping some garbage, that's all."

What continued to bother me was that the man I called Baldy and the Valley professor were still out there and likely positioned to continue the strike on AmeriCan should Assad and Big Nose fail, which they did, dead that they were.

I called Jack's office and although his assistant tried to put me off, saying he had been on the phone for the past hour with Washington, I explained who I was again and that I had just taken out two terrorists. I got the impression she thought I was some kind of nut or glory hound and made the whole thing up. "No, really," I told her. "Just put him on. He'll want to talk with me."

Jack finally came on the line and I filled him in on my day so far at the office. When I conveyed my concern about the third terrorist and the teacher, he said not to worry about one of them. A man identified as Ahmed Omari was spotted and taken into custody by an agent on a rocky pinnacle overlooking the AmeriCan plant. He looked just a little too suspicious sitting there with an SA-7 missile on his shoulder. The man had somehow evaded the locals while driving Assad's Nissan the night before on back roads from Lewisburg to Charleston. Jack said if it hadn't been for my brilliant analysis of the plot, my speculation about the check-valve gunner and my dogged persistence, they would never have thought to add the high ground on the south to their protective barrier around the factory. Well maybe the word wasn't 'brilliant,' but it was something similar. Ahmed had been taken out with a single sniper's bullet through the shoulder that had supported the missile. But he did manage to survive. Unlike Khalid (you remember DAG), they did find identification on him … his student ID from Valley Community.

It was now close to noon and after the State Police arranged for road kill removal, I thought to call Joey's cell to ask him to go by and check on the ladies at Wolf Laurel, but he didn't answer. I also called the inn for Adrianna, but there was no answer on her cell or the house phone. It caused me immense concern that I was unable to reach both of them, considering the Arab teacher was still out there somewhere.

Just after twelve thirty, I limped the old truck back onto 219 and to the airport where I had left my farmer friend sitting in the middle of the asphalt. The parking lot was flooded with State and County vehicles plus two government cars which likely belonged to an agency team from the Southwest Virginia FBI. Obviously, everyone was either inside the terminal or the flight academy working the grisly scene, except two troopers, one of which stopped me as I pulled into the lot. I flashed my State Department ID, told him I was looking for Lieutenant Williams, and he said to park "over there," which was ironically the space beside of my Suburban. The trooper eyed my Dodge Ram, wondering, I'm sure, as to what a State Department agent was doing driving a beat up old pickup.

I took another moment to ring Joey's and Adrianna's cells and there were still no answers. I then called Cora at the house and she said Joey was at the funeral home as far as she knew. So, I called the shop. Lester Basham, Joey's associate, said he arrived about noon at the shop and both Joey and the family car were gone and didn't know where. It did seem rather strange that I wasn't able to reach either Joey or Adrianna, and now that Lester told me Joey was missing in action, I began to get concerned.

And then something else entered my brain as I sat waiting to go in to talk with Williams. I knew Assad had discovered my true last name from Adrianna's ledger ... and that had stayed with me. I had no doubt he and the others had figured out my connection with the funeral home and Joey. My blood was running cold again.

Chapter 21

Instead of going into the flight academy to give Williams a personal account of my day's work, I transferred to the Suburban and drove out to Wolf Laurel. Upon entering the parking lot I saw that the McGowan and Sons Continental was there. My mind now eased that Joey had thought enough to go by and check on Adrianna, I strolled on up to the front door and flung it open. When I entered the lobby and saw Joey, Adrianna and Lottie sitting in the dining chairs, the urgency of the matter didn't immediately register in my brain, mostly because my eyes had to adjust from the bright sunlight to the darkened room. But then a sudden sensation of stark dread came over me. I saw that they were all seated in a straight line and bound to their chairs with duct tape.

"What the hell?" I exclaimed, reaching for the Glock.

"Bruce, watch out!" Joey yelled, unfortunately too late. I first saw the shadow cast across the floor by the figure behind me and then I felt the cold muzzle against the back of my neck beneath the left ear. At least I assumed it was a gun, but I wasn't going to ask questions right about now.

The man shoved me toward the center of the room before I could grasp the handle of the Glock and yelled "Take out the gun with your fingertips and place it on the table, McGowan!"

Turning around, I came face-to-face with *Fearless Leader*, Navab Abouzar. In his hand was a 9 mm and it was still pointed at my head. Carefully, I grasped the Glock at the grip with my fingers, pulled it from its holster and laid it on the edge of the dining table.

"Now lock your fingers behind your head and sit in that chair." While digesting the imperativeness of the moment, I was struck by the fact that his English was very good.

I did as instructed and looked at my brother and the two women. None of them appeared injured, but they were sure as hell scared.

"Sorry, Bruce," Joey said. "He came into the shop and put a gun to my head. Then he made me drive him over here."

"Shut up, infidel," said Abouzar, now waving the gun in Joey's direction. He then picked up my Glock from the table and shoved it into his pants. Turning his attention back to me, the professor stared a while before giving me an evil half-smile. "So you are the man called Bruce McGowan."

"And a very good reason I'm called that, asshole. It happens to be my name."

"You have a profane mouth, McGowan. I suggest that you curb your sharp tongue or I will take great pleasure in cutting it out before I kill you." The grin turned into a snarl. "You are the government man responsible for the destruction of our plan."

"Well, I do what I can, you know."

Calmly, he switched the 9 mm to his left hand and slapped me across the face with the back of his right hand. I immediately tasted the blood that poured from my lower lip.

"Enough with the jokes!"

I stared at him fiercely. He was right. This was not a time for frivolity.

At that moment, Burt the fur ball, who had apparently just awakened from his midday nap on the office couch, sauntered in. Although he took notice of the scenario, he obviously did not understand or appreciate the predicament we were all in. Nor did he sense the element of danger. After all, he was used to strangers being around. He went to work as usual on my pant leg, whisking his tail back and forth to solicit some stroking. I did start scratching the old boy behind his ears, then apologized to him under my breath, "Sorry about this, Burt."

Grabbing a handful of Burt's skin and fur behind his neck, I flung the cat straight into Abouzar's face. Burt, of course, had extended his claws to latch onto anything in preparation for a landing and Abouzar yelped. Unfortunately, the gun went off and I immediately felt a fiery pain shoot into my left side. The ladies screamed, Burt bolted from the room and Abouzar shoved the hot muzzle into my forehead. I thought for sure he would pull the trigger again and this time repaint Adrianna's dining room wall red. But I guessed he wasn't through with me just yet. His face was a bloodied mess as nearly every one of Burt's claws had dug in.

The bullet seemed to have gone into my washboard abdomen at an angle, out my side and into the floor. But the blood was pouring and I grabbed a cloth napkin from the dining table to press it first onto the entry wound and then the exit. Abouzar also grabbed a napkin to press against a series of lacerations around his right eye, nose and mouth. His black beard had caught much of the blood and had turned a bright red in places. Burt and I had obviously pissed him off as he suddenly kicked me in the left side right on the exit wound. I think I screamed like a little girl from the pain. The corners of Abouzar's mouth turned up into a snarling half-smile. I guess if Burt had still been in the room, his nine lives would have been used up at the expense of a 9 mm slug.

"How does that feel, infidel?" Abouzar continued applying pressure against a half dozen cuts, a few seconds at a time.

I didn't respond, but my gut hurt like hell. I straightened up in the chair and laid on him my most squalid glare. "What do you want here, Abouzar?"

"Ah, you know my name; but I do not think you know everything about me."

"I know you're a goddamned sheet-head ... or should I say Muslim *shit* head who likes killing Americans. I thought you Islamic bastards were supposed to be peace-loving. Well, guess what, prick, all I've seen out of you assholes is violence. Islam is nothing more than a religion of hate-mongering psychopaths."

"Such language and blasphemy from a man who is about to die. Maybe you should pray to your God for forgiveness."

I didn't respond.

Abouzar studied me a moment, like he couldn't believe I wasn't blubbering and begging for my life. Then he continued. "I will tell you who likes to kill. It is your government who continues to make war on the people of Islam. You kill our religious leaders, our women and our children as though they are nothing but maggots."

"Mmm ... maggots, you say? Yeah, that's about right."

I believe he wanted to go ahead and kill me then and there, and here I was making it easy for him. How stupid is that?

"I should first cut out your blasphemous tongue, McGowan. Then you will beg with only grunts for me to end your life."

I figured then I had better back off with the insults and stall for both time and opportunity to rush him.

"Where are you from, professor?"

He looked puzzled from my question, but answered anyway. "My home is Saudi Arabia, if you must know. Which is where I will be returning within hours after you are dead."

"So, when is the last time my country invaded your country and killed your people, genius?"

"Do not worry about where I am from, infidel. I am a brother to all of Islam in all countries. Even those here in the United States. Your country persecutes my brothers in all lands."

"And for good reason."

I winced after that retort, fully realizing that the comment was not exactly 'backing off.'

Abouzar placed the 9 mm within inches of my forehead and cocked the hammer. Adrianna gasped and let out a cry that sounded much like a small bird. I probably shouldn't have pushed him like that. We had been having such a nice little conversation.

He smiled again, mirthlessly, and softened his eyes. "You think that antagonizing me will cause me to become irrational and I will lose my composure. And in my weakness, you will try to take advantage." He walked casually around me several times, all the while keeping the gun trained on my head. Working the muzzle over the back of my neck, he taunted me, and on one occasion bumped it into my skull. He then circled me like a wolf paralyzing its prey with fear. I may have been a bit afraid, but unlike the defenseless lamb, I waited for just that one opportunity to spring onto *him*. However, it wouldn't be easy. He had the gun and all I had was my cat-like agility and wit.

Again, he seemed to take great pleasure massaging my forehead with the muzzle of the 9 mm. The hammer was cocked and with crossed-eyes I was taking note of the pressure of his forefinger on the trigger. All I would have to do is flinch and my brains would be laid out on the dining table for everyone to examine. I felt little beads of sweat breaking out on my face as Abouzar continued to smile that demonic smile and ridicule me. Somehow, though, I knew he wouldn't pull the trigger … not just yet. He had plans for me. I knew he would eventually plan to kill me, but he first wanted me to watch him kill Joey, Adrianna and Lottie. And maybe even Burt, if he could find the feline. One by one he would put a bullet in their heads or cut their throats, taking his time with each, relishing the look on my horrified face. But he had to figure that after the first killing, I would lunge for him and then he would have to go ahead and end my life.

Suddenly, he moved away from me and stepped behind Joey, pulling a large knife from a sheath that hung from his belt. I turned and froze in fear, contemplating what he was about to do. He held the knife high in the air as though he was prepared to plunge it into Joey's neck. The blade gleamed like a mirror as it caught a ray of the afternoon sun peering through the window. But then he lowered the knife and laid the blade across Joey's throat. "You killed my brothers today, McGowan, and now I will kill yours. His blood will be on your hands."

Adrianna cried out, "No, Mr. Abouzar! Please don't do this."

And then Lottie spoke. "Please listen to her, Mr. Abouzar. I beg you. If you must take a life, then let it be mine. I'm seventy-four years old and have had a good life ..."

"Shut up, old woman. I am talking to the infidel. Do not worry; your time will come. Before the hour is over, your blood will soak into this floor along with the others." The blade now made an indentation in Joey's neck and Abouzar's mouth drew up into a wicked smile again. "McGowan. You will get on your knees to beg for your brother's life. You mock my religion and my prayers, so you will now pray to Allah, the one and only god. Perhaps *he* will have mercy on your brother."

Slowly, I got down on my knees and watched as Abouzar tightened his grip on the knife. He now grinned gleefully at the thought of seeing me humbled. A small amount of blood oozed from Joey's neck. I knew Abouzar would still kill him whether I prayed or not. He would kill us all. I bowed my head until my nose actually touched the floor. Muttering some words that included the name Allah, I dropped my hands to the floor in front of me as I had seen

Muslims do in their prayer rituals. "Please," I begged. "Please don't do this. Spare his life."

"That's it, McGowan," Abouzar said, smiling. "But, alas. Allah does not hear you. How can he answer the prayer of an infidel? You have failed. I will now take pleasure in watching your brother's head fall to the floor. Look at me, infidel. I want you to see it, too."

I brought both hands back along my side and then slid my right hand up under my jean cuff until it touched the .380 holstered on the inside of my boot. Slowly I formed my fingers around the grip of the gun, knowing I had only one chance, one shot. And it had to be accurate.

Then I called to him. "Abouzar."

"What. What is it, infidel?"

"Do you love your God?"

"You have no right to ask such a question, but if it is important for you to know before you die … yes, I love Allah with all my heart."

"Then you will be prepared to give him my regards."

"What?"

I raised up quickly, still on my knees, and fired without aiming the one shot that struck between his thick eyebrows. The report was so deafening in the small room, pain shot through both of my ears. Abouzar's head snapped back and the knife fell harmlessly from his right hand. The body then disappeared behind a terrified Joey.

"Son-of-a-bitch!" Joey yelled. "I think I felt the bullet whiz through my hair. Do you realize how close that was?"

"You're welcome," I replied.

I stood and went first to Adrianna, who was now crying and shaking, cut her loose with Abouzar's knife, and gave her a quick hug and a kiss on the forehead. Then I cut the tape from Lottie and hugged her as well. I thanked her for her bravery and for offering up her life for Joey's. Both ladies quickly ran to the veranda for a breath of fresh air and to get away from the D.B. who was now leaking all over the floor.

"I suppose you want loose as well, little brother."

"If it's not too much of a bother."

I looked down at Abouzar who was now wearing a very large eighth hole in his head. Black-red blood slowly pooled beneath him. In his death stare the look of surprise remained. He was getting Adrianna's beautiful wood flooring all goopy, bleeding like that. But so was I. The cloth napkin I had jammed between my belt and entry wound was totally soaked with my blood. Anyway, I sliced the duct tape off of Joey and ruffled his hair.

"Thank God for the backup gun, Brucie. Cut it pretty close, didn't you?"

"I live for drama, Joey boy."

He didn't respond to that, but went immediately to a mirror on the hall wall to check out his hair. "Damn, I do believe I have a new part."

Joey doctored me up temporarily until he could get me to the hospital. Before we left, I shoved Abouzar's body into a broom closet down the hall and asked Adrianna and Lottie to go along with us. I was concerned about both of their emotions, and just in case, hoped the Greenbrier Valley Hospital had a psychiatrist on staff. They sat in the waiting area like zombies, saying nothing, while I was getting patched up.

I hate hospitals. There's always an atmosphere of funky, nauseating smells ... like disinfectant, not to mention the odor of hospital food as it rolls by on a cart waiting to be gagged down by the patients. And people are sick. People are in pain. People die. Of course I was *one* of those people. Sick with nausea and experiencing throbbing pain in my side where by the way I started leaking again. I was sure as hell hoping I wasn't one of the *dying* people. But I pretty much figured that wouldn't be the case, considering these were mosquito bites compared to the bullet that had smacked me in the lung a few years back.

A TV on the wall continued to broadcast WTC commentary, showing the same videos over and over of the towers burning, then going down. Joey called Cora, finding her safe and unaware that anything at all had happened at Wolf Laurel. He didn't tell her, either. And wouldn't, that is, provided everything that had happened the past three hours or so in Greenbrier County were temporarily contained by the locals until further notice.

When I came out of the O.R. I smiled at Adrianna to ease her fear that I had somehow crashed and expired from my gut wounds. She jumped up to hug me and the tears began. Joey gripped my shoulder and winked. "How do you feel, big brother."

"Like an idiot. I should be more careful and look for people with guns when I walk into a room."

While I was at the hospital I decided to check in on Candellera. I made my way down the corridor past the double doors that led to X-ray and Radiology and then by the door that said *Maternity,* under which was a brass plate at the door edge that read *Push.* For some reason I thought that was a bit funny and broke out into a smile. A pretty nurse happened by and returned the smile, thinking it was for her. It kind of was. For a while I paused at the nursery window to make faces at the newborns. But lollygagging like I was, I wasn't getting any closer to the trauma ward and Candy's room.

Expecting to see Candy on his back with his leg hoisted on a weighted pulley, he was actually sitting up in a vinyl chair by the bed in the process of yanking an IV from his arm. When I appeared at his door, his eyes immediately started to glisten. Tough guy was having a tender moment.

"Bruce …" That's all he could say. He had been watching the endless footage of the burning WTC towers on the TV.

"How're you doing, man?" I replied.

He just nodded *okay,* and bit his lower lip to regain his composure. My shirt was still open and he noticed the surgical wrapping around my waist. "What happened to *you*?"

"More holes, Candy, thanks to Professor Abouzar."

"You found him."

"He found *me*. Saved me a lot of time and trouble."

"Well you're still here. Where's he?"

"Stuffed in a closet, bleeding all over the floor back at Wolf Laurel."

Candellera gave me a puzzled look, so I filled him in on the events of the day. He listened intently like a wide-eyed child at storybook time.

"Damn good job, Bruce."

"Just another day at the office," I replied.

He became sullen again and diverted his eyes back to the TV on the wall. "I got a call from Chuck earlier. Said he thought the boss went down with one of those towers. Virginia, Abu, everybody."

"I heard," I said. There wasn't much more I *could* say.

This was the first real opportunity I had throughout the day to watch the footage other than when the tragedy first unfolded. I was stunned speechless. With one sweep of the death scythe, an estimated three thousand innocent people had disappeared. Although I had seen a number of horrific aftermaths while with the Bureau ... to include the Branch Davidian inferno and the Oklahoma City Federal building bombing ... what I was seeing on the screen was well beyond my capacity to not only comprehend, but accept as reality. My heart would not leave my throat. My blood felt like it was frozen.

Candy and I didn't say more than a half dozen words thereafter. But momentarily I stood and shook his hand and said I had to go.

Adrianna and Joey were waiting outside for me. And it was time for the professor to come out of the closet.

On the way back to Wolf Laurel I called Harlan Williams to inform him of what went down at the inn and he arrived within ten minutes with a squad of troopers. We pulled Abouzar out of the hall closet, finding him looking as dead as I had left him. Maybe a little paler.

The lieutenant let out a whistle, followed by "Good God Almighty."

I turned to him and planted my steely blues on his. "This all has to stay sealed for a while, Harlan. I know the flight academy massacre will get out, but the official account can't contain the word 'terrorists.' We have to keep a lid on it for now until the Bureau and State Department *make* it official. If we don't, there will be more panic and paranoia in the streets than this country can handle. My team will ultimately dispose of all the Arab bodies, including the one at the airport. My brother, Joey, will put them on ice for now. And we'll square it all away with the Bureau. The fracas that went down here … never happened."

"Then how the hell do we explain all this, Bruce? How will the murders at the flight academy be explained to the media and everyone else?"

"Some crazed loon went on a killing spree, distraught with what happened in New York and you're still looking for him. I don't know. Use your imagination. If that doesn't work, just say everything is classified."

"That's not fair to the families of the flight school people and the security guard."

"There are a lot of things about today that are not fair, Harlan." I grasped him by the elbow and drew him away from the troopers.

"My boss and members of my unit were in the World Trade Center today. *That's* not fair."

We studied each other a moment and he nodded slightly. "Sorry, Bruce. I didn't mean to ..."

"Look, Harlan. Let's say people around here learn there was a terrorist nest right in the heart of good old Greenbrier County. Everybody who bears any resemblance to a Middle Easterner will be suspect. That may lead to a hell of a lot of undue persecution and maybe even vigilante-ism. Remember, that happened right after Pearl Harbor. To America, every Asian was Japanese. Innocent people got hurt ... even killed. A lot of innocent people could get hurt right around here. Let's keep a lid on all this. Once the Bureau and State Department agree on what to put out, it will then be official. And that will be *your* story as well."

"Guess you Feds thrive on making shit up, don't you? Is any of what trickles down to the American people and us poor slobs at State and Local ever the truth?"

I smiled ... actually, rather sheepishly. "Occasionally."

Harlan was not humored. "Then you guys get us something soon, Bruce. Okay?"

I didn't respond except with a slight nod. He walked away shaking his head. "Come on, fellows," he said to his troopers. "The coroner will clean up here. I'll explain how we will handle this on the way back."

I called Jack again to fill him in on what had transpired and that the last piece of the puzzle (Abouzar) was now in place. There didn't appear to be any other players. That is, except the Jamestown maid. Ahmed had been taken to the Kanawha County lockup to await the Zulu boys who would interrogate him before his transfer to Gitmo. His brain would be siphoned for every minute detail of the plot as well as his affiliation with the bastards who brought down the

World Trade Center. I still had a hard time accepting the reality that such attacks had actually occurred on American soil, not to mention the resulting death and destruction. I could swallow such horror and devastation happening in places like Beirut or even Paris, but not in our safe, free and protected land. Was this just the beginning? Will Americans now live in constant fear? A nauseous tremor suddenly formed in the pit of my stomach, but it was not from my wounds. It was from pure consternation.

Adrianna and Lottie had gone on to their respective quarters. When Joey carted Abouzar's corpse off to McGowan and Sons, I trekked upstairs and rapped on Adrianna's door. After a few moments it opened. Her expression was stoic. Her eyes, reddened. I could tell she was still visibly shaken, if not traumatized.

"Are you okay?" I asked.

She nodded and turned away. I followed her to her bedroom.

"I … just think I need to lie down a while," she said almost in a whisper. The ordeal seemed to have sapped her strength *and* her voice.

I sat on the edge of the bed and held her hand. We didn't say anything for a long while. Her clock read ten past four. Funny. It seemed later. The day had been long … and arduous.

"Will you be all right if I leave you for a while? I need to take a drive and clear my head. I also need to try getting up with my team."

"I'll be fine. Just tired, that's all."

"Okay. I'll be back after a while." I kissed her on the forehead and slipped from the room.

I drove downtown along Route 60 and took account of what initially appeared to be a ghost town. There were a couple of people here and there talking to one another on the sidewalk, but most of the businesses had closed up and the spaces by the parking meters were hauntingly void of vehicles. I guessed that people were sent home by their employers earlier in the day to be with their families and they were all glued to their tubes. One would have thought there had instead been a nuclear strike and what few citizens were left were wandering the streets aimlessly or huddled together in the safety of someplace underground.

I wasn't able to reach Chuck and the others on my cell phone and there was only a recorded message on the land line at my Washington office. Suddenly, I felt very alone and thought about calling up Jack or Harlan again to reassure myself I wasn't the only player left. My blood was running a little cold again.

About five-fifteen I turned down Seven Bridges and back into the Wolf Laurel parking lot. Pulling in behind me was Joey in the Lincoln. I got out of the Suburban and waited for him to dismount.

"You're back," I said. "You worried about me?"

"Not *you*. You're the guy with nine lives, remember?"

"No, that's Burt."

"Did you find Burt? Last time I saw him, he was a little pissed."

"No, he's probably cowering under a piece of furniture somewhere."

"I was actually checking on the ladies."

"I guess they're okay. I was just out for some air and some deep thinking."

I walked toward the south side of the inn and into a small garden. Joey followed.

"Cora wants you to come to the house for dinner tonight."

"You didn't tell her anything about today, did you?"

"Nope. But I did tell her that members of your group were in one of the Trade Center buildings and you haven't heard anything."

I walked deeper into the garden and Joey sensed somehow that I wanted a little solace. He stayed back a bit and leaned into a masculine elm. As I digested this day of carnage I thought again about

Lionel Byrd. What really happened to him, Virginia and the other members of our team? I had to wait for news about them as did thousands of family members about their loved ones. I settled down on my knees amidst the beautiful mountain laurel and wood poppies to not only say a prayer for Byrd, but also to give thanks for our deliverance from the jaws of death today. Then I stood and looked deeper into the forest past the green-black cypress and ever reddening Japanese Maples and on into the haunted crevices of my mind where I saw a city burning. I closed my eyes to dispose of the vision.

"Are you coming, Brewster?" Joey called from behind me. "The wind's picking up and with all those holes in you, I think you're starting to whistle."

"Yeah," I replied. My voice cracked a little.

"Why don't you go up and ask Adrianna and Lottie to join us at the house. There's plenty of food and Cora wouldn't mind."

I thought perhaps that was a good idea. It would probably be what all of us needed. A little love. A little family time.

We went inside and sought out the ladies. At Joey's insistence they reluctantly accepted the invitation. They didn't need to be alone. And family … anyone's family … would be good medicine.

There were feeble smiles all around as we sat at the dinner table. It was a good country meal of Salisbury steak and milk gravy. But there was a hollowness deep inside of our stomachs that food just wouldn't satisfy. Cora said *grace*, but it was more of a prayer, like you'd hear in church. Adrianna and Lottie still appeared to be in shock from not only their horrific experience at Wolf Laurel, but what happened in New York, Washington and that field in Pennsylvania as well. But there was no mention of any of it at the table. The room was quiet save the clatter of forks on china as we ate.

And then from the open windows of the dining room, across the meadow and into the valley, we heard the faint tolling of the Methodist Church bell followed by the melodic pipes ironically chiming out *Great Is Thy Faithfulness* and a song from the Civil War era called *The Vacant Chair*. I wondered if there would be a vacant chair at the Byrd household this evening. We all picked at our food for a while and then Lottie, Adrianna and I thanked Joey and Cora for the dinner. We left just before seven for Wolf Laurel.

The ladies went on inside, but I pulled out my cell phone and remained a while on the veranda. I tried calling the Byrd house and a couple of guys I knew that were still with the Bureau in New York, but there was no service. So many emotions were tearing away at me ... anger, frustration, immense sorrow and even fear. Fear that people I really cared about were dead. Fear that we were now facing a future of terror in our country wielded by a faceless, conscienceless enemy, bent on causing our streets and gutters to overflow with American blood. I felt helpless, even lost. And I couldn't even begin to imagine how helpless and horrified the people of New York were.

I laid on Adrianna's couch trying to get comfortable in a position where my wounds wouldn't hurt so badly and trying to digest everything that had happened this senseless day, September the 11th. We both watched the network news and shook our heads in disbelief at all the stories coming out of New York. President Bush had made a compelling statement and vowed swift and terrible retribution for the attacks. No mention was made by the media about the plot on AmeriCan or the taking down of the terrorists in our area. The West Virginia Bureau and State Police had obviously adhered to my direction that these events would be considered classified for the time being and not parlayed in any fashion or form to the media. It was unfortunate and ironic that on the same day thousands of American citizens fell victim to the worst terrorist attack in history, two employees of a flight school and an elderly security guard in a rural area of West Virginia were murdered by an unknown assailant who tried to rob the academy. The story of these murders, as horrendous as they were, would be greatly over-shadowed by the 9-11 tragedy, buried somewhere on page ten in the Gazette and mentioned as a side note on network news, soon forgotten.

While I was in deep contemplation my cell phone went off and I saw a familiar number on the screen. I took a breath and exhaled slowly.

"Darlene."

"Hi, Bruce. Just wondered if you were okay. Where are you?"

"Not in New York, if that was what you were wondering." I immediately thought how abject that sounded and shook my head at myself. "Good of you to call. What's the matter … you worried about your ex-husband?"

"Something like that."

"Well, I am okay. I wasn't in New York or D.C. when the planes hit. My boss may not have made it out of one of the towers, though."

"I'm sorry, Bruce. That's … awful."

"Yeah." I paused. "You doing all right? It's been … what, six months since we talked?"

"I'm doing well. That is, up until today. This is all so surreal. God I hate the people that did this."

"Real bastards, they are. I hope they're frying in Hell right about now."

"My mind is totally blown today, seeing it all on TV, hearing everyone talk about it. As a matter of fact, *I* don't even want to talk about it."

"I know," I replied. "Enough said. What are you doing these days?"

"I'm working down in Fredericksburg for a CPA. Exciting, huh?"

"Very. You been taking care of the 3000?"

"Ned keeps it up. He had to put a master cylinder on it recently."

Damn, I hated that. Another man driving my Austin Healy. He can drive Darlene all he wants, but not my baby. It's just not right.

"When do I get it back?"

"With all that's happened, you want to talk about your old car?"

That did not merit a response.

She continued. "The car is mine, Bruce. You remember it was the only tangible property you had and I had to get something."

"You got the apartment ... and the TV."

"We didn't *own* the apartment, Bruce. I still had to pay the rent for months, you know. And the TV was ten years old. Anyway, you always cared more about the stupid car than you did me. It doesn't surprise me you're bringing it up again."

The car is not stupid.

"Okay. Let's drop it," I barked. "Sorry I brought it up."

She was silent for a while, then said softly, "I do wish Caroline wasn't entering the Bureau. This is *definitely* not good timing, Bruce. She'll be exposed more than ever to danger. And I can thank *you* for that, you know."

"Believe me, Darlene. You're not telling me anything I haven't thought about ... and not just today."

She sighed. "I know. I'm sorry. You may *be* a lot of things that have irked me to the end of my rope, but you've always been a good father and I respect you for that. I won't lay any guilt trips on you."

She says that, but let something happen to Caroline, God forbid. I may as well go ahead and put a bullet in my brain. Before Darlene puts one there.

I needed to end the conversation as I was getting even more depressed, what with the talk about Caroline and my 3000.

"Well, gotta go," I said. "Be safe. Thanks for the call."

"Goodbye, Bruce. Would be good to see you sometime again soon. Stop by when you're in Woodbridge."

"Yeah. Maybe some day I will."

I checked my cell phone again and saw that I had missed a call from Caroline while I was talking with her mother. Quickly, I returned it.

"Hi, Sweetheart."

"Dad, I was worried about you. I knew you had been chasing leads on Middle Easterners in your area and when those planes hit … I just didn't know whether you were still in West Virginia or had gone to New York before …"

"I'm fine, still here in West By Gawd. How are you managing?"

"We're all on edge here. They've briefed us a couple of times, but otherwise, we're watching TV like everyone else."

"Are you sure now that you want to continue on with the Bureau?"

"More than ever, Dad. If I ever thought about quitting before, today gave me new resolve. I want these people to pay and hope to hell I'll have a shot at bringing people like that to justice one day."

"Good for you, Caroline. But that won't make me sleep any better."

"I know." She paused for a few moments. "I love you, Daddy."

"And I love you, sweetie. Take care."

I dabbed a tear from my cheek.

Lottie left about noon on Wednesday after her son arrived from South Carolina. Over the breakfast table, she said she'd never forget either one of us and thanked me for saving her life. And again I thanked her for offering up *her* life in exchange for *ours*. She replied, "A lot of things ran through my head while I was sitting there, Skip. I just kept praying and thinking about what Jesus would do. And then I remembered what Jesus *did* do. He gave up His life, so why shouldn't I do the same for my loved ones?"

I hugged her and kissed her forehead. She hugged me back and then embraced Adrianna, telling her that she'd try making Wolf Laurel a yearly event. She then pulled me off to the side and whispered in her softest, folksy voice, "That little girl loves you, Skip. I see it in her eyes every time you walk into the room. Sweet as fine Muscadine wine, she is. Now don't let her get away from you. You hear, boy?"

"Yes, ma'am," I replied obediently. "I'll keep that in mind."

She kept her eyes on mine, cocked her head to one side and nodded quickly in that stern manner of hers. And she was gone.

I then looked down and saw that Burt was back and rubbing his face on my leg, looking for a bit of scratching or a piece of bacon. Obviously, he had forgiven me for tossing him onto a man with a gun.

Later, Jack Fuentes, along with an agent from Southwest Virginia and I went to McGowan and Sons where we found Abouzar's van. From papers and other contents we were able to determine the exact location of the professor's house which wasn't in Crows at all. It was further east and north in the woods near Goshen. A bounty of findings to include a blueprint written partly in English suggested that it was the intent of the Cessna pilots to fly directly into the chlorine and cyanide tanks. They would simultaneously fire the blasting caps with a hand crank, exploding the C-4 strapped to their waists a split second before impact. As I suspected, the lone terrorist was to be the check-valve. If the Cessna missions failed for some reason, Ahmed would fire the SA-7 missile into Storage Tank B which would set off the secondary explosion of Storage Tank A. Ahmed was in position to perish either way, as were they all.

And in checking all of the terrorists' vehicles and Abouzar's house, we were able to establish there were no suitcase nuclear devices, thank God. There was just some good old-fashioned C-4 strapped on the two would-be aviators … and lots of it.

In a back bedroom of Abouzar's house we also discovered the body of a woman, the young maid, naked and sprawled across the bed. Her throat had been cut and the sheets were soaked red with her blood. In the Islamic balance scale of good and evil, Abouzar had committed his one last sin at the expense of this young woman before his plan to kill us all at Wolf Laurel, the act of which would allow him to gain his ultimate reward. The maid's body was ravaged and debased, sexually. Her horrified expression revealed the last traumatic moments of her life as the blade slid across her neck, jugular to jugular. She was no more than a subjugated pawn, a necessary means to their end. Women not only are disempowered, but are in fact an enemy. As they are responsible for the sinful lust that men have, they weaken and bring down the moral man. Her punishment in death would acquit the man; he would be vindicated and his sin forgiven through her blood.

Professor Abouzar was one of Bin Laden's hand-picked lieutenants who was to methodically over the next several months execute one of several planned missions. The targets would be key population centers, towering plazas, shopping malls and of course industries that manufactured armament and munitions to supply the U.S. military as it made war on Islamic factions. There was literature that suggested Abouzar was not only an Al-Qaeda strategist, but had also taught in the Afghan training camp, Derunta al-Ghuraba.

It would be weeks later when we found out that the nineteen Islamic hi-jackers of Flights Eleven, One Seventy-Five, Seventy-Seven and Ninety-Three trained on aircraft like the Cessnas in several flight academies like the Ross Academy at small airports in the eastern and southern regions of the United States. Mohammed Atta, for example, learned the controls at Briscoe Field in Gwinnett County, Georgia, and in Venice, Florida. Although the controls on the small aircraft differed from a 737, the principles of operation were similar. Atta would have practiced buzzing Atlanta's Peachtree Plaza and Bank of America building in rehearsal for the WTC attack. I don't know why I hadn't seen the kamikaze attack coming. The puzzle pieces had been there all along ... the map, the flight lessons, the plan. Unfortunately, I just couldn't connect the dots. Thank God I finally woke up and took down the terrorists just in the nick of time.

But then what would haunt me forever was the fact that if I had figured out the actual aircraft attack plan, I would have sent the information through channels which in turn would have alerted every airport to tighten up its security. Then again, who would have known these maniacal bastards would have taken over airplanes with box cutters. Still, I would continue for weeks and months to feel in some way responsible and it would make me a very disconsolate and brooding soul.

At five-thirty Wednesday evening, my heart received that *good* shot of adrenaline that I had needed the last couple of days. My cell phone rang and the voice of Lionel Byrd was on the other end. He had made it out of the first tower just seconds before it fell. Gathered up with him were Virginia and support members of the team. Covered with debris and the blood of other people, they had walked out of Manhattan along with thousands of others. I told him I had worried and prayed about him and he thanked me for that. And then he said it was time for me to get back to Washington. He had already talked with Chuck and boys and they were leaving as we spoke. Candellera was scheduled for transport to Walter Reed on Friday morning.

There were pockets of Islamic terrorists still out there to hunt down. Zulu would reconsolidate and collaborate with several other CTT teams to be part of a task force made up of select operatives from the CIA, NSA, NSC, CTC and the FBI to strategize in seeking them out. With all those egos in the room, there were sure to be all the dynamics you would expect to find on a high school girls cheerleading squad or back stage in a beauty pageant ... jealousy, back-biting, in-fighting, dirty looks. Not good when everybody in the room packs heat.

CHAPTER 22

My cell rang again just before seven. It was Jack.

"Bruce. We have a situation over in Mingo County I'd like to get you in on."

Well, Jack was certainly living up to *his* end of the bargain where it came to the 'information sharing' code that he had earlier established with me. I can't say that I had been totally forthright with the guy along the way, being the covert, not to mention selfish butt that I am. But it kind of goes with my job. Of course, I had come around in the eleventh hour just before our world started to cave in.

"Yeah, Jack. What gives?"

"We have a report from State Law Enforcement that a Middle Eastern man did not make it home yesterday from his job at a gas company. He was involved in some kind of altercation at work with a couple of other employees Tuesday morning a few minutes after the terrorist attacks. He left the building and his wife and two children have not seen him since."

"Sounds like this one could go either way. The guy could have fallen victim to some good ol' boy profiling who helped him drop out of society. Or he could be part of an actual terrorist element, and not taking any chances on being found out, decided it was time to get the hell out of Dodge."

"Perhaps, but these folks are really family-oriented and I would doubt this guy would just abandon his wife and children."

"Did the wife report him missing?"

"Yes, and according to the locals she seems legitimately upset he didn't come home."

"So, Jack, what would you like me to do?"

"Can you meet me over in Mingo? I'd like to talk with the wife, the gas company foreman and some of the employees."

"Now?"

"First light tomorrow."

Well. Just when I thought my Tour of Duty was over in the great WV, it appeared there would be yet another party for me to go to.

"Okay. I *was* planning to head back to Washington tomorrow, but this could be worth a look."

"That's what I hoped you'd say, you being the only Terrorist Czar I know. Meet me at Lovejoy's Shop-and-Go at 0630 on Highway 3-8, eight digit grid coordinates Sierra Lima 82503742."

"I love it when you talk all official like that, Jack."

"Goodbye, Bruce."

Adrianna and I sat in the car that afternoon like a couple of teenagers at Jim's Drive-In just west of Lewisburg. Being a sensible eater and connoisseur of the more healthy fare, she was struggling with her hot dog. Of course, I had already wolfed down two. The aroma of these puppies took me back a few years … thirty-five or forty to be exact. The grilled weenie, the ground chili, cole slaw and steamed buns all worked together to tantalize and delight my olfactory senses.

For the first time in a couple days we were actually enjoying ourselves. "You're a cheap date, Skip McGowan," she said. Her giggle was back and so was my smile. For some reason, the grieving City of New York seemed so far removed from my mind like the whole thing was a product of one of my nightmares. The attack on our nation was only in a new movie I saw called something like *World War III in America*. Funny when you're sitting and eating the All American hot dog in the front seat of your car with a your honey, the plights and tragedies of the world seem safely far away. Like we will always be pampered and sheltered in our perfect little Utopia nestled in the small hills of West Virginia. The defense mechanisms were at work. Denial, repression, displacement, reaction formation … you know, all the Freudian escapisms.

That evening we took in more TV, saying very little, depressing ourselves watching the continuous network footage of human interest stories intermingled with recovery efforts. We finally turned off the tube and sat in drained silence like two old married people, then went to bed. We kissed each other good night and lay quietly until I heard her slow, heavy breathing. Then sleep came over me as well.

I jumped up at four, took my shower and sat at Adrianna's desk in my jockey shorts, plotting my route and coordinates. It would take me a couple of hours to make the rendezvous point, so I had to zip. I kissed my sleeping bunk mate on the forehead and closed the door behind me.

It was six-twenty two on the Suburban's digital clock when I pulled off Route 38 into the gravel parking lot at Lovejoy's. Coming out of the minute saver with two cups of coffee in his hands was Jack in a ball cap of some kind. A briefcase was slung over his shoulder. Even though all he would be able to see was my headlights, he walked directly toward my truck. I was not only impressed with his punctuality, but his recognition skills in the morning twilight as well. When I stopped and threw the shifter into 'park,' he opened the passenger door and got in. "Black, right?"

"Right," I said, taking the cup from his hand.

"How are the wounds?"

"Sore, but I'll live." I waited for some kind of smart-alec retort like 'what a pity.' But that wouldn't come from Jack. Jack was not me.

He tapped the right side map light and opened his briefcase to retrieve a notebook and map. "If we take 38 to Barksdale and go right at the stop sign in town onto 213, Taggart Natural Gas will be on the right. They start work at seven. The foreman is a guy named Bill Hanley and the CEO is Dennis Mazeroski. There are twenty-four operators, surveyors and site crew that work there and in the field. Three female employees are in the front office doing the dispatch and bookkeeping functions."

"Holy Horse Turds, Batman. You've done your homework. So, what kind of underwear will the women be wearing … cotton or nylon?"

Jack ignored my smart-ass question and continued on. "Although the State investigators have already interviewed several of the employees, we'll hit them again. We know the Arab employee's name is Yaheem Barat. Some kind of altercation went down Tuesday on the gas company grounds and we need the blow by blow account."

"You want to play good cop or me?"

"Neither good nor bad, Bruce. We're just here to obtain facts and assess the information. And … it would be good to learn Mr. Barat's whereabouts."

"Gotcha," I replied, making a finger and thumb gun, then pointing it at him.

Agent No Nonsense motioned me on with a flick of his hand.

At five minutes past seven it was fully light when we entered the gate to the gas company. Jack dismounted first and re-arranged his gun and shoulder holster inside of his jacket. He was dressed in a tan golf parka, black Levi's and a Nike ball cap, appearing rather

GQFBI, if there is such a thing. No suit and tie today. We both looked almost like we fit in around these backwoods. Almost. I was similarly dressed, but if either one of us resembled a good ol' boy, it would be me. Jack was too pretty and his duds, too perfect.

We entered the door that read 'office' and were immediately greeted by an ancient looking woman with a cigarette drooping from a pair of prunish lips. There were so many wrinkles in her face, I felt an urge to return to Wolf Laurel and iron something. And I was not the least bit interested what fabric her underwear was.

"What can I do for you," she barked in a raspy smoker's voice.

Jack flashed his ID and badge and responded, "I'm Special Agent Fuentes of the FBI and this is Mr. McGowan of the State Department. We need to talk to Mr. Hanley or Mr. Mazeroski."

"Is this about that Arab feller? If it is, the State cops were here yesterday about him." She accidentally on purpose allowed a stream of smoke to engulf Jack's head. He was definitely annoyed.

"That's something I will discuss with the two gentlemen, ma'am," Jack retorted curtly.

Way to go, Jack.

The woman looked him over with indignant eyes, then pressed a buzzer. "Just a minute," she replied gruffly. "Bill, the FBI's out here. About Yaheem." She glared at us for a moment and then turned sideways toward her computer screen. She made it quite apparent she was done with us.

Directly, a large balding man appeared in the interior doorway and approached us with an out-stretched paw. "Bill Hanley," he began. "You're FBI?"

"That's correct." Jack introduced himself again and then me.

"Both the company president and I gave our stories to the State Police, Mr. Fuentes. You don't have them?"

"I do. But we want to hear it from *your* lips, sir. Not second hand."

Hanley sighed and sat down in one of the lobby chairs. We took two others. "All right, then. Shoot."

"Tell us about Mr. Barat."

Hanley settled back, exposing a humongous gut. His flannel shirt was under enormous stress and between the buttons, three gaps formed, exposing his white tee shirt. At any moment one of the buttons could go and put an eye out.

"Well, he's about thirty, has an engineering degree and been with the company about a year. Got referred to us by a guy at West Virginia Tech. He went to school there, you know."

"I understand he has a wife and two small children."

"That's what his personnel file says."

"Have there been any problems with him?" I stepped in.

"Nope. Good employee. He's in the office here about a third of the time, but spends most of his work day checkin' out the gas wells or followin' up on leaks."

"Can we get a look at his file?"

"Guess so. There're some HIPAA stuff we gotta consider, but you all bein' Feds, it don't matter none."

Hanley disappeared for a couple of minutes and returned with Barat's personnel shield. "I got some things to do. Can I leave you fellas with that?"

"Before you go," began Jack, "tell me what kind of altercation went down here on Tuesday."

Hanley sat back down on the edge of his chair, putting even more stress on his Dun-lap *and* the buttons. I think it was Jack who was in the line of fire.

"Well, Tuesday morning, nine-eleven, you know, all of us was here and Yaheem and a couple others were ready to hit the field. Somebody heard about the planes flyin' into the towers and we turned the TV on. Bad, bad deal." He paused and shook his head. "We were all just stunned and nobody was doin' any work. After we heard who was responsible for it, one of the guys, John Sisko, started spoutin' off about A-rabs and towel heads and all these Muslim bastards were a bunch of goddammed camel fu ..." He stopped short. "Well, you get the picture. Then he said the U.S. ought to put a bomb on the whole Middle East and vaporize every one of them. I didn't even think about Yaheem when John was goin' off like that. I looked at him and could tell he was gettin' hot under the collar. Well, anyway, Yaheem said something like, 'we are all not terrorists, Sisko. Most Muslims love peace and do not condone violence and especially murder. Perhaps you should consider your own people like Timothy McVeigh before you begin condemning Arab Americans.' I guess that set John off even more. He started yellin' and told Yaheem to get his f'ing ass out of his sight. Then Yaheem said he was going out to a site anyway and away from bigots like Sisko. He left and didn't return on Tuesday and still hasn't. We just thought he quit. Then the cops came by my house Tuesday night and told me Yaheem never went home."

I was studying Barat's file as Hanley was talking. Yaheem appeared to be clean on the surface. He came to the United States from Libya on a Visa when he was twenty three, worked in Pittsburgh as a carpenter's apprentice, brought his young wife over, apparently then had some kids, moved to Montgomery, West Virginia, and began pursuing an Engineering degree, finishing out in three and a half years. Unlike Assad and boys, this guy was a for real student and appeared to be seeking the American dream. I seriously doubted there was any connection to an Islamic subversive group from reading about him, but I could be wrong.

Jack continued his questions. "Is Sisko here today?"

"He called in sick. Second day in a row."

"Uh *huh*.

"Funny," replied Hanley. "A couple of other guys called in as well."

Jack and I looked at one another with raised eyebrows. About that time Mazeroski came out. He was tall and slender, silver-haired, and wearing a suit. Obviously he didn't run in the same circle with Hanley or eat the same foods.

"Gentlemen, Bea (the receptionist) told me you were here. Is Bill giving you what you need?"

"Yes, sir," said Jack. "What is your take on the missing Barat?"

"I don't rightly know. He's been a good employee ... very smart and very dependable. I think a couple of our boys may have come on too strong with him. It was uncalled for. Yaheem doesn't deserve that, no matter what happened on 9-11. I expect he's probably quit ... and wouldn't blame him. I talked to the State fellows yesterday and told them my feelings about the boy. He's not of the same fiber as the people who made these attacks, gentlemen. He's just another hard working immigrant trying to make a good living in the land of opportunity."

"I'm sure that's the case, sir."

We continued with our barrage of questions and it became more and more apparent that something ill had befallen Yaheem Barat. Maybe he had everybody but John Sisko fooled, but I had a feeling that it was Sisko or one of his buds who somehow made this guy disappear.

Satisfied we had what we needed, we thanked the Taggart fellows and left the office. When we were just short of my Suburban, we turned to see Mazeroski on our heels.

"Gentlemen, may I add something else? I didn't want Bill or Bea to catch any of this, but I felt I needed to share something else with you about Sisko."

We were all ears.

"I've heard he and one other of my employees, Jarod Cummins, are involved in some kind of para-military group they say is nothing more than a hunting club. I've seen some of their Klan-ish looking propaganda floating around in the past about Blacks, Jews, Mexicans, Muslims and anybody that doesn't look like a WASP."

"And you know they're connected how?" I asked.

"Talk, Mr. McGowan. I may be isolated from everyone around here because of my position, but some things still get to me."

"Okay. So where does Mr. Sisko live?" asked Jack.

"Not far from here. Go north on this road about six miles and you'll see a dirt road on the left. I think it's called Farley Road. There should be a sign. He's about the third house down that road. I've only been there once and that was two or three years ago, so I could be wrong. You should see a blue Ford pickup in the driveway."

I asked "Would you know where this para-military camp is located?"

"Not really. I hear they call it a hunting camp. And I do know there's some kind of hunting camp on Jewel Mountain. I imagine someone in that area could clue you in. Near a town called Petersville about fifteen miles further north."

"Is Cummins here today?" I asked.

"No. He called in yesterday and said his aunt died and would be going to Huntington for her funeral."

"Imagine that."

"I don't check up on employees when they say they have a death in the family. I just wouldn't think a man would lie about something like that."

"Maybe not about a guy's mother, but aunts and uncles don't have the same status and are expendable," I added.

"Thanks, Mr. Mazeroski" Jack stood and put out his hand.

I thrust mine toward him as well and asked one more question. "What about Sisko? What do you think of him?"

Mazeroski shuffled his feet in the gravel and looked down. "On the job, generally dependable. But he's a rogue and we have had a couple of problems with him."

"Such as?"

"Has come in drunk or hung over a couple of times. And he invited one of the other men outside one day after some kind of argument over a gambling debt."

"Salt of the earth kind of guy, huh?" I responded.

"Not my blend of salt. I expect one day I'll have to cut him loose and then all hell will break loose."

"I guess that's it, then," Jack said. "Thanks. If you think of anything or hear anything else, here's my card."

We entered Farley Road a few minutes later and on Mazeroski's best recollection found the third house on the right. There was no blue pickup in the driveway. I figured it was Sisko's place, all right, since there was a large Rebel flag on the double wide attached to a flag stand by the door.

I got out first and led Jack to the door. After I rapped sharply, we heard the thumping of footsteps on the trailer floor. The door opened and a frail 40-ish woman in a housecoat appeared. Her left eye was swollen and blackened and when she opened her mouth to speak, I could see she was missing some teeth … either knocked out by her husband or she had never owned a toothbrush.

"Yeah?" she greeted.

"Good morning, ma'am," I touched the bill of my cap. "We're with the State Highway Department and are talking with homeowners about the State's plan to blacktop Farley Road. Is your husband in?"

Jack looked at me and turned his head. I think I saw a bit of eye rolling.

"No, he ain't?" Her eyes widened. "You all really gonna pave this road?"

"Well, that's the plan, but we have to run it by everyone who lives on this road."

"Damnation! I've been prayin' for that to happen. When you gonna do it."

"Well, we have to get everybody's permission. I'll need your husband's signature." I looked at my faux notebook. "Your husband's name is …"

"John. John Sisko."

"That's what I have written here. So, he's not around today?"

"No, he's … at the doctor's."

I suspected Mrs. Sisko had been ordered earlier in the morning by the mister to tell anyone and everyone that, given that he was 'out sick.'

"Oh, I'm sorry. Hope it's nothing serious. There's some bad stuff going around."

She nodded, deciding not to say any more. I expect she didn't like lying as she seemed a nice enough soul, but I had to dig a little further.

"Well, we have to get on. Got several other people to see and then get over toward Jewel Mountain. There's a road going up to some kind of hunt or fish camp there that people have been after the State to improve."

"Oh, yeah. My husband goes up there to hunt most every weekend all year long."

I actually think she did not know that hunting season is *not* year round and although I hate taking advantage of people who are not as bright as three watt bulbs, I had to do it today. "You know, I've been looking to get back into hunting and maybe I'll check out the hunt club. What's the name of it, do you know?"

"I don't know much about it. When John leaves the house for the camp, he don't say too much. I think it's just called The Jewell, you know, after the mountain?"

"Great. Do you know if anyone's up there today I can talk with?"

"Prob'ly. You may even catch John …" She stopped, knowing she was about to give her husband's whereabouts away. "… maybe this weekend, if you wait and go then," she recovered.

"Maybe I will wait and check out the road at the same time. That way I'll kill two birds with one stone. Well, thank you, ma'am." I touched my bill again.

When we turned to walk away, she yelled after us. "I can't wait to see this road paved. Thanks."

I actually hated the deceit I had wrought on this little lady. She would be looking in vain every day to see the road crew set up with their equipment only to realize that one very special prayer in her life would never be answered. I felt bad about that. Then I thought about something else. I hoped she would not see that my Suburban sported a District of Columbia tag when I was pulling away.

At about nine-forty, we stopped at a gas station at the base of Jewel Mountain for fuel … another cup of coffee. Jack sat in the SUV while I went in. I guessed that he about had his fill of my fabrications. There was a good ol' boy behind the counter who looked as though he could belong to the Jewel Mountain Boys Club, so I had to be coy about my questions. After paying for our coffee, I struck up a conversation.

"Great country, man. A guy could retire here."

"God's country, we call it. Where you from?" he asked.

"Over in Virginia, up D.C. way. I don't get to see this part of the world much. When you're stuck behind a desk six days a week and all you see is buildings, this is like driving through the Garden of Eden. Is there some good fishing around here?"

"Yep. We got Moon Lake up Kettle Creek not too far and a couple of pretty nice streams just off fifty-seven. You fish?"

"Don't have time for it; but I have done a little hunting, mostly up in Pocahontas County."

"Yeah, I've been up there. Snagged an eight pointer about five years ago."

"Much hunting around here?"

"When the season opens up, man, it's like Grand Central Station."

I took a sip of my coffee and chose my words carefully. "I'm just returning from a family reunion over in Matewan. My uncle said he's come over this way and met up with some guys at a hunting camp on Jewel. I guess he meant somewhere around here."

The man looked at me from beneath the bill of his Red Man cap and placed his paws on the counter. I figured right then and there I had somehow given myself away. He stared for a few seconds and then said, "Yeah, they's some kind of camp up Hog Hollow a couple of miles from here. I heerd there's some fellas that go there all times of the year and hang out. Don't know if it's really a hunt camp, though." I wasn't quite sure why he was sharing all this with a stranger.

"Hmm. Maybe it's just a place to get away from the wives and do a lot of drinking," I replied.

"Well, I really don't know much about anything up there." He knew he probably said too much to me in case any of the other store patrons were listening. Obviously, he wasn't a charter member of the 'club.' And if these people *were* backwoods militia, they wouldn't take kindly to storekeeps spreading any idle gossip around about them.

"Anyways, good talkin' to you, sir." He quickly broke off the conversation and turned his attention to a burley man behind me in camou who by the way was eyeing me rather suspiciously.

I returned to Jack and the Suburban and handed off one of the coffees … the one I was not drinking from.

"What did you find out, Bruce?"

"I think we may have found the area we're looking for. If my suspicions are correct, we may have some home-grown militia camped out in them thar hills. Will any of your boys be ready to roll if we find a bunch of guns up there?"

"May be difficult to scrape everyone together at once without an Op Plan or rendezvous time. Better chance to draw in the State for something like this."

"Let's see how this goes and if there is evidence of either some illegal activity or we find that Sisko and Company have snatched or disposed of Barat, we'll back off and bring in the locals."

I think this excited Jack. He looked over at me and nodded. "All right. I'm game. Let's go."

I found Hog Hollow Road at the base of Jewel Mountain rather handily and after throwing the Suburban into 4 wheel drive, started up what appeared to be an old logging road. There were no signs indicating we were on the way to a hunting camp or any other kind of camp. Soon, however, we began to see some *No Trespassing* signs. The road quickly deteriorated and some of the tire track ruts actually turned into trenches.

After covering what seemed to be two miles, we came upon a gate on which there was posted a much angrier sign than the others: *Absolutely No Trespassing. Violators Will Not Be Prosecuted. They Will Be Shot.* About as angry a warning as I have ever seen. I was getting ready to get out to open the gate when suddenly a figure dressed in authentic military woodland camouflage stepped from around a thick oak and bore down on us with an AR-15. He was about six feet tall, had a full black beard and two fierce peepers.

"Stop where you are and turn off your engine. Now!" he barked.

I did as commanded since I already had enough guns trained on my person in the past couple of days. And some of them were spitting stuff at me.

"Excuse me, sir," I said. "Please lower your gun. We were looking for a fish camp up here."

"There ain't no fish camp up here and you're trespassing. Assume you assholes can read."

I looked over at Jack and said, "Looks like we got a bum steer about this place, Jack." I then turned back to the guard and added, "We were told there was a lake up here ... Moon Lake, I think."

The man edged closer to the truck and eyed me menacingly. "That's over near Coalburg, more'n ten miles from here." He looked past me at Jack and then back at me again. "And you faggots don't look like you're up here to do any fishin.' So, what are you sweethearts really up here for, huh?"

I ignored the comments and spread my map over the steering wheel, pretending to mull it over. "I don't know, Jack. I think we took the wrong road." I then looked at the guard. "Sir, will you please point out where on the map we need to go?"

The man lowered his rifle and pushed his head half through the open window on my door. No sooner had he made the mistake I hoped he would, I reached over with my right hand and slammed his nose down on the door frame. Blood immediately spurted from his nostrils. I released the handle with my left hand and kicked open the door. As the man went sprawling onto the ground, he dropped the firearm. I jumped out and kicked him in the groin as he rose to get up. Although he yelped in pain, he still tried to upright himself. Swiftly, I swung the knife part of my hand across his throat and hit hairy meat. As the man lay on his back, gasping for air, I pounced onto him, pulled my Glock and placed the muzzle against his forehead. It felt good turning the tables for a change. Two days ago a now defunct professor had a gun against *my* head.

"Put your hands behind your head and interlock your fingers!" I ordered.

The man appeared to be choking on his blood and as a result of my shot in his Adam's apple, he was getting very little air. I turned his head to the side so that the blood would drain. Jack came up from behind to join me.

"What's your name?" I barked.

"H … Horace," he coughed.

"Horace what?"

"Tim … mers. Timmers." More coughing.

"Where's your camp Horace?"

He didn't answer.

I pressed my left thumb against his Adam's apple, still training the Glock on the forehead area between his eyebrows. "You have three seconds to tell me, Horace, or your brains will be feeding the crows. One two three," I counted very quickly and cocked the hammer.

Horace immediately unlocked his fingers and pointed to his left. "Just over that hill … about a hundred yards … (cough). You're … hurting me, sir."

"Trust me, I'm *not*. Now, are there any more guards like you?"

"One," he rasped.

"Is Sisko in there?"

Timmers looked surprised and his eyes widened. "You … you know Sisko?"

"I know him and people like him. Is a man named Cummins there with him?"

He hesitated, then nodded.

"How many total men are in the camp?"

"Four … five. No, four."

"For your sake, we'd better find four. Now I have one more question, Horace. And you'd better give me a straight answer. If you believe I won't kill you, better think again, asshole."

He nodded again. Jack knelt down by us and I believe he was actually ready to stop me if necessary. Now *his* eyes had widened.

I looked at Jack. "And you know I will."

I returned my attention to Timmers' wanly face. "Is a Middle Eastern man named Barat there as well?"

Timmers' eyes were now showing fear. "Yes, sir."

"Is he alive?"

"Yes, sir."

Amazing how one can command such respect when the muzzle of a 40 caliber Glock is laying lovingly against a person's forehead.

"You've been very courteous and helpful, Horace," I said. "My sweetheart here and I now wish you sweet dreams." With that said, I cracked him on the right side of his head with the butt end of my gun. The ugly thud made Jack wince.

I stood and turned to Jack. "Let's go ahead and call for troopers and then move in."

"Move in before they get here?"

"Yes. Are you still game?"

"I am."

Jack's Bureau phone was still hanging on his dash back at Lovejoy's, so he used my cell to contact the 911 operator, asking to be dispatched to the Mingo detachment. After getting the unit sergeant on the horn, I heard him explaining the scenario and giving directions. Meanwhile, I had secured my .308 from the cargo area of the Suburban and moved into the woods around the gate. Leaning against a tree that sported a sign with a skull and crossbones painted on it, I peered into my binoculars through a patch of maples, spotting the other guard, also in woodland camos. Beyond him approximately fifty feet further downhill into a clearing was a small shack that appeared scores of years old, perhaps made of chestnut. A number of pickups were parked off to the side, one of which was a blue Ford. No other bodies were in sight and I assumed they were inside the building.

Jack slipped stealthily behind me and I handed him the .308. "Have you ever used one of these?"

"Just once, in a weapons familiarity class."

"Good enough. Follow me down at a distance. You've got my back. There's a guard at seventy-five yards. A shack is beyond that. I'll take the man out, but if someone else materializes … well, you know what to do. Once I take down the guard, come down the hill quickly."

Jack nodded. If I were him, I'd be questioning me as to who was actually in charge of our little covert deal. But Jack knew he had been scarcely more than a desk jockey and dealing mostly with white collar crime. I'm not sure he had ever even been in the woods; and then knowing what I was capable of, he likely chose not to challenge me for the command job.

The guard near the shack was certainly not expecting anyone to get past Timmers and appeared to be less than vigilant. He had set his rifle down and was sitting on a tree stump, digging into a pouch of Red Man. As quietly as I could, careful not to step on any dry twigs, I moved at a crouch around behind the man. He may have heard me make some kind of noise as he turned his head sharply in my direction. I immediately dropped down and after a few moments, he returned his attention to jamming the wad into his mouth. His AR-15 remained propped against a tree

Slowly I moved to within five feet of the guard. At the same time he heard the cock of my hammer, I said softly, "Don't move." I was pretty sure he had swallowed his chaw as I thought I heard him gag. "Now stand up and keep your hands where I can see them."

When he stood and put his hands up, I grabbed his rifle. "Now turn around."

Slowly he turned and I holstered my Glock, now training the rifle on the guard's head. "How many inside?"

"Three," he replied.

"Three plus the Arab man?"

He nodded.

"Thank you," I said, then gave him a horizontal butt stroke on the chin with the stock of the weapon. He dropped with a groan and didn't move again.

Jack came up behind me, eyeing the sleeping guard, and looked at me with a frown on his face.

"He's not dead, Jack."

"So, what now, Bruce?"

"We need to go ahead and move in on them. If they come out and find the two guards in a supine position, they'll shoot first and ask questions when the smoke clears. We can take them, Jack."

He nodded.

I went through the guard's pockets and found his wallet. It wasn't Sisko. The man's name was David Burke. I had an idea.

"Jack, position yourself by the door and be ready to take down anyone who comes out."

"What's the plan?"

"I'm calling them out."

"What? Bruce, they're not in a saloon and this isn't the Wild West."

"Not far from it."

Jack frowned and rolled his eyes again. I was sure he got that from his wife.

He moved next to the door, leaned against the siding and brought up the .308 into position.

I checked the magazine in the guard's AR-15 and sought cover by a nearby tree facing the shack. I figured the people inside wouldn't be able to detect the difference in the voice. I then yelled, "Hey, Sisko. Hey, you guys come out and see this!"

Shortly, the door opened and all three men tromped down the steps and onto the turf. They had no weapons in hand, thinking that the camp was still secure. Obviously, the guard had seen something interesting, like a UFO. I stepped from behind the tree and Jack got the drop on them from behind.

"What the hell …?"one of them exclaimed.

"On the ground! Now!" I barked. The men dropped, automatically placing their hands out in front of them.

"Jack, go check on Barat." I then tossed the rifle and drew my Glock. One by one I placed the muzzle of the Glock against the men's cheeks and searched them for weapons. Two of them had .45 automatics in their leg pockets, which I confiscated.

Momentarily, Jack came out of the shack with a very frightened Middle Eastern man, hands bound with duct tape. He had been beaten badly and both eyes were nearly swollen shut.

Jack took out a small Buck knife and cut the tape from Barat's wrists. "Mr. Barat, I presume. I am Special Agent Jack Fuentes, FBI. We're pleased to find you."

The man could hardly speak, partly from his tears, but also because his mouth was cut and swollen. "Thank … you."

"All right, which of you is Sisko?" I began barking again.

One of the men, apparently scared poopless, pointed to the bearded one in the middle. I then pressed the Glock into the back of Sisko's neck. "Get the hell up!"

Sisko stood, looking rather indignant. "What do you people want? We ain't done nuthin."

I walked up to him and started what I thought would be a meaningful dialogue. "Your militia days are over, asshole. How does kidnapping, assault and battery and terrorism charges sound to you? Jack, would you like to read them their rights?"

"Love to, Bruce."

When Jack approached Sisko, the man spit in Jack's face. "How's that, Spic? They let anybody be FBI these days. Next thing you know, towel heads like Barat there will be agents. I guess what happened on Tuesday don't mean shit to you, you Muslim-lovin' pricks?"

Jack took out a handkerchief and slowly wiped his face. Then he did something that absolutely rocked my world. Obviously, he was impressed with the way I had handled the guard by the shack. He smiled and said "Hey, Sisko. Lights out." Suddenly the butt of my .308 swung up and crashed into Sisko's jaw, certainly shattering it into several pieces. The man sunk to his knees and fell on his face. I saw *nothing*.

We then heard the sound of vehicles, one of which crashed the gate. Blue lights were flashing and reflecting all through the woods. The troopers had arrived, not that we would have ever needed them.

An ambulance was called in for Sisko who had resisted arrest. The two guards had awakened from their naps and were presented silver bracelets by the posse. Jack and I then walked with Barat back to my Suburban.

"Mr. Barat, we need to get you to the hospital," I said.

"No. I just want to go home to my family."

"You could have some internal injuries, you know."

"I don't think so," he replied. "I am all right. Just flesh wounds as your TV cowboys say."

We smiled. "Committing hate crimes is a Federal offense. You know you will have to testify against these men. Will you be up for that?"

"I will. You know I will." He paused before getting into the truck. "Thank you for coming to get me. You restore my faith in

American people. I want you to know, no matter what these men did to me, I am proud to be here in this country. I would never say or do anything to hurt the American people. I hate what the terrorists did in New York and Washington. I believe all people have a right to live and worship, but I know that some of my people don't. My family and I will stay here and enjoy the freedom given to us."

"We wouldn't blame you if you didn't, Yaheem," I said. "What these men did to you took away your freedom …"

"And you both gave it back to me." He held out his hand. I actually felt like bawling … not only for him, but for the 3000 plus people who were also victims of terror and weren't so lucky. And when Sisko spouted his bigoted venom, it was like he held a mirror up to my own face. It made me think of some of my comments about the Middle Eastern society over the past couple of weeks. Guilty as charged.

We took Yaheem home. When his wife heard the vehicle approach, she ran from her doorway and into his arms. Two toddlers followed. He looked at us and smiled the best he could, given his swollen lip. He also mouthed the word, "Thanks." Tomorrow he would go back to work and things would be different. I was sure that Mazeroski would see to that.

On the way back to Jack's Crown Vic, hardly a word was spoken. Then Jack cut the stale air. "Good job, Bruce."

I didn't respond for a moment, but then said, "I guess you saw me at my worst."

"No," he replied. "I saw you at your *best*. I learned quite a bit today from you. This may have gone down differently if we had a Bureau team running the show. There likely would have been loss of life and we may not have gotten Barat out alive. It's amazing these guys were taken out without us firing a shot."

"You're a good wing man, Jack."

We shook hands and I do believe that his grip had improved since the first time we met. He actually popped a couple of my knuckles.

We stood for a couple of moments leaning against the Crown Vic, arms folded and looking down. I really liked the hell out of Jack and I do believe he reciprocated the feeling. But, over the past couple of weeks I'm sure he had reason to ponder how complex, enigmatic and confusing of a guy I was. Ruthless, yet compassionate. Austere, yet affable. Obnoxious, yet delightful. Sometimes, all at the same time. I'm often even confusing to *myself*. But I do believe Jack learned something from me at any rate ... it's neither a Bureau requirement nor emotionally profitable to be a tight-ass 100% of the time.

We seemed a bit awkward saying goodbye, shuffling the toes of our shoes in the gravel. But then we nodded and turned away from each other. When he opened his driver's side door, I called out to him. "Hey, Jack."

"Yeah."

"Say hello to Diane for me."

He smiled and nodded again. "You bet. See you in the funny papers, Bruce."

And *I* smiled.

The troopers found a roster in the cabin of the militia numbering twenty-three men. Each was later rounded up and charged, although it was apparent that only the five men on site had actually kidnapped and assaulted Barat. A cache of about twenty rifles and handguns was found, which did not include the weapons that the men had in their vehicles and at home. Obsolete U.S. Marines training and field manuals were also located in the shack, along with a variety of pyrotechnics and ammunition. Beyond the clearing where the cabin sat the militia had cleared off brush to build a 100 meter known distance range complete with targets. A few days later the cabin was bulldozed and signs were posted, *No Trespassing by Order of the Federal Government.*

Chapter 23

▼

And yes, I know how lonely life can be
The shadows follow me
And the night won't set me free
But I don't let the evening get me down
Now that you're around me.

—*Don McLean*

Some time around seven I turned down Seven Bridges and into Wolf Laurel. I was hungry and because I had had my cell phone off all day, I hadn't talked with Adrianna about any dinner plans. I hoped she hadn't succumbed to any invitation from Dan. Of course, as long as I was in the picture, he was going to steer clear of me. I'm sure he wasn't ready to get smacked around again.

As soon as I reached the top step of the staircase, she opened her door. "Well, how was your day today?" she asked. "Have you been off saving the world?"

"Something like that. Have you eaten?"

"Waiting for you. I tried your cell a couple of times. I thought you just blew me off."

"No way, my dear. How about you and I making this a special night out? Dinner and a little dancing at the Greenbrier?"

"Really? Why? Is this some kind of special night?"

"I don't know if you'd call it special, but I *am* going back to Washington tomorrow."

Her eyes sank and she turned to go back inside her room.

"If you don't mind, Skip, can we just stay here? I'll fix us a nice dinner." In five seconds she had gone from *bubbly* to the *ice blues*.

I followed her to the kitchen where she took out a roaster. I could see the melancholy in her face clean through the back of her head. "Come on, now. You knew I'd be leaving. Remember, I was all set to go a couple of days ago."

She nodded without reply.

"I *do* have a job in D.C., you know."

"There are damsels in distress around here, too, as you have found out. I think I saw an advertisement just the other day in the paper for a knight in shining armor." She actually smiled. A little.

I smiled back. It was the first set of smiles of the evening. "But I think the kind of job you'd *want* me to have would make me a knight in shiny Armani, you know, politician, professor, used car salesman …"

"Used car salesman dressed in Armani?"

"Well, I'd have to show these people around here how to dress, wouldn't I?"

Her smile widened. Now just a little more, but still all not that much.

While she busied herself in the kitchen over the next hour, I slipped into the sofa chair and dialed Birdman's cell.

"Just checking on you, boss. How is everyone?"

"We're managing, Bruce. I moved my family temporarily into an apartment down in Alexandria. I have a meeting with Mr. Big (I took it to mean the President) on Saturday about the people who did this and to determine if there are any remnants out there. By the way, congratulations on taking out the element in *your* area. You were right on the money about that nest, the factory, everything. That would have been catastrophic."

"The least I could do."

"And I also got word through the Fabulous Boys system that you handled a home-grown threat in Mingo today."

"Jack and I handled it."

"Good work. Assume you'll be back tomorrow? I want you in on the Saturday meeting to brief the boss."

"Should I wear a coat and tie?"

"I insist."

"Okay. Turtle neck it is."

"See you in a couple of days, Bruce."

I didn't even turn on the TV that evening. I could only take just so much of the scenes of rubble and smoke in New York, the hole in the ground in Pennsylvania and that missing section of the Pentagon. Anything I needed to know beyond that would come to me through official channels.

Somehow, Adrianna's mood had managed to retrogress as the evening wore on. We sat picking at our food, not saying much and it appeared that the emotions associated with fear, separation and loneliness would rule out in the end. Occasionally, we would lift our wine glasses to take a sip (or a gulp in my case), but most of the beef and greens remained uneaten.

I broke the ice. "You do know how I feel about you, don't you."

"I think so," she replied softly. "But what does it matter? I'll be here ... you'll be there."

I didn't respond, but kept staring at my plate.

I guess she took that as apathy. She scooted her chair back and picked up both of our plates. A moment later I heard them clamor inside the sink. I couldn't leave it at that, so I finished sucking down the wine and as she was facing the kitchen window, looking out into the night, I slipped my arms around her waist. Laying my cheek against hers I whispered in her ear "I do love you."

It had been years ... maybe never ... since the last time I said that to a woman. That is, other than my daughter.

The night was again bittersweet for us. We made love to one another with such fervor, it became at one point volatile, even desperate, like there was a finality to it. We lay spent and perspiring, gently stroking, talking, laughing, and then silence. Her eyes glistened in the soft light and occasionally she would dab them with a corner of the sheet.

"Is this *it* for us?" she asked.

"You know it's not."

"I don't want to go back to being lonely. I've kind of gotten used to having you around."

"Well, there's always Dan."

She slapped me playfully on the abdomen, careful not to bust open my new stitches. "That's not nice," she chided. Then she paused a few moments and shuffled her body, turning away from me. "But, he *will* always be around, you know."

And I wouldn't.

For the longest time after that we were silent and still. I began to make love to her with the tips of my fingers, running them lightly over the back of her neck, shoulders, breasts and tight belly. Where the side of my head crushed the pillow, I could hear my heart thumping in my ear. My brain came within inches of asking her to marry me. But then I knew I'd have to seek out some meaningless vocation that was foreign to me, and for a hell of a lot less money. The community college was now looking for a new teacher, but I'd have to become buddies with Paul, and that made me very afraid. Afraid I may become just like *him*. But at least people would not be putting holes in me.

I placed my lips close to her ear and buried my nose into her hair. Inhaling deeply, once, I drank in her sweet scent. "It's impossible right now, you know," I whispered.

"What is?" she asked, still facing away.

"Coming back here anyway soon."

She was quiet again for a moment, then said, "a coeur vaillant rien d'impossible."

"What?'

"Nothing is impossible to a willing heart."

I didn't respond. My heart was truly willing, but for now and likely years to come people like me would be needed by our country. I did know that I wanted to spend the rest of my life with this woman, somehow, some way. She would never give up Wolf Laurel and never condone being married to a counter-terrorist agent who flitted around the world ninety percent of the time at a beckoned call. And anyway, I would miss the excitement and action, now that our world was ever more dangerous. My kind was needed out there. The kind of evil we now experience in this world has the determination of a cockroach colony. As we knock down two or three, hundreds more will spring up.

Nothing more was said. She wriggled into my body and I held her tightly against me. It would be so easy to love this woman and take her into my life. She may even domesticate me to a point where I got used to living an uncomplicated life. A safe life. But whereas I would be happy with *her*, my mind and my body would begin to die inside. I would be like a stone-sober drunk going through the DTs. She would sense that and soon come to realize our mistake. We would both feel guilty for different reasons. She, because she coaxed me into a safe and sane relationship; and I, because I would ultimately leave her.

Sometimes I dread the thought of sleep taking me over. One of the last thoughts I have before losing consciousness is whether the dream will come that night, and if it does, will it give me a break and wait to materialize until at least five or six. That night, however, the dream monsters invaded shortly after one-thirty, and as usual, it opened my eyes and left me in a cold sweat. The badly mangled

Vietnamese child stumbling from the burning hut this time formed the word *why* with her horrified lips. It was strange; she had never done anything but scream before. Now, she confronted me.

As I knew I wouldn't get back to sleep right away, I arose and eased myself quietly into Adrianna's cushy sofa chair near the bed. It began to rain, which served to perpetuate and further memorialize the dream, reminding me of the monsoon rain that fell on the village that horrific day. I closed my eyes, finding the girl and the rain still affixed to my brain like an appendage, but with special effects going on outside my window. The girl just wouldn't let this thing die. For thirty years she and her mother had haunted me and now it was my turn to ask *why*. Considering the number of people I had sent to their graves, not just in Southeast Asia, but in the last few years in the good old USA, why hadn't any of *them* materialized in my dreams?

Adrianna stirred, reached over to find my side of the bed empty, and then sat up.

"Skip, is anything wrong?"

"Naw. Just having trouble sleeping, that's all." I looked toward the window. "The rain puts a lot of people to sleep, but sometimes I just like to sit up and listen to it. It's like experiencing a nocturnal symphony, sweet and intoxicating."

Although I couldn't make out her face in the darkened room, I knew she was smiling. I heard the smile in her voice. "There's that *poet* coming out again. I love that about you, Mister Tough Guy."

"Sorry I disturbed you," I whispered. "I'll go sit in the living room for a while."

"That's okay. If you're still going to sit up, then you can keep watch over me while *I* sleep. You make a pretty good protector, you know."

"Yeah. Gotta keep guys like Dan Laramie away from your bed."

"Goodnight, bad boy." I heard the mattress creak and groan as she settled back under the sheets.

I squared my bill at the front desk on Thursday morning, said goodbye to Juanita, and took Adrianna's hand in mine as we strolled out the screen door and onto the veranda. We stopped for a moment and turned to one another in silent reflection.

Then she threw her head back and smiled. "Take care, hero. Keep away from bad guys, okay?" She picked up my right hand and placed something in it. It was a small box wrapped in some very familiar paper with a pink bow.

I laughed. "I knew somehow I'd get it back. What's inside?"

"Something you'll need. I searched high and low before finding it. Open it later."

"Okay."

We stood for a few more lingering moments, looking into each other's eyes. Then after a parting, almost emotionless kiss, I left her standing on the veranda. She leaned her body into one of the porch support beams, keeping her sad, unwavering eyes on me as I loaded the Suburban. I stopped before entering the vehicle to look back at her and threw up my hand. She did the same, then turned and went back inside.

I swung by the funeral home once again to visit with Joey before leaving town. He was already at work draining the darkened blood from an old codger who after eighty-nine years gave up on living. I waited in the office until Joey had finished pumping in the formaldehyde, after which he came out to give me a bear hug. "Bye, big brother. I'm proud of you." Then he drove his index finger into my chest. "Next time, don't cut it so close. I've always liked parting my hair on the left side. Seems like you do everything with a dramatic flair."

I smiled. "I live for drama. It is only the drama in my life that saves me from the throes of apathy. Call me anytime, Joey boy. Kiss the girls for me."

"When will you be back?"

I shrugged. "Maybe Christmas. I plan to spend a lot more time with Caroline after she gets through her training. But then they'll probably assign her to Boise or Waco, and I'll be off spanning the globe even more looking for subversives."

"Well, don't be a stranger around these parts. We love you and I *know* the beautiful Mrs. Wolf does."

"See ya, Joey." I gave him a playful shot in the shoulder with my fist and walked away.

As I passed the sign at the apex of the long, upward grade that read *Thank You for Visiting West Virginia. Drive Safely,* I felt a sudden sense of loss. A part of it was leaving my family, the lovely Adrianna and her Wolf Laurel; but also, today I was leaving beautiful Greenbrier. During the first twenty years of my life its velvet farmland, grand hills and genuine people had become indelibly ingrained in my blood. And in these three weeks, as paradoxically passionate and tragic as they had been, I felt like an alcoholic, having been over thirty years off the bottle, suddenly falling off the wagon of the world to enjoy yet another taste of Greenbrier's sweet nectar.

I knew I was getting close to Covington as the pungent odor of the old paper mill filled the cabin of the Suburban. After running the door glass up with my left index finger, I reached onto the seat for my bottle of Evian. Instead, I found the silken paper of the present Adrianna had given me. For a moment I just held it in my hand, wondering what was inside, like a kid studying an interesting-looking package with his name on it under the Christmas tree. My curiosity finally getting the better of me, I opened it with my right hand and immediately began laughing out loud. It was a box containing a bottle of Hai Karate.

And there was a note attached.

> "*Something to keep the girls away.*
> *Love,*
> *A*"

I then drove further east and north, and after the smile had long dissipated from my face, I allowed the TV images of the smoldering ruins of the fallen towers to once again haunt my brain. Although the tragedies had made us fearful, causing us to question our safety and vulnerability for the first real time since Pearl Harbor, they had also summoned within many of us an anger and a thirst for vengeance. And for the first time in many years all of us will have had a rekindled sense of patriotism. But then I wondered how long *that* would last, being the fickle and complacent society we had become. When the World Trade site and the Pentagon were restored, America would go back to business as usual. The horror may never be totally forgotten, but it wouldn't take long until Americans were lulled back into a false sense of security.

There was still a ravenous craving in my soul that would go unsatisfied, unrequited, until my country no longer needed me and I had nothing left to contribute. But my country would indeed need me and people *like* me in CTT, the CIA, FBI and other agencies, to seek out and destroy America's new enemy. Who knows? There may even one day be a new department in the government dedicated to securing and protecting our homeland.

I fully intend one day to return to Adrianna and Wolf Laurel. She will be the one person who can help me get beyond myself; and I pray to God that when I am through serving my country *and* myself, she will still be there.

> *There are stars in the Southern sky*
> *And if ever you decide you should go.*
> *There is a taste of time sweetened honey*
> *Down the Seven Bridges Road.*

—Eagles

A forewarning

When I come for you, I will not be hiding behind a woman or a child. I will come at you head-on, full force and without reservation. I want you to know that I am very good at what I do and can snuff out your life in a split second with a single forty-seven cent bullet. You may not hear me or see me; you may run to any corner of the earth to evade me, but I *will* find you. I may not be as eager as you to give up my life for my country, but by God I will gladly sacrifice my life to protect my people from people like you.

—Bruce McGowan—
U.S. Department of State

About the Author

Lee Martin is a native West Virginian, now living in the Atlanta, Georgia area. After a career in the United States Army, which included a Vietnam combat tour and for which he was awarded the Bronze Star and Vietnamese Gallantry Cross, he retired with the rank of Colonel. He has a Masters and Doctorate in Counseling, is an adjunct professor at a Georgia university teaching a battery of Psychology courses, and works part-time as a Marriage and Family Therapist.

Made in the USA